Painted Women

A Warbonnet Mystery

by

Robert Kresge

Rob Kresge
2012

ABQ Press Trade paperback Edition 2011

Cover Design by Matt Kresge

Author's website by Darren Wheeling of www.blackegg.com

www.abqpress.com

ABQ Press
Albuquerque, New Mexico

ISBN 978-0-9838712-1-7

Author's Notes

The following persons named or characterized in this book are real:

--In Laramie:
    Albany County Sheriff Nathaniel Boswell,
    Mrs. Crout of the Frontier Hotel,
    Doctor Finfrock,
    and Mrs. Ivinson.

--On the Yellowstone Expedition:
    Professor Ferdinand Hayden,
    Jim Stevenson,
    William Henry Jackson,
    Thomas Moran,
    Anton Schonborn,
    Steve Hovey,
    Albert Peale,
    and Potato John.

--Mentioned in passing:
    Albert Bierstadt.

All other persons are fictional and are not intended to represent anyone living or dead.

To my wife and first reader, Julie

To Matt and Annick and Amanda

To Darren for his help and creativity

To Judith for her faith in me

*To Roy Zarucchi and Carolyn Page for their helpful comments
And to the members of my critique groups who saw
the earliest draft of this novel:
Pari Noskin Taichert, Penny Rudolph, Mike White,
Penny Rogers, Roz Russell, and Karen Timm*

Prologue

June 12, 1867
Manzanita, Texas

The buzzards flying over town should have warned him, but Monday Malone only figured that out later. A week later, when regrets and tears came way too late to do anything differently.

Buzzards never flew over Manzanita. But on this stifling morning there were buzzards aplenty. Monday could see them descending over the buildings when he was a mile away over the hot, dusty, north Texas plain. Looked like they were landing in the main street. Where were the people to clean up or shoo the damn things away?

He'd been riding for more than two hours. His foster father and sister hadn't returned to the ranch yesterday. This year's wave of Indians, outlaws, and Comancheros wouldn't be put off by a one-armed man and a beautiful girl. Since their brother Tom was out with most of the ranch hands chasing rustlers, Monday had buckled on an old Army Colt Pa had brought back from the war and taken the fastest horse in the corral. But even holding to an anxious trot all the way, both horse and rider were parched. These plains baked and the earth cracked open in protest at the assault of the pitiless sun.

Monday wasn't surprised to find things quiet when he approached the water trough behind the hotel. Folks tended to stay where it was cool when the town roasted on days like this.

He began to be concerned when he found the trough nearly empty. Johnny always kept it half full for guests and their mounts. Monday got down, took off his hat, and wiped his brow. He pumped a few inches of water into the trough, drinking a little himself and leaving his horse to enjoy the rest.

Time to find Pa and Mary Ellen. Better try the hotel first. They must have stayed there last night.

He went up the alley next to the hotel and looked to his right. Buzzards were gathered around something in the middle of the street. He couldn't see what they were eating, but a hat lay in the dust near their feast. Not a good sign.

A bottle crashed out of a front window of the saloon next to him and landed in the street. A young woman in a faded blue dress stumbled out of the saloon, turned left and ran up the boards toward him. She held the front of her dress together as she ran. Her long dark hair was matted and uncombed and her face was either bruised or she'd been cry-ing—or both.

She didn't seem to see Monday until he cried, "Mary Ellen!"

She stumbled, caught herself with one hand at the corner of the saloon, and saw him standing in the mouth of the alley. He could see some buttons had been torn off her dress.

"Monday. Oh, God. Get out of here! Run!" She staggered forward and into his arms. She smelled of tobacco smoke, sweat, and whiskey. Over her shoulder, he watched two men come out of the saloon, the younger one in the lead, holding another bottle by the neck. He made a show of searching the street for her, then broke into a leer when he saw them.

"Who the hell are you, cowboy? And why ain't you dead if you're out here?" He turned to the older man. "Rafe, I thought you and Pinkie had all them men locked up in the hardware store." As the older man squinted at Monday and Mary Ellen, the young man turned back to them with a cold look. "Reckon we got to kill one more then." They advanced down the walk.

Monday pulled Mary Ellen back and pushed her up the hotel stairs. "Get up there, Mary Ellen. You'll be all right in the hotel. Who are these men? Why were you in a saloon with them?" He backed up a few steps behind her.

"Monday, they killed the sheriff, and Reverend Walsh, and some more men. You can't go up against them. Come up here with me." She pulled his right arm, but he shook her loose and slipped the hammer loop off his holster. Monday looked down at the two men.

The younger one reached the bottom of the stairs. He took a long drink from the bottle and wiped the back of his right hand across his mouth.

"Turn loose my girl, damn you! We wasn't finished yet." He laughed and tried to set the bottle down, but dropped it into the dirt instead, where it toppled over. "Damn!" He looked up at Monday. "You made me spill that whiskey. I'm gonna love killing you."

"Billy," the older man said. "You been drinking too much. Let me go get Deke or Pinkie. We'll take care of this feller."

"Shut up, Rafe. Looks like my gal likes him. Let's see what she thinks of him with a big hole in his belly."

He went for his gun and he was fast. Monday never would have beaten him except that Billy hadn't taken his hammer loop off. As it was, Billy cleared leather, but Monday shot him in the chest and he fell first onto his rear, then onto his back. Billy's pistol went off as he hit the ground, and the bullet thunked into the front of the hotel.

The man called Rafe drew and snapped off a shot at the couple now retreating up the stairs. The bullet tore up splinters just in front of Monday's left boot. Monday squeezed off a shot in return that sent the man dodging back to the corner of the saloon. Before he could fire again, Monday and Mary Ellen scrambled through the upper door into the hotel hallway. They backed down the hall and found the stairs to the lobby. As they neared the bottom of the steps another man came in the front door with a drawn gun. When he raised it, Monday fired and the man's hat flew off. His return shot sang through the air between them, too close to Mary Ellen.

"Back, we've got to go back!" Monday cried, shoving Mary Ellen up the stairs. As they made their way down the hall, Rafe swung open the door at the end. Monday fired at him and Rafe dodged out of the opening. The door swung closed. Monday tried a door to a room overlooking the street. It was unlocked.

"Quick! In here," he said, pulling her inside. Together, they slid a heavy dresser across the door. They could hear Rafe yelling to someone and the sound of running feet.

Monday went to the window, but couldn't see the street past the hotel's second floor balcony. Then he remembered he'd fired four of his five shots. He pulled Mary Ellen to the floor and sat down beside her, fumbling in his belt pouch for powder, balls, and caps.

He leaned over and kissed her briefly, then he turned his attention to his pistol.

Once Monday had the powder in the cylinders, he could put the balls in by feel. While his hands worked automatically, he looked more closely at Mary Ellen. She had a great bruise under her left eye and dark welts on the left side of her throat. He couldn't see a hint of the white shift she always wore under her dress. Both forearms were bruised, and she was barefoot.

"What happened to you? Where's Pa?"

"Pa's all right, last I knew. They didn't worry about a one-armed man. We'd just left Doc's office when they grabbed us. They locked all the men in the hardware store yesterday morning. Monday, there are six of them. Or five now. You just killed Billy Lassiter. He's the little brother of their leader, Deke. They're not going to—"

The window over their heads broke in a shower of glass. The bullet buried itself in the wall behind them. Monday pushed Mary Ellen flat and pulled the thin mattress off the bed to lay over her. When he leaned forward, he could see a man across the street with a rifle. Monday ducked back, finished loading, then rotated the cylinder, putting caps on each nipple. All six chambers, something he hadn't done since the Major had taught him how to shoot. Another shot crashed into the door from the hall outside. The dresser kept the bullet from flying into the room.

Monday eased over to the edge of the window, but couldn't see a good target. Off to his right, beyond whatever body lay in the street, he could see the hardware store. He wondered what the men in there thought of this gun battle out here.

4

"Where did you spend the night?" he asked over his shoulder.

"In the saloon," came the listless reply. She wouldn't look at him. "With Cora, Angie, and Maria. They took turns with us all night long. They made me . . . . It was horrible." She blinked back fresh tears.

Then a gun went off close to the open window and splinters flew from the window frame. Someone was on the balcony.

"They got us boxed in, Mary Ellen. Stay under that mattress. Hope we get some help before long. I count three of them shooting at us right now. That might leave only one or two—or maybe none—watchin' Pa and the other men."

He looked at her, but her brown eyes seemed lifeless. She clutched the front of her dress.

"I'm glad you killed that Billy," she said, looking at the floor between them. "He was the worst. When I wouldn't . . . , when I wouldn't do what he wanted, he burned me with a cigarette." She peeled open the dress a little to show him an angry red spot above her left breast.

"They came to us at all hours of the night. I lost track. Early this morning, I could hear Angie screaming 'til they slapped her. Even after she quit screaming, they kept slapping her. I didn't see her this morning. She may be—"

Another shot crashed outside. They ducked, but this one didn't come into their room. There was more yelling, running feet, and shots. They could hear Rafe on the outside stairs. More shots, then the sound of someone tumbling down the stairs. Monday and Mary Ellen looked at each other. Had the men got out of the hardware store? He put his arm around her.

"Mary Ellen, it's gonna be all right. Pa will kill these men or drive them off and me or Tom will catch any that get away."

"I don't care, Monday. It don't matter any more. Not from about midnight on. It's all done now, all gone. You remember I came into town to see Doc? Well, he said—"

"Hey, you in the room," said a voice from the hall. "This is Zack. You still alive?"

5

Monday got up cautiously, still watching the window. "Zack, that you? What's going on out there?" He moved to the dresser.

"Monday? Your Pa's got them on the run. We killed three so far, not counting that Billy you shot. We're hunting their leader and another feller right now. Wanna come outta there?"

Monday hauled Mary Ellen to her feet and together they slid the dresser to the side. When they opened the door, Zack Hibben shook him by the shoulder.

"Good going, Monday. Art and some of the other boys are looking in the saloon for the girls now." He looked past Monday. "Good God, Miss Malone. They done . . . . Oh, my." He couldn't hide his shock at Mary Ellen's appearance.

They took a hunched over Mary Ellen down to the lobby, arriving just as Major Charles Malone strode in through the front door, pistol in his right hand. The left sleeve of his shirt was pinned to his shoulder. "God, Mary Ellen, honey. I was scared we'd never find you. Cora and Maria are all right, but Angie . . . ." He trailed off.

"They killed her, didn't they, Pa?" Her eyes should have blazed, but they still looked lifeless. "I guess I knew it this morning. There were so many of them, so many times." She didn't faint, but her knees buckled. All the men jumped for her, but Monday caught her and held her up.

"Pa, why don't you take her someplace safe? Zack and me'll find this Deke and that last man." Blasts of gunfire from behind the hotel indicated at least one of the raiders might have been spotted. "Go on out the front, Pa! Come on, Zack."

They headed for the back door. The guns had gone silent now, and Art and two other men were dragging a body from behind the hotel stable. They dropped him as Monday approached. Art casually shot the body again.

"Son of a bitch," Art said, and kicked the corpse, too. "All that's left now is Lassiter."

They all whirled back toward the hotel at the sound of a scream. Mary Ellen! Monday ran for the back door of the

6

hotel. "Watch the sides, boys," he called as he disappeared inside. No one in the lobby. Both front doors stood open.

"Malone, you in there? They tell me you killed my brother Billy. Well, your Pa is laying out here with a cracked skull, and I got this girl who says she's your sister. Come on out here!" Monday stood in the doorway. He could see the Major's body lying in the street. A tall man with a black mustache and crossed gunbelts held Mary Ellen tightly with his left arm. Monday could see the glint of a knife in that hand. His right hand held a pistol.

"Well," Lassiter called, "Are you comin' out or do I have to cut this girl?"

"I'm coming out. Let her go." Monday walked down the front steps and directly toward Lassiter. Into what should have been the last few seconds of his life.

He tried to get a clear shot past Mary Ellen. He couldn't. As Lassiter raised his own pistol, Monday instinctively turned his left side toward the outlaw, dreading what was to come.

Lassiter's bullet caught Monday high in the left shoulder and sent him sprawling, his gun flying out of his hand. He heard Mary Ellen scream his name.

At the sound of more gunfire, Monday struggled to sit up. His left arm was numb. He got to his knees and saw Lassiter unhitching a horse on the far side of the street, taking fire from both sides of the hotel. Monday couldn't find his own gun. He started to crawl toward Mary Ellen. Lassiter rode past him, riding low. None of the shots hit the tall man and he galloped out of town chased by a swarm of bullets.

Mary Ellen lay on her left side facing Monday, the front of her dress shiny with fresh blood, Lassiter's knife deep in her stomach. Carefully, Monday turned her onto her back and placed her head in the crook of his right arm. His left arm would barely move and was nearly useless. He couldn't feel any pain. Mary Ellen's tortured face burned him worse than any bullet.

"Don't move, Mary Ellen. Doc'll be here soon. *Doc!*" he bellowed over his shoulder.

"I wanted to tell you, Monday, in the hotel. What happened to me." She closed her eyes and gasped in pain. "Take it out, please. Hurts so bad."

"I can't, Mary Ellen. You'll bleed worse."

"It don't matter any more. I'm dying. Please. Take it out for me."

He hooked two fingers of his nearly limp left hand around the cross guard of the knife and eased it out as gently as he could.

"Ahhhh. That's better. Better now. But I'm so cold."

"Mary Ellen, you can't die. I'll surely die if you do."

"No, Monday. You have to live. Hear me? You have to live for all of us now."

"Mary Ellen?" He kissed her, but felt her lips go slack. "No! Don't go, Mary Ellen. *Don't go!*"

When her bloody hand fell away from the wound in her belly, Monday put his head back and screamed at the sky. Such was the sound of his agony that no one dared approach him, not even his friends. They waited for the doctor.

1

Early June 1871
North of Warbonnet, Wyoming Territory

Monday Malone checked the angle of the lowering sun and considered how he would shoot the Hotchkiss boys. If it came to that. They were hunkered close together at their campfire, not a hundred yards down the hill from him. Probably thought they'd picked a sheltered spot, safe from prying eyes. They'd used dry wood in an effort to avoid telltale smoke.

Smart boys, Monday thought, but not smart enough. They'd built their fire atop damp grass and that thin wisp of smoke had steered him in this direction. Then he'd smelled their fire. Monday had left his horse on the other side of the hill, taken his rifle from the scabbard and the bag of leg irons from his saddlebag, and crept up until he'd had to belly crawl. This spot he'd picked, beside the trunk of a wind-twisted tree and just under some silver sagebrush, gave him cover to see the two men.

Cletus was standing while his brother squatted. Cletus had a dark beard and Verle just a three-day growth of whiskers.

Three days. That's how long Monday had trailed them from the outskirts of Warbonnet. Three days since they'd hit Charlie Simmons, the assayer, over the head in his office and taken a small bag of nuggets. Mrs. Simmons had said it was small, but it was larger than the meager poke the Hotchkiss boys had brought with them. They'd been prospecting in the

9

hills south of town since early spring and they'd evidently got little color to show for their work.

Too bad he was out of town when the robbery occurred, Monday thought. He might have caught up to these boys sooner. Boys! Cletus looked to be about forty and Verle must have been in his thirties. Everybody around town called them the Hotchkiss boys. At twenty-three, Monday wondered if they called him the boy marshal behind his back. Monday took off his black hat and ran his fingers through his damp sandy hair.

Time to act, he reckoned. Cletus took the little coffee pot from the fire and was stepping over to where Verle squatted, holding out his cup. Perfect. They were only a foot apart now. Monday put the rifle into the hollow of his right shoulder, squinted into the sight, held his breath, and fired.

The coffee pot flew out of Cletus' hand, spraying both men with scalding liquid. Verle swore and stood up, reaching for his pistol even as his left hand wiped his face. Cletus knew better and stayed put, making no move toward his gun. Monday jacked another round into his Henry repeater.

"Don't move! This is Marshal Malone from Warbonnet and I've got you covered. Stay as you are." The light breeze had blown away his telltale powder smoke before they could look for him. Monday hoped his hiding place—and the fact they'd recognize the boom of a rifle—would keep them from trying to draw. He stayed prone.

"Cletus," Monday called to the pair. "I want you to take two steps away from Verle—to your left. That's it. That's good. Now keep that right hand out where I can see it and unbuckle your gunbelt with your left hand. Verle, you just stand easy. OK, now throw that belt far to your left." He turned his attention to the slower brother.

"Your turn, Verle. You do the same thing with your left hand. That's fine. Now throw your gunbelt off to your left. Good. All right, Verle, you turn around and face the same way your brother is looking. Both you boys clasp your hands behind your backs where I can see 'em. That's it. Now hold still. I'll be down there directly."

Monday stood up silently, and picked up the bag of leg irons. He made his way down the hill carefully, keeping one eye on both men while avoiding making any noise that might give them some idea how close he was. When he dropped the bag by the fire with a clank, the brothers jumped.

"Well, that'll do, you two. You led me a tiring chase the last three days and I plan for us all to get some sleep tonight and start back to Warbonnet tomorrow. Looks like," he paused and glanced at the pan on the fire, moving it to one side with his foot. "You even saved me some beans and bacon. Your hospitality will go over big with the judge in Laramie when he tries you boys for murder."

"Murder," Verle wailed, slightly turning his left shoulder. "We didn't kill nobody, just hit him over the head."

"Shut up, you damn fool," Cletus snarled. "He's just tryin' to trick you into confessin'."

"Your faith in me is well-placed, Cletus. He's right, Verle. Mr. Simmons wasn't dead when I left town—but he could be by now. I've known a few men to succumb to having the barrel of a .44 Colt bent over their skulls. But I do thank you for 'fessing up to that hit on the head. That and the bag of nuggets I'll probably find in your saddle bags is all the county will need to put you boys in the pokey for a lotta years."

"All right, fun's over," Monday said, picking up the bag of clinking leg irons. "Move to that lone tree." They walked about ten paces away from the fire. "Sit down now on opposite sides. Verle, do you know what 'opposite' means? Not next to your brother. Over here, facing him. That's nice. Now lie down like you're fixin' to take a siesta and put your hands behind your backs again."

With that, Monday laid down his rifle, drew and cocked his pistol, and shook out the leg irons. First he clamped the end of one restraint to Cletus' right ankle, tight over his boot, and the other end to Verle's left ankle. Then he circled the pair and repeated the procedure on the other side of the tree. Keeping his pistol leveled, Monday checked both pairs of boots for knives and came up with one from Cletus' right boot.

11

Neither one had a hideout pistol. Finally, he stood, uncocked his own pistol, rotated the cylinder to the empty chamber, and holstered it.

"Now, I'm gonna bring my horse over here to keep yours company. Don't you boys get any ideas of climbing that tree while I'm gone." It must be forty feet high, Monday reckoned.

Monday brought his big buckskin horse down to the camp and unsaddled him, then left him to graze with the Hotchkiss horses. Their nags looked played out and grateful for rest. Monday pulled his spoon from his saddlebag and went to see if the beans and bacon were scorched. Cletus and Verle argued all during his brief meal, but he didn't let that affect his appetite. He drank water rather than make more coffee in his own small pot.

Monday unrolled his blanket next to a log Cletus had used for a seat. He remembered the boys' blankets and took them over to the tree. He held them up and they gestured which one belonged to whom. As he started back to the fire, Verle began to whine.

"Marshal, can I go over in them weeds and take a pee? I got to go."

His brother snarled.

Monday said, "In the morning, Verle. Hold it 'til then."

"Well, what if I cain't?"

"Then just turn over a little and do what you gotta do on the downhill side. But I'd think twice about that if I was you. Too much pee around a campsite might attract bears."

"Bears? Grizzlies? Oh, no. I'll hold it."

Monday grinned. No grizzlies on these rolling grasslands.

"And Verle. Just in case you're tempted to stay up all night and jaw with your brother, too much talking has been known to attract the Sioux—or the Cheyenne. These are their hunting grounds, you know."

Verle opened his mouth to say something, but thought better of it and closed it with a snap.

Monday went to water the horses. Since the Hotchkiss boys hadn't hobbled their mounts, he fashioned two pair from some old rope hanging next to Cletus' saddlehorn. He didn't

12

need to hobble his own horse; Lightning was too well trained to wander at night. Finally, he collected the gunbelts and the one rifle the boys had carried and dumped them next to his blanket.

He checked to be sure there was enough wood. No clouds in the sky. Should be perfect sleeping weather, now that the Hotchkiss boys wouldn't be making any more noise. He checked his pocket watch. Eight-thirty. Too early to sleep, but enough light to read.

Monday got from his saddlebag the copy of Mark Twain's *Innocents Abroad* that Kate Shaw the schoolmarm had lent him. She claimed to know Twain personally. Monday had to admit the man had real wit, even if he couldn't understand every word in the book. Kate had promised to lend him a book about some ship that traveled under the ocean when he finished this one.

He lay down and read for a half hour. He was more tired than he'd thought, so he put the book away and turned his feet toward the smoldering fire. He took a canteen over to Cletus and Verle and bade them a quiet good night.

As he sat down on his blanket again, Monday thought of Kate and the birthday present she'd given him. That had let him track smart the last three days, allowing him to rest Lightning from time to time. She gave him a pair of shiny brass Liverpool binoculars in April, reminding him of the danger they faced last summer from a killer with a telescopic sight on his rifle.

"Use these," she'd said, "when you're looking for someone dangerous. Perhaps they'll help keep you from harm."

He'd been touched at the time, but never had any real use for them until now. Monday had picked up the Hotchkiss boys' trail just north of the Mastersons' Arrow Ranch and their tracks had been easy to follow that day, almost straight as an arrow, you might say. Then as the hills got steeper, Monday found the true value of the binoculars. Every time he came to a hilltop or ridge, he got down off Lightning before reaching the skyline, lay down, and scanned the opposite hill for his quarry, especially any sign they might be watching their back trail.

Yesterday, he'd seen Cletus—easy to spot with his dark beard—let Verle take the horses on a ways while he laid beside a boulder watching the valley they'd just crossed. After about an hour, Cletus stood up and beckoned to Verle, who brought up their horses. Once they left, Monday was able to cross the valley quickly and picked up their trail as the light began to fail. Today, he'd made up more time and caught them finishing their supper.

Monday took off his boots and wrapped himself in his blanket. He put his hands behind his head and thought of Kate again. Then he stopped. Thinking of Kate last night and dreaming of her had probably caused him to have the Mary Ellen dream again, for the first time in weeks.

He'd never gotten over Mary Ellen's death, or his responsibility for it. They'd been raised together as brother and sister, but for a few days that spring of 1867, when they were nineteen, they'd become something more. Secret lovers. And the child created in their passion had led to Mary Ellen's death. If she hadn't gone to Manzanita that day with Pa to see the doctor and the preacher, she wouldn't have died when the Lassiter gang took over the town.

Every time he had that dream, Monday tried to think of ways he could have changed the outcome, how he should have died instead of Mary Ellen. If he'd ridden in more cautiously. If he'd taken her directly to his horse and left town right away. If he'd stayed with her and let Pa and the other men search for Lassiter. The only sure thing he'd figured in the last four years was that if he hadn't turned away from Lassiter at the last minute, he would have taken that bullet in the heart and Mary Ellen might have lived. At least he wouldn't have had to watch her die.

Since her death, he'd ridden three cattle drives from Texas to Kansas. Mary Ellen's brother Tom had cheated Monday out of his share of the ranch when Pa died in '69. So Monday went on one more drive last year, then quit and headed for Montana, hoping to leave bitter memories of his lost ranch in Texas and dreams of Mary Ellen behind.

14

Even that hadn't worked out as he'd planned. During his three-day ride with Marshal Sam Taggart escorting that pretty new schoolteacher Kate Shaw to Warbonnet, he'd witnessed Taggart's murder. Then he'd let Kate persuade him to help her solve it. In those two short weeks, he'd come to care for her and she'd convinced him to stay on in Warbonnet after they found the killer.

Now he was a full-time lawman and had surprised himself by surviving long enough to pick up some of the skills this job demanded. In the last year, he'd only had to shoot one man, and that was to wound him. Now he'd tracked down two bumbling but dangerous robbers and would have to get them back down to Warbonnet and on to the county seat for trial.

The Hotchkiss boys weren't going anywhere tonight. He chuckled, turned on his side, and went to sleep.

2

Warbonnet

Kate Shaw trotted Windy to keep up with Becky Masterson's horse. They'd finished their Saturday afternoon ride from Arrow Ranch and headed south, back to Warbonnet. The school teacher was only an inch or two taller than her young friend, but her borrowed roan, larger than Becky's black pony, made her look much bigger. Kate reached forward to pat Windy's neck and her long blond ponytail brushed her shoulder.

Becky reined in a little so they could ride side by side again.

"I was trying to tell you," the younger girl said, "I got another proposal this week. From that other lieutenant at Fort Fetterman. You know, Doug Walsh. She tossed her auburn curls,

"But I told him he'd have to wait a bit. There were other suitors in line ahead of him." She laughed and slapped her reins against her jeaned leg. Becky wore pants when she rode and one of her father's checked shirts.

"I swear, Becky, you'll soon have half the fort lined up at your house to pay you court. The line of men from Warbonnet would stretch from town halfway to your ranch as it is."

Becky laughed again. "You talk as if I'm the only belle at the ball for the church dances. I'll bet you get five or six proposals a month yourself."

Kate grinned. "Oh, nowhere near that many. In fact, if you leave Roy Butcher out, then I've only had five or six since I got here."

"Roy? The old man who drives the freight wagon down to Laramie? I can't believe he'd dare ask you more than once."

"Roy is wonderful. He reminds me of my grandfather back in Buffalo," Kate said. "Why, he told me perfectly seriously that he'd be a good catch. He doesn't drink or gamble and if I'd marry him, he said he'd give up chewing tobacco. Can you imagine? He told me he was going to be persistent and he's asked me, regular as clockwork, every month since last September." She cinched up the cord of her straw hat a little under her chin, then thought better of it and slid the keeper down and let the hat fall back to dangle between her shoulder blades.

"I hope you don't get only the older men asking you, Kate. You have so many dance partners to choose from."

"Well, Sean Finnegan has asked me twice, when he's been in town. He says an older man would do me good. More experienced and, he says, not as likely to stray." Kate laughed at her friend's expression. "Stop fishing, Becky. I really haven't had any offers from men my own age."

Her own age. Kate would turn twenty-one this fall. She supposed that meant men in their twenties. There were quite a few, not so many in town, but more at the ranches, the mines, and Fort Fetterman.

"Well," Becky went on, "I've been asked by men only a little older than we are. By that gambler who came through here last month, and," she paused for emphasis, "by Monday Malone!" Laughing, Becky moved her pony a couple of quick steps to the left to avoid Kate's swat as she leaned out of the saddle trying to reach her.

"You little liar! You know very well if he had, you'd have ridden all the way to town just to tell me."

"I wouldn't have done that right away. First, I'd have accepted. *Then* I'd have told you."

"No, first you would have kissed him," Kate teased.

"Maybe I already have!" Becky shied her horse away from Kate again.

Kate swatted the air playfully. Becky would already have told her if she had, just as she'd told Kate about kissing Lieutenant Beamish last fall. Besides, Monday Malone seemed to have all the emotions of a block of wood lately. He fidgeted with his hat whenever he saw her these days and often wouldn't meet her eye when they spoke.

"Kate, when are you gonna let me give you a pair of jeans like mine for riding?"

"Oh, Becky, I could never—I have to think of my position. The schoolteacher can't be seen wearing trousers."

"Oh, pooh! We hardly ever see a soul on our rides. How would anybody know? You wouldn't scandalize the town if you just wore pants at our place."

"But you've told me the secret of riding comfortably in them is to wear, to wear those short drawers you made. I have to hang my laundry in town behind the boarding house, Becky. I could never. . . ." She trailed off, thinking.

"What's the matter, Kate?"

"Oh, nothing. Probably nothing. It's just that I've had some of my laundry go missing the last couple of months. I seem to come up short a pair of drawers some weeks. I'm going to have to give Roy an order for more the next time he goes to Laramie."

"Well, if he proposes as often as you say, you'd better put that order in a sealed envelope. I'd just die if I had to order new drawers through a man, especially one of your beaus," she teased. Becky's cheeks colored a little and Kate was pleased to see some things could still embarrass her young friend. Becky sometimes seemed so worldly at eighteen.

"At least I'm not hoping to run off with an entire expedition of men, Kate. You were miles away there for a minute. I'll bet you were thinking of the Hayden trip again, weren't you?"

18

"Uh, no. Actually not. Although I do have to think about packing. It's less than two weeks before I leave, if I can go at all. It still depends so much on Mr. Moran and Mr. Bierstadt."

Although most of Warbonnet knew she hoped to go with the Hayden survey party, Kate had shared the story of her deception only with Becky and Corey Masterson at this point. Professor Hayden had passed through Laramie a couple weeks ago with the bulk of the expedition to Yellowstone. Sean Finnegan, who'd been hired as guide for the Yellowstone part of the journey, had told her the expedition was going to begin in Utah, doing geologic surveys for possible railroad routes while working their way up into Montana and then into northwestern Wyoming. The two invited guest artists—the famous Albert Bierstadt and the less well-known but promising Thomas Moran—would come through Laramie by train weeks after the main body of explorers. Sean would convey the artists, by train and a series of stagecoaches, to Ft. Ellis, Montana to rendezvous with the rest of the party.

But it wasn't certain that either artist would actually accept the invitation. Kate had heard about this uncertainty when she'd been in Laramie a few weeks ago on a shopping trip with Becky and her handsome older brother Corey, one of Kate's frequent dance partners. Professor Hayden was in town at the time, picking up supplies for the journey with most of his men.

Kate had heard wonderful stories about Yellowstone. She longed to see the land she'd read about in the Washburn expedition's glowing reports published earlier this year, but she knew no geologic survey would take a woman along. Then she had a sudden inspiration and decided to act on it immediately. School would be over soon. Her plan just might work.

She had to work hard to talk Becky and Corey into supporting her plot. Although Kate didn't have any of her Warbonnet sketchbooks with her, she bought two in Laramie and worked furiously overnight to fill the pages with some better than passable work. She sent a note to Professor Hayden the morning before he finished his planning and left town, an application purporting to come from her brother, a young man named Kenneth Shaw asking to fill a place on the expedition

19

as a sketch and watercolor artist if either of the painters failed to show up. She'd coached Corey to pretend to be Kenneth, and the three of them went to Hayden's hotel.

Hayden had admired the sketches and, since Corey looked more than strong enough for the journey, had invited him to go along if there were a vacancy.

"The larger our party, the better deterrent to Indians we're likely to meet," he'd said.

Becky was looking at her strangely. Kate had been uncharacteristically silent for too long.

"Oh, Becky, I was so nervous Professor Hayden wouldn't like my sketches or believe Corey. I'll be all prepared to go, but I'm sure I shall sit in the Laramie station on pins and needles when the artists arrive on that train."

"There is the small hurdle, Kate, of convincing whoever does show up that you—a mere woman—should go along as an artist because your brother 'Kenneth' broke his arm. Even if you convince the painters, Kate, I still can't see Professor Hayden taking you with him when they leave Fort Ellis. It will be a great waste of your time, not to mention hundreds of miles by train and coach."

"Perhaps I've learned some things from you that will stand me in good stead," Kate teased. She batted her eyelashes and looked demure as she said this and they both laughed together. How good were her powers of persuasion, Kate wondered. She was really no charmer like the young beauty riding with her.

Becky stood up in her stirrups for a moment. Kate knew they were getting close to the Platte River and town. Her friend was probably checking the distance for their favorite part, the race to and through the river. The second girl usually caught all the splashes from the lead horse, normally Becky's little Darby. Kate saw Becky grin and begin to ease back down into her saddle. Kate didn't wait, but set herself to steal a jump and kicked Windy's flanks.

"*Hiyaah!*" she yelled, exulting in the thrill of his acceleration. She'd become an excellent horsewoman in her rides with

Becky and Corey. Kate didn't need to look back; she could hear Becky call to Darby.

Kate pulled on her cord and drew the hat up from between her shoulder blades. She took it in her left hand and swatted Windy on the rump with it. Just over the next rise now, there was the Platte, shimmering in front of them.

Crouched low over Windy's neck, Kate talked to him, urging him on. Now she could hear Darby's hoofbeats close, off to her left. She took the reins in her right hand and waved her hat far out with her left, hoping to make Darby shy away, maybe throw him off stride a bit.

She was rewarded with a shout of, "Kate, you rat!"

When the land dipped down to the river, she and Becky raced across the final flat section. Windy began to blow, but Kate hadn't started him too soon. She'd learned what he could do.

She headed him for the ford. One last thunder of hooves and he hit the water at full extended stride. Kate heard Becky squeal as she was splashed. There, Kate thought, that'll pay her back for teasing me about Monday.

Kate waited until Windy had run two or three strides out of the river on the far side before slowing him. Her cheeks were flushed and she had fire in her eyes as Becky came riding up.

"You shouldn't give away your intentions like you did, Becky. Someone could take advantage of you." Kate put her hat back on.

"Oh, they could? You're not going to lecture me about men again, are you, Kate? You, who've had ever so much more experience back East than a small town girl?" Becky used her "la-di-da" voice, then laughed and patted Darby's neck. They rode their horses at a walk up River Street toward Joe Fitch's stable.

Kate didn't rise to Becky's bait, but she took off her deer-skin gloves and rubbed the back of her scarred left hand with her right. Kate had had some experience with a man once. Not good and not to be repeated. She didn't like being reminded of it.

21

She loved the way her hair had lightened to gold in the Wyoming sun, but was afraid the weather here was coarsening her. She couldn't ignore the sunburn on the backs of her hands.

They pulled up at the water trough at Fitch's Livery. It was dry.

"Loser pumps," Kate said, dismounting and taking her reins over Windy's head so he could drink more easily.

Becky pumped, while Kate tucked her gloves into the waistband of her split riding skirt. From hat to damp, spattered boots, she decided she looked like she belonged here, like she'd always been a Wyoming woman. She was tanned a little now, not freckled like Becky. Her mother would have chastised her for not wearing gloves whenever she left the house, as a proper lady should. How ironic that she only wore gloves went she went riding. And astride a horse rather than sidesaddle, "as a proper young lady should."

She wasn't living up to her mother's standards, but not to Wyoming's standards, either. Becky and Martha were her only two real friends and the town council had turned down her request for funds to start a library. Warbonnet would never be as comforting as her home town.

Warbonnet lacked so many of the cultural opportunities of Buffalo. Art classes, exhibits, musical performances, fashions, handsome men all dressed up, dances in a real hotel ballroom. And news. People from other cities bringing new ideas and new possibilities that whetted her imagination.

"Are you sure you won't come to Martha's with me for supper?"

"Nope. I've got to get back for all the chores Ma lets me put off when you visit."

Kate laughed, but her forehead wrinkled in concern as she gazed at the sun, now lower on the horizon.

"Don't go worrying about me," Becky assured her. She patted the rifle in the scabbard by her saddle. "Corey says I'm such a good shot now, I'm my own best escort. Will you come again next week if you're not off to Laramie? Corey really wants to ride with you next time. Just you and him." She grinned. "And he wants to help you learn to shoot, too."

"Of course, if I can," Kate grinned back, thinking of Corey's arms around her as she aimed a rifle. She hugged Becky and the girl rode off with Windy in tow.

Wyoming seemed like such an exotic place before she'd come here. Now for the past year it seemed Wyoming was standing aloof, like a club that wouldn't let her join. Despite all her efforts, she was still treated as an outsider here. The thought of going home to Buffalo came to her again.

Kate took the gloves from her waistband and beat some dust off her skirt as she walked out into the street, around the horses tied up at the saloon next door. She wasn't about to walk up on the boards beside the saloon where she might be tempted to look into the windows—or worse, where the men in there might see her and accost her. She turned the corner onto Main Street and admired one or two horses as she made her way to the end of the saloon's second hitch rack and prepared to step back up onto the boards. Then she stopped; something had caught her eye.

Kate walked back carefully. There! One dusty pinto twitched its tail. She spoke quietly to calm it as she raised her hand and traced the brand on its left flank. A Circle M. Monday's brand. From Texas. He'd told her there were many common brands and one could see a lot of similar marks in cow towns like Abilene and Ellsworth. But what if this horse—and its rider—was from Texas?

"What are you doing standing in the street, Miss Kate? One of them horses might kick you." A small voice came to her through her thoughts.

"Oh, Buxton, I didn't see you. Did your mother send you to look for me?"

"Yes, Ma'am. Supper'll be ready directly. Did you have a nice ride in with Miss Becky?"

"We did, thank you." Better than usual, Kate thought. She hardly ever won a race. "Buxton, I'm glad you turned up. I need you to do a little favor for me. Will you?"

"Well, I guess so. Supper won't be ready for a while. Do ya need me to get something for you?"

"Not something. I need you to get some*one* for me. Do you think you could go in the saloon and ask for someone? The schoolteacher can't be seen going in there."

"Nor any lady, Miss Kate. Nor any son of my Ma's, neither. I'd have to eat standing up for a week if she was to learn I'd done so much as put my head in that door."

"Well, she wouldn't be so upset with you, since I asked you to help, Buxton. After all, she's preparing supper way back up the street and I'll stand lookout for you." This made Kate feel like a little girl back in Buffalo, when she'd conspired with her sister and brother.

"Wow, would you do that, Miss Kate? I always wanted—I mean, I wondered what goes on in there." Monday had been encouraging the boy, bringing him out of his shyness by calling him "Buck" instead of his proper name. Kate realized she was probably not helping Buxton's moral education, but there was no one else around to help her.

"Well, don't you loiter in there, young man. I just want you to carry a message, then come right back out. Do you hear me?" Kate tried to sound as stern as she'd learned to be with her pupils this past year. "I just need you to ask Mr. Stratman to send out whoever owns this pinto horse with the Circle M brand."

"A Circle M? Really? Like on the marshal's horse? OK, Miss Kate. You stand guard now."

With that, Buxton plunged through the door like he'd been entering saloons all his life. Kate was suddenly concerned that she might not be able to get him back out as easily. But she needn't have worried. He returned in a minute, rubbing his eyes.

"It's too smoky in there. Mr. Stratman said he'd tell the man you wanted to see him. I better get back now. Hope I don't smell too much like smoke." Kate smiled and sniffed his hair, then sent the boy on his way. When she looked up, a young cowboy stood on the boards with the door swinging

24

closed behind him. He took off his hat as he stepped down to her.

"Whoo-ee. You must be Miss Shaw. Barkeep told me you'd asked for me. Ma'am, I seen some pretty women in saloons before, but I ain't never had one that looked like you come drag me outta one."

He talked like Monday. This must be what passed for manners in Texas, Kate supposed. She sized him up—tall, hefty, slightly bowlegged, with short dark hair. His clothes looked dusty and rangeworn. As befit his profession, he smelled like he spent a lot of time around horses. She held out her hand.

"Yes, I'm Katherine Shaw. I'm the schoolteacher here in Warbonnet. Can I ask you about your horse, Mister . . . ."

"Rollins. Ben Rollins," the young cowboy said, taking her hand. His hand had hard calluses for someone who couldn't have been more than a year older than she was. "He's a mighty fine cowpony, Miss. I call him 'Speck,' short for 'Speckled.' But I'm afraid he ain't for sale."

"It's his brand I really wanted to talk to you about. Is that Circle M from Texas?" Lifting his eyebrows, he admitted that it was. Kate nodded and steered him across the street to the bench in front of the bank, so no one would see her talking to a stranger close by the saloon.

"Our marshal, Monday Malone, has told me about the brand and about the Circle M Ranch."

Ben told her how he'd ridden up to Laramie with a trail herd to deliver cows to Dave Masterson and the new ranch south of town that belonged to Mitch Cullinane.

"I'm supposed to be up here scouting the trail, so we can deliver them beeves in the next week or two, before they eat up all the grass around Laramie. When I found out in Laramie that Monday was the marshal up here now, I couldn't believe it. We used to ride together and I made sure it was me that got to come scout this trail. I wanted to see him, but they tell me he's off chasing outlaws right now."

"Yes, I'm sorry. He may be out another few days or so." Kate prayed that Monday would return safely. Outlaws. Indi-

25

ans. Buffalo stampedes. Everything in Wyoming was more dangerous than home. She forced a smile. "But you'll be back when the herd comes, won't you? He'll be so glad to see you."

"Well, yes, Ma'am. I will. But that won't do as good. I was hoping to see him now. I got some real bad news for him. News that won't keep as long as a week. I was fixin' to write a note I could leave at his office." He nodded toward the jail, next to the bank.

Kate's heart sank. What more bad news could there be for Monday, an orphaned survivor of a wagon train massacre who'd been raised by a foster family? She knew that Monday's foster father, mother, and sister were all dead now.

"I can write that note for you. What's happened that you came all this way to tell him?"

"Well, this is hard for me to say to a lady of quality, Miss. But his brother Tom's in jail in Laramie. They say he killed a wh—a woman there three days ago. When I saw Monday's name on a sign on the wall in Sheriff Boswell's office saying he was marshal up here and a deputy sheriff for this county, well, I came as soon as I could. Thought he'd want to know. Maybe he could do something." Ben looked down at the street, avoiding meeting Kate's eye.

"That didn't sound so hard to say to a lady, except the part where you didn't want to tell me about this woman he's accused of murdering. What did you leave out, Mr. Rollins?"

Ben jerked his head up to look at her.

"I, uh, Miss Shaw. She isn't—wasn't—a respectable lady, Ma'am. She worked in a place, well . . . . "

Then Kate understood. What had Anna Green told her they called such women in New York City?

"She was a woman of, shall we say, 'temporary affection'?"

Ben relaxed, relieved to be let off the hook. "Yes, Ma'am, that's it. 'Temporary affection.' They say he killed her one night and they're fixing to try him and hang him for it."

3

Warbonnet

Monday Malone locked the Hotchkiss boys into one cell, after he'd had them drag the other bunk in there. He intended to keep the second cell empty in case he had to arrest anyone else while he already had two "guests."

He found Buck Haskell while he was on his way to Doc's office and asked the boy to tell his mother the marshal had two prisoners who'd need supper. After the boy left with the message, Monday remembered he hadn't ordered a meal for himself. He'd missed Martha's cooking. Maybe he could get some leftovers from Kate in Martha's kitchen later. He went on to Doc's office.

"No, it's not murder yet," Doc Gertz told him. "In fact, I think Charlie Simmons is mending well. May be up and around by next week. Got a head as hard as some of those rocks he studies." He pushed up his glasses and brushed his gray mustache.

"Can he talk, Doc? I need to have him confirm the bag of nuggets I found on the Hotchkiss boys. It'd be good if he could identify the two of them for me, too. Judge in Laramie will want to have that out of the way—if Charlie's up to it."

"I think you'll find him conscious. But you'll have to take the Hotchkiss boys to him. I don't want him out of bed for a while."

Monday decided he'd haul the nuggets and the boys down to the Simmons place tomorrow. He said goodbye to Doc and

27

headed out on his last errand. He was glad he'd got back before dark. Kate had left a note on his desk saying she needed to talk to him. He put the nuggets into the big safe at the bank overnight and made his first check of the saloon. No trouble there. Only two customers at this hour. Wouldn't be full dark for a while. He stepped into the street and headed up toward Martha Haskell's boarding house, hoping to find Kate there.

But he stopped at the end of the saloon. There was Kate talking to Jane Odom about thirty feet up the street. Both women stood sideways to him, but he was sure Kate noticed him.

Wind came up between the buildings and whipped Kate's skirt out like a flag, molding the garment to her legs. Her long hair streamed out behind her, too, and Kate reached both hands up to the back of her head, trying to gather it. The sight of her in profile was too much for him and he felt the old familiar feeling return. This is what he got for thinking of her by the campfire the other night. He pulled his hat off and held it in front of him in both hands.

"You know, I sometimes think the same thing about Miss Kate," a voice boomed from a shadowy chair on the boards at the end of the saloon. "But I hafta use a bigger hat."

Monday jumped as if he'd been shot. He peered into the shadow of the porch, but once he saw fringed leggings, he knew who'd spoken.

"Sha—Sean Finnegan. When did you get back in town?"

"Yesterday afternoon. Sorry I missed helping you track down them two bastards. They give you any trouble, young marshal?"

"Nothing I couldn't handle. I got 'em both locked up right now. Just waitin' to see Miss Kate."

"You know, boy," the gray-bearded scout said, leaning forward on his tilted-back chair and holding his beer glass carefully. "Not everybody in this town can see through you as keen as I can. If you got calico fever for Miss Kate, why don't you tell her how you feel? Some day she's gonna choose a husband, and if you're the only man in town who ain't asked her, well . . . ." He didn't need to finish the thought.

"Aw, Sean. I ain't got the cattle or the good looks Corey Masterson has. And I ain't got Jonah Barnes' education. I don't think I can just waltz up to a lady like that and . . . ."

"You ain't exactly without prospects, Malone. You got that little scrap of land the town council rewarded you with after you solved that murder last year. And I heard you bought a little more."

"Yeah, the council gave me a hundred and sixty acres and the ranch buildings. They let me buy another chunk the same size east of the north road. They gave Miss Kate the section just north of mine. Oh, here she comes."

Kate left Jane Odom and walked toward Monday. She still held her long hair behind her head with both hands. She looked good from this angle, too. Monday swallowed hard.

Sean Finnegan winked at Monday from his chair.

She stepped down from the walk into the street and said to Monday, "We really do need to talk right away. How about your office?"

"Uh, no, Miss Kate. I got two prisoners in there and I don't want men like them seeing you. Here comes Buck with their supper. I go down to the river for target practice some evenings. How 'bout I collect a couple things from my office and we'll go talk down there? Of course, if you'd rather not be seen going down to the river with me . . . ."

"I've lived in this town for almost a year, and I can go any-where I want," she teased back. "Go and get your guns."

Monday went into the jail with Buck while Kate waited. The marshal came out a few minutes later carrying a bucket with an extra pistol, cans, and some old newspaper in it. Buck spoke to Kate and went up the street toward home.

"I hope you didn't let Buxton take in their trays. You know his mother wishes you and his friends wouldn't call him Buck."

"No, Miss Kate. I fed them. But I ain't fixin' to even let them hear your voice back in those cells. Let's go to the river and talk."

Kate didn't say anything as they walked down to Monday's target area, a sandy, shaded stretch. Across the river was a high bank. He could see if anyone came into the line of fire on the far shore.

"Now," Monday said, putting down his bucket and taking out the cans and paper, "what's this important news you got for me that can't wait?" He placed the cans and some stones atop a driftwood log to hold the sheet of newspaper. It had a big black dot in the center of the page. He came back to her after stepping off about twenty paces.

"It will keep a few more minutes," Kate said, brushing off another log and spreading her skirt before sitting down. "I don't want to spoil your concentration. Let's talk when you've taken advantage of the light and finished your shooting."

"It'll be a while before I do any actual shooting. I generally practice a few moves before target practice. Since I gotta pay for my own ammunition, I only squeeze off about five rounds each evening."

With that, Monday took his loaded pistol out of his holster and put it carefully in the bucket. Then he took the other gun, made sure it wasn't loaded, holstered it, and tied down his leg thong. He shook his right arm a little to loosen up, then drew smoothly and cocked his pistol, pointing it at the paper target. He returned the weapon to his holster and made a half dozen more draws.

"Goodness," Kate said. "I do believe you've gotten faster. I just blinked as you started that last one and I heard you cock your gun before I opened my eyes."

"Well, thank you. I reckon I owe most of the new speed to you. This latigo rig gunbelt you gave me at Christmas makes for easier and faster draws. Doc timed me last month with his stopwatch at eight-tenths of a second from touch to cock and fire. He said wearing this holster is a double-edged sword, though." Monday drew and cocked another half dozen times while he spoke, never taking his eyes from the row of cans.

30

"That's quite a literary allusion Doc used. Do you know what he meant by it?"

"Well, I don't know what an 'al-lusion' might be, teacher. But I been readin' those books you lent me, and I'm learnin' new words all the time. Doc said he meant that if a lawman wears a fast draw holster, it might give him an advantage in speed. But it also means that ornery men might figure from my rig that I'm a fast gun, so I gotta practice more often to make sure this here holster don't get me in trouble with really fast *pistoleros*." He grinned at her. "So far, so good."

Monday put the empty gun into the bucket and took out the loaded pistol. He holstered it carefully and faced the cans again.

"You brought new cans to use tonight, just for me?"

Monday eased his stance and turned to talk to her. "Nice of you to say so, but no, I used these cans last week. Didn't hit any of 'em, so they're good as new. I'm thinking I do better now when I use the newspaper. It lets me see how close I come to my target."

With that, he turned, drew, and fired at the newspaper, all in one motion. Kate jumped.

Monday holstered his pistol again. "There, see that? I only missed the center of my paper target by about two inches at this distance. If I kept firing at the cans, I'd never know if I came that close." With that, he drew and fired, drew and fired, until he'd fired all five rounds. Then he walked over to the bucket and put his pistol into it.

"I generally fire one pistol, then load the other to carry tonight and tomorrow. I'll clean the one in the bucket when I get back to the office. What did you want to tell me that brought you down here for my target practice?" He remembered Sean Finnegan's warning. "You're not going to tell me you're getting married, are you?"

"Why, no. No, I'm not. Why would you ask such a thing?" Her look of amazement quickly turned to a frown. "It's not my future I want to talk to you about. It's about your past. Something I learned yesterday."

31

Monday gave her his full attention.

"Yesterday, I met a young man from Texas, right here in Warbonnet. His name is Ben Rollins and he said he knew you from Manzilla."

"Manzanita. Ben's folks own the ranch bordering mine. Ours. I mean Tom's." Monday cleared his throat. "Go on."

"Yes, well, he told me he came to Warbonnet to scout the route for the Circle M herd. It seems your brother contracted to bring cows up here for Dave Masterson and Mitch Cullinane. The herd is down in Laramie right now." She stopped speaking and seemed to watch his face for some sort of reaction. Monday lowered his head so she couldn't see his eyes.

"Oh. So Tom's in Laramie too, I take it." He holstered his pistol and tried to keep his voice steady.

"Yes, but he's not at liberty. That was the rest of Ben Rollins' message. He couldn't stay indefinitely, but I got the whole story out of him before he went back to Laramie. Your brother's in jail. For murder. They say he killed a young woman named Francine down there. A 'soiled dove'."

This time, Monday raised his eyes and looked at her.

"I don't recollect using that term in front of you—or any other lady."

"You didn't. We *ladies* have our own sources of information. Ben said she'd been murdered one night, stabbed with your brother's knife. He said Sheriff Boswell thinks he has an ironclad case. They expect to try him in about two weeks." Kate stared hard at him now. "You know what they'll do if he's found guilty, don't you?"

Monday couldn't meet her eyes. He began to collect his unblemished cans and the riddled sheet of newspaper. "Yeah," he said at last, in a voice so low she probably couldn't hear him. "Reckon in that case, they'll hang him." He returned the items to the bucket, picked it up, and looked at her without expression.

Kate stood up and faced him in obvious distress. "Is that all you can say? They're going to hang your brother and that's all?"

"He made it clear to me more'n once he don't think of us as brothers. I don't owe him nothing now. Seems like the law ought to run its course." Why couldn't she just give him the bad news and let him think about it in private?

"How can you say that? You may have been adopted, but you were raised with him. You have the same last name. You were both brothers to, to Mary Ellen." She stepped back a pace when she said the name, as if afraid of his reaction.

"Mary Ellen's dead, Kate. Major Malone and my ma are dead, too. Just as dead as my real parents, whoever they were. I don't see—"

"Oh, don't you? Tom is the last kin you have left. As marshal of Warbonnet, you're also a deputy sheriff of Albany County. That means you can look into this murder. What if Tom didn't do it? Do you want him to hang for a crime he didn't commit? Can you just turn your back on him because of the way he's treated you, the way he took your share of the Circle M Ranch?"

Her bossing him around always made Monday hot under the collar. "Kate, I don't want to go mess around with Sheriff Boswell's evidence, just so you can play detective again."

How dare you? She stamped her foot. "I thought we knew each other better than that! This has nothing to do with me. I hope to go to the Yellowstone country with Professor Hayden in another couple of weeks. This has to do with you. Ben came here to tell you because he thought you would care. What do you suppose will happen to the ranch if your brother hangs?"

"I hadn't thought about it. Don't know if it would come to me or what might happen."

He was quiet for a few moments. Kate seemed to be seething quietly.

"I see what you're driving at, Kate. If I do nothing and let Tom hang, am I doing that because I want the ranch for myself? It must seem that way."

"No," she said, reaching out and touching his arm. "I never thought such a thing."

33

"Maybe not. But someday you would have. I reckon I'll go check out Tom's story when I take the Hotchkiss boys to Laramie. Might leave as early as tomorrow morning. I wouldn't want this issue to come between us, Kate. I wouldn't do anything to lose your respect."

Kate took her hand away. "This has nothing to do with any feelings I may have. I don't want you to look into your brother's case because you think I want you to. I want you to do it because you think it's the right thing to do."

Monday began to walk up the shallow bank, but turned to look at her.

"That's the trouble with you, Kate. You always think people are better than they really are. All of us."

She picked up her skirts and walked up to Monday, then stopped and looked at him.

"No, I don't think that at all. I *know* every person is better than he or she thinks they are. Your brother Tom, for instance. So are you, Monday Malone. Better than you think you are. I know you'll do the right thing. Pretty soon, you'll know it, too."

They walked back to town in silence.

4

Laramie

Monday stopped his horse at the hitching rail in front of the Albany County Sheriff's Office. As he got down and tied off Lightning's reins, he glanced back up the street at his straggling party. Cletus and Verle Hotchkiss moped along, Cletus in the lead, as usual. They had no reason to look forward to arriving. Verle looked around like he might miss the sight of a busy street for the next few years. A good thing, Monday thought, that Charlie Simmons recalled Cletus as the one who'd hit him as he brought the nuggets out of his safe; maybe the judge would go a little easier on Verle.

Bull Devoe brought up the rear of the little procession. Monday was glad the huge black man had business down here in Laramie and agreed to the dollar-a-day special deputy's rate to help him keep an eye on the Hotchkiss boys for these last three days. He chuckled at how Bull had scowled at the pair and never put his rifle in its scabbard. Cletus would probably like to kick himself for not trying to escape when they had only Monday to contend with on their way into Warbonnet. That is, he would kick himself if there weren't leg irons fastened under his horse.

The boys steered their mounts to the same hitch rail and waited quietly while Monday tied off their reins. Then, while Bull stayed mounted on his huge sorrel—the only horse in Warbonnet strong enough to carry the big blacksmith— Monday knelt and unlocked their leg irons. Bull's presence meant he didn't have to worry about being kicked in the head at this point.

"So, Malone again, eh? See you brought in a pair this time. Won't work. You can't swap two o' them for yer brother."

Monday straightened up. He didn't need to look at the speaker. "'Lo, Bowman. Nate still paying you to keep the office swept out?" Then he turned to look at Reese Bowman, the most recently hired of Laramie's three deputy sheriffs.

"Naw, I get to do real work. Things stay busy down here, not like in that little one-horse town you bunk in." Bowman tried to lean casually against a porch beam, but his round form and short legs made that pose difficult to maintain.

"You sayin' Warbonnet's a one-horse town, deputy?" Bull cut in. "You insulting my horse here? I might have Rusty sit on you. He'll be so happy to get me off his back, he'd likely be grateful to sit on a soft sack of grits like you." Monday smiled in spite of himself. He saw Verle was relieved that Bull spoke gruffly to someone besides him and his brother. Monday removed their leg irons and helped both of them down. Their handcuffs clinked and rattled.

"Sheriff in, Reese?" Monday asked, trying to seem more friendly to the little deputy. "I'd like to get these two 'guests' signed in soon as possible. Maybe get a bath, have a beer."

Bull grunted in assent to the bath, but Monday knew he didn't drink. Bowman opened his mouth to say something smart, but when the big blacksmith scowled at him, the little deputy evidently thought better of it.

"Naw, he's over at the judge's. Dutch'll take care of you. He's got the office." With that, Bowman came down the steps and tried to swagger around the Hotchkiss boys. But when Cletus raised his manacled hands in front of him and shook his chains, the deputy did a little half-step to his right and scuttled off up the street without looking back.

"Why don't you take the horses over to the livery, Bull, and get a jump on me for a tub at the bath house? Reckon I'll be along in a little while." He grinned. Bull had said the bath

36

house got a real large tub last winter, one that could accommodate him and both his feet, too.

"Sure you can handle these desperadoes up the stairs and through that door?" Bull teased. "I'd be glad to keep 'em covered a mite longer." Cletus sneered at Bull, but Verle moved up the steps quickly, dragging his unlocked leg iron. Monday waved Bull off and opened the door. As he ushered his prisoners inside, he saw the big black man unhitch Lightning and take the boys' horses, too. Not for the first time he wished Warbonnet could afford Bull as a permanent deputy.

The longest-serving deputy sheriff in the county welcomed Monday as he closed the door.

Dutch van Orden, all six-foot-two of him, uncoiled from a chair and smiled when he saw who followed the prisoners in. "Monday. Hey, you're a sight for sore eyes. Wondered how soon you'd be down here when you got the news about your brother." Dutch pointed to a steaming cup of coffee on the desk. "Just blew on that one a bit. Ain't touched it yet. Take it. I can pour me another one."

"What about us?" whined Verle.

"Later, boys," Monday said, fishing the keys to their shackles out of his vest pocket. "After we get you tucked in and the paperwork done, I'd be glad to bring it to you myself. You been so well-behaved and respectful all the way down here."

Cletus shot him a look under straight black brows, but Verle looked as if he'd just had a reprieve. Dutch and Monday guided them back to the first empty cell, where Monday removed their handcuffs and leg irons and Dutch locked them in. Back in the outer office, Monday settled down with the offered cup while Dutch got himself a new one. The deputy smoothed his thick mustache that sandy-haired Monday envied, then blew on his cup as he began to write down particulars on the new prisoners.

Monday hauled out the papers he'd brought. He surprised himself at how good he'd gotten at the legal niceties of his job. At least nobody in Laramie criticized his spelling. He took care not to show the paperwork to Kate, though. The teacher

37

would make him copy it over. Dutch looked at his report and signed a receipt for the two prisoners, their horses, and gear.

"I heard Bowman riling you outside. Sorry your brother's got himself in a peck of trouble. You want to talk to him now?"

Monday knew Dutch's concern was real and he wanted to be of help. The two of them had ridden three days into Cheyenne territory last fall in search of a bank robber. The Cheyenne found him first. He and Dutch were nervous bringing the remains back and the shared tension of that trip had made them friends. Monday had confided a bit about his family to Dutch during the ride back. Besides Dutch, only Kate and Jonah Barnes, the circuit-riding preacher who called once a month in Warbonnet, had any idea of the state of Monday's relationship with his brother Tom. He hadn't told anyone the whole story.

Monday sighed. He guessed he'd put it off long enough. No way around it now.

"I reckon I'd better. Any chance of some privacy back there?" He waved at the cell block door.

"Sure. Sheriff's had him in that last cell next to the back door. The two we locked up in the front are our only other guests—until things get busy tonight. Nice of you to offer, but I'll see the Hotchkiss boys get coffee and grub."

"Bull or I will bring their guns over this evening, after we get settled in." Monday took a deep breath and glanced at the door into the cells. He'd been dreading this moment. "So, same drill as before?"

"Right. You know Nate's rules. Visitors have to hang gunbelts beside the door. Let's go." Dutch picked up his keys again and led the way. He locked Monday into the back of the jail and returned to his desk.

Monday walked to his left, around the central block of four cells, and worked his way to the left rear of the building. He could just make out a form sitting on a bunk in the last cell. The man had his back to him, his elbows resting on his drawn-up knees, looking at the small barred window. He turned his head at the sound of Monday's spurs.

"Early for supper, ain't it? Oh. It's you." Tom Malone was broader and taller than Monday. Four years older, too, but the dark hair he'd shared with his father and sister still didn't have a touch of frost.

"Grew a beard, huh? Don't think I could've picked you out of a crowd, Tom." Monday didn't see the stool that usually sat by the back door. He held his hat in his hands and began to rotate it nervously. What he had to say wouldn't take long anyway.

"Had an easier time raisin' these whiskers than you woulda," his brother said. "Are you shaving twice a week yet?" With his opening pleasantries out of the way, Tom went on. "Once they told me you were a lawman north of here, I figured you'd be by some time to gloat. What's the matter, cowboyin' too tough for you up here? Or the winters too cold?"

Monday looked down at his hat. "I never got to Montana after all. Found a town I liked here in Wyoming. Helped solve a murder last year and the town council asked me to stay on permanent. I got a little land already, but it don't compare to Texas, Tom."

"I reckon not. How much land you got?"

Monday spoke softly, reluctant to tell his brother the truth. "Uh, three hundred and twenty acres. Council will let me buy another one-sixty if I want."

"Five hundred acres? Circle M's more than five hundred square *miles*." Tom's sarcasm stung, but Monday tried not to show it. All those five hundred square miles belonged to Tom now, since he and a Manzanita lawyer had denied the existence of a will Pa had once shown him.

"How you holdin' up?" Monday asked, trying to act as Kate would want him to.

"How do you think? Food ain't bad, but there ain't nothin' to do, 'cept think. Smitty comes by once a day. He's gettin' ready to run the rest of those beeves north to the buyers soon. He still remembers you." Tom grinned wolfishly.

Monday looked up at his brother now with a spark in his eyes. He'd never been able to best Tom at anything, and Tom had used his foreman Smitty as the instrument of Monday's humiliation during the last two cattle drives they'd made. Monday didn't think he feared Smitty the way he used to.

"I'll be sure to look him up when I need to scrape my boots. Tom, I didn't come down here to gloat. Somebody I know thought I could help. Somebody who don't know you and thinks she knows me. I thought . . . ."

"That you could help get me out of here? Forget it. You'd have to bust me out. Smitty's talked about that. Maybe after the last cattle are turned into cash, he might try it. The hands are game. But no, there ain't nothin' you could do to make anything any better. Best you be on your way. I don't need your help." He pulled his feet up onto the bunk and turned his back, resting his elbows on his knees.

Monday put his hat on. "You might help me a bit, then. Did you do it? What they said?"

Tom didn't speak for a while.

"I don't know. Can't remember. I was dead drunk that night. I'd been sober enough earlier to enjoy Francine's favors. All them girls out at Fricker's Hog Ranch got real pretty French names. Plenty of men swore they saw me leaving her place. Went to some saloons, had a few, then took a bottle back to the hotel.

"Next thing I knew, they're bangin' on my door and draggin' me down here. Said they found my knife in her. Had my initials on it. Can't say I didn't do it. Only, if I did, I don't recall why I woulda done it. I liked Francine. A lot." Tom looked out the window. Monday wondered if "a lot" meant anything, coming from his brother.

"I'll go talk to the sheriff about the evidence," Monday said. "See if they got any witnesses." But he was disgusted with himself for feeling relieved. He'd seen Tom drunk a few times. He recalled once in Abilene when Tom had slapped a saloon girl hard enough to knock her down. Tom hadn't recalled that incident either when Smitty and Ben Rollins mentioned it to him later. It looked like his brother was guilty all right. Monday could go back and tell Kate that he'd tried.

40

"Well, I'm sorry, Tom." Monday stood up, preparing to leave. He couldn't think of anything else to say.

"I'm only sorry to be hung so far from home. From Ma and Pa's graves. From Mary Ellen's." Tom stood up and came to the bars. "You know I never asked you for nothin'. This is real hard for me. If you could see your way clear, would you make sure the boys take me back to the ranch and plant me behind the house, on that little rise with the family?" In the dim light, Monday couldn't read his face.

"If it comes to that. Sure. I'll see to it."

"No need to go all that way yourself. Unless you hanker to throw yourself on Mary Ellen's grave again." Monday could only make out Tom's unblinking eyes.

"Don't spit out her name like that, Tom. She was my sister, too."

"Your *sister?* No man treats his sister like that. Just send my body back. I ain't askin' anything more. Even you couldn't screw that up."

Monday backed away, choking down a reply. He wanted to say he'd return, that he'd see Tom again before the trial, but he couldn't speak. He stumbled back to the cell block door and rapped for Dutch. The deputy took one look at Monday and bit off whatever he intended to say. He offered coffee again, but Monday declined.

"Maybe I need a drink instead. Ain't had but one whiskey in the last two years, but by God, I'm ready."

"Don't start, Monday." Dutch was a family man who hardly drank himself. "Go have a bath and a meal. Get a good night's sleep. You'll feel better in the morning."

Monday shook his head, wiped his eyes, and sighed. "Guess I will. But I ain't done here yet. I oughta find out some more about the murder. Who found the body? Who made the arrest? I need to find out where and how it happened."

"Well, you're in luck. Bowman got there first that night. He had evening rounds. But he left the scene of the crime right after he took a peek, so's he could arrest your brother back at his hotel room." Dutch leaned back in his chair. "I

41

was home at the time, but Nate asked me to go right out there and see to the girl and take notes. What can I tell you?"

"For starters, who reported finding the body?"

"Suzanne. She's one of the other girls there. Said she heard a scream from Francine's room. Found the door open and went in when she got no answer to her call. She found Francine starin' at the ceiling with the knife still stuck in her."

"Where was the body?"

"In her bed. She'd been workin' that night. Didn't have no clothes on. Looked like somebody who'd been with her stabbed her."

"Reckon I can go over to this Hog Ranch later. Can you tell me what the room looked like?"

"Sure, Monday," Dutch said, pulling a notebook from a drawer. "Uh, stand over here by the front door. Now, see how our door swings in? Opens to the right. The door would bump into the foot rail of Francine's bed when you swung it open. Now, if you're standing in the doorway . . . ." Dutch consulted his notes.

"There on your left is the first corner of her room. Then there's a wall running away from you. No furniture right there, just clothes pegs and a couple nails along that wall, starting close by your left shoulder. Beyond that, there's a humpbacked trunk. Then the next corner of the room—right here," he said, pointing to a place in the imaginary room he was constructing for Monday. "There's a standing screen. Reckon Francine changed clothes there."

"A girl in her profession? Why would she need a screen? Why would she consider modesty?"

"I dunno. Didn't think about that," Dutch said. He consulted his notes again. "Dark green fabric with little white curlicues on it."

"Well, coming out of that second corner behind the screen, there's a window, right across from the door. No particular view; it looks down on a hitch rack. Hmmm." The deputy moved his finger down the page.

"Next to the window is a dresser with a mirror over it. Then there's a washstand with pitcher and basin." He paused and brought the notebook closer to his face. "Almost forgot. Found a chair behind the screen, tipped over on its side. Matched the dresser and the mirror."

"Uh, let's see," Dutch went on. "After the wash stand, the third corner, then a little table came next, with a lamp on it—still lit when I got there, before you ask me. With a red fringed shade. Then over here in this corner," he indicated the front wall of the jail, having come to the fourth corner of the room now, "this is where her bed would be, headboard up against the third wall, foot rail down here where the door would come round and hit it."

"What kinda bed?" Monday asked.

"Oh, uh, brass. Big one. Come all the way from St Louie, this Suzanne said."

"With a tall footrail then?"

"Yeah. Stood more than a foot above the mattress as I recall."

"How big a bed? One person or two?"

"Two," Dutch said. "I understand some customers could pay to stay all night. That's rare, though, according to Suzanne. She said the girls prize their sleep." Dutch looked up. "You know, Monday, when you come outta the cells a minute ago, you didn't look or act like you. Now with all these questions, you seem more like your old self."

"OK," Monday said, grinning at Dutch's implied compliment. "Guess I am feeling a little better." Orienting himself to the small room Dutch had described, Monday pointed to the last corner and along that wall. "Now where was she on this bed and in what position?"

"Over here, against the fourth wall,' Dutch said, pointing. "Flat on her back. The knife—hand me yours, would you? Thanks. She looked like this and it was in her like this." The deputy obligingly lay down close to the wall and held the knife horizontally over his heart, with the point toward his shoulder, the edge toward the wall and the handle toward the door.

43

Monday froze with his hand outstretched. "Just like that, Dutch? I mean, she was over against the wall with this foot-high rail between her and the door, on the far side of a bed as big as that?"

Dutch glanced up at Monday like he sensed something was up. "Yeah, just like this. I saw her myself and I stayed with Doc until he took away the body. Why?"

"And you're sure the knife was in that exact position? Not just standing up in her, like somebody had reached over and stabbed down on her?"

"No. It lay nearly flat. Doc said it pierced the heart, though. He said death was near, uh, instant something. And I got the position right here in my notes. You could read the initials 'TM' right on the handle."

Monday came over to where Dutch still lay. "*What?* You mean you could see the initials with the knife in that position?" He couldn't believe it. His mind began to race.

"Well, sure. See, you got your initials on the handle here. Well," he said, bringing the knife up to his eyes, "Yours has a Circle M on it, not your initials. What's the matter, Monday? What's got into you?"

Monday turned slowly around the room Dutch had described for him, pointing to various things and talking to himself. Dutch got up off the floor and brushed himself off. He handed the knife back to Monday.

"Monday, what's wrong? You got me spooked now."

"Dutch, Tom didn't do it. He really didn't do it. Somebody set him up, but the killer made a couple mistakes. Look here." Monday put his knife back in its sheath, then took his gunbelt from its peg and buckled it back on. "Look here. What do you see?"

"Nothing special. What am I supposed to see?"

Monday turned to his right so Dutch could see the knife on the left side of his belt. "See where this knife hangs, on my left side? Look here at my brand mark. See which side of the handle that's on when I draw it? It's against my palm. Which hand did I draw it with, Dutch?"

44

"Uh, your right. You reached across to draw it, same as I would."

"That's right," said Monday, stepping close and placing the blade flat on Dutch's chest over his heart again, point toward the shoulder and edge away from them both, parallel to that wall Dutch had told him about. With the Circle M design showing.

"Dutch, that woman was sprawled as far from the edge of the bed as she could be, with a footrail nobody'd be likely to climb over. A man laying right on top of her stabbed her, maybe while they was havin' relations. Look at my hand resting on the handle, Dutch. Think about her position on the far side of that bed. She was killed by someone right-handed. Tom is a lefty."

"What?"

"Left-handed, Dutch. If you got his gunbelt, you can check it out. A lefty like Tom carries his gun on his left side and his knife on the right, opposite of you and me. When he carves his initials on a knife, they should be on the other side of the handle from those on the knife of a right-hander like me. When he reaches across himself to draw it—like we do—it comes out in his left hand, with his palm against the initials," Monday said, switching the knife to his other hand.

"If I want to stab someone like you found this knife in Francine, I can't reach across her with it in my left hand and put it in the way you found her." He switched hands again to show where the initials should be on a lefty's knife. "Somebody right-handed stabbed her, probably while he put his left hand over her mouth." So how did anybody hear a scream, he wondered.

"I'll be damned, Monday. You might be right. I got his gunbelt here in this drawer." He took it out and they both looked at the knife in the sheath. No initials. Then Monday pulled it out and turned the handle over.

"Nobody carries his initials against his hip like this, Dutch. This ain't his knife. Tom's been framed. I gotta talk to the sheriff." Monday handed the gunbelt back and went out the door.

45

5

Laramie

Monday found Sheriff Nate Boswell coming out of the judge's office holding an unwieldy sheaf of papers tucked under his bushy brown beard. He helped Nate by taking half the burden.

"Thanks, Monday. Good to see you again. You come down here to see about your brother?"

"Not exactly, Nate. I brought you a couple hold-up artists. Or at least they fancied themselves artists." Monday secured a few fluttering sheets. "I woulda been down here with them today or tomorrow anyway. When I got the news about Tom, I admit I came a little early."

"Well, I'm right sorry about his case. Did you already get a chance to talk to him?" They headed toward the jail. Nate's long beard and frock coat moved in the slight breeze.

"Yeah, but he didn't have much to say in his own defense. Come inside and let me tell you what Dutch and I discovered. I gotta tell you, though, I ain't compared what I think I know to the actual scene of the crime." He held the door for Nate and they went in.

#

Ten minutes later, Nate sat at his desk, sliding Tom's knife in and out of its sheath, holding it first in his right hand, then in his left.

"Damn. *Damn!* You make a good case, Monday. If all this hangs together, I guess we haven't got the right man. You gonna check things out over at the Hog Ranch?"

"He'd better try to do that tomorrow in daylight, Nate," Dutch said. "Business is probably pickin' up over there about now. Place'll be crowded and all the beds will be filled for the next few hours."

"All right, then. What do we do about your brother? Can't just let him go on the basis of what you figured out. Judge'd never stand for it. We need to find a better suspect."

"I know, Nate. I'll need time to smoke out the real killer. If we were to let Tom out right away, he'd bull around out there and we might never find whoever we're looking for. Or the murderer might kill Tom himself this time. Reckon we gotta leave him locked up a while."

"Hmmm," Boswell said, stroking his beard as if in thought. "I guess we ought not to let anybody but the three of us know about this new information. Won't that be cruel to treat Tom that way, though, not lettin' him in on the secret?"

"Well, maybe. But I'm trying to save Tom's life. Reckon you could keep him locked up for his own safety."

Sheriff Boswell stood up.

"Suppose I can tell your brother at the right time. I'll take that responsibility."

They shook on it and Monday left with a lighter heart than when he'd come to the jail. Glad, in fact, to have something to work with, anything better to tell Kate than that his brother was probably guilty and his case looked hopeless. He'd better find a way to tell Kate. He was prepared to just walk away from a guilty Tom, but now he'd have to live up to her standards if he was going to see justice done and keep Tom from hanging.

Kate. Monday thought about her as he closed the door of the jail. The envelope she'd entrusted to him! He'd forgotten it. He touched his shirt pocket under his vest. Still there. But would the dry goods store still be open? He checked his watch and hurried down the street. Mrs. Ivinson had pulled down the shades and was showing the last customer out as Monday hurried in.

"I'm sorry, but we're closing up. Can you come back tomorrow?" An imposing woman, with faded hair that must have been red at one time.

"Well, yes, Ma'am. I can. But I need to pick up this order before I leave town. Can I leave this with you and get the order tomorrow?" He passed her the envelope, glad to have the clinking coins in it out of his pocket.

Mrs. Ivinson examined the wax seal on the envelope to see that it was still intact. "What's the order, Marshal?" she asked, reading his badge.

"Uh, I don't know, Ma'am. It's from Miss Katherine Shaw up in Warbonnet. She didn't tell me what she ordered. Something unmentionable, I'd guess." He started to grin, but stopped.

"Indeed," she said, frowning at him in disapproval of his using even that term. "Well, if we have what she wants, come back around noon and I'll have it wrapped up for you."

Monday thanked her and let her close up. He should go over to the bath house. Bull would be wondering what had happened to him. But he had one more errand to run.

# # #

"Evening," Monday said, stepping into the telegraph office. "You're not fixin' to close yet, are you?"

The clerk looked at him over his glasses. "Nope, not for another hour. You could send a real long telegram in that time." Monday thought that was probably supposed to be Western Union humor, but the clerk didn't smile.

"I don't, I mean, I won't have a wire that long." The clerk gave him a sheet of paper and a pencil. Monday wrinkled his forehead and set to work. Ten minutes later, he handed his draft to the clerk.

"Let's see," the man said, making a face and peering at Monday's penmanship. "Hmmm. I think we can save you a little money. You ever sent a wire before?"

"Once. It was hard work then, too."

"I imagine so. Fortunately, they pay us well to help customers like you. First, I'll just put the second 'n' in innocent for you." When Monday opened his mouth, the clerk quickly said, "No charge for extra letters. We charge by the word. Now, presumably this K. Shaw will know what you're talking about here?"

"Yes, sir. It's about a matter we discussed back in Warbonnet."

"All right, then. Let's save you a few words and a little money here. Instead of 'I am looking into the matter,' let's try just 'am investigating.' That'll save you four words. You do understand what 'investigating' means, don't you?" he asked, peering at Monday's badge.

"Course I know what it means. I just couldn't come within a mile of spelling it is all." This man did as well at embarrassing him as Kate did. He was relieved to fork over his money and get out of there. A bath, a meal, and a good night's sleep. Dutch's remedy. Monday would start investigating tomorrow, even if he couldn't remember how to spell the word.

6

Warbonnet

A half hour later, Kate Shaw gathered up the last of the supper dishes and handed them to her landlady, Martha Haskell. Martha's son Buxton burst through the back door.

"Miss Kate, Miss Kate! Mr. Wyler said you got a tellygram. *A tellygram!*" The boy was out of breath.

She and Martha looked at each other, startled. It couldn't be good news. The station had opened in April after the Army restrung the old lines knocked down by buffalo and Indians four years ago, before there was a town here. Kate had gotten two congratulatory wires, one from her parents and the other from Miss Bishop, the head of her Normal School. There was no reason for anyone to send her a telegram now except bad news. The worry must have shown on her face.

"Go on, Kate. Go on down and see what it's about. I can finish up here. In fact, Buxton can take your place." The boy rolled his eyes in response and flopped into a kitchen chair.

"I can't imagine that it's anything but bad news, Martha."

"Why does it have to be bad, Kate? Don't you have a sister? Perhaps she's going to get married. And what about that writer friend of yours?"

"Anna Green? I hadn't thought of her. Perhaps she sent news of a success in New York City. Thanks." Relieved a little, Kate took off her apron and stepped into the hall to check the clock. "Do you think the telegraph office will be open for another ten minutes?"

"I can't think Enoch Wyler does enough business to close up on the only customer he probably got today. Go on, now, before he does close."

Kate looked at herself in the little hall mirror. A few stray hairs had worked their way out of her bun and her cuffs had gotten in the dish water. Well, no help for it, now. She thanked Martha again and went out the kitchen door. She'd better stick to the back yards, she decided. At this hour, she might be slowed down if she met too many people she knew. She lifted her skirts and ran, dodging chickens and hoping she wouldn't meet any ill-tempered dog.

She slowed to a walk to catch her breath and came out between the Simmons' house and the assay office. Maybe the telegram was from Monday. Oh, no. He would have arrived in Laramie today. He would only wire her this quickly if his brother had already been tried and hanged by the time he got there. Had she sent him straight into disaster?

Craggy-faced Enoch Wyler stood on the boards in front of the little office in a white shirt with sleeve garters. In the tradition of Western Union, he slept in the back of the office. He put his watch away as Kate came up to him.

"Sorry, Mr. Wyler. I didn't mean to keep you open past closing."

"That's all right, Miss Shaw. Anything for you," he said, smiling. He handed her a sealed sheet. "Don't look such a fret. It didn't seem like bad news to me."

That was the problem with telegrams, Kate thought after she'd thanked him and started back up the street. Two telegraphers would always know your business. She stopped to open it. From Monday, just as she'd feared. Her heart sank, then rebounded as she read the message.

"To K. Shaw, Warbonnet. Stop. Brother innocent. Stop. SB agrees. Stop. Am investigating. Stop. Signed Monday."

He'd even figured out how to tell her the good news without alerting the clerks. They wouldn't know from the signature "Monday" that the brother's last name was Malone.

51

And SB. That must be Sheriff Boswell. If he'd said Nate, or his nickname "Boz," the news would have been all over Laramie by now. And Monday was going to pursue the matter.

She couldn't read any emotion in the short telegram, but she hoped he felt as pleased as she did. Right this very moment. The immediacy thrilled her—to think that he'd written out this note minutes ago in a town three days' ride from here. The message made it seem like he was right next to her. With this new service, her home back East didn't seem so far away. She pushed thoughts of Buffalo away.

Kate stuffed the message between the buttons of her bodice. Telegrams were such a novelty out here that she didn't want anyone to see her carrying the distinctive yellow sheet and ask about it.

She smiled as she started back to the boarding house. Tomorrow, the fact that she'd gotten a wire would be all over town. So few were received in Warbonnet that Buxton and Mr. Wyler were bound to talk. But she'd figure out how to avoid revealing its contents.

Her mother had told her more than once that she was too secretive. Kate had always loved secrets as a child. She stopped smiling when she touched the scar on her left hand. She recalled how she'd lived a secret life for nearly five months after Stuart's death.

A secret life that almost killed her.

7

Laramie

Monday got up early. He had lots of that "investigating" to do today if he wanted to leave for Warbonnet tomorrow morning. He smiled as he brushed lather onto his face and remembered the meal he and Bull ate last night. They hadn't smiled about it at the time.

# # #

"Let's sit over by the window, Bull, and watch folks passing in the street. We never get to do that in Warbonnet." As they made their way to their seats, Monday pegged his hat on the back of one chair. A waiter came hurrying over.

"Uh, excuse me. But I'm afraid you can't sit there." Bull sighed, but Monday didn't understand.

"Why not? This table already spoken for? Don't look like you're crowded in here tonight."

"No, it's not that," the waiter said, glancing sidelong at the big blacksmith. "It's just, well, you see, we're not supposed to serve Negroes in here. The owner—"

Monday finally caught on. "We don't want you to serve us Negroes. We want to eat some steaks. If you can serve beef, you can serve us." He turned to their table, but Bull caught his arm before he could sit.

"Ain't no use arguin' with the man, Monday. At least he's being polite. I been treated a lot worse in better places. Let's go."

"No, wait a minute," Monday said, shrugging off Bull's hand—no easy task. He turned to the waiter. "Does it make a difference if this man is my guest? I'll be paying the bill."

"No, I'm sorry. But the owner gave us strict instructions that we aren't supposed to seat, um, certain types of people. *Eep!*" He made a mouse-like noise when Monday grabbed his shirt front.

"So it's really all about seats, is it? Well, we don't want to sidestep the owner, but we just came in off the trail from War-bonnet, had baths and all, and we really had our hearts set on a couple of your biggest steaks. Tell you what we're gonna do," Monday said, letting go of the man.

"We're going to take two of these unused chairs and go out back and have ourselves a little picnic. You bring two steaks and potatoes out the back in about ten minutes, all right? Coffee, too."

When the waiter nodded and made as if to leave, Monday held up one hand. "Bull," he said over his shoulder, "how do you want your steak?"

"Well done," said the big man, chuckling. "Just like what you're trying to do here, Monday. Well done."

"I'll take mine a little pink in the center. Reckon you can do that?" he asked the waiter. The man backed away, nodding. Monday and Bull each picked up a chair and took them around back, where they set up a couple balks of firewood to form a makeshift table.

"Air seems fresher out here, somehow, don't it," Monday asked Bull while they waited.

That amused Bull, but Monday wasn't mollified.

"Monday, I 'preciate what you tried to do in there, but black folks run into that kind of treatment all the time. I'm accepted in Warbonnet from church pew to supper table because folks there know me. But here in Laramie, I'm just

54

another, well, I ain't gonna use the word. Remember what I said about havin' this happen in other places?"

"Reckon you can tell me which places those were, Bull? I wouldn't want to throw my money away where folks are so narrow-minded they can look through a keyhole with both eyes."

# # #

Remembering Bull's laughter at that last remark made Monday smile this morning as he wiped the last of the shaving soap from his face and looked at his reflection in the little hotel mirror. He'd agreed to meet Bull this afternoon and see where Francine was murdered.

"How are you gonna meet me there around noon, Bull, if they won't serve you a steak in this eatery?" He'd spread his hands, the knife and fork emphasizing the question. They were sitting out by the woodpile.

"Listen, Monday," Bull said, cutting some more steak. "The owner and those gals who work there don't care if you're black, white, red, or a Chinaman. They judge a man on three other colors—how much gold, silver, or green you have. Trust me. I'll see you there."

# # #

Monday had a quick breakfast, then went looking for Doctor Finfrock, figuring he'd be up early. After an exchange of pleasantries, including an update on Finfrock's colleague in Warbonnet, Doctor Friedrich Wilhelm Gertz, Monday got right to the point.

"Doc, I want to ask you some things about that girl who was stabbed out at the Hog Ranch. Her name was Francine. Don't know her last name."

"I don't know it either," he said. "All the girls have taken French first names. I understand many of them later move on and get married somewhere else. Not using their true names in their line of work helps them when they try to become

55

respectable. And it lets them preserve a private part of themselves they don't have to share with all the men they service."

"I recall some girls like that in Abilene used fancy names, too. Tell me, Doc. I got the position of the knife, the location of the body, and the layout of her room from Dutch van Orden. Do you recollect how the knife was placed in her?" Monday handed him his own knife.

"Dear me," the doctor said, examining it. "Except for the Circle M on this knife, I should say it was the murder weapon."

"No, it ain't, Doc. But all the Circle M cowboys bought knives just like this in Abilene after our first cattle drive. I reckon new drovers buy 'em there, too. Nearly everyone in the outfit that came into Laramie must have a knife like this. And most of them probably carved initials or other designs into the handles by now."

"Well," Finfrock said, handling the knife gingerly, "this was the exact position of the knife in her chest." He demonstrated the same positioning that Dutch had shown Monday.

"Then, Doc, it looks to me like someone would've had to put the knife into her from this position." He stood closely in front of Doc and used his right hand to grasp the handle. "If that someone had stood at the edge of the bed and reached over—"

"Then the knife would have been more vertical and the blade would have been away from the wall, like you'd do if you made an overhand stab," Doc finished for him. "But to be in the position we found it in, it would almost have to have been inserted by a person who was right on top of her." He demonstrated the angle.

"And with his—or her—right hand, Doc?"

"Yes, exactly. No other way. Why?"

"My brother's left-handed. He couldn't have killed that girl. When I pointed that out to the sheriff, he agreed to let me look into things."

"Well, that's interesting. I think everybody in this town figures your brother did it. And they're not happy with him. That Francine was a most popular girl, I am informed. If you're

56

looking into this killing, then here's something else I found, quite by accident, when I looked at her body after I removed the knife. I suppose Deputy van Orden told you there was very little visible bleeding."

"Yeah, he said that."

"The killer got her heart on the first thrust, sliced it nearly in half. Death was instantaneous and any bleeding was only into her chest cavity. That's what makes the second thrust so interesting."

"Second thrust? You mean the killer stabbed her again, when she was already dead?"

"Or two people stabbed her once apiece. I can't explain it. When I first took the knife out, I carefully noted the angle. It was too shallow to have killed her right away. That's when I found the other wound, the one that really killed her. The second stab didn't appear to have been made in haste, just slid back in, close to the same position as the first thrust. Like it had been sheathed in her deliberately, so we could see the initials more easily. But for some reason, the killer took the knife out, then put it back in."

# # #

On his way to the jail, Monday thought about the possibilities Doc raised. An uncertain, reluctant killer? Or a mean killer who'd enjoyed stabbing this girl more than once? A second person who came into the room after the killer had left? Why would a second person remove the knife and then put it back in her? Why would anyone stab her twice?

And if the first thrust killed her right away, how had she managed to scream? Had she seen the knife coming and managed to get a sound out before the killer covered her mouth?

Monday's head was swimming with these questions when he got to the jail. He asked Sheriff Boswell for the list of the girl's belongings from the inventory sheet and scanned it.

"How much money did Francine have in her room?" he asked.

"Money?" The sheriff looked at Dutch and said, "Didn't come across any money, did we?" The deputy shook his head.

"This was after she'd been working a few hours at, what, two dollars a man?" Monday asked. "She should have had maybe twenty dollars in her room."

"Coulda been more than that," Dutch said. "These are really professional man handlers out at the Hog Ranch. I understand they sometimes got three dollars a time. This Francine was really fresh, they say. She'd only been in town a couple months. Said she came from New Orleans and claimed she was well trained there. She might've earned a bit more than the other girls."

"Well, there's been many a working girl killed for her day's take before this. Until we find out more about where she kept her stash, I wouldn't rule out robbery."

Sheriff Boswell turned to Dutch.

"Run that down and any other leads you think might pan out. I'm mighty impressed—and a mite peeved—that Dutch and I didn't notice that. You ready to leave Warbonnet and come down here and be a full time county deputy?"

Monday shook his head and they shared a laugh over the offer. Dutch poured Monday two cups of coffee and let him into the cells after Monday hung up his gunbelt by the door again.

Monday passed one cup through the bars to Tom. They blew at the rising steam. Tom broke the silence first.

"Well, I see you're back. Couldn't get enough of me yesterday, huh? Smitty'll be by in a little while. Reckon I should charge admission. Might be able to afford a better shirt for my hanging."

Monday regarded his brother coolly and didn't speak for a while.

"Tom, I found some evidence in this case that don't hold up. I pointed these out to the sheriff and he agrees with me. He asked me to look into this murder. I don't think you did it and I aim to figure out who did and why."

"Like some snoop in them dime novels? Listen, I told you I was with Francine that night and I got to drinking later. I couldn't swear I didn't do it. And if I'm not convinced, how you gonna convince a jury?"

"I don't know yet. I ain't got any experience with juries," Monday said. "But I think you could help me. I need you to recall some things. Like who else liked Francine, came to see her of an evening?"

"Well, most of the Circle M outfit was sweet on her. Young Ben when we first got to town, although he said he didn't go back to her after his first time. Smitty was almost as regular with her as me. So was Sandy Sutter. In fact, Sandy was jealous of Francine's other customers. Spent a night in jail after he beat up some poor dry goods drummer. You remember Sandy?"

"Yeah. Anybody else?"

"Hmmm. Only one I recollect bumping into on her doorstep regular-like was that chubby little deputy."

"Reese Bowman? Bowman was a regular customer?"

"Guess he was. I don't recall seeing anybody else go in or out of her room more'n once. Of course, the girls were into each other's rooms all the time. Sometimes when one girl would be entertainin'—or just about to—they'd borrow each other's clothes, slap on some different perfume, replace a lost garter."

"Sounds like you spent so much time there, you could run the place, Tom," Monday chided him. "One more thing. How much did you pay Francine, and where did she keep the money? Was it two dollars a time?"

"Sometimes three. I got to tell you, little brother, if I got to hang for knifin' a woman, I'm glad I had my way with that one a dozen times or so. I didn't know what talent was until . . . ." He broke off and sighed. This wasn't like him, Monday thought. Maybe it was thinking of hanging.

"Tom, I need to know where she kept her stash of money until she turned it over to Fricker, that fella who runs the place."

Angry again, Tom splashed the rest of his coffee against the back wall of the cell.

"Well, I don't think I recall where she kept her damn cash. Ask one of the girls or your friend Bowman. Or, better yet, why don't you stick around and ask Smitty? I bet he'll be real cooperative." Tom turned his back and brought his legs up onto the bunk again.

Monday sighed and stood up from the stool, taking both coffee cups. "This ain't over yet, Tom. I'll be down here a time or two, I reckon. Might hafta return to Warbonnet for a few days, but you'll see me again. They ain't fixin' to hang you anytime soon."

# # #

After that difficult meeting, Monday was glad to get out into the sunlight again. He checked his watch and went down to Ivinson's store. The proprietor's wife said Kate's order was ready. If he'd just wait a moment, she would wrap it up for him.

"Thank you, Ma'am. Would you do something for me first, though? You still got some of that real nice French soap I bought from you last fall?" He remembered Kate's joy when he gave her some last Christmas. A black lace mantilla for her birthday and fancy soap for Christmas. They weren't nearly as nice as the gunbelt and binoculars she'd given him.

"The wrapped soap that smells like peaches?"

"Yes, Ma'am. That's it."

"I think we still have a few bars left."

"Would you put one in with that order? Charge me for it, of course."

"It's rather expensive, you know. Fifty cents a bar."

"All right, put in two bars then. Here's a dollar."

She gave him a brown paper package tied with string. It was sort of soft and he could feel the bars of soap inside. Maybe some of them frilly camisole things Kate wore, he thought, and almost grinned in front of Mrs. Ivinson. He

60

thanked her and stepped outside, nearly colliding with Reese Bowman on the duckboards.

"Whoa there, Malone. Slow down. Don't want to get cited for assaulting a peace officer, do you?"

Monday was about to compare running into Bowman to slipping on horse manure, but caught himself in time. He didn't know why he was getting so worked up. Maybe it was just because he couldn't reach through the jail bars far enough to smack some sense into Tom. He needed information from the deputy, but how to get it without arousing his suspicions? Monday knew he'd have to act like Bowman's long-lost friend.

"Say, Reese, I'm right glad I ran into you—or almost ran into you. I'm fixin' to visit the Hog Ranch before I go back to Warbonnet. Reckon you could tell me how much I should carry for the tariff?"

"Well, if you just want the regular treatment, then you only need to take along a couple a bucks. But if you want the 'New Orleans Special'," he winked, trying to look sly, "then you might want to tote an extra dollar. It'll be worth it. Ask for Suzanne, now that Francine's gone. Too bad your brother done that to her. We all liked Francine. She was a real breath of fresh air in this little town."

Little town, Monday thought. Laramie had more than seven hundred souls at last count, to Warbonnet's hundred and fifty. He steered the conversation back to money.

"Well, Reese, if I take three, is it all right to use coins? I understand some ladies tuck that money away in places that only folding money ought to go." Now it was Monday's turn to wink slyly. He hated himself for playing Bowman's game.

The little deputy chuckled. "Naw. You can carry coins. Francine was the most experienced girl there and she always put her stash under the chamber pot. Said no one would think to look for it there. I know Suzanne and some other girls picked up that trick from her."

"Thanks, Reese. You been real helpful. I'll mention your name when I talk to Suzanne."

The deputy walked off beaming. Monday tucked Kate's package under his arm and went to get his horse for the ride out to the scene of the murder.

8

Laramie

Monday arrived at the Hog Ranch that afternoon. He'd learned what the locals called it when he'd ridden through Laramie to Warbonnet last summer. Brothels in Wyoming were located on the outskirts of the few good-sized towns like Laramie and Cheyenne and near Army posts. Decent folk wouldn't allow such establishments in the city limits and gave them the nickname for the same isolated locations where farmers raised pigs.

Dutch told him those women received cold treatment in town. They weren't welcome in restaurants or hotels, nor in most stores, but usually one afternoon a week was reserved for them to do their shopping. The proper ladies of Laramie made sure their children were in school or at home during the Thursday afternoon shopping days when the soiled doves came to town. Today was shopping Thursday. With most of the girls in town, Monday should have no trouble looking around the place.

As he rode up to the Hog Ranch, Monday noticed its newly painted sign, "The French Quarter." He shook his head at the fancy name on the two-story log building and tied Lightning next to Bull's sturdy horse. He remembered the big man's confidence that he would get in. Among the horses at the rails were a dozen with US Army brands and a few with the Circle M brand. Knowing the natural curiosity of cowboys in a strange town, Monday didn't dare leave Kate's parcel sitting on Lightning's saddle, so he took it with him.

He found Bull seated at a table where he could watch the door. The big man waved Monday over. He grinned when he saw the other two men at Bull's table.

Ben Rollins stood up and hugged Monday, practically knocking the marshal's hat off. "Monday, it's been too long. You look great, though. Wyoming cooking must agree with you."

"Yeah, well, folks up here don't know nothin' about chili or sourdough biscuits, but I get by." Then he shook hands with Sandy Sutter, not an old friend, but they'd ridden a couple cattle drives together.

"How are your folks, Ben," Monday asked as he pulled out a chair.

"Pretty much the same as ever. Mama's head has gone white now, but Daddy's still got his red hair and beard." Ben sipped at the last of his beer. "I ain't married yet and I hear from Bull here that you ain't either. We been talking about that Miss Shaw I met when I came lookin' for you in Warbonnet."

Monday frowned. "In here? You been talking about Miss Kate in a place like this? Ben, we never discussed ladies we knew back home when we were in places like this in Abilene and those other cow towns." He tossed his hat and Kate's parcel on the table and scowled at Bull. Monday reckoned the big blacksmith should have known better and controlled the conversation with the two cowboys. Bull spread his hands to indicate they were going to have their say anyway.

Monday put up four fingers to signal the barkeep he'd pay for another round of beers. Among the soldiers at the bar were two black men in uniform, probably from Fort Sanders. Buffalo soldiers, Bull had said they were called. That explained what he'd said about how easily he could get into this Hog Ranch. The owner would welcome any soldier's money.

When Bull confirmed all the working girls were still shopping in town, Monday pumped Ben and Sandy to catch up on news from home. Then he steered the conversation to Laramie and to Tom's fix.

"Mr. Tom, he was with Francine that night," Sandy volunteered. "I was next to see her. He stormed out of there past me, with a face like thunder and punching his hat. You know how he does that? He's hell on hats."

"Any idea what upset him?" So Tom hadn't looked happy when he left Francine. But he'd told Monday that he liked her a lot.

"Not right then, I didn't. But when me and Francine were together, she told me not to be drinking too much if I expected to perform with a lady."

"Now that's interesting," Monday said, sipping his beer. "I understand Tom didn't come back. He had a few more drinks here and then went back to town."

"That's right," Ben offered. "I saw him have two at the bar over there before he got on his horse and headed back to Laramie. Reckon he might have had a few more there."

"He did," Sandy said, running his fingers through his dark hair. "Smitty sent me to check up on him. I found him at the Alhambra and helped him back to the hotel. He could walk, but not straight. I came back and told Smitty."

"Did Tom still seem angry? Did he mention Francine at all?"

"Nope, not by that time. Just singing the dirty version of 'Yellow Rose' for everybody to hear. He let me guide him up to his room and help him off with his boots. I hung up his gunbelt for him. When I turned around, he was out like a lamp."

"Was his knife in its sheath on his gun belt when you hung it up?"

"I seem to recollect it was."

"And I don't suppose you could lock the door to his room?"

"Naw. Not from outside. Mr. Tom, he likely had his key somewhere."

"What about this Francine? I understand she was popular."

"Popular?" Sandy asked, and for once looked troubled. "Like ice cream on the Fourth of July. You didn't just wander up to her room. Had to have a reservation with the boss, Mr. Fricker, for the first few hours each evening. Nobody just walked in on Francine. The other girls, you could always get one of them."

"What about you, Ben? What can you tell me about Francine?"

Ben blushed to the tips of his ears. "Well, I only went to her the once, when we first got here. She was awful pretty, with light brown hair. Said she came from a big fancy house in New Orleans. Didn't have no French accent, though."

"How come you only went to see her the once? You find another girl here? I remember in Abilene two summers ago . . . ." Monday broke off and grinned.

"No, not any other girl here," Sandy cut in with a grin. "Ben's found himself a quality lady and he's spending his money on her."

Ben frowned like he resented Sandy's kidding, but he spoke softly.

"Yeah, I did. Second night we were here. We came out of the steak house and there was this lady—just a girl, really—on the front porch of the hotel, tryin' not to cry. She had a suitcase and was sittin' on a trunk. I stopped to talk to her, but the boys wanted to have a hoo-rah with me, so I sent 'em on their way. Waited to talk to her 'til after they left. I thought maybe she'd judge me by their remarks and go inside, but she didn't."

Ben looked up at the ceiling as if it helped him remember that evening. "Said her name was Lynn. She'd come all the way from Boston. Her parents were dead and her uncle was taking her to San Francisco. She was gonna be a singer there." He sipped some of his beer and looked at Monday now.

"But some men held up the train between here and Cheyenne. When her uncle tried to keep their tickets and money, the robbers shot him dead. They made a clean getaway. Federal marshal from Cheyenne formed a posse and chased 'em into Colorado, last I heard. Lynn decided she'd wait here to see if they got any of her uncle's money back. She didn't have a way to get to San Francisco and had no money for the hotel either." He sighed and slid his glass around.

Then he looked at Monday again. "I been paying for her room since then and not spending anything over here, 'cept maybe a beer now and then. Mr. Fricker's been fronting her a dollar a night to sing here, but she can't make enough for a ticket to San Francisco that way. So she's been learnin' . . . ." He trailed off and just looked at his beer glass.

"Has she been learning what the girls here do, Ben?" Monday asked softly.

"Yeah, sorta. Learnin' without doin' it. Yet." Ben wouldn't meet his eye and pushed his beer glass in circles again. "She's seen enough that she doesn't want to do those things. But it might be the only way she can save enough for a ticket. When I run out of money, her singing won't pay for her room and meals. She's already in debt to Fricker."

"I shouldn't say this," said Sandy, saying it anyway. "But all the boys seen Ben's gal and like her a lot. They're hopin' to be with her when Ben's money runs out. Mr. Fricker even gave her her own French name. Introduces her as 'Danielle' when she sings each night."

Monday expected Ben to hit Sandy, since he balled his right hand into a fist. But instead, Ben looked over the marshal's head and his features changed to a look of disgust. Monday looked across at Sandy, who suddenly showed worry —or fear.

The marshal heard the distinctive sound of boots with Mexican spurs and big rowels as someone came through the door behind him, walked up to their table, and stopped. Monday slipped his right hand under the table and took the hammer loop off his pistol. He sure hoped his holster was slippery today and not sticky. He couldn't tie down his leg thong without attracting notice.

"Hello, Smitty," he said, without turning.

A deep voice behind him said "Hello, Monday, you son of a bitch. Heard you got tired of eatin' dust and put on a star."

Monday sighed and got up. He turned to face the newcomer.

Smitty had an inch on Monday and maybe twenty pounds. His hair had as much salt in it as pepper now, but his thick black mustache was as dark as ever—and big, too, because of his long upper lip. He had his right hand on his holstered pistol.

"Last year, you said you'd kill me if you ever saw me again, kid. Still feel the same way?" He showed yellow teeth beneath the mustache, seeming to savor the situation.

"Well," Monday started, "I see I'm at a big disadvantage right now. Your holster's already tied down." He gestured at his own. "Mine's not. And I see you got your hand on your pistol. I don't." He showed his right hand palm outward down below his own waist. "And I see you already slipped off your hammer loop."

Smitty froze, his hand still on the butt of his gun.

"Now, we got ourselves a situation here, Smitty." Monday pulled back his vest with his left hand to show his star. "See, I'm a marshal back in Warbonnet, but only a deputy sheriff here in Laramie. I don't know what the sheriff's thinking would be if I were to shoot you right now."

"What I'm gonna do here, Smitty, is give you a chance to smile and take back what you called me. So the bartender over there with the scattergun behind the counter thinks we're still friends." Monday pointed toward the bar with his left hand, but never took his eyes off Smitty's. "Why don't you just smile now and say you're sorry? I ain't that kid you tried to drive into the ground all the way from Texas."

Monday smiled, hoping to get Smitty to do the same, but the other man just spun away and walked to the bar. As Monday released the breath he'd been holding, he heard a click behind him. He turned to see Ben Rollins lay his pistol on the table, having just let it off cock.

"Thanks, Ben. I was hoping I wouldn't need anyone to back my play." Monday raised his empty hand to eye level and was pleased to see it wasn't shaking. He remembered being beaten senseless by Smitty more than once when he'd gone up against the older man on their first cattle drive together.

Sandy nodded to them and went off to join Smitty and some other Circle M cowboys at the bar.

"It riles me that that damn Sandy would hoo-rah me about Danielle. I mean, Lynn," Ben said. "Sandy was so sweet on Francine that he got in a fight with some townie over her. Sheriff put him in jail overnight. I heard some of the boys say he was jealous of anybody she was with. But I don't recall him sayin' he was in love with her."

Whatever else Ben meant to say was interrupted by a flurry of giggles and pleasant female voices. The girls of the Hog Ranch arrived in a whirl of bright dresses, hats, boxes, and parcels. They headed for the stairs to the balcony that ran along the rear of the bar room. All but the last one, who came over to their table.

She looked about nineteen and had long brown curls and huge dark eyes. She looked like she was amazed at something. You could see white all around her pupils. When she smiled at Ben, she showed dimples.

"Hello, Ben. I don't think I know your friends." Ben introduced Lynn. She held out her hand to Monday, Eastern-style, not like a handshake, and then to Bull, saying "Mr. Devoe." Not every white woman Monday knew would take a black man's hand. He liked her instinctively.

"I really can't stay. I have to go learn about rouge and face powder and putting up my hair today." She grimaced. "I already know how to do my own hair, thank you. But I'll be down again in a little while to practice some new songs with the piano player. Will you still be here?"

Ben glanced ruefully at his empty beer glass, as if he knew the bartender would suffer only paying customers. He opened his mouth to respond, but Monday stacked up three quarters on the table.

"Sure, Miss. Ben will still be here," he said.

69

She and Ben moved off a little way to say their goodbyes and Monday spoke softly to Bull.

"I can see why Ben's caught calico fever. If his mama Ann ever got a look at her, she'd get Lloyd to sell a chunk of their ranch just to help her get that train ticket to Frisco." Lynn left Ben and went up the stairs.

"You been doing a pretty fair job of pumping those boys for what they know," Bull said as Ben returned to the table. "You gonna go talk to that Suzanne now?"

"I reckon I ought to," Monday said, rising and picking up his hat and Kate's parcel. "Which one was she?"

"The one who went up the stairs first. Long dark hair, red dress, and. . . ." Ben used both hands to make an unmistakable gesture.

Monday grinned. "Oh, that one. Yeah, I did sort of notice her. Can you keep an eye on Smitty as long as he stays here?" Monday asked as he stood. "Which room will be Suzanne's?"

"She has the one at the end of the hall, looks back toward town," Ben said.

Bull gestured toward the parcel on the table. "You wanna leave Miss Kate's order with me?"

"Nope, I better not. She acted so particular about it and that Mrs. Ivinson was so fussy, I figure I better ride close herd on it 'til we get back to Warbonnet. I'll see you in a little while."

As Monday walked toward the stairs, he heard raised voices at the bar and turned in time to see Sandy Sutter hit the floor. Smitty reached down and snatched his knife back from the downed cowboy, who was rubbing his jaw. Smitty sheathed it and dropped a plug of tobacco onto Sandy, who caught it before it hit him. Monday couldn't hear what the mustached foreman said, but he moved to the end of the bar. Sandy got to his feet a little shaky, brushing tobacco scraps off his shirt. The Circle M foreman must be as touchy as Monday remembered about anyone borrowing his gear.

Monday climbed the stairs, walked past three rooms, and knocked on the last door before the hallway ended at the front of the building.

70

"Not yet," came a woman's voice. When he identified himself, the dark-haired woman opened the door. As soon as she saw him, she put on a knowing smile.

"I didn't mean I wasn't doing business yet, honey. I just meant I wasn't dressed to receive gentlemen." She'd taken off her hat, but was still wearing her street clothes. "Come on in. You stand out there too long, some other girl will latch onto you. Ain't none of them can do for you what I can."

Suzanne stood out of his way, opening the door just enough to force Monday to squeeze past her.

"Long as you're here early, honey, would you help a girl with her buttons?"

Monday put Kate's parcel on the bed and touched the buttons at the back of Suzanne's dress lightly. This woman he'd seen downstairs was only a couple years older than he was. He hesitated.

"The buttons on a woman's dress are like piano keys, dear. You can't make music until you touch them. I need to change into my working clothes. You gonna help me or not?"

Monday fumbled with the buttons until he figured she could undo the rest. His mouth felt dry and he longed for another beer. Or just a cup of water.

"I won't be but a minute. Whyn't you sit over there 'til I get comfortable?" Suzanne went to the dresser and got out something small in an even brighter red, with black ruffles on it. Then she went behind the screen. Monday looked about for a chair and noticed with a start that this room was laid out like Francine's. In fact, the fabric on the screen was a green paisley pattern. Maybe this was Francine's room. Everything looked like Dutch's description, except for the lack of a chair. Monday went over and sat on the edge of the bed, facing the dresser and the window.

"Did this used to be Francine's room? I had it described to me."

"No," came the curt reply. "It used to be *my* room. Then Fricker gave it to *her* when she arrived. Now it's mine again. It's one of the larger rooms and it has the best brass bed and mattress in the place." The red dress went up over the screen. The little red something disappeared. In a moment, Suzanne came out in a frilly red thing with black lace that left her shoulders and legs bare.

Monday tried to stand, but his spurs were entangled in the edge of the bedspread. Suzanne waved him to stay seated and he did so, moving his boots in an effort to free the spurs. She picked up a hair brush and brushed a few strands, looking into the mirror.

"You're movin' your feet back there like you want to dance. Would you like to dance with me? Saw your badge when you came in. Are you a deputy, like Reese Bowman?" She replaced a few hairpins.

"No, Ma'am. I'm Monday Malone, the marshal in Warbonnet, and one of Sheriff Boswell's deputies down here when he needs me. He's got me lookin' into Francine's murder. Reckon you could answer some questions for me?"

"Sure," Suzanne said. "I ain't got to go to work for an hour or so. Plenty of time." She put the pins and hairbrush down, turned to him, and smiled. Monday swallowed hard and played with his hat.

"Uh, Ma'am. Miss Suzanne. Are you sure you don't want to put something else on?"

"No thanks, Malone. I'm comfortable like this. How about you?"

He could feel his face getting red. He hated it when women made him blush; usually it was Kate or Becky. "Tell me about Francine. I understand she'd been here just a couple months."

"That's right, she came here in the spring, from New Orleans. But I expect you've heard that already."

"Was Francine her real name?"

"We all take workin' names. French, mostly, even though we ain't got no accents. The fancy names make the men feel good. Francine's real name was Gertrude Fortnum. Not too fancy, huh?"

"No, not as fancy as Francine or Suzanne. Or Danielle."

72

"Oh, you met her, have you? She sings real good, but Mr. Fricker's got plans to have her work upstairs." Suzanne put her hands on her hips now.

"She's been watching us at work and Fricker plans to break her in himself, he says, when the time comes. Poor girl is awful embarrassed about seein' all the things we do. I don't think back in Boston she even knew there were such places. But a good-lookin' girl like her, all alone, with no money for a ticket out of here, well, there ain't many things she can do."

"Has Danielle watched you work?" He had to look at the floor when he spoke. He couldn't meet her eyes, the hungry way she looked at him without blinking.

"Sure, she watched me a few times. Watched Francine mostly, though, since this is the biggest room. But nobody's supposed to know she's been learning. Mr. Fricker didn't want any of our gentlemen to see Danielle upstairs yet." Suzanne purred the last few words and moved over to the bed. She sat down on Monday's left. He tried to move over a little, but their combined weight on the edge of the mattress made it sag, making it hard for him to edge away.

He tried to think of another question.

"Can she make enough money singing to buy a ticket to San Francisco?"

"I don't think so," Suzanne said. "She's gonna have to work up here sooner or later."

Monday wanted to ask her to confirm what Bowman had said about Francine stashing her night's money under the chamber pot below the bed, but at that moment, Suzanne took the hat off his lap and hung it on the tall brass foot post.

"You know, honey, I don't have to go to work for another hour or so. Mr. Fricker lets us be real friendly with first-time visitors. Then they become regular customers and spend more time and money here." She ran her right hand up and down the lapel of his vest.

"I don't . . . , I mean, I can't." Monday tried to get up and end the conversation. Suzanne put a hand on his leg and kept him from standing. Then she reached for the buttons on his jeans.

73

Monday thought of Kate again and stood up abruptly.

"Thanks for your help, Miss Suzanne.   Reckon I got everything I came for."

# # #

Monday rushed out the door of the Hog Ranch to find Bull Devoe prepared to mount up. He couldn't meet the big man's eye.

"Let's get out of here and go back to town, Bull."   He yanked Lightning's reins loose and swarmed into the saddle, already turning away from the rail.

"Hold on, Monday. You're in too big a rush. Where's Miss Kate's parcel?" Monday flailed around behind him to feel the top of his bedroll as Lightning danced a circle nervously. Her parcel wasn't there. His heart sank and he could barely speak.

"Bull, I left it upstairs in that Suzanne's room." Bull just looked up at him and waited. "But I can't go back up there and get it. Not now. I don't suppose . . . ."

Bull sighed. "Sure, I can do it. I recall Ben saying it was the last door at the end of the hall." He handed the marshal his reins and went back inside. Monday let out a big breath and then took another one, slowly. He never should have gone to talk to Suzanne alone. Lord, what a fool he'd been.

Bull was back in a minute or so and handed Kate's parcel up to him. Monday felt it carefully. The bars of soap were still in there and the string was intact.

Bull got aboard his big horse slowly. "She had a message for you." He grinned and added: "She said you're welcome to come back when you can take more time."

9

Warbonnet

Kate hurried down Main Street. Monday had returned from Laramie this afternoon. He hadn't been able to say too much over supper in front of Martha and the children and Joe Fitch, their guest this evening, but he'd promised to tell her all he'd learned at the jail. They wouldn't have much time. Baths started at eight o'clock and Monday said he wanted one, too, after the ladies finished theirs. He'd told her the three-day ride north had been hot and dusty. Kate would ride down the same trail to Laramie tomorrow.

She found Monday at his desk, slowly writing in a notebook with a pencil. When she came in, he rose from his office stool and indicated she should take it. He crossed the small room and sat on his bunk.

"Thank you for sending that wire," Kate began. "I was certain it was bad news and I regretted having sent you into heartbreak, if they'd already tried and carried out sentence on your brother."

"Good thing I got there when I did, Kate. Nate Boswell told me they were originally fixin' to try Tom startin' yesterday. Looked like it was all sewed up and he'd probably have been found guilty the same day. They mighta hung him today." He looked at his notes, then took a deep breath as if he were gathering his courage.

"I know we had some sharp words before I left town and I said some things about you interfering. On the way back here,

75

I had a lot of time to think about what I said. And what you said. Tom really didn't do it, Kate. You were right—about me, I mean. You had me pegged." He kept his head down and wouldn't look at her.

"I was just figuring to go down there and ask a couple questions and then say goodbye. But when I saw how things were and explained my reasons to Sheriff Boswell, he agreed Tom couldn't have done it and let me, um, investigate." Once he got those words out, he met her eye.

Kate brushed hair back from her face. "I didn't know anything about the circumstances, Monday. I just felt you owed it to yourself to talk to Tom one more time, guilty or innocent. What are the details of the crime? If he's innocent, can you get him released?"

"Not until I find the real killer. Men of Laramie are all stirred up over Francine's murder and Tom looks guilty to them. Nate's holding him in jail as a precaution, he called it. I got maybe another few weeks, and I'm going to have to do a lot of the work up here, from my notes. The marshal of Warbonnet can only traipse off to Laramie if he's on county business."

"I have to leave for Laramie tomorrow morning myself, with Sean Finnegan," Kate reminded him, hesitating. Monday didn't know how fragile her hopes were. If she didn't get to go to Yellowstone, would she have the courage to come back here and pack up to leave Wyoming? She had a lot riding on whether Yellowstone could sway her decision on Wyoming.

"We're going to meet the guest artists. Then, if I'm lucky, catch the train and join the rest of the Hayden expedition in Montana to Yellowstone. If you think of anything more you need to ask down in Laramie before I leave tomorrow morning, I could always, well, I mean, I don't want to interfere."

"Oh, that's hogwash, Kate. You don't interfere. I recall how we worked on the murder of Marshal Taggart last year. I can't think of all the things you do. I'm gonna need your help."

Kate didn't say anything, but just looked at Monday for a moment. He clutched his pencil as if he might break it. His forehead was creased, whether from worry or concentration, Kate couldn't tell. He sat forward on his bunk as if he were anxious to tell her things.

If she didn't get to go to Yellowstone, she'd at least try to stay in Laramie for a while and ask some questions of her own. Before she had to decide whether to come back here and pack.

Monday told her about his interview with Tom, including his brother's uncertainty about whether he'd actually committed the murder. He passed her his copy of the layout of Francine's room and told her what Dutch had recounted to him of the scene of the murder, the parts that convinced him the girl had been killed by someone with his right hand because of the position of the bed and the knife in the body.

She turned the drawing to get a better look at it.

"I see you have a chair drawn here between the edge of the screen and the dresser, but then you crossed it out. Why?"

Monday began to pace the length of the office slowly, as if it helped him remember. "I was there, Kate. I visited the room later. There's another woman in there now. Anyway, the chair may not have been by the dresser that night. Sometimes it's kept behind the screen."

At this point, Monday ran his fingers through his hair as if frustrated. "And one more odd thing, before I forget to tell you. Francine was stabbed twice, Doc Finfrock said. Nearly in the same place each time, but at different angles. He said the first wound—the deepest—probably killed her."

Kate's father was a doctor and she'd helped him treat a few accidental stab wounds. She made a note of Monday's account of the first deep cut, then the second, shallow one.

If he was confused by the two wounds, Monday didn't show it. He filled her in on everybody he could think of who might be a suspect, counting them off on his fingers

. Reese Bowman, who spent entirely too much time at the Hog Ranch and claimed to know all the girls. He might have killed Francine out of jealousy, or if he'd been bribed by Fricker to provide a longer presence each evening beyond what a deputy normally would, maybe Francine knew about that and threatened to tell the sheriff.

Smitty, the despised foreman of the Circle M, who'd also been a regular customer of Francine's, but Monday couldn't think of why he might have killed her, much as he'd like him to be the guilty one.

Sandy Sutter was a regular visitor, too, and said to be jealous. He had much less money to spend than Tom or Smitty. And Francine's take for that night was missing. Someone might have killed her for it. Someone who needed money.

He finished with Ben Rollins, who needed cash to help his new girlfriend.

"Oh, I don't want to believe that," Kate said. "I liked Ben when I met him. Why would he do such a thing?"

Monday told her about the Lynn/Danielle situation. He thought Ben might have been driven to protect the girl and get her out of having to observe the girls "at work."

"I don't want it to be Ben neither, Kate. He's a couple years younger than me. Ben always danced with Mary Ellen when we had *fandangos*—all-night Texas dances—at his ranch or ours, or in town." He stopped and glanced at the back wall for a moment, as if savoring a memory. "But I can't rule someone out just because he's my friend. We found that out the hard way a year ago."

Kate was silent for a while, jotting down notes of what he'd said about those he'd identified as suspects. She looked at the list, then up at Monday.

"Are you sure the killer must be a man? Were any of the other girls jealous of Francine—of her success or her looks?

"That didn't cross my mind at first, Kate. But yeah, I reckon Suzanne wasn't shedding any tears over Francine's death. I reckon Suzanne inherited a lot of Francine's regular customers, too. Francine came up here from New Orleans in the spring and became the most popular girl in the place. She got Fricker—he's the owner—to give her Suzanne's room. Suzanne's got it back now that Francine's dead." Monday didn't explain how he'd learned all that.

Kate sighed and put her notes down. "The last I read, Wyoming has about three thousand men and only about three hundred women. I guess I should be grateful there's no Hog

78

Ranch in Warbonnet yet." She waited to see how he'd react to that, but he only stroked his chin as if in thought.

"Monday, as the marshal, you're supposed to say, 'don't worry, Kate, there won't ever be one of those dens of sin here in Warbonnet.' Don't you want to say something reassuring?"

Seeing her concern, he just grinned. "No chance of that for a long time, Kate. Railroad don't come through Warbonnet, or hadn't you noticed? Not enough soldiers or money here to attract the big spenders those girls follow. Besides, them places ain't illegal; they're just sort of tolerated."

Kate wasn't mollified by that answer, but she refused to give him the satisfaction of having "got her goat."

"Well, anyway, I'll see what I can find out from Ben and this 'Danielle' of his when I get to Laramie. I may have only a day or two. I'll write you a letter if I find out anything." She brightened and gathered her notes. "And I'll write to you from Yellowstone, if I get to go. Will you write to me? About your investigation, I mean."

"Sure I will. Don't know how you'll get any mail in, but I imagine you'll have a chance or two to send letters out." He came over and reached into a desk drawer.

"This here's your parcel. I didn't want to hand it to you at Martha's door, the way you and Mrs. Ivinson were so secret about it and all. I figured there's something in there you didn't want me to know about. But I took a little liberty with it."

"Indeed? How dare you unwrap something—"

"I never," Monday pleaded, raising both hands as if in surrender. "I let Mrs. Ivinson wrap that bundle up and it ain't hardly been out of my sight ever since, but I never opened it. I got some nice things for you in Laramie and had her put them in before she wrapped it all up. Hope you like them and that you use them soon. Might even take them to Yellowstone with you."

Kate felt the parcel carefully. Some hard square things were in the center. Probably some kind of soap. Why had she been so suspicious? She was so quick to jump to conclusions lately. Perhaps she was feeling at loose ends since the school term ended. Too much time to think about whether to give up and leave Wyoming.

"I'm sure I shall appreciate them. But I must run if I'm to make ladies' bath time. Don't forget, yours is scheduled right after Buxton. I'll see you in the morning before Sean and I go."

Kate thought about her clothes as she walked back to Martha's. She was glad Monday had returned as quickly as he did. She needed this package to have enough underwear for the trip. She had two riding skirts now and would probably wear dresses only when she rode in a wagon, or on the train or a stagecoach. She took the package up to her room, then helped Sally pour hot water into the tub from the heavy boiler, first for Sally herself and then for Martha.

When it was Kate's turn, she went up to her room for fresh clothing. She felt around in the parcel and found two bars of imported peach soap. How thoughtful of Monday. She smiled and held one under her nose.

Back down in the kitchen again, she stripped and got into the hot water. When would she get a bath this nice again? It would be pleasant to lie back and really soak, but Martha had only a hip bath and Kate had to leave her long legs outside the tub when she bathed. Professor Hayden had said there are natural hot springs in Yellowstone. If it were only true, she thought, dreaming of a huge pool of hot water.

Abruptly, Kate looked at the kitchen clock. Almost nine. Monday would be coming for the men's baths at any moment. She'd best be washed, dressed, and out of the kitchen before he arrived. It was nice to take her time as the last woman in the hot water, but she didn't want a male audience. She'd secured all the kitchen window curtains before Sally's bath.

Kate dried off, put on a shift and robe, and hurriedly toweled her hair. She pulled the cork on the tub and let it empty through the floor drain. Monday and Buxton would have to haul the heavy boiler for their own hot water.

As she went up to her room, she heard Monday knock at the kitchen door. Buxton let him in. Sally said good night to Kate and went to bed. In her room again, Kate reached into

80

the partially unwrapped parcel for the other bar of soap, to put it in her Yellowstone baggage. She jumped when something black fell out of the bundle onto the floor. She was startled, but she didn't scream or even yelp. There was no sound from Martha's or Sally's rooms.

When the black material didn't move, Kate bent down to pick it up, and almost dropped it in shock. It was black lace underwear! A camisole that was all lace, like that "mantilla" shawl Monday had given her. And a pair of matching drawers —even shorter than what Becky wore under her jeans!

Kate bristled. Where had Monday bought such things? How had he gotten Mrs. Ivinson to put them in her parcel? She was so angry, she found herself squeezing the underwear like it was Monday's neck. How dare he give her something so scandalous? And he'd had the temerity to suggest that she take them to Yellowstone!

Yellowstone. What should she do with this black lace underwear? She was off to Laramie in the morning and Martha would have the run of her room. Lord above, what if her landlady found these?

Kate had an inspiration. Reverend Jonah Barnes wasn't due here for another week or so. She kept a locked trunk in the spare bedroom the preacher used when he visited. She took the lacey items across the hall toward the back of the house. As she let herself into the darkened room, she wished she'd brought a lamp, but a beam of light came up through the floor. Curious, she got closer and saw that the corner of a small rug was turned up and light shone through a knothole in the flooring, probably from the kitchen directly below.

Kate went to the little beacon, stretched out on the floor, and looked through the hole. There was Buxton, just leaving, all freshly scrubbed. Then came Monday, putting the last of the hot water into his tub. He was dressed only in his union suit. Now he turned toward her peephole and began to undo his buttons. Kate jerked her head up in alarm. Spying on Monday like this wasn't right, even if he had just offended her.

She knew what a good Christian girl should do. Kate got up quickly and went to the door, then paused with her hand on the knob. She closed the door quietly, locked it from the inside, and returned to her vantage point.

Of course it wasn't right to do this. But hadn't Monday spied on her in her bath on Box Elder Creek last July, just before Sam Taggart was killed? Wouldn't this just be turn-about as fair play? Kate remembered with a grin how she and Lacey Ferris had gone to the boys' swimming hole one July afternoon. That was the summer before Stuart joined the army. Before he died.

Kate tore her thoughts from Stuart, blinked rapidly, and put her eye closer to the hole in the floor. Monday was sitting on a bench now with his back to her, peeling off his union suit. When he stood up, Kate could see he had dimples above his buttocks. She almost laughed, but shut her mouth before any sound came out. Monday took two steps over and sat down carefully, dangling his even longer legs outside the tub. Monday soaped himself rapidly and washed and rinsed. Just like a man, to rush through anything pleasurable and be off to get dirty again.

Then Kate strained to hear. Monday was singing off-key, probably some dirty cowboy song. All she could catch were a couple words in the chorus, "yellow" and "Texas." She thought he sang badly when they were in church, and this solo per-formance confirmed her assessment.

Kate was debating. Maybe she'd seen enough. She ought to do the good Christian thing and break off this sordid spying. But then she remembered how angry she'd been over the black underwear. The issue was finally decided when Monday found he couldn't reach the towel where he'd left it on the bench, so he stood up and took a couple of steps to pick it up. She gasped and quickly put the heel of her right hand between her teeth so she wouldn't make another sound. She put her left hand between her breast and the floorboards, certain that he'd be able to hear her heart thumping against the floor. Like that Poe story.

Monday was toweling his face and hair. As he finished with his face and began to towel his back, she saw him look down to the far end of the bench. Then he moved out of her sight for a moment and returned. He was holding something white.

Oh, no. It looked like—it couldn't be! He had her camisole, the one she'd just taken off in order to bathe. Kate gasped. She thought she'd brought all her laundry upstairs. What was he doing? Monday brought her camisole to his face and kept it there, smelling it. Then he laughed, put the camisole back on the bench, and sat down to finish drying his feet.

Kate didn't want to leave the room. Not even to move, for fear she'd make the floorboards creak. So she waited while Monday pulled the plug on the tub and got dressed. Then, to her horror, he picked up her camisole. He was taking it! Was he the one who'd pilfered her drawers from the wash line? Oh, this was terrible. First the black lace underwear, and now this. She'd never suspected him capable of such things.

But wait. He hadn't left the house. The sound of creaking steps meant he was coming up the back stairs, trying not to make any noise. She went to the door quietly and opened it just a crack. Monday came along the hallway without seeing her and stopped in front of her bedroom across the hall. Monday tapped quietly and waited. When there was no answer, she saw him hang the camisole over her doorknob, back away silently, and head down the back stairs.

Kate let out the breath she'd been holding. Had she misjudged him? No, she hadn't. Here was the proof in her hand, in black lace. She forgot about hiding it in the trunk for the moment and went to her own room when she heard the back door close downstairs. This time, she held up the lacey evidence and let the lamp shine through it. Merciful heavens! It was even more sheer than she'd supposed.

That damned Monday! "I bought you a couple things I know you'll like," he'd said. "Maybe you'll take them to Yellowstone." She wasn't going back across the hall to the trunk tonight. Perhaps in the morning. She put the underwear by the lamp and prepared to blow out the flame, when her bare foot stepped on something crinkly.

Kate picked up a scrap of paper. Where had this come from? Had it fallen out of her parcel? Out of the black underwear? She unfolded it and read "To Francine. A.S."

A.S.? Who the devil was A.S.? None of the suspects Monday had named possessed those initials. Kate would have to look into what this meant when she got to Laramie. She blew out the lamp and went to bed.

# # #

The next morning, Kate helped Buxton load her valise into the wagon that white-whiskered Roy Butcher would drive to Laramie. Monday and Sean had already put her trunk aboard. Monday was looking like his normal self this morning. He didn't seem to have grown horns or anything. He hadn't asked about whether she liked his "gifts" either, something she'd expected him to do. But his reticence wasn't fooling her one bit. He probably had to act innocent with these other men around.

Roy had closed the tailgate of the wagon and was getting on his seat. Sean Finnegan raised his hat to her, then set it back on his gray head and climbed onto his horse.

"Well, Miss Kate. If you turn up anything in Laramie, be sure you let me or the sheriff know." Monday had his hat in his hands and was rotating it nervously.

"Don't worry. I shall," she replied coolly. "In fact, if I find out anything urgent, I'll wire you." She moved to climb up the wheel to get to her seat, but Monday put both hands on her waist to hoist her up. She struck out at his hands in sudden panic.

"Don't! Don't touch me! I mean, I can do it myself. Get up myself." When she clambered onto her seat and glanced back at Monday, he looked like she'd kicked him.

Kate was in a quandary. How should she treat Monday now? He'd always been so kind and considerate before. She'd meant to ask him about "A.S." and that black lingerie before she left, but now she was too angry and this was too public. She could send him a note from Laramie if she wanted.

84

Kate didn't do more than offer a weak wave when the wagon lurched away, off to Laramie. And off, she hoped, to a month in the Yellowstone country, if her plan worked. To spend a month or more with men from the East, civilized folk. Would just a short time with them be the tonic she needed to tough it out and stay here? Or would they talk her into abandoning Wyoming and going back East?

10

Laramie

Three mornings later, Kate left the Frontier Hotel for the Laramie jail. Monday had told her to stay away from Tom when she was down here. Moran and the other artist, Bierstadt, were scheduled to arrive later today. That would give her nearly a whole day here in Laramie to talk to Tom and, if she were lucky—and circumspect—maybe even to see Suzanne. And what gave Monday the right to tell her what to do or not to do, after what she'd seen in Warbonnet? He'd been presumptuous enough to give her a scandalous gift.

She'd thought about what that meant as she traveled with Roy and Sean. She wasn't as sure now, having found that A.S. note, that Monday had given her the underwear. But he'd brought it from Laramie, hadn't he? Her feelings for him were so conflicted. Just like her feelings for Wyoming.

It was easier to understand how she felt toward Roy and Sean. Between them, the two older men had proposed to her nearly a dozen times, but they'd been polite and restrained with her in each other's company on the trail, like two senior roosters circling the new hen in the yard. She grinned as she approached the jail.

Kate hadn't figured out how to arrange to speak with Suzanne yet, but she'd told Sean Finnegan what she intended and asked him to help figure out a way. She ought to meet Suzanne at the Hog Ranch so she could see the murder scene. Monday hadn't actually told her not to do that. He probably

86

never thought she'd try such a thing. Kate wasn't sure how she would handle herself in that kind of place. She regretted going against Monday's wishes in visiting his brother, but she hoped she could help the investigation. Besides, why had he told her not to talk to Tom?

Dutch van Orden had told her last night that Monday and Sheriff Boswell agreed she shouldn't have access to Tom. Dutch said he had no choice but to carry out the sheriff's orders. But he also let slip that one of their suspects, Reese Bowman, was the day deputy today. Sheriff Boswell didn't usually get to the jail 'til eight o'clock or so, Dutch said. Kate arrived promptly at seven.

Reese Bowman looked up from a pile of papers when Kate entered. At first, he didn't act like he was going to stand up, but then he took a second look at her and got to his feet, slicking his hair to one side.

"Ma'am," he said. "What can I do for you? Sheriff ain't here yet."

"Well, if you're Deputy Bowman, then you're the man I really came to see." Kate could have used a smile on him, but she wanted him to let her back into the cells as quickly as possible. She could always try to assess Bowman later today or leave him to Monday. Her time in Laramie might be limited.

"I'm Kate Shaw from Warbonnet. Monday Malone may have mentioned me. I'm here to see Tom Malone."

"Whoa up there, Miss. The sheriff and your marshal done ordered us all not to let you in to see his brother. You know I gotta carry out the sheriff's instructions."

"Yes, of course, Deputy, but I hear the sheriff won't be in for an hour yet. Couldn't you see your way clear . . . ."

"No, Ma'am. It'd mean my job if he found out."

"I don't think Tom will tell him, and I certainly shan't. Isn't there a way you could let me back there for, say, half an hour? I'm prepared to buy you a cup of coffee while you wait for me." Kate plunked two dollars on the desk. Bowman rubbed one hand across his mouth. Perhaps he was thinking about more than coffee, perhaps something else two dollars would buy. Evidently, Bowman made up his mind. He

87

scooped up the money, took the keys from a peg by the door, and unlocked it for her.

"All right, Miss. Just a half hour. Sheriff always likes to look in on the prisoners first thing, even before he's had his coffee. This one back here's Tom Malone's cell.

"Hey, Malone, get up. You got your pants on? You got a lady visitor."

"Now, Miss," Bowman continued almost without pausing for breath, "here's a stool for you. And over here next to Malone's cell is the back door. It's got a slip lock on it. If you hear me rattling the keys in the door out there again, you got maybe a count of ten to get out the back way. Reckon you can do that?"

Kate assured him she'd keep their bargain a secret and Bowman scuttled away to watch for the sheriff.

She turned her attention to the cell and saw that Tom Malone had come over to the barred door now. She didn't think she ought to offer her hand, so instead she sat on the stool and composed her skirt. Malone remained standing.

"Good morning, Mr. Malone. I'm Katherine Shaw, the schoolteacher in Warbonnet. I'm a friend—an acquaintance, really—of your brother and thought I might be able to help him in his investigation. He's working hard to clear you of the murder charge, but he can't spend all his time down here in Laramie."

"Well, I tell you what, Miss Shaw. When he was in here last week to see me, he made it sound like he was my only hope. But since then I've learned that somebody else knows who the real killer is. I only have to get some money together when the rest of my herd gets delivered to Warbonnet and I can pay for that information. So I may not need your precious Monday's help any more."

Kate sat up straight at that. Her 'precious Monday,' indeed. "You must be comforted by such news, I'm sure. Can you tell me who told you this? I'm sure I could wire for money from Warbonnet to help you pay this woman sooner." Kate deliberately used the word woman in hopes Tom would bite on it.

88

"Weren't no woman, Miss Shaw. It was a man told me that. But I'll not be giving out his name, even if you were to try any more tricks. I want to get out of here without your help—or Monday's." He sat down on the end of the bunk so he was more nearly at eye level with her.

"Why are you so stubborn where your brother is concerned? I declare, even though you two don't look alike, stubbornness is certainly one trait you share."

Tom curled his lip under his beard. "Let me give you some free ad-vice, teacher. Monday Malone ain't worthy of a fine-lookin' gal like you, a real lady. I can tell. He ain't worth your concern and no virtuous woman should let trash like him anywhere near her."

"Why, he's always been a perfect gentleman." Well, usually. Until lately. "I cannot think why you would warn me in such a manner."

"You know all about our sister, Mary Ellen?" When Kate nodded, he pressed on, "*All* about her?"

"Well, I know mostly about her death, I'm afraid. How she was killed by bandits in your town about four years ago."

"Well, I'll bet he didn't tell you he got his own sister pregnant, did he?" Tom asked fiercely, his dark eyes more intense now.

Kate reeled back on her stool. She raised one hand to her heart. Monday couldn't have. Oh, God! But wait, wait, she told herself, trying to sort things out, seeing Tom grinning at her discomfort.

"I don't believe you," she said at last, calming herself. "I know enough about your family to know Monday isn't related to you and Mary Ellen by blood. He was an orphan, rescued by your father from the ruin of a wagon train. That means she wasn't really his sister and I doubt you're telling me the truth. Monday wouldn't—"

"You don't need to doubt me, teacher. He tell you why she and Pa were in Manzanita that day?"

"Why, yes. I recall he said they'd gone to attend church."

"Not to church. To see the doctor. When he confirmed her condition, she and Pa were gonna see the preacher, but to set a wedding date, not to go pray and sing."

"But if your father was willing to see them married, didn't they have his blessing?" Kate was grasping at straws, trying to find some way to keep her sympathy for Monday having lost his sister.

"It ain't moral, teacher. I ain't no regular hymn-singer, but even I know that if you're raised nineteen years with a girl as your sister, you don't repay your family by sneaking off behind the barn. Doc confirmed she was gonna have a baby and they were heading to see the preacher when the Lassiter gang rode into town. Mary Ellen was the first thing they saw and I reckon you must know the rest of the story if Monday's told you anything."

"I know they kept her and some other girls all night in the saloon and treated them shamefully. I think he said they killed several men and one of the girls. Then when Monday arrived, they started shooting at him. Monday was shot and the leader of the gang, Lassiter, stabbed Mary Ellen right in front of him."

"Well, he told you most of that true, I reckon. He couldn't see the last part too clear, so he doesn't know what I found out. Lassiter didn't kill Mary Ellen, not on purpose."

"He didn't? Then what happened? Monday was there. Surely—"

"I got this later, after I got back from chasin' rustlers, from Cora Wallace, one of the girls who saw the whole thing. Cora told me what Mary Ellen confided to her at the saloon when they were together. The doc told her she might have a hard time keepin' the baby and said not to do any more of what she and Monday had been doing up to that time. But then those men in the saloon gave her more of that in one night than Monday could have in a month. Cora said Mary Ellen bled a lot in the morning and she was sure she'd lost the baby.

"Anyway," Tom went on, "out there in the street, Cora said Monday turned sideways to Lassiter and raised his left shoulder, knowing he was gonna get shot. Mary Ellen knew it, too, and I guess with havin' lost the baby and havin' just seen our Pa get hit over the head and not knowin' whether he was alive or dead, she must have figured, well . . . . "

Tom drank from a cup by his bunk, as if the story affected him, too. Kate wished she had something to drink. How much of her half hour was up?

"She must have known Lassiter was going to kill Monday, 'cause Monday couldn't get a clear shot at him. Cora said Mary Ellen cried out Monday's name and then took Lassiter's hand in both of hers and pulled that knife right into her." Tom broke off and went over to stand by his small window. He was silent for a few moments. His voice sounded different when he resumed. "She screamed then, and her sudden weight must have pulled Lassiter's aim off. He hit Monday in the shoulder and only wounded him. Turned out to be Lassiter's last shot. With everybody shooting at him, he was lucky to get out of town. So Lassiter didn't kill Mary Ellen. She killed herself. For Monday. For a man who'd treated his own sister like she was some girl at the Hog Ranch.

"He wasn't worth Mary Ellen's life," Tom said with vehemence. "And he sure as hell ain't worth any of your concern for him, Miss." Tom moved back and sat on the middle of his bunk, not looking at her.

Kate choked back her sobs. She fumbled a handkerchief out of her reticule and tried to stem her tears, but she couldn't stop crying. Oh, God, Monday, she thought, forgetting her suspicions of him. Losing his sister had been so much worse than she'd imagined—and she'd been so much more than a sister to him by then. Oh, the pain he must have felt. Must still feel. No wonder he hadn't told her the full story. She got out a second handkerchief and tried to breathe slowly and deeply to calm herself.

"So," she tried, then swallowed and tried again. "So Cora saw all this and told you later. Did she tell Monday, too?"

Tom wiped his eyes on his sleeve. "No, my Pa and Monday were laid up a while at Doc's afterward. Doc checked out Cora and Maria, the other girl who survived. They were both so ashamed, they left town soon after. Cora stayed for Mary Ellen's funeral, but she never told Monday what she told me."

"But you went to see Cora? That was very kind. Then you must have told Monday—"

"I never told him nothing. He was pretty eaten up by then, blaming himself—like he should have. I wasn't gonna tell him anything that might make him feel better about what he'd done, what he'd caused."

Kate sat in stunned silence. She'd thought nothing Tom said could shock her any further. But Monday never learned the exact sequence of events, never knew of Mary Ellen's sacrifice for him. And Tom had done nothing to help him. He was as rotten as Monday had said. But at least he'd tried to comfort Cora.

"What became of Cora and Maria?" Kate asked in a small voice as she wiped her face.

"Well, Maria went back to her people near El Paso. Never heard if she had a baby from that night. Cora found out she was pregnant a month later. Her folks sent her away to have the baby. I heard she turned to workin' in a place like the Hog Ranch in Fort Worth."

"How horrible! Why would she have to do that? It wasn't like what happened to her was her fault. What did you say to her about it?"

"I told her leaving would be for the best. See, I didn't just go to see her because we were neighbors. Her and me had been sweethearts a long time. We'd been fixin' to get married later that summer. But her night in the saloon changed all that. No man wanted her after what had happened. Me neither."

Kate couldn't get a sound out. She was past tears, but she couldn't breathe. She fought her way to her feet, clutching the bars, trying to think of something to say, when all she wanted to do was to scream at Tom, to use the few really dirty words she'd learned, to hit him and hit him and hit him again.

Just at that moment, keys rattled in the lock of the cell block door and loud voices were raised. The sheriff!

92

Kate staggered to the back door and wrenched it open. She slipped out silently and closed it behind her just as quietly. There was a bench across the little alley and she sank onto it gratefully. Her body was wracked with sobs, but no tears came this time. She knew she was going to be sick. She couldn't fight the feeling any longer.

11

Laramie

Kate went back to her room at the Frontier to wash her face and see to her hair. Thank God she'd managed to keep her dress clean, the one she'd chosen to meet Bierstadt and Moran in. She wrote a quick letter to Monday, though she hadn't learned much yet that she could share with him. She did tell him that someone with the initials "A.S." may have been involved in Francine's murder, but refrained from mentioning how she'd found that out.

She had one possible new angle she could pursue herself. Tom was obviously a man who made enemies. Could Cora or her relatives despise him for his treatment of her? Despise him as much as Kate did? Could they reach this far, from Texas to Wyoming, to frame Tom for murder? If so, why wouldn't they just kill him?

Perhaps one of the Circle M cowboys here in Laramie had been in love with Cora and harbored a grudge. If that were the case, why hadn't that man rescued the woman from her current life? Kate couldn't see an answer yet, but with Monday looking so close under his nose for a killer, she thought there might be a motive a lot further away—perhaps as far away as Texas. The motive for Sam Taggart's murder they'd solved last year had been in Kansas.

That decided her. Kate still had time before the train was due to arrive. She went to the telegraph office, got a blank form, returned to the hotel dining room, and ordered coffee.

94

This was going to take some economical writing, unless she wanted to spend a fortune on a single message to Texas.

This wire wasn't going to go in a direct manner. She and Monday had asked Mr. Wyler about other telegraph stations when the Warbonnet office opened. Everyone Kate might want to send messages to was served by a local office. But Monday learned that the closest town to Manzanita with telegraph service was twelve miles away. That meant this telegram would have to be sent onward from that station by mail or messenger to reach Manzanita, where Kate felt the answer might be. She'd learned from Ben Rollins that Monday's old friend Zack Hibben was now a deputy sheriff himself in the little town.

A half hour later, she had a message both concise and sufficiently bland not to pique the interest of a telegraph clerk.

"To: Deputy Hibben, Manzanita, Texas

"Tom Malone jailed for murder Laramie. Stop. What is status of Cora Wallace. Query. Reply soonest. Stop.

"Signed Kate Shaw, Laramie, Wyoming."

Zack would send his reply—letter or telegram—to her in Laramie. All mail for Warbonnet was held here anyway until Roy Butcher picked it up every two weeks.

The clerk didn't seem interested in the contents of her telegram. Kate paid him for the wire and a little extra for sending it on at the other end and waited until he sent it. Then she added a quick note to her letter to Monday that would alert him to any response that might arrive from Texas. She found Roy Butcher, who promised to take the letter back to Monday in Warbonnet on his return journey tomorrow morning. Monday would probably get her note before any answer to her telegram arrived.

# # #

Kate was too late to catch the two artists at the train station, but she knew they'd be staying at the Frontier, too, so she made her way back there. She was inquiring at the desk when a man in Eastern garb came down the stairs. He had long dark hair and a neatly trimmed full brown beard. He seemed to be

95

in his early thirties, handsome and untouched by gray. The clerk identified him to her as Thomas Moran. She went to him and, having no one else to make an introduction, as would have been proper back East, boldly introduced herself.

Moran looked at her with an artist's appreciation.

"I've read about you, Mr. Moran. I saw your painting 'Ruins on the Nile' when it was exhibited in Albany. And I've admired your more recent work, 'The Woods Were God's First Temple,' but I've only seen that reproduced by Currier and Ives."

The artist beamed and took her hand again. "Miss Shaw. Professor Hayden told me about your brother's work and was impressed with the sketches he saw. Is he with you?" Moran glanced about the lobby. "He would be well received at Fort Ellis, since Bierstadt declined to make the journey and Professor Hayden has allowed room for another artist."

Kate's heart leaped within her. She felt so light-headed that she rose onto her toes, sure that she would float away. The opportunity to tell her carefully crafted lie about the fictional brother that Corey had portrayed for Professor Hayden brought her back to earth.

"My brother Kenneth was much concerned whether there would be a place for him. Is Professor Hayden aware that Mr. Bierstadt is unable to join you?"

"Yes, he knows. When I sent him a telegram from Chicago, he bade me be sure to bring your brother along."

"Ah, well," said Kate, launching into the lines she had practiced for so long and prayed she might use. "I am sorry to inform you, sir, that my brother Kenneth fell off a horse last week and broke his right arm. He wished me to tell you that he very much regrets not being able to travel with you." She took a deep breath as Moran frowned.

"However, all is not lost. I myself am a passable sketch and watercolor artist. I have brought a number of sketch books with me." She indicated those she held at her left side. "I took the liberty of bringing a trunk of clothes and some supplies with me. Do you think Professor Hayden would take me as a substitute for my brother?"

Moran shook his head sadly, but Kate pushed on before he could reply.

"Of course, I realize you could not commit him to such a decision, but your recommendation would carry so much weight." She stopped, rather more breathless than she had intended. She quivered with nervousness, but held his gaze steadily and didn't bat her eyes, as Becky had urged her to do.

The painter must have been skeptical, and was probably weighing his words. Kate stepped back a pace, as if to remind him how he'd studied her form just a moment ago. She hated appealing to him in this way, but he was the first hurdle she would have to cross.

"I don't hold out much hope for your request, Miss Shaw, but I will look at your sketch books over luncheon before deciding. Will you not join me?"

After they ordered, Moran went through all her books, pausing at several points and asking questions. After the meal, they stayed at the table to converse. At length, Moran took her hand in both of his and looked her in the eye. Kate did not object, but was glad the dining room was almost empty.

"If it were up to me, Miss Shaw, I have seen enough to say yes. These sketches are the work of a young artist of great promise. We should feel fortunate to have such an accomplished eye to augment what my paintings and Jackson's photographs will illuminate for the American public."

"Really, Mr. Moran? You actually think my work shows promise? I haven't practiced much since leaving school. I had no idea . . . ." She looked at him more closely.

"However," he said. "And this is a very large however. You must realize that as leader of the expedition, Professor Hayden will have to make the final decision. His last wire said that he will now be out of telegraph reach until he gets to Fort Ellis. You would have to take quite a gamble and invest some time and discomfort to go there with me to hear his judgment.

And then you would have to accept it as final. What do you say to that, Miss Shaw?" He finally released her hand.

Kate's heart rose within her. "Yes, I'm willing to do that, Mr. Moran, to travel with you as far as Fort Ellis and abide by the professor's pronouncement. I hope my work will stand on its own merit. I will add to these notebooks under your eye as we travel, so that you'll be able to assure him I have not misrepresented Kenneth's work as my own."

"That thought never crossed my mind, Miss Shaw. I hope you'll get used to calling me Thomas. We might be riding together for a few weeks."

What an honor, she thought. Moran was already one of the foremost landscape painters of this generation.

"Yes, yes, of course," Kate said. "Oh, I've been so excited for the last few weeks—at Kenneth's going, of course—and apprehensive of my own prospects since his accident, but I will abide by Professor Hayden's ruling when he sees my sketches. You may rest assured I am not in any way a weakling nor encumbered by any of the concerns he may have for my sex. I will not be a burden and shall endeavor in all ways to be a credit to the expedition."

Kate glanced up at the dining room door just as Sean Finnegan came in. She couldn't talk freely in front of Moran about the adventure she had planned for this afternoon, but she introduced the two men. Sean supported her story, as she had pleaded with him to do if she were successful here in Laramie. She told Moran that Sean had been hired as a Yellowstone guide, since he'd been there some years before; Professor Hayden had other guides for the Utah and Montana portions of his journey. Eventually, she and Sean excused themselves, saying they had some last minute errands to run this afternoon, and would see Moran at supper.

Another westbound train was due tomorrow. Her heart soared.

12

Laramie

Kate and Sean went down to Dillon's livery, where the scout had rented a horse for her. To her delight, he'd hired Valentine, the gelding she rode from Laramie to Warbonnet last year. He helped her into the saddle and led her south out of town, over the railroad tracks. After a few minutes, they encountered Ben Rollins and another cowboy waiting for them at a bend in the road. Ben introduced the other man as Sandy Sutter, an odd name, Kate thought, for someone whose dark hair was nowhere near sandy, as Monday's was.

"Now, Kate," Sean began. "You know I disapprove of what you're doin' this afternoon and if Monday ever finds out about this, he'll skin me and fry me in hot grease. The three of us are gonna stand guard here on the road to the Hog Ranch. You go around these trees to the right and ride down to the little creek bed, about a quarter mile. Then turn left and you'll come up on the place from the back. Fricker's expecting you and he'll get you upstairs to see Suzanne without anyone else seeing you." Sean squirmed in his saddle.

"We'll tell anyone comin' in that a few dozen railroad men have filled the place up and are spoiling for a fight. That should send some of the early birds packing. You might have as much as an hour, Kate. When you're finished, don't just ride up here to us. You don't want it known in town you was ever out here. Just follow that creek to the railroad bridge, then follow the tracks back to town. After an hour or so, we'll

99

look at the hitch rail behind the Hog Ranch for your horse. If he ain't there, we'll figure you went back to town and I'll find you at the hotel."

Kate left them and rode Valentine around the trees and followed the creek bed. She wondered what this Hog Ranch would be like. The name put her off, but would the building be a palace of sin, with gold chandeliers, red velvet curtains, and big windows? Would it have discreet alcoves and big columns? She'd always imagined a place like this should look like the illustrations of harems she'd seen in books like *The Alhambra*.

Her spirits fell when she rode out of the creek bed at the back of a two-story log building. This was the short side. She could see a few windows along the second floor on the long side. There were some flea-bitten horses tied out front. A balding man with bushy side whiskers was waiting at the back door to tie up her horse and help her down.

"Howdy, Miss Jones. I'm Harvey Fricker. Sean Finnegan told me all about you. I never met a female reporter before, but I hope your Denver readers enjoy your story. I'm afraid our little rancho here won't hold a candle to those silk and velvet palaces you got in Denver."

Kate smiled shyly. She hoped a shy smile might dissuade Fricker from further conversation. If she were a real reporter, she ought to have a notebook with her. All she had was a couple sheets of paper and a pencil in her reticule. To her relief, Fricker didn't ask any questions but bustled into the building and showed her up some stairs. As they walked along a sort of balcony over the main room, she looked down onto the gaming tables and bar. A few men were playing cards. One man, with a dark mustache and graying hair, might have looked up at her over his cards, but Kate couldn't be sure.

Fricker led her to the end of the hall and knocked at Suzanne's door. The woman who opened it wore a red dressing gown. He introduced Kate as Vera Jones. Kate smiled ruefully at that. Trust Sean Finnegan to put a twist into what he'd made up for her. Vera—truth. A good name for a journalist, but also appropriate for someone seeking the truth about a murder.

Suzanne didn't meet Kate's idea of a courtesan. She appeared to be in her mid-20s, more fleshy than glamorous. Fricker left them alone.

Suzanne had evidently been about her toilette when she'd answered the door. She smelled of a recent bath, but wore no perfume that Kate could detect. She dragged the only chair out from behind the corner screen that Monday had described and offered it to Kate. Suzanne sat on the bed, where she could see herself in the mirror over the dresser. She picked up her hairbrush and began to wind and tuck her hair up into elaborate coils.

"So, shoot, lady. Whatchya starin' at? Never been in a place like this before, I'll bet. Good thing, too. I wouldn't want you working here. Tough enough with Francine, but those men downstairs wouldn't give any of the rest of us a tumble if you were to let that golden hair down."

Kate felt her face grow warm, but busied herself with extracting paper and a pencil stub from her handbag. "I, I'm not really Vera Jones from Denver. I'm just here today from Warbonnet and then I'm traveling on to Yellowstone tomorrow. I know you've answered some questions already for Marshal. . . , um, Deputy Sheriff Malone, but I wonder if I could ask you a few more. I'm sort of helping him out in his investigation. Sometimes a woman can think of things to ask that no man ever would."

To her surprise, Suzanne gave her a big smile, showing clean but uneven teeth. "Ain't that the truth? Well, you took in old Fricker with that song and dance about being a reporter. Makes you sort of a spy, don't it? All right, Missy. We're gonna get along fine. Ask away."

Kate had organized her questions and started out with Francine's background, how long she'd worked at the Hog Ranch, and who her most regular customers were. There were few surprises; her notes tallied with what Monday had learned. One new disclosure was that Deputy Reese Bowman hadn't been able to afford to see Francine very often, nor any of the other girls. But since Francine's death, he'd been to see Suzanne nearly every night.

"He followed Francine around like a dog when she was down at the bar sometimes, but she told me he'd only been with her once or twice. Acted like he couldn't afford it."

Kate asked her about Ben Rollins. Suzanne said she'd seen him, but had never had him as a customer. When Kate asked about Smitty, Suzanne brushed some powder from the inside of her left upper arm and showed Kate a fading bruise there.

"Smitty wants what he wants when he wants it. And most often he wants it a certain way, too. Oh, I'm sorry. I didn't mean to be so forward saying that."

Kate felt the heat of another blush. She changed the subject to the other girls. Nothing in Suzanne's litany of names and backgrounds suggested any of them felt the jealousy toward Francine that Monday said Suzanne had exhibited. Finally, they got to Danielle.

"Well, if it's any comfort to you, Miss, Danielle can blush quicker and deeper than you—and she's been here more'n two weeks now. It amazes me she isn't red as an Indian all the time. You'd like her singing, if you could stay to hear it. This ain't no life for her, doin' what we do. I sure hope some angel flies down and spirits her off to San Francisco like she wants. That Ben Rollins comes to hear her sing and I understand he's helpin' her some, but there ain't much a poor cowboy can do."

"I've heard Danielle sometimes has to observe what the girls do, as part of her training."

"That's right. She ain't actually spread her own wings yet, so to speak, but Fricker says she only has money to hold out another couple a weeks. I hope he don't . . . well, if Fricker's gonna get her pearl anyway, she ought to give it to that nice Ben Rollins first. Oh, there I go again. I'm sorry."

Kate didn't blush at this. She'd seen enough horses mating since she came to Wyoming. And she'd sneaked one of her father's medical books, Doctor Youman's *Illustrated Marriage Guide*, to her room for several nights when she was sixteen.

She tried to steer the conversation back to a less inflammatory topic. Like murder.

"Who discovered Francine's body?"

"Well, I reckon I did. I heard a scream, and when I come from around the hall corner—my room used to be along the front of the house that way," she gestured out the door and to the right. "I found the door open and Francine just lying there looking at the ceiling. Reese Bowman came hurrying up the front stairs to see what the matter was. When he come in, I went down a ways to tell the other girls. Them and their customers were standing in the hall by this time."

"Well, thank you, Suzanne. If I think of any more questions . . . ." Kate rose and was about to leave when she saw Suzanne take a black lace item out of a dresser drawer. That reminded her.

"Suzanne, when Monday Malone was here . . . ," she started, uncertain how to proceed.

The woman smiled broadly again. "You're Kate, aren't ya? I should have figured right away."

Kate sat back down in shock.

"Oh, you're wonderin' how I know your name. It was writ on the package that Monday left on my bed." Kate gasped. Monday had brought her package in here? He'd left it on this bed? Had he been in this bed with Suzanne? She didn't want to think about that. She put both hands to her hot cheeks. She'd been trying so hard not to blush, to seem like a woman of the world. Suzanne was busy at the mirror and didn't see her reaction.

"See, he ran out of here in a big hurry and left that package behind. I peeked inside and saw it was filled with plain white drawers and a couple bars of fine soap. Francine had this little outfit that wouldn't fit me. I don't think she'd even unfolded it. I just put it in the package and tied it back up. I gave it to that big black fella, Bull, who came for it a minute later. You look about Francine's size. Did they fit you?"

Kate jumped up so quickly, the chair fell over backwards. She turned and busied herself picking it up and putting her notes back into her handbag. Then Monday hadn't given her that underwear. But it might be worse. He'd been alone in this room with Suzanne. She calmed herself and tried to side-track the woman by asking another question.

"Suzanne, do the initials 'A.S.' mean anything to you?"

"Nope. 'Fraid not." She put down her hairbrush and turned to Kate.

Kate's mind raced. Suzanne didn't seem to know that the note with those initials had been with the black lingerie.

She felt her composure return. Suzanne didn't let her keep it very long. She came forward and took Kate's hands between hers.

"Miss, I gotta say that man of yours has probably been true to you."

Before Kate could object that Monday was hardly "her man," and now could never hope to be, Suzanne went on. "I was bent on seducing him right over there where he was sit-tin'. He was tryin' to resist, but I had some powerful argu-ments, you might say." She crossed her arms under her breasts.

"Anyway, when I was trying to persuade him, he sighed this name 'Kate,' almost like a prayer he figured would protect him."

Kate felt behind her for the chair. Suzanne seemed to sense her panic.

"Oh, not what you think, Miss. What you fear. Your shy Mr. Malone jumped up soon's I touched him. I told him to come back and see me again, but he was out of here like a shot. Reckon that's how he forgot your package." Suzanne stood up and touched Kate's arm in what she probably thought was a reassuring gesture.

"You don't have to blame him for what didn't happen here. It was my doin' and I thought I was being clever at the time. But now that I've met you, I'm sorry I was so forward with him. And I ain't felt that way in years."

Kate began mumbling a farewell and thought about mak-ing a dignified exit. But as she opened the door, a black-mus-tached man in cowboy garb came in and put hands on her chest—her chest!—and pushed her back into the room, closing the door. Kate raised her hands, covering her breasts with her forearms. How did he dare touch her like that, even in a place like this?

"Who's the new girl, Suzanne? You been breakin' her in like Danielle? When do we get a taste?" He sneered at Suzanne and then turned to Kate. "I'm Smitty, Blondie. Let's see that hair down." He reached for the pins in Kate's hair, but she turned her head away. She didn't dare move her hands from her bosom.

Click. She and Smitty turned at the sound. Suzanne was pointing a derringer at Smitty's chest. Suzanne didn't say anything and she didn't blink as she held the gun with both hands. Smitty stepped back a pace from where he had Kate pinned against the footboard of the bed.

"This here's, um, Miss Vera Jones from the Denver newspaper. She was just asking me some questions about this place for a story. I think she'd like to leave now, Smitty." She twitched the little gun to indicate he should back away from her guest. When he did so, Kate squeezed past him, her forearms still crossed over her bosom, and went out the open door. As she fled down the balcony, she could hear Smitty's voice.

"You don't need to use that thing on me, Suzanne. You open for business now?" Kate heard the clink of coins.

"Well, I'm not really dressed yet."

"Hell," Kate heard Smitty say as he closed the door. "You know you don't hafta go to no trouble for me."

13

Warbonnet

Liza Crandall played "Immortal, Invisible, God Only Wise" over again as a recessional, but to no avail. No one filed out of the little schoolhouse that functioned as a church one Sunday a month. Outside, the rain was coming down in sheets and nobody was anxious to leave.

Nevertheless, Monday Malone and a few men took their slickers off the pegs by the main door and went to fetch food and drink from the porch of Martha Haskell's nearby boarding house. The church fund relied on the monthly Saturday night dance and the box lunch auction after the Sunday service. God didn't want to dampen their good time, Reverend Jonah Barnes had assured his flock this morning. Everyone needed the rain and only the second half of last night's dance had been washed out.

When the food and drink had been brought in and set on tables hastily constructed from a couple of benches and the movable floorboards from the dance, Monday peeled off his slicker and thought about the noon meal. He almost swore at the weather, but Reverend Barnes—Jonah, he reminded him-self—was coming this way. Monday pegged his wet hat and stared out the streaked window. He wondered what Kate was doing right now.

"Yes, I miss her, too." The voice at his elbow jerked Monday from his reverie. Jonah leaned in next to him and squinted out at the low clouds that brought delight to the farmers in his congregation. "But cheer up. The rain falls on the just and the unjust alike. She'll be fine."

How could Jonah read his mind that easily? "Who do you mean?"

Jonah smiled as if he shared a secret. "Kate Shaw," he said. Liza finished the recessional and began to tidy up her music. "You know that last tune? Liza is a good pianist, but she played it like a hymn."

"Uh, it is a hymn, isn't it? We sang it this morning."

"Yes, strictly speaking, it is a hymn. But when Kate played it back in February, she made it sound like a triumphal march. She does that with many of the pieces she plays, even Chopin sometimes. She puts more drama into what she plays than the composers intended." They looked away from the window and at each other. The table was almost ready and Ike Hauser, acting as auctioneer, took his place at the lectern.

Monday wanted to ask if Jonah could recall every hymn Kate had played at each service, but then closed his mouth. He knew Jonah was sweet on Kate, just as he himself was. No doubt Jonah could recall each hymn she'd played in the last eleven months, and probably remembered which dresses she'd worn to church each time, too. Good thing he was a circuit rider and not living here all the time.

The auction went more quickly than usual. The rain had kept many people home, but three cavalry lieutenants now vied for the box lunch Becky Masterson had prepared. Hers and Kate's lunches were most prized among the young officers, cowboys, and occasional visitors; high bidders got to sit with the ladies who prepared the meals. Becky looked glad to be the sole center of attention this morning. Monday won the bidding on Maria Torricelli's lunch and there was enough for him and Jonah. She'd made some of that "pasta" stuff. It tasted exotic to Monday.

"I look forward to seeing Kate during my visits here," Jonah said. "I think I miss her piano playing as much as I miss her singing and dancing." He sipped some water. "I miss conversations with her most of all."

"If you'd had Kate to talk to on Friday night, you couldn't have joined me for that little target practice down by the river. I never figured a preacher to be such a keen rifle shot." The gangly preacher looked like a young Abe Lincoln. He'd been quite a sight holding a rifle.

Jonah grinned. "When I was a boy, I was a fair hunter. I even put some ducks on the table—and they're a hard target. I haven't fired a rifle in years, and never touched a repeater like yours. It took me back a few years. I'm grateful for the experience, but I'd rather have spent Friday evening talking to Kate. No offense."

"I imagine I have a slight advantage over you, Monday," he continued. "When I return to Warbonnet in a month, Kate will be back. I routinely go a month at a time without seeing her. This long separation must be much more trying for you." Jonah looked down at his dinner. Was he baiting Monday?

Monday swallowed and considered his answer. How could Jonah know how he felt about Kate? He tried to pay equal attention to Becky and was all set to dance with her last night when the heavens opened up. That's what he got for delaying his pleasure. If only he'd gotten to her when her dance card was fresh.

"Yeah. Sometimes I get to see Miss Kate two or three times a day. I been worrying that she's all right. I know it's only been a week or so, but . . . . " He trailed off and looked at his own plate, working Maria's bread through the tomato sauce.

"Don't you think she'll be all right, Monday? You did everything you could. You sent Sean Finnegan off to Yellowstone with her. If you couldn't go yourself, you couldn't have picked a better man to protect her from bears and wolves."

"It ain't just bears and wolves, Jonah. There's two-legged critters, too." Monday worked on the last of his pasta and bread.

"You mean Indians? I can't imagine they'd harm Kate. Our Sioux neighbors have become quite fond of her. I heard her referred to in one village east of here as 'Zhi-zhi Pahin'."

He paused, clearly conscious of the fact that Monday couldn't speak Lakota. "That means 'Golden Hair'. They think she's 'good medicine.' They say that despite white hunters' depredations, the buffalo have seldom been so plentiful as this spring and summer."

"Well, I ain't just worried about Indians, Padre. There's many a man would give a lot to go away with her for a month or more. Some of the men in that group are married, but if she makes it onto that expedition as she hopes, she'll be the only woman they take along."

"Then those men will be sorely outnumbered, even if there are forty of them. Kate can take care of herself. You watch. She'll probably come back and tell us how she had to rescue Sean Finnegan from a bear or something."

Monday nodded and laughed. They each ate a cookie, then Jonah spoke again.

"How is your murder investigation coming along? I heard about that in Laramie two weeks ago. It must be going somewhat well, since they don't seem to be in any rush to try your brother."

Monday took another sip of water. Didn't take long for the whole county to learn his business. Why did they need this new telegraph, if Jonah could carry news from town to town?

"Well, it's hard to do a proper investigation when I'm three days' ride from Laramie. But I send letters and wires when I can. And I'll be down there and back here before you get back to Laramie." Monday ran his hand through his hair, dampened by the rain despite his hat.

"I'm leaving soon to help guide them cows up here. They've eaten so much grass south of Laramie, you'd think grasshoppers had stripped the place. This rain will fatten the grass for 'em up here, so I guess it came in the nick of time. The just and the unjust, like you said."

"Do you have any suspects you're most keen on?" Jonah asked. "The girls at the Hog Ranch are anxious to make sure her killer is not still on the loose and is not one of their, um, regular visitors."

"Why, Reverend," Monday said in mock amazement. "I didn't know you knew about Laramie's little Sodom and . . . whatever." He grinned at the young preacher.

Jonah stroked his small beard. He didn't seem embarrassed. "Know of them? They're my smallest flock. Mrs. Ivinson and the other ladies of Laramie society will not let them attend regular services, so on the one visit I make to Laramie each month, I hold a special service just for them on Monday afternoon. At the Hog Ranch. Kate knows all about it."

So that might be how Kate had heard the words "soiled dove," Monday thought. A small mystery solved.

Jonah went on. "You know how Kate is never satisfied to help someone a little when she can help them a lot? Well, when she heard about the Monday afternoon services, she gave me two spare McGuffey readers to take down there. I've been teaching a few of the girls to read after the service. Francine, the murdered girl, was in that class." He sighed and put his plate aside.

"The ladies of Laramie didn't want her to have a regular funeral either, so I couldn't use the church there. We had a special graveside service for her. Our little class is the poorer without her enthusiasm."

"So Francine was a new reader," Monday said. "That's something I didn't know. Can't figure out what good it does me, though. Kate says these little bits of facts are like them puzzle pieces, you know, the ones in funny shapes? Anyway, she says you don't have to make sense of them right away. You can just put 'em aside and bring 'em out later if you find a place where they might fit. Sort of like that 'A.S.' clue she sent me in her last letter."

"A.S.? What kind of a clue is that? Are they someone's initials?" Jonah's interest sounded genuine. Monday recalled the young preacher had read those Poe stories Kate had mentioned. She'd tried to get Monday to read them, too, but there were some words in them he didn't understand and he hadn't wanted to ask Kate. He'd stick to Twain.

"Kate sent me a note before she left Laramie and said the letters A.S. might be important. I only know one 'A.S.' in this case and he's one of my leading suspects."

"Well, who is it? Can you say?"

"Sandy Sutter. Some folks would figure you get a name like that from your hair color, but Sandy's has always been dark. His nickname is short for Alexander. I don't know how it makes him any more of a suspect, though. Kate didn't tell me how she'd run across them initials. I sure hope she writes me again from Yellowstone. Sean said there'd be a few chances to send and receive mail."

"I hope so," Jonah said. "I've written to her twice."

"I'll send her a letter, too," Monday said. "Never wrote one before, but then I never had anyone to send a letter to."

He and Jonah helped take down the tables as folks left. Monday used the work time to let his mind wander, thinking about Sandy Sutter and the murdered girl, Francine. He'd already learned he was a frequent customer of Francine's. What could have come up between them that Kate thought Sandy had killed her? Was Sandy involved in some other way? How could Kate just suggest the initials to him and ride off to Yellowstone?

At least he was thinking of what Kate knew and what she told him and not how she looked and how she felt when he danced with her. If he was going to miss her, he ought to think more about her detective skills than her charms. That's what she would tell him, he knew. Still, there was a lot more of her to miss than her sharp mind.

14

Fort Ellis, Montana Territory

The stage coach rolled into Fort Ellis on a hot, dusty afternoon. After the long ride from the Ogden train station, down in Utah, this would be Kate's moment of truth. She'd practiced lines for every eventuality. And she'd changed into her riding skirt and put up her hair into a severe schoolmarm's bun this morning. With her riding skirt, boots, gloves, bandana, and hat with horsehair strings, she didn't look like any greenhorn from the East. She hoped she just looked determined. Like a Wyoming woman should.

A grinning Sean Finnegan offered to buckle a gunbelt around her waist, but she declined.

"I only want to look like I can take care of myself, Sean. Not like I'm spoiling for a fight."

She gathered her sketch books as they picked up their luggage. Sean and another man carried her trunk. Moran offered to go and find Professor Hayden, but Kate touched his arm and asked him to wait until the coach had fresh horses attached and southbound passengers aboard. When it was gone, and she couldn't be sent packing immediately, then she would make her case to Professor Hayden. And be well and truly stuck if he said no.

The expedition must have gone well up to this point. Professor Hayden and Jim Stevenson, his right-hand man, sounded like they were in good spirits. Moran found them on the veranda of the hotel and, according to Kate's request, introduced himself to them first, while Kate watched and listened, off to one side, out of sight. He and Sean and the others affirmed their readiness to head out to Yellowstone the next day. As instructed, Moran waited until Professor Hayden asked about the other artist. Since Albert Bierstadt hadn't been able to join them, had Moran been contacted by a K. Shaw in Laramie?

"Yes, we met at the hotel. This K. Shaw struck me at once as a capable and dedicated artist, but also, as a Wyoming pioneer, appeared to have been tested by this territory, inured to hardship, and unafraid of danger. In short, a worthy addition to Jackson and myself—and of course your topographer, Anton Schonborn." Moran nodded to Schonborn.

"Good, good. I saw that in the young man myself," said Hayden, looking around. "Where is he?" At that moment, Kate stepped up onto the veranda and walked slowly up to the group, her boot heels the only sound in the sudden silence.

"Mr. Moran is understandably reluctant to tell you, Professor, that my brother Kenneth met with an unfortunate accident two weeks ago that left him unable to ride and unable to sketch. I presented myself to Mr. Moran in Laramie and he thought my work had sufficient merit that I should be considered for Kenneth's position, my gender notwithstanding." She opened her two best sketch books and set them on Professor Hayden's table.

"I too am a 'K. Shaw,'" she continued. "Katherine rather than Kenneth. I am completely equipped and ready for this expedition, Doctor. I throw myself on the mercy of the court." She bowed her head and then raised it, staring quietly at him. She hadn't smiled at all and hoped seriousness of appearance and speech were the proper ways to begin.

Everyone began to speak at once. Sean and Moran added to the general babble. As Hayden tried to restore order, Kate saw Schonborn and Jackson, the photographer Moran had pointed out, come to the table and pick up her sketch books. Kate knew Schonborn was an accomplished artist, but serving as the expedition's topographer. Would his presence in the expedition diminish her chances? They turned pages and showed each other certain drawings while Professor Hayden

113

tried to deal with the tumult. At length, Jim Stevenson thumped a bottle on the table and Hayden was able to speak.

"I recall meeting you in Laramie, Miss Shaw, when I met your brother. I deeply regret that you have traveled all this way for nothing. No matter your credentials, I cannot take responsibility for having a woman, a young woman, *an unmarried woman*, along on this journey. Why, even Mrs. Jackson only went as far as Ogden with us and I know Mr. Jackson would not want even his wife to have to face—"

"Hell." Sean Finnegan cut in. "I'll take responsibility for her, uh, comportment. She can ride and shoot, she don't complain about bad grub nor poor weather, and Injuns and wild critters don't scare her none. Not all the men you brung can say that, I'll wager. And as for having such an attractive woman along who might corrupt your party, she's turned down dozens of proposals and ain't found a man good enough for her yet. I don't think you need to worry about her."

Sean brandished his rifle. "I can vouch for her and I'll make sure you don't have to worry about your own men. How about it? You need a good guide inside the Yellowstone country. I'm the man you wanted for that job. You were expecting another pencil and brush artist, I understand. Well, this is the woman for that job." Sean stood practically gray beard to brown beard with Professor Hayden. And he'd remembered the comportment word Kate had given him.

Hayden looked ready to argue, but Jackson took his arm. The photographer and Schonborn talked to him and pointed out pages in the sketch books.

"They're all her sketches," Moran interjected. "I can vouch for that. I've watched her work. You've seen her brother's work already. If you think her material compares favorably, you ought to consider her on those grounds alone. Open your eyes to her abilities, sir, and never mind her appearance." Professor Hayden looked at the sketch books again.

Kate risked a quick smile at Moran. He and Sean had been more eloquent than she dared hope. After more talking with Jackson and Schonborn, Hayden consulted Stevenson, who pointed to the map and nodded in response to some whispered questions.

"All right," said Hayden, leaning on the table, now strewn with maps and Kate's sketch books. "This is how it is. I perceive how the tide is running on this matter. I shall engage you as a sketch artist and water colorist, Miss Shaw, for the period of one week on a trial basis." He held up his hand when Kate opened her mouth to speak.

"That is how long it should take us to get to White Mountain Hot Springs, said to be the gateway to Yellowstone," Hayden continued. "I shall render judgment on your art work and your comportment when we get there. If both are satisfactory, to me and to these gentlemen—" He indicated Moran, Jackson, and Schonborn. "You may continue with us into Yellowstone and return here when Mr. Moran leaves us. Is that agreed?"

"Yes, sir," Kate said. "I agree to your terms and shall bow to your judgment when you render it." No smile, no unbending. Just a level gaze. She hoped she was playing this scene correctly.

"All right," Hayden continued. "Sean Finnegan has spoken well of you. I hope I hear no complaints from you about any of the men in this party." He thought for a moment.

"A government expedition like this cannot afford any taint of scandal in Washington. We shall carry you on our books only as 'K. Shaw.' While we may later be pleased to have had a female perspective on our findings, I do not wish Mr. Peale or any of the others making journals of our exploration to record that we had an unmarried female accompanying us. Do I make myself clear to one and all?" After a general murmur of assent, the group began to break up.

"We rise at five tomorrow, Miss Shaw, to break camp. Breakfast is at six and we shall be on the trail by seven. Pray do not keep us waiting." As Hayden turned to consult Stevenson, Jackson, and Sean, Kate went off with Moran to take care of her gear. Professor Hayden's last remark rankled her, and she didn't intend to swallow the implied criticism.

# # #

The next morning, most of the men got an early start and finished packing up after breakfast. Riders and wagons set out just after seven, with Sean riding next to Hayden at the head of the column.

"I didn't see Miss Shaw at all this morning," Hayden said to the scout, glancing back after the first mile. "Was she confined to her bed with the vapors or some such?"

"I'm sure she took your words of yesterday evening seriously, sir. But I ain't seen her neither."

At that moment, they rounded a bend in the trail. Hayden reined in as he saw a rider waiting for them. Kate Shaw sat with one leg cocked over her saddle horn, balancing a sketch book on the knee of her riding skirt. She made a couple more pencil strokes and then looked up at them and the line of wagons and horsemen strung out behind them.

"You're a little late getting under way this morning, aren't you, gentlemen?"

Hayden coughed to cover a laugh and grinned through his beard.

15

Montana Territory

Kate was feeling inordinately proud of herself this morning. The expedition was now three days out from its Montana jumping off point. Professor Hayden had said last night that they must be only a day or so from the Yellowstone country, based on Sean's estimate and guidance from last year's Washburn expedition.

She'd ridden a horse the whole way, despite being offered a place in one of the supply wagons. The larger wagons might not be able to go much farther and pack animals would soon have to carry their food, tents, and Jackson's delicate photographic equipment. But she'd proven she could keep up with her male counterparts. Often, when they rested, she hadn't even got down from her saddle. Sean had told her they were impressed. They didn't know how stiff she was.

"You haven't held 'em up none," he'd said one evening over the embers of their fire. "In fact, they're beginning to wonder if you're really a woman, since you don't ask for no special treatment or nothing."

"I have had buckets of hot water to wash in delivered to my tent for sponge baths, Sean; I think that qualifies as a special consideration. But I take your meaning." No doubt some of the campfire laughter had been at her expense.

"Yes'm. But I also told 'em you're a Wyoming woman. You don't expect no special treatment. You showed 'em a thing or two when your horse trod on that snake two days ago

117

and quickstepped sideways. They were talking about racing you and your mare up to that point, but you got her under control right smartly. Now I'll bet they think they might as well rassle a grizzly bear as take you on."

Kate smiled at that memory. Her horse had been startled by a snake and so had she. But she'd spent so much of her energy and concentration getting her horse under control that she quite forgot to be scared. When she got her mare to calm down, she'd been so angry that she slid from the saddle, broke off a dead tree branch, and went back to look for the snake. It was generally agreed around the campfire that evening that the snake had been wise to leave the area.

All that riding with Becky and Corey Masterson had done her a world of good, she thought. The brief sponge baths got her clean, but she didn't have to take long soaks to ease her stiffness. Now she rode as if she'd been born in a saddle. She thought briefly of Monday. Maybe he'd think she was as good a rider as Becky now. Almost a Wyoming woman.

This morning, Kate had taken a place between a supply wagon and Jackson's wagon. A sudden disturbance caused the whole column to come to a halt. She eased her mare out to the right with a sure hand and kicked her to move forward.

She came up next to Thomas Moran. Sean Finnegan and Professor Hayden were a little farther ahead, stopped facing a tree line of low pines. With a start, Kate saw a dozen painted Indians on horses at the edge of the trees on the right. She may have mastered her aversion to snakes, but still held an abiding fear of Indians. Since coming to Wyoming, Monday and Sean had bandied about stories that made her hair stand on end.

"We just saw them, Miss Shaw," Moran was saying. "Or rather, we saw them when they wanted us to see them. All I know is Sean just said the word 'Lakota' and went out to talk with them."

Sioux, Kate thought. That couldn't be right. This was the country of the Lakotas' mortal enemies, the Crow. Or as they called themselves, the Absaroka—children of the big black bird. She recalled Sean had been married to a Crow woman at one time, but she forgot whether that was his first or second wife. He'd told her far northwestern Wyoming and southwestern Montana was Crow hunting grounds. She looked at the Lakotas' painted faces. Monday had taught her that painted horses and bare faces meant a hunting party. These Indians had painted their faces for war.

Kate watched Sean dismount and leave the reins of his horse with Professor Hayden so he could talk to the chief of this band on foot, using his voice and sign language to make himself understood. Out of the corner of her eye, she was pleased to see that none of the men drew or even touched a weapon. Sean and Professor Hayden had drilled into them that no matter what kind of temporary advantage forty white men, some armed with repeaters, might gain, the expedition would have to retrace its steps in a few weeks and couldn't afford to have hostile foes along their return route.

She strained to hear Sean say, "This is a war party all right, but they're here to raid the Crow for horses. They'll leave us alone if we give them some powder and shot. They don't need bullets; only a couple of 'em have repeaters." Hayden nodded and Sean asked Steve Hovey, the wagon master, to fetch a small powder keg and a bag of shot.

Kate let out the breath she'd been holding and shivered. She'd seen Indians a few times in the vicinity of Warbonnet. But here they were in the middle of Indian territory. Maybe they wouldn't need to fight today. They couldn't outrun determined pursuers in this increasingly hilly and wooded terrain, not with their wagons. She thought she could see more Indians looking out between the trees. Kate swallowed her fear and tried to look at least as calm as Moran next to her. Another test she had to pass.

When Sean spoke again to Hayden, she heard him say, "They're nervous, you see. The Crow have been hitting them hard all spring. They're hoping they can turn their recent bad medicine into good medicine. Good enough to make their enemies think twice about going south for Sioux and Cheyenne horses. The chief says—"

Sean broke off when the chief in the tree line said something, pointed one-handed with his rifle in the general direction of the company, and rode out of the trees. All she could

119

catch of what Sean said to Professor Hayden before breaking off to talk to the chief was "Uh-oh."

After some vigorous verbal and sign communication, Sean turned back to Hayden and this time acknowledged Kate with a glance. "Seems the chief has noticed we have a woman with us. He thinks that's a good sign. Despite our Army escort, shows we may not be a war party. Not even spies. He wants to look at her, maybe speak with her. They don't usually do this. I don't know if it's a good sign or if there'll be trouble." Professor Hayden beckoned Kate to ride forward.

When Moran moved to ride with her, she gestured with her left hand for him to stay where he was and kicked her horse forward. She hoped she wouldn't have to speak. Her heart was in her throat. Her best friend in Buffalo, Lacey Ferris, had scared her with tales of what Indians would do to white women they captured. Sarah Wakefield's favorable memoir of her six weeks of captivity by the Sioux, a book Kate's mother had sent her, was cold comfort now.

She reined in next to Professor Hayden and looked first at Sean and then at the chief. The latter wore straight vertical lines of black and white paint below his eyes. He had a few white handprints on his scarred bare chest. And his calves were painted bright ocher. He didn't blink when he looked at her. He was nearly naked, with just a flap of deerskin at his waist. She swallowed hard and looked away from his broad, muscular chest. She tried not to blink when she met his gaze.

"Kate," Sean said softly, standing between her horse and the chief's. "This is Red Legs, a war chief who's leading this raiding party. He saw you and asked to see you up close." He broke off as Red Legs said something. "He wants you to take off your hat. I don't think that's a—" Kate took off her hat and shook her long blond hair free before Sean could offer any more advice. She looked the chief in the eye again. Fear had made her mouth dry.

Sean and the chief spoke for a minute. "He's inclined to let us go our own way. He's heard some other bands of Sioux and Cheyenne tell about *Zhi-zhi Pahin*, the golden-haired woman of the whites' town way to the south. He hears you have great

120

good medicine and he fears to anger the spirits by harming you or us. That's the good part. Now he wants to touch your hair for good medicine in the coming raid. I don't think that's a good idea neither."

Kate kicked her mare and rode up alongside Red Legs. At this distance, she could smell him. The overwhelming impression she had was of horse sweat and wood smoke. She met his gaze and reached out for his hand. She guided it to her hair, and he ran his fingers through it. The Indians in the tree line murmured in low voices. Red Legs spoke a single word and the talking stopped. Kate had a sudden idea. She pointed to Red Legs' knife at his hip, then combed out a lock of hair with her fingers.

As Red Legs drew his knife, Kate heard Sean Finnegan's intake of breath behind her. Kate pointed to Red Legs' horsehair reins and then pointed to the lock of hair she held out. The chief appeared to understand she was offering him yellow hair that he could weave into his horsehair reins. He cut off the lock with one sure, smooth stroke. He put the hair away into a rawhide parfleche, a pouch he wore at his hip, and went to sheath his knife. Then he thought better of it and reached up and cut off a lock of his own black hair and laid it in her palm. He didn't smile with his mouth, but the corners of his eyes crinkled in amusement.

Kate said without looking at Sean, "Tell Red Legs my hair will be strong medicine, but only to steal horses, not to kill. If he has to kill anyone to get horses, the medicine will vanish—go away. Can you tell him that?" She said two Lakota words she'd learned, "*wastay pezuta*"— good medicine—and made a sign language gesture, pointing her finger and the ground and rotating it in a circle. Good medicine in this place.

When Sean made sure she'd been understood, Red Legs asked a question in return. Sean said, "He wants to know what you know about stealing horses." He grinned up at her.

Kate didn't smile and kept her eyes on Red Legs. "Tell him I stole a horse a year ago." That stopped Sean before he could mount his own horse. She remembered taking that young cowboy's roan gelding in a desperate bid to keep Monday from being killed. When Sean translated that, the chief grunted another question.

"He wants to know if you were armed. And if the man you stole it from was armed."

"Yes, he was," said Kate, remembering the pistol the young cowboy had carried. She recalled her shame upon finding out later that the rifle she'd threatened him with hadn't been loaded. "And I guess I wasn't."

Sean knew the tale; the whole town had heard it before school started last September. Red Legs' eyes twinkled as he heard Sean tell the story in a voice that all the Indians could hear.

The chief said a few words, then turned to rejoin his braves in the tree line. He waved to Sean that the party should proceed.

Kate sat still and waited for Sean to mount and join her. She put the lock of the chief's hair into her reticule that hung from her saddle horn. They waited as the rest of the expedition moved past them. The Lakota band sat in the tree line and watched. She knew from earlier conversations with Sean that they would be counting the men and rifles in the expedition.

"Red Legs was impressed, Kate. You stole your first horse and faced down a live enemy at the same time. He thinks your big medicine must come from having done that—sort of 'counting coup.'"

"You done real good with him, young woman. You sure you didn't live out here in some previous life? There's no way I woulda figured you could do like you just done, you being a greenhorn only a year ago." He spoke without looking at her as they sat side by side watching the motionless Sioux.

"Thanks for the vote of confidence, Bill Cody," she ribbed him. "I didn't know what I was doing; I just went on instinct." And acted as she imagined any other Wyoming woman would have. Thank God she'd paid attention to Jonah Barnes on sign language and learned a few words of Lakota from him.

"Well, your instinct's holding up pretty good. We're sort of sitting here acting as a rear guard while the expedition moves on past us. That's what plains Indian warrior societies do—Dog Soldiers and the like. We're sending 'em a message that we're so strong we have a woman as a Dog Soldier. Sort of, you might say—"

"Don't say it, Sean. I don't like that word. Let's just sit here and not look hostile. What was Red Legs saying just before he broke off?"

The old scout's deeply weathered ruddy face couldn't show a blush, but Sean was quiet for a moment, as if considering. Finally, he said, "Red Legs called you *Zhi-zhi Pahin Maku*. He was telling his braves why he thought the Sioux and Cheyenne really like you. It was a crude comment, really. You couldn't tell that from his men's reaction; only Indian children laugh."

"What does it mean? I know *Zhi-zhi Pahin* means 'Golden Hair.' What is *Maku*?"

"Uh, Kate, please, you don't want to know."

"Sean, remember what you said. I'm a Wyoming woman, remember? No special considerations."

"But Kate . . . ."

"Tell me. If I have another Indian name, I ought to know it." Now that the last wagons had rolled by and the Indians had vanished, she turned to look at him.

He took a moment, as if collecting his thoughts to choose his words carefully. "Red Legs said that Golden Hair—that's you—could, um, nurse many babies. That's their way of noting a woman's, uh, charms." He raised both hands and cupped them in front of his chest.

Kate was glad there was no one else around to see Sean's gesture.

"Well, then, I'll take that as a compliment. But Sean, mark me well. Don't let me hear the word '*maku*' around the campfire, all right? That's a secret between just you and me—and twenty Sioux." She kicked her horse so they could rejoin the column.

She thought she heard Sean whisper the single word "mercy" as she passed him.

At the next rise, Anton Schonborn was waiting for them. Sean trotted by, eager either to get to the head of the column—where a scout should ride—or to get away from her. Kate wasn't sure which. As she tucked her hair back under her hat, Schonborn doffed his.

"I don't know how close we were to death back there, Miss Shaw, but you certainly have charms to soothe the savage breast." Kate looked at him sharply. Was he just quoting a cliché or had he heard what Sean told her?

"I was just lucky." Kate blushed. "The Sioux must have been ready to cut a woman some slack today."

"You're too modest," Schonborn went on. "I get the feeling that if you hadn't been with us, we might be feeding the buzzards right now."

Kate eased her horse's pace and looked back. Not only were the Sioux not following them, there was no indication they'd ever been in that tree line. They'd vanished like smoke. "What are you getting at, Mr. Schonborn?"

"I'm proud to travel with you, Miss Shaw. I just wish we could get beyond the Miss Shaw-Mr. Schonborn stage. Since we've just been through our 'baptism of fire,' so to speak, couldn't we become Kate and Anton now?" He grinned through his fashionable black beard.

Kate began to feel the effects of the strain of the last few minutes. Her hands shook on the reins. She had actually had an Indian touch her. She'd been terrified at that moment, but now she felt strangely calm and confident. What had Monday told her? If you can do what you're most afraid of—and if you survive—you receive the gift of courage afterwards. She sighed.

"All right, Anton. I'd be pleased to have you call me Kate. So far, Sean has been the only one who dares call me by name. As a Wyoming woman, I guess I should expect men to use my first name without requesting permission, but you have nice manners. Thank you for asking."

"I'd like to ask you something else, too, Kate. Or ask you to consider something." He paused as if weighing his words. "We all—and I particularly—value your contribution to this expedition and the fresh eye you'll bring with your sketches, so I don't want you to take this the wrong way. Have you thought of being on the opposite side of a sketch pad, of having your portrait done? You'd be a striking subject, especially with the steel I've seen in your eyes today."

Kate felt herself relax and smiled at him. "Actually, I've been thinking that very thing. The Wyoming sun, wind and snow have been weathering me. I thought I ought to have a photograph made before I look too old. I intend to approach Mr. Jackson."

"Not a photograph, Kate. Jackson's black and white works are fine for rough impressions, but I meant an actual painting. A way to capture the real you—at this time and in this place. Don't you have family you'd like to give such a portrait to?"

Kate was flattered. "I don't know what to say. I know you do mostly sketches and landscapes, but to have a portrait done here would require extraordinary effort and the expense would be beyond my means."

"Well, not a real oil painting right away," he said. "No one here, not even Mr. Moran, has brought any of that gear. Takes too long for oil paint to dry. But I could do sketches and perhaps a water color or two, and you could ask Mr. Jackson for a photograph. I'm no portrait artist myself, but I know many such back in New York who could work from sketch, photograph, and a water color. Would you be interested?"

Kate thought for a moment. "Yes, I'd like that very much. I could give it to my parents for their twenty-fifth anniversary. But I'm afraid I couldn't afford to pay an artist the customary fee for such a painting."

"Oh, that's all right," he said lightly. "I'm sure, with the prestige that will come from the work of this expedition, we'll work out something reasonable for the fee my artist friends might charge. There's a lot of Yellowstone to see. I'm sure we'll find a fittingly majestic backdrop for your beauty. Shall we get ourselves back among the wagons before we encounter more Indians today?"

Kate shivered. They spurred their mounts and trotted ahead.

16

Laramie

Monday tied Lightning's reins in front of the Laramie jail. He'd rather have headed for the bathhouse, since the ride down from Warbonnet had been unusually grueling, but he had business at the lock-up. He'd used all that saddle time to mull over how his five leading suspects could have killed Francine. Three days' ride had brought him to Laramie, but he'd gotten nowhere with his suspect list. He'd had a week in Warbonnet to think about the case, too. Maybe Kate had done better since she went off to Yellowstone. Could be he was smarter when the schoolteacher was around. "Perhaps so," Kate would have said. He grinned just thinking of her.

All his suspects could have done it. Now he was back in Laramie and hadn't figured out much of a motive for any of them yet. Except that Suzanne had been jealous of Francine and Sandy had been sweet on her. But dozens of men had liked her and used her, he'd heard.

Monday wanted to ride north with the Circle M herd day after tomorrow. Another three days in the saddle and then three more to get back down here to do some of that "investigating" before Kate returned from Yellowstone. He'd probably need the extra time, unless Kate wrote him with some fresh ideas.

This was a good moment to visit the jail. If he'd timed this right, the day shift should be changing and he might get to talk with Tom, Dutch, or Sheriff Boswell.

As luck would have it, Deputy Reese Bowman was alone in the office. He told Monday that Nate and Dutch had just gone home. Monday decided to make the most of the situation. He could at least talk to Bowman without fear of interruption. Bowman asked if Monday had time to play a little cards or if he'd come to see his brother again. The deputy pulled out a cribbage board and a deck. Monday went down to the Alhambra and brought back a bucket of beer and two glasses. Nate might not approve of drinking on duty, but hell, beer wasn't drinking, and anyway, Monday needed to get the little man talking.

Bowman was not only pleased Monday would spend some time with him, but seemed genuinely touched that he would pay for the beer, too. When the deputy offered to let Monday cut the cards, he declined, hoping Bowman would assume it was because Monday trusted him. No harm in that, Monday thought. They were only playing for a penny a point. He ought to be able to lose a dollar, if it came to that much. After a couple games and near the end of their second glasses of beer, he began to probe.

"Say, Reese, how come you draw night shift all the time? Don't seem fair to have one man lose all that sleep." He knew the answer. He just wanted to get Bowman talking.

"Aw, it ain't that bad. Sheriff, Dutch, and Cal are all married, you know. They got wives to go home to. I get a little extra for working nights—and it ain't for all night, either. I only got to work 'til two, an hour after the saloons close." He took a gulp of beer and wiped his mouth with the back of his hand. "Then I'm supposed to make one more round of the Hog Ranch before checking the prisoners and lockin' up. I get to sleep in in the mornings. I reckon I'm used to it by now. Ha! Two points for turning a jack!" He moved his peg on the board. Bowman had won one game, lost one, and was ahead in this one now.

"What about that night of the murder? You know, when you discovered the body and made the big arrest?"

Bowman puffed up visibly. "Well, I seen right away that Francine was dead. And not ever'body woulda guessed that, with so little blood. But her eyes were staring at the ceiling and she wasn't blinking. I put my hand on one of her bosoms to see if she was still breathing. If she was, she'd have slapped my hand away. She was still warm."

Monday counted out the points in his hand and moved his peg a paltry six holes. Feeling a woman's breast to see if she was still alive. He hoped his feelings weren't written on his face right now.

"How did you happen to connect Tom with her death? Not every lawman could have found clues as quick as you must have."

The little deputy practically glowed, both at the praise and at the ten-point hand he counted out. "Well, ever'body in the place knew your brother Tom had words with Francine that night. We all figured it must have been about his perform-ance. He'd had too much to drink when he'd gone up there and then he had a few more when he come down. 'Course, it was really the knife that was the giveaway—the *dead* giveaway, you might say." He grinned at his small joke, counted his crib, and passed the deck to Monday.

"Oh yeah, Tom's initials," Monday said casually as he shuffled. "You were able to see those all right? It wasn't too dark or nothing?"

"Nope." Bowman scooped another beer from the bucket for himself. "The lamp in the room gave enough light to see the initials white against the black handle. They was thin, but real clear."

Monday recalled he and Tom had bought their knives on their first cattle drive, in 1868. They'd carved their handles in turn, using each other's knives. Though they were no longer close a year after Mary Ellen's death, they hadn't been enemies yet. Three years of use since then ought to have worn the new-ness off Tom's initials. Time had certainly made it harder for Monday to see the Circle M he'd carved on his own knife. Did that mean the carving on the murder weapon was fresh? Was that why Bowman noticed it so quickly?

"Did you search the room for any other clues?"

Bowman nearly spit out his beer in his haste get his glass down. "No. No, I didn't touch nothing," he coughed. He seemed sensitive on that score. Had Dutch or Nate questioned him about Francine's missing proceeds for that night?

"I didn't look around much. There was no need. Figured I had my man. Just had to go find him." It sounded to Monday like Bowman was in such a hurry at that point that he wouldn't have noticed whether the chair behind the screen was tipped over, the way Dutch found it a few minutes later. Monday didn't ask.

"How'd you know where to find Tom so quick?"

"Aw, that was easy, too." Bowman crowed with pleasure when Monday turned over his crib and could only count two points for a pair of threes in it. "Sandy Sutter was just coming back in. When I said I needed to find Tom Malone, he told me he'd put him to bed a little while before. He took me right to Tom's room." He gathered in the cards for his turn to deal.

"And you found him asleep when you got there? Who went with you?"

"Well, he was probably fakin' sleep if he done murdered that girl and had just come back. That's what I figured. As to who, well, let's see. Sandy was there and Jimbo Cobb, and . . . oh, we come across Tom's foreman Smitty near the hotel. He went up with us, too."

"Who noticed Tom's knife was missing from the sheath on his gunbelt?"

Bowman finished dealing and grinned. "I did. Course, that's what I was looking to find."

Monday recalled Sandy had said Tom's knife was still in its sheath when he'd hung up Tom's gun belt after putting him to bed. Tom's room had been unlocked. Anyone could have got his knife. Unlikely he'd have gotten up and gone back to kill Francine if he'd been as drunk as he said. Had he been faking drunk to set up an alibi, sleeping it off in his room?

They ended their final game. Bowman won twenty-five cents on that one, nearly skunking Monday, who hadn't been concentrating. The deputy generously poured the last of the beer into his opponent's glass.

"You know, Malone, I think it's a shame we never got along better. The sheriff's always singing your praises, how you captured this fugitive or that horse thief, or some such. Seems like when you come to town I'm either working or sleeping and you end up talking only to Dutch or Cal. When the sheriff puts together posses, I'm always left behind to mind the town." He put the cards away. "I sure would like to get some tips from you on what it's like to track someone—and how to get the drop on somebody. I practice, but I'm a better shot than I am a fast draw."

Monday was touched. The little deputy did seem to lead a lonely life. He promised to talk to him again before leaving town. When Reese went down to return the beer bucket, Monday let himself into the cell block and took the last of the beer in his glass back to Tom.

Maybe that was what Kate had been trying to tell him about Sandy. That he'd had access to Tom's knife. But why had she just referred to Sandy's initials? And what did it matter if he had access to Tom's knife? Monday figured the murder weapon wasn't Tom's. The initials were on the wrong side of the handle for a lefty like his brother. And thin and shallow, like someone had scratched them in real recent.

Tom didn't seem glad to see Monday, but he was grateful for the beer, even if it was a little warm and a little flat.

"You any closer to getting me out of here?" he asked, with no preliminaries.

"No. I mean, I got the sheriff convinced you didn't do it, but it's gonna be hard for him to just let you go if he ain't got the real killer to put in here."

Tom wiped his lips after another swallow of beer. "You talk to that cute little schoolteacher yet? I told her you might not have to bend your brain too hard on my case. I got me someone who knows who the murderer is. We're just dickerin' on the right price for that information. Five hundred dollars seems pretty steep to me. I'd like to dicker with him a bit, but if it comes right down to it, it's my life. Reckon I'll pay it if I have to."

Monday was stunned. Kate hadn't even mentioned she'd talked to Tom. And after he'd warned her not to. He felt the flush as his face turned red.

"Well, I thought she hadn't told you. Your face gives all that away. Anyway, she was a mighty pretty piece of work, but she couldn't trick me into telling her who I'm talking about. Now maybe if she'd got a key and come in here, we could have worked something out."

"You bastard!" Monday flung himself against the bars, reaching for Tom. Tom grabbed his right wrist and held it in a vice-like grip.

"Some lawman," Tom said. "You oughta learn to control your temper. And control yourself around ladies. She's too good for the likes of you, you know. She won't think much of you, considerin' what you done to Mary Ellen."

"You didn't tell her, did you?" When Tom just raised one eyebrow at him and grinned, Monday returned to the problem at hand.

"You can't bust out of here by holding my arm, Tom. I ain't got no gun or keys and I'll be damned if I'll—"

Abruptly, Tom let him go. "Run along and play detective for a while." He drained the last of the beer. "Much obliged for this. I'll buy you a round when I get out." He gave Monday the glass.

Monday left the jail as soon as Bowman returned. He put off that bath and rode out to the Hog Ranch. He knew he probably wouldn't run into Suzanne during her prime working hours, but he hoped to find Sandy or Ben. Tom had his salvation pinned on his mysterious informer. Monday wanted to help, but his brother was so hostile. Would Kate have better luck?

Ben was there, but no other hands from the cattle drive.

"Oh, hullo, Monday. Figured you'd be back in town soon. Lookin' forward to having you help guide us north. One trip to Warbonnet don't make me an expert on that trail."

Monday ordered beers for them both. He wanted to ask Ben about Sandy and whether he would have had a reason to kill Francine and frame Tom, but Ben shushed him.

"Wait. In a bit. Danielle—Lynn—is coming on to sing again." They settled down, but the men at the bar made some rude remarks they couldn't quite hear. Ben held his beer glass in white knuckled hands.

"I can't . . . . It tears me up to hear them say those things about her, just to see her have to work in a place like this. But Fricker warned me if I punch out one more customer or make what he calls a scene, he'll ban me from the place. Lynn is too good a moneymaker for him. I hope he just lets her sing."

Monday could tell from Ben's intensity while he watched Danielle that he'd do almost anything to get her out of here. Had he gone into Francine's room and stolen her night's take the night of the murder? That wouldn't get him but twenty dollars or so, probably not enough to make a difference. Did Ben know who the killer was? Was he Tom's mystery witness, hoping for a five hundred dollar windfall? Instead of talking to Ben about Sandy, maybe Monday should be talking to Sandy about Ben.

For now, he just listened to Lynn finish "Like a Nightingale" and start "Green Grow the Lilacs." What a nice voice she had. Too good for a place like this. If Ben felt about this Danielle like Monday did about Kate, there might be enough reason to steal, if not a motive for murder.

17

White Mountain Hot Springs

Kate lowered herself gently into the hot water that bubbled from a spring and joined a creek she had found. It was still a little too scalding. She didn't want to be cooked, so she moved away and found a warm spot. What luxury! A bath that she didn't have to heat the water for. Much better than the tepid sponge baths she'd endured this week. This eddy had everything she could have wanted, except a roof over her head and walls to keep out prying eyes. Still, it had more privacy than the commercial bath hut they'd encountered, which so far served only male bathers.

Almost all the explorers were out collecting, photographing, sketching, and surveying, in what had become their daily routine. She had Sean Finnegan and his rifle to keep peeping toms at a distance. Of course, since Sean had asked her to marry him more than once, she knew she couldn't entirely trust him to keep his eyes in the other direction. *Zhi-zhi Pahin Maku* indeed! It was a good thing she'd worn an old shift under her robe. That got her modestly into the water and she'd placed a towel with them for after the bath, when she'd be more exposed.

But for now, Kate let all her cares fade away with her aches and minor pains. This water was heavenly. She watched the breeze move the nearby tree tops and was grateful for the warm day. Otherwise, she might catch a chill at Yellowstone's altitude. Even in summer.

These geysers and hot springs were the most impressive things she'd seen since leaving Niagara Falls. From a white fairy mountain of little stairsteps to powerful columns of shooting water, there were cascading basins of water of every temperature and color, wrapped in whirling mist. For a moment, she imagined herself as Lady Rowena in *Ivanhoe*.

She'd had trouble sketching the geysers to get a realistic feel for the huge fountains of water and clouds of steam. Thomas Moran had advised her to concentrate only on one element at a time. Since these geysers went off fairly regularly, she'd learned to sketch columns of shooting water, then fill in their cloudy tops and plumes of vapor with the next eruption.

Kate applied the peach-scented soap Monday had given her while she watched a hawk circling overhead against a few clouds in a brilliant blue sky.

Couldn't bathe like this at Niagara, she thought. No place but Wyoming.

"You really ought to use binoculars, Miss Shaw, if you hope to see that hawk more clearly," said a man's voice, alarmingly close.

Kate whirled at the sound, barely remembering to cover her breasts. Quickly, she sank to her shoulders in the dark steamy water as Anton Schonborn stepped around a bush with binoculars at his neck. She doubted he'd been bird watching.

"Anton, this is a lady's bath. I understand the gentlemen will bathe this evening. Would you please leave? And how did you get past Sean Finnegan, my guard?"

"Ahhh, as to that," Schonborn gestured off to other shrubbery on his left. "Mr. Finnegan is otherwise occupied, I believe. I brought along a bottle of good whiskey and persuaded him that I could take over guard duty for a little while." He found a rock at the edge of Kate's stream, and sat down next to her robe, shift, and towel. Her retreat was cut off.

"Sean," Kate called out. "How can you do this to me? I'll remember this, if I ever get out of here."

"Don't be too hard on him, Kate. He probably can't hear you anyway. I left him after he took his second swallow from the bottle. You can chastise him after he wakes up."

"*Mister Schonborn*, don't take that tone with me. This is not funny. I do not want a man sitting next to my bathtub while I am naked."

"Not naked, Kate. Nude. It's a term artists use."

Kate thought of how she'd spied on Monday Malone in his bath. She caught herself smiling, then regretted showing Schonborn any sign of amusement. Was this intrusion God's punishment for her peeking at Monday in his bath? She'd been expecting some sort of divine retribution for what she'd done that night.

"I am not feeling like any Greek Diana right now, sir, and if you were the gentleman you profess to be, you'd excuse yourself and leave."

"You know, Kate, I've been thinking about what you said about a portrait you'd like to give your parents. We plan to make many sketches and watercolors of the Yellowstone country in the next couple of weeks and with those, Jackson's photographs and whatever Moran creates, there will be tremendous interest in the sights of this country. Catching you at your bath like this raises an interesting possibility."

I'll bet it raises something, she thought. Desperately, she tried to imagine how Becky would try to get out of this situation.

"What sort of 'interesting possibility'?" Only her head and shoulders showed above the dark surface of the slow-moving stream.

"Well, I'm sure you know that artists have a schedule of fees that they charge for commissioned works, like portraits or paintings of some rich man's home or family."

She already knew that. What was he driving at?

"Kate, you're being very modest this afternoon, but I should like to assess what kind of Diana you would make. Could you at least show me your back?"

"Only if you promise to leave." She turned her back on him and stood up slowly, showing him only her back. She submerged herself again before turning to face him.

"Thank you," Schonborn said. "You would indeed make a splendid painting or sculpture. That's what I wanted to talk to you about. I think you might have difficulty meeting an artist's fee for a portrait, so why don't we strike a bargain? I can sign up a friend or two of mine to paint your portrait if you would consent to being my model here for a figure study against some lovely backdrop in Yellowstone."

Kate arched her eyebrows. "What is a figure study?"

"You must know that artists often employ models for sculpture and paintings. Good models are so hard to come by that groups of artists often must share them. The discerning eye may see that the same young woman appears in several works by different artists. It is an honorable profession to which many young ladies—"

"I'm sure you mean young women, sir. I doubt if any lady would so display herself."

"Oh my, but they do. You see, an artist often alters the face in a painting or generalizes the features of a model. In 1865, the daughter of a prominent judge posed for a colleague of mine. One cannot tell from the finished work that it is Libbie Hargrove, but I have seen his sketches and a smaller painting. Since I know the young lady—happily married to a doctor now and the mother of two sons—I can attest to the truth of the story."

Kate frowned. "So you propose that I pose undraped for you here and for your friends in New York City in return for an oil portrait for my parents?"

"Well, I don't expect you to say yes right away, Kate. But I hope you wouldn't rule it out al-to-gether." He chuckled at his little joke. "And you could be decorously draped, if you wish, rather than nude. Will you think about it?"

Kate remained silent. She ought to be outraged at his effrontery. On the one hand, the thought frightened her. But on the other, it could be a deliciously wicked adventure. If she dared to pose modestly draped for Schonborn, she'd have to share the secret with Lacey Ferris and Anna Green. What good was skirting scandal unless you could tell your oldest and closest friends?

"What do you say? Have we got a bargain?" Kate began to move toward him, still demurely submerged, when there came a loud *click*.

"I reckon that's about far enough, Miss Kate." Sean Finnegan emerged from the shrubbery and pointed his rifle in Schonborn's direction. The artist raised his arms high in a "reach for the sky" gesture. Kate giggled and kept well below the water line, with arms crossed in front of her.

"Sorry, Anton. But this Venus is not going to rise from the waves for you today. Thank you, Sean. Have you been listening long?"

"Naw, only the last minute or so. Mr. Schonborn's whiskey sent me to answer the call of nature, but when I returned, I heard what this polecat was proposin' to you. I don't know what you've been thinkin', Miss Kate, but maybe you got a little ahead of yourself."

"Yes, I fear I did, Sean. Thank you for your timely intervention. I am not feeling my ordinary self right now."

"How did you withstand the effects of that bottle of whiskey?" asked Schonborn. "You should have—"

"Well, yes, at one time, I mighta. But Marshal Malone told me that if I let anything happen to Miss Kate on this trip, I oughtn't to plan to return to Warbonnet. So I just had two pulls and I've saved that golden ambrosia—fine whiskey, sir, really fine it is, too—for later."

"Thank you again, Sean. Why don't you take Mr. Schonborn and yourself over past that stand of pines and I shall finish my bath and dress, using those bushes as a screen. Potato John should be ringing the supper bell soon."

"We should talk again, Kate." She just turned her head away and let him go. She didn't want either man to see her grin.

Kate whistled while she finished washing.

Artists' model. Hmmm . . . . A way out of Wyoming and back to New York. But only if she didn't want to go home to

Buffalo. If she chose the model route, she could never return to her family. Definitely not to her family.

18

Near White Mountain Hot Springs

Kate relished this time of the evening. Supper was finished. She'd bathed and put on fresh clothes. She'd done her laundry this afternoon, ahead of a dozen men. The camp was festooned now like a ship with pennants on its lines. She'd answered mournful pleas this evening and darned eight socks and repaired two shirts and a pair of trousers. Why did men assume that just because she was a woman, she was good with a needle and thread? Her mother would be amused at her popularity as a seamstress. How would these men have coped if she hadn't come along?

Still, this journey was a relief from all the housework, laundry, and ironing she helped Martha Haskell with every week. Why couldn't the men on this expedition fend for themselves? Couldn't they be more grateful for the drudgery she did for them? The other artists and Jackson the photographer weren't asked to do such scut work.

She turned to the letters she could write in these free hours before bed time. Most of the men had gone to bathe over at the Hot Springs. Some were drinking or playing cards. Professor Hayden and Jim Stevenson, his second in command, were planning the objectives of the next few days. The expedition would leave for Tower Falls tomorrow, then go on to Yellowstone Falls and eventually to more geysers and the big lake Sean had told her about.

Kate said good night to half a dozen men on her way to her cot in the only one-person tent in camp. Of course, she had to share it with ammunition, food, and other supplies that Mr. Hovey, the wagon master, wanted to keep dry. She was conscious of her status and grateful for the solitude. The men seemed relieved when she left them each evening. They could get to their card games and their drinking and not have to watch their language any longer.

She didn't light a candle to undress and put on her shift and robe. No sense taking any chances someone would see her silhouette on the canvas wall. She put a board across two flour kegs and formed a writing desk, then pulled over another keg to sit on.

The camp was quiet. Some of the men were taking advantage of their bath time at the hot springs. She could hear deep tones of talking men and the occasional laughter that meant card games and off-color jokes. Kate had learned to absent herself after supper. That got her out of dishwashing.

There was no sign that whatever had been scaring the horses for the last two nights would be active tonight. She'd wormed out of Sean that bear tracks had been found only a hundred yards from the tents. The expedition had dined on bear this week, but Kate declined. She was particularly appalled that the hunters had killed two cubs along with the mother.

Tonight, all the food and anything else that would smell good to roaming bears would be strung up in bags in nearby trees. Nobody expected any repeat performance, since all the temptations would be out of reach tonight. And a good thing, Kate thought. Sean wouldn't tell her, but she'd overheard him tell someone else that the tracks had been those of a grizzly, not a smaller black bear. "Big as a pie plate," Sean had said of the tracks.

Some of the men hauled food into the trees using flour sacks as bear bags, but others put things in old socks before stringing them up. Ugh, Kate thought. She wasn't going to consign her beloved peach soap to the inside of someone's dirty sock. Kate rewrapped it carefully and put it in the tray of her trunk. She swore she could still smell it even after she'd closed the lid, then smiled as she brought her forearm up to her nose. She smelled wonderful when she used it. That

140

reminded her of Monday, who'd given her two bars for her birthday and now two more, for no special reason, he said. He'd also given her a black lace *mantilla* at Christmas, sent all the way from Texas, he claimed.

Kate frowned. She loved wearing the *mantilla* to church sometimes, but now it reminded her of that black lace underwear in the same package as her drawers and the peach soap. She remembered she'd been furious when she opened that package from Laramie, without thinking how Monday could have found such things. She'd been relieved to find out Suzanne had inserted the fripperies into her package, but then furious at Monday again to think he'd been with one of those women. She felt about Monday the way she did toward Wyoming, alternating between exasperation and affection. Right now, smelling the peach scent on her arm, this was a moment of deep affection.

That made Kate think first of her own bath this afternoon and then of Monday's, when she'd peeked at him through the knothole in the ceiling. She would never have let Monday stay at her bath and talk to her the way Schonborn had presumed to do back at the stream. But the man was a competent artist himself and knew more artists in New York City. Like the more sophisticated Moran, Schonborn appreciated all the finer things that she loved. He represented a breath of civilization, a touch of home in a desolate land that hardly compared to Buffalo.

Kate would not have found her flirtation at the stream acceptable in another woman. Thank heaven for Sean's arrival. She was ashamed now that she'd enjoyed it and allowed Schonborn to remain.

Remembering Monday after his bath and her own situation made Kate flush. She felt her hot cheeks with the back of her hand and hoped she wasn't coming down with something. She took off her robe and just sat in her nightgown. It was still warm this evening.

She was beginning to recall the details of Monday's form very clearly now. Kate had better think of something else, if she wanted to fall asleep tonight. She got out her writing materials. Kate decided to savor her mood and write about Monday to her oldest friend. She'd write a letter to Monday later.

Kate addressed the first of her three envelopes to Lacey Ferris in Buffalo. She described her journey thus far and dwelt on White Mountain Hot Springs, the first of the promised natural wonders they'd encountered. She'd made several sketches for the expedition yesterday and replicated a small one for Lacey's envelope.

Remembering her scandalous conversation with Schonborn by the stream, she briefly considered telling Lacey about it. But she decided instead to share that juicy secret with another friend, Anna Green, who was living in New York City and trying to get her poetry published. Anna lived far from Buffalo now and would know about artists and models and could appreciate Kate's mixed feelings about Schonborn's offer for her to pose.

She decided to tell Lacey about peeking at Monday in his bath. After all, she and Lacey had spied on Stuart and other neighbor boys when they were swimming—how long ago? Heavens, was it seven years now, the summer of 1864, before Stuart went off to the war? She shivered at that thought. Her flush evaporated and she pulled her robe around her shoulders.

Kate recalled how she'd felt when they'd crept away undetected. Lacey wanted to go back and steal some of the boys' clothes. She remembered how similar her feelings at observing Stuart were to those she'd experienced peeking at Monday. Kate began to warm to her subject and waxed poetic, writing quickly.

Kate laughed so hard at this that voices outside asked if she were all right. Canvas walls had big ears. She decided she'd better tone down some of her language or control her reaction. Perhaps this was a lingering effect of the afternoon bath.

After a few more lines to Lacey, Kate set that letter aside and started on her missive to Anna Green. She told Anna as much about the country as she'd told Lacey and included another small sketch. Then she summarized as well as she was able Schonborn's visit to her bath and his proposed bargain. Anna was a woman of the world, nearly four years older than Kate, and she had a career in New York. She of all people would understand Kate's dilemma.

Writing all this down made Kate pause and consider what Schonborn had suggested in exchange for getting friends to do her portrait. Could she trust the man to be professional while sketching her in that vulnerable position? Or would he treat a posing session as a tryst?

She knew Anna could never get this letter and provide advice before Kate had to make her own decision, but it helped her to write some of this to a trusted friend. By confessing to these thoughts now, she'd have to explain her actions to Anna later. Knowing that might help Kate decide the wisest course for herself between now and then.

Kate finished the letter to Anna by asking her some questions about Francine's murder. Anna knew all about Poe' stories and French police novels. She asked her friend several questions about possible motives. Kate considered jealousy the likeliest reason for Francine's death, but elements of it didn't look like a crime of passion. The substitution of a knife meant to look like Tom Malone's, for instance. Francine's missing money. Her scream when she must have seen the knife, before the first and fatal blow came down. Why was there a second wound and why was the knife left behind?

What a puzzle. Kate pinned some hope on Deputy Sheriff Zack Hibben in Manzanita, who might shed additional light on Tom Malone's past. That had been the key to finding the secret motive behind Sam Taggart's murder last year. Monday was good at sifting clues in Laramie, like he'd done at the ranches, farms, and mines near Warbonnet during their Sam Taggart investigation. But Kate knew she was better at probing hidden motives, secret jealousies, and harbored resentments.

Suzanne could have killed Francine if she were jealous of her success. But why would she frame Tom Malone for the crime? Just to turn suspicion from herself? Sheriff Boswell had said no woman had yet killed anyone in Wyoming Territory. Not like back East, where poisonings of husbands, knifings of lovers, and drownings of children were becoming as much a woman's endeavor as a man's.

Kate reluctantly ended her letter to Anna, leaving it unsealed like Lacey's. She might add some more lines tomorrow before a rider took the mail back to Fort Ellis.

She decided she could turn her attention to writing to Monday now if she confined herself to a wholesome subject like murder. She certainly wasn't going to confide to him any of the secrets she'd shared with Lacey and Anna. Ladies simply didn't tell those secrets to men, not even gentlemen. And it would be stretching propriety to call Monday Malone a gentleman.

Kate told Monday of her good health and described the steaming geysers and the lovely and dangerous hot springs they'd found since her last letter to him a week ago. Then, hoping he wouldn't be offended, but knowing he depended on her help, she began to suggest several possible lines of inquiry he could pursue before her return.

"I know I mentioned the importance of the initials 'A.S.' to you, but I'm uncertain how or even whether they may be connected to the crime. I know you told me not to approach the women at the Hog Ranch, but being a good detective is not limited by one's sex. My gender gives me certain advantages and I was able to exploit them to have a long conversation with Suzanne before I left town with . . . ."

She'd mentioned talking to Suzanne. She didn't care if it made Monday angry. He had no business telling her what a woman's place was or what a lady couldn't do. He wasn't her mother, or even Martha Haskell, who'd been fussing over her of late.

Kate realized she'd become flushed and shed her robe again. Was her frustration stoking her inner fires or was it Monday Malone? Why was she letting thoughts of him inflame her tonight? Finding out Kate had talked to Suzanne would be likely to upset Monday. He'd probably worry that Suzanne had told her they'd had relations—or nearly had relations. Let him squirm as he thought about that, she decided. She picked up at her stopping point.

144

"I left town with . . . members of the expedition. I didn't tell you in my last letter, but before I left Laramie, I sent a wire to a deputy sheriff in Manzanita, hoping for some information in your brother's past that might shed light on Francine's murder. I hope you won't think I'm interfering in any way in your investigation, but his return letter or wire may provide some help of the type we received when we looked into Sam Taggart's murder last summer."

"I talked briefly with Ben Rollins and his lovely Danielle," Kate wrote. She should probably cross that out and write "Lynn," but she was close to the end of a page. Kate checked her candle and yawned. Close to the end of her ability to write, too. She tried to clear the cobwebs from her mind and find a way to finish this letter to Monday. She glanced at Anna's and Lacey's letters; they were still unfinished and unsigned.

Kate urged Monday to talk with Ben some more. It might be difficult or impossible for the young cowboy to find enough money to take Danielle away from that awful Mr. Fricker. She didn't believe Ben capable of murder, but she worried that he might hold up a bank or do something even worse.

She capped her ink and blew out her guttering candle. She'd finish the letters tomorrow morning. As she lay down and pulled the blanket over her, she thought Monday would talk to Smitty and that Deputy Bowman without her suggesting them. She shivered when she remembered Smitty pawing her bosom at the Hog Ranch. What a disgusting creature! She was grateful no one else there had mistaken her for a woman like Suzanne.

That made her think. Schonborn wanted to see her the way Smitty had wanted to see her. Though their motives were different, that made her compare herself to Suzanne. Jonah Barnes taught reading to the women of the Hog Ranch, some of whom hid their former lives and went on to respectable marriages.

Painted women who papered over their pasts. Should Kate model for Schonborn? Would that lead to becoming a model for a group of painters? That might mean descending into a world of paint herself, perhaps never to emerge. Would

145

painted canvas cover her step into modelling and propel her into an uncertain future? With the turmoil of those thoughts, she drifted into fitful sleep.

# # #

Noise woke her. It wasn't dawn yet. There was a wind rising. No, not a wind, a rumble of some kind. The horses were crying out in panic. Her tent billowed as if in a storm. Was she dreaming? But the sky had been clear tonight.

Abruptly, the sky came into her tent. A gaping rent appeared in the fabric over her head. Through the gap, she saw the stars were undisturbed by any wind or clouds.

Then the stars were blotted out by a vast bulk above her and she closed her eyes in sudden apprehension. There was a roaring in her ears, in her head, and from without. Shouts and yells came to her and she was dimly aware of the flickering of torches. Warm breath blew on her bare shoulder. The strap of her shift had slipped off. She tried to pull it back up, but a huge and hairy hand pushed hers away. That awful man Smitty? How had he found her in Yellowstone?

A massive form pushed against her creaking cot and she felt a tongue licking her bare shoulder. All the shouts and yelling and neighing were drowned out by a lone voice screaming. Some hysterical woman somewhere was wailing and crying out. Why didn't someone stop her? Why didn't . . . .

Kate opened her eyes and looked up into a huge muzzle of yellow teeth and reeking breath. Her last conscious thought was that she'd become hoarse.

19

South of Warbonnet

Monday Malone got out of his bedroll, stood up in his union suit, stretched, and yawned. Not dawn yet, but sounds and movement in camp had roused him. Bastiano, the old cook, had a fire going under the big coffee pots and the sound of his putting the dutch oven under the coals reminded Monday that sourdough biscuits would be ready soon. That woke him as reliably as a gunshot would have.

Coming along on this three-day drive had been a real revelation to him. He thought he'd remember all the good times of the first drive, when Jim Squires had been Major Malone's foreman and trail boss, and when at twenty years old, Monday had taken care of the *remuda,* the cowboys' horse herd. But it hadn't worked out that way. Maybe you couldn't relive the pleasant experiences of your youth. There were too many new faces on this drive and everyone was surly, probably because Tom Malone wasn't along to ride herd on Smitty. All Monday's Smitty memories had pushed out his recollections of happier times.

Sandy Sutter and a couple of the other boys were getting their gear together to go out and relieve the last night watch. By custom, the morning relief would eat before the rest of the outfit. Monday took advantage of this opportunity and picked up a bridle that Sandy dropped and walked with him toward

the horse picket line. Perhaps he could get some more information on Ben Rollins or Smitty.

"You don't have to do that, Malone. I can handle it."
Sandy carried the saddle in his right hand and reached out
with his left. Monday ignored the gesture.

"It's no trouble for an old trail mate, Sandy. Besides,
seein' the *remuda* again might bring back some memories.
How has this drive been, compared with the others we used to
ride on?"

"No better, no worse. Just longer. Course, that means the
payout will be a bit higher."

"An extra month, right? For bringing part of the herd this
much farther north. Did you get a partial payout in Kansas?"

"Yeah, we got our first two months' wages there, same as if
we were paid off at the end of a usual drive. Guess your
brother didn't want to carry that much cash all the way up
here. He wired the rest of it back to Texas. Anyway, some of
us drank up our pay, some gambled it away, some spent it on
women. I did," he leered. He found his favorite mount and
dumped his saddle. Monday handed him the bridle.

"How about Ben Rollins? What did he do with his money?
I know he has a lady friend in Laramie now, but he don't seem
to have much to spend on her." Monday held the reins after
Sandy put the bit in the horse's mouth. Sandy saddled up
quickly, with the cowboy's usual economy of motion. He
talked while he worked.

"Well, he didn't spend much of it on ladies or drinking.
You know his folks don't hold with that. I recall there were
some gamblers fleecing any cowboys stupid enough to join
their games. Ben fancies himself a poker player. I think he
mighta lost some of his pay that way.

"You can do that, you know," Sandy said, grunting as he
tightened the girth, "Piss away your pay, even if your pa owns
a good-sized spread of his own." Monday took the implied criticism. Sandy wasn't just talking about Ben; he also meant
Monday himself. When Major Malone owned the Circle M, his

sons Tom and Monday always had deeper pockets than the rest of the hands.

Seemed like Sandy had some kind of burr under his saddle today, something bothering him. He rode for the Circle M when Smitty made Monday ride drag on his last two drives, eating dust and flies all day at the back of the herd.

Those were the summers after Smitty, the new foreman who'd replaced the dead Jim Squires, had tried to break Monday for no apparent reason. Tom, who rode at the point of the herd as top hand, had done nothing to improve the situation. Monday stood up to Smitty twice during the first of those drives, once on the trail, and once, when he was drunk, in Abilene. The result had been the same both times; Smitty had beaten him to a pulp. After that, Monday had felt like a whipped dog, and on his last drive the next summer, hadn't dared challenge Smitty again.

He'd quit after that last drive and pushed on up here from Kansas, hoping to find work in Montana. Instead, he'd picked up a badge temporarily in Wyoming and Kate Shaw had prevailed upon him to stay. Hell, she always prevailed in everything she did. You couldn't win an argument or a contest with Kate. That set him to wondering what she was doing right now.

Suddenly, Monday realized he was alone with his thoughts. Sandy had left and walked his horse back to the chuck wagon for his grub.

Monday decided to check on Lightning before he went to breakfast. The horse was glad to see him, but was stepping funny. Monday bent to check his right rear leg and saw that the horse's fetlock was severely bruised. How had that happened? Lightning had been fine last evening before Monday turned in. He'd have to let the horse recover today and ride one of somebody else's remounts.

He got short shrift with a replacement horse. After breakfast, Smitty let him have someone's worthless end-of-string, played-out nag. But they were only half a day out of Warbonnet. Monday would leave Lightning with Joe Fitch when he got to town and use Sam Taggart's bay mare.

Monday saw Ben over breakfast, but he didn't have much to say this morning. If Ben had gambled away some of his wages from the longest part of the cattle drive, he might be just about broke by now. Tom probably didn't intend to pay any of them very much for this part of the drive. So how was Ben hoping to raise train fare and get his Danielle out from under Fricker's thumb?

As to Ben's silence this morning, Monday knew the disease. His friend had calico fever and pined for the woman who'd given it to him. He felt it himself in the weeks since Kate had been gone. Jonah had been right. He consoled himself with the thought that the preacher might have as bad a case as his own.

Everybody put their bedrolls and pistols in the wagon. Only a couple hands would carry guns in case they were needed to signal or to turn a stampede. Monday kept his rifle and pistol with him now as a matter of routine. Cowboys might leave their guns in the wagon, but lawmen always went armed. His weapons wouldn't get in his way. He had no real duties, no strays to bring back. He rode near the center of the herd and tried roping a steer every now and then just to see how well he'd kept the skill.

About noon, they went over the last couple of low foothills that separated the mountains from the Platte River. Monday noticed his borrowed horse was favoring his left rear hoof. There was a clear space in the middle of the herd, so he got down quickly to take a look. The hoof was bleeding, and in a minute Monday saw why. Someone had placed a short nail sideways between the hoof and the horseshoe. The nail head had finally worked its way back toward the softer part of the hoof and now dug in a little with every step his horse took. Damn. He was just this side of lame. Monday looked around to see if he could walk this horse out of the herd and not put any additional pressure on that sensitive hoof.

At that moment, someone began firing. A bullet felled Monday's horse, shot through the neck. Monday reached for the rifle in his scabbard, but it was under the dead horse. He couldn't get it out. Then he heard a dreaded sound. Pistol shots. A lot of them in a row. The cows behind him bellowed and began to run. Stampede!

He turned to see the leading steers only a hundred yards from him and closing fast. He was in the cowboy's worst predicament. Unhorsed in the middle of a stampede. He couldn't see through the rising dust who might have fired those shots, but it didn't matter at this point. Death was bearing down on him, bawling and rolling reddened eyes.

20

Near White Mountain Hot Springs

Kate woke up screaming. Or she imagined she woke up. Twice, maybe three times. But each time it was still dark. A gentle wind was in the trees and the stars were bright. She drifted off again.

Finally, birds woke her. Sunlight streamed through the pines overhead. She was in a sitting position. Some kind of lumpy chair. But she couldn't move. Strong bonds encircled her. And something furry was at the nape of her neck. Smitty! No, the bear!

She sat bolt upright and tried to break her bonds, but it was no use. She was held fast by someone's arms. Her head was at a slight angle and she could see fringed leggings below her own leg. Sean Finnegan! She was sitting on his lap. She struggled to get free. She kicked a shin with her heel. Her left shoulder hurt as she tried to use that arm.

"Whoa. Hold on there, Miss Kate," the old scout said softly from behind her head. "You're not well. You oughtn't to be—"

"Let me go, Sean! Why are you holding me like this? Professor Hayden will not approve."

"Well, he did approve this, bein' as how I rode in here with you and I volunteered for nursemaid duty if it came to that. Now, stop struggling! You're gonna hurt yourself. I got a good reason for holdin' you like this. But I ain't gonna tell you 'til you calm down. What'll it be?"

"All right. I'll hold still, but you'd better unhand me or have a good explanation." Kate looked around. In front of her were pieces of her cot, her broken trunk, and some scattered clothing. Her tent was nowhere to be seen. And there was hardly anyone about. One wagon, some horses and only a few men packing Jackson's bulkier photographic supplies. She breathed deeply to calm herself, conscious of how the fresh mountain air felt thin and cool today.

"Now," Sean said. "What do you remember about last night?"

"I remember putting aside my letters, blowing out my candle, and going to bed. I think I was having some bad thoughts as I went to sleep. Perhaps I had a nightmare."

"Yeah, it was a shaggy brown nightmare, 'bout eight feet tall. You had a grizzly come into your tent last night. Probably the same one that's been scarin' the horses. They were all in a tizzy last night and we went to see what was troublin' 'em. There was hardly a man in camp when he clawed his way through your tent."

Kate remembered the roaring and the hot breath—and those teeth. She shivered, clutched her robe around her, and threw herself back into Sean's embrace so hard she hit his chin with the back of her head. She looked wildly around, but the campsite looked normal. No bear.

"Ow," Finnegan said, moving his chin away from her. "I thought you was so all-fired anxious to be up and about."

"Perhaps not. I think I remember the bear. Why did he come into my tent?"

"Nobody knows that but you, me, and Schonborn. Remember that peach soap you use? We think he was attracted by the smell. We didn't say nothing to the professor."

"But I put that soap away in my trunk."

"And look what he did to your trunk. Lucky he didn't splinter you like that. You smelled like peaches to him, I reckon. I been smellin' it for hours, sittin' here holdin' you."

"Was holding me like this necessary, Sean? I mean, I appreciate your concern, but—"

"Miss Kate, you was plumb out of your head. You were all arms and legs and screaming and crying. We couldn't get you to settle down and we didn't want you hurtin' yourself, 'specially not once we patched you up. How's that left shoulder feel now?"

Kate looked at her left arm. There was a sling around her forearm, slightly disarranged by her struggles. Her shoulder throbbed slightly.

"What happened to me? I remember the bear breathing on me, then he licked me. At first I thought he was someone else and I just struggled, but when I saw those teeth . . . ." She shuddered.

"We figure he got into your tent and was sampling your peach preserves, so to speak, when you woke up and screamed and scared him."

"*I* scared *him?*" At this point, she noticed a handful of men had begun to gather. She reached out to rearrange her robe and shift, but her left arm hurt. She gasped at the pain.

"Scared him enough that he scratched or bit you. Professor Hayden thinks it's a claw scratch. Anyway, when we got him off you—"

"How did you do that? Did you kill him?" Kate hoped she wasn't showing anything more than her bare feet. She pulled the robe tightly about her as the men gathered round.

Three or four men laughed. Potato John, the cook, said, "No, Miss. But I'll bet this morning that bear wishes he was dead." That led to more raucous laughter. Sean tried to explain, but another man cut him off.

"We done shot that bear three or four times, but it didn't faze him. I was reloadin' my rifle when Sean here grabs it and makes for that bear. I told him, 'Sean, I only done charged it with powder. I ain't put in no bullet yet.' Didn't slow Sean down none. He put a cap on the nipple, stepped through that torn canvas, lifted the bear's tail, and jammed that rifle barrel into his, well, uh, up under his tail. When he fired the powder charge, that bear roared like an explodin' steam engine and tore outta here, draggin' what was left of your tent and

154

moanin' bloody murder." The man laughed and slapped his knee. Other men were holding their sides or wiping tears from their eyes at the recollection.

"I imagine it must have been quite amusing," Kate said frostily.

"Yeah," Sean said quietly behind her. "They been coming by every few minutes to check on you, but mostly to try to hang new nicknames on me. Most of 'em are unprintable and have to do with what you find under a bear's tail. You don't want to hear any of 'em." The men took that as a signal and moved away to finish getting ready to leave.

"When we dragged you out of the wreckage," Sean went on, "I was feared maybe you were dead. There was so much blood on your shift. But your, uh, breathin' apparatus was working fine. You couldn't scream no more, but you made these wheezy noises like a tea kettle. Professor Hayden figured that was a good sign. We got lanterns goin' and our committee of doctors worked to patch you up."

That's right, Kate recalled. The expedition had four medically-trained doctors, including Professor Hayden. "Do I have a broken bone?"

"Naw, just a real good scratch. 'Bout three inches long and half an inch deep. Probably from a claw. We cleaned the wound with whiskey before the professor put the stitches in. You hollered a lot at the sting of the whiskey, I recall, and you were jumpin' around so much, he was a-feared he'd never get needle and thread into you. Finally, Schonborn gave us some sherry and that seemed to do the trick." She couldn't see him, but she was sure Sean was grinning. The other men had drifted off and begun to move the wagon and packhorses away.

"You poured alcohol into me when I was unconscious? A defenseless woman?"

"Hah. Defenseless, my Aunt Sally. I was against it, but the doctors overruled me. Schonborn said it would work and it did. After you sputtered the first dram, you musta liked it, 'cause Professor Hayden was able to get nearly a cupful into you."

That must be why her mouth tasted like an old sock this morning. And her head hurt.

Kate asked what the doctor's prognosis was.

After she explained "prognosis" to Sean, he told her Hayden had recommended rest, sleep, and not using the arm for a couple days, while the stitches were fresh. Kate reached under the strap of her shift and touched the stitches. They'd bled a little because of her exertions in the last few minutes. She looked at her shift. Hardly any blood on it. That could only mean one thing.

"Sean, who put me into a fresh nightgown?"

"Uh, Professor Hayden himself. He felt responsible for lettin' you come along. And he said he couldn't ask his men to do anything he wouldn't do himself. He put out the lantern and did it in the dark. Made the rest of us turn around." Kate tried not to blush and hugged herself. Well, better a doctor than one of the wagon drivers, she supposed. She was tired and thirsty.

"Sean, can I have some water? I'm hungry, too."

"I'd think so," Sean told her. "It's goin' on afternoon. You sure been sawin' away, calling out all kinds of things."

"Indeed?" Kate was suddenly all ears, her thirst forgotten.

"Yeah, well, the first couple times, you just screamed and thrashed. Then you told somebody named Smitty to stop doin' something. You called my name out once. Oh, and Becky Masterson's too. That Monday Malone is a lucky devil. You called for him a half dozen times, I reckon."

She had? What did that mean? She'd fallen asleep thinking about the murder. Or was she thinking about Monday in his bath? No, that was earlier. She couldn't recall.

Sean brought her some cool water and some leftover breakfast. The last of the pack horses was getting ready to pull out. Sean had her horse and his and a packhorse tied nearby. He tossed his stool onto the last wagon as she drank and ate. After the meal, he showed her the fresh clothes he'd laid out—riding skirt, blouse, drawers, camisole, stockings, and boots. Her hat was on her horse's saddlehorn. She was about to ask how she would get dressed with no tent, but Sean went and stood with the horses and looked the other way. The horses formed a screen.

"You don't need to worry about your letters, Miss Kate," Sean called over his shoulder. "I found 'em where the bear had knocked over your little desk. He didn't break your ink bottle. I put your letters in their envelopes. Rider took the mail to Fort Ellis this morning."

Kate froze.

"Did you read any of those letters as you put them into the envelopes?" Her heart was in her throat.

"Couldn't, Miss Kate. I can read printin' fairly good, if I squint. But I can't read script at all. Looked like you write real pretty." Kate let out her breath. She didn't want a man to see the secrets she'd confided to her friends.

She slipped out of her robe and shift and struggled to dress. Her stitches pulled a little. Aside from her hot springs bath, this was the first time she could remember taking her clothes off outdoors. Today she only felt embarrassed, not at all daring. Perhaps life as an artists' model wouldn't be for her after all.

As Kate tied her robe and shift into her bedroll, she thought about the bear attack. She ought to have expected something like that. God's punishment for having spied on Monday in his bath. But wait, maybe the bear was retribution for her having let Schonborn nearly coax her out of her bath. Perhaps God sent the bear for both her sins. Worse, maybe God wasn't done punishing her yet.

First Indians, then a bear, now she'd have another scar. Perhaps Schonborn was right and Wyoming was beating her down. Was going to New York the answer?

Sean helped her into her saddle, so she didn't have to use her left arm. They followed the wagon and pack horses, trotting to get to Tower Falls before the evening meal.

21

South of Warbonnet

Monday retreated a few steps to the body of his horse. He drew his pistol and tried to pick out a likely steer amid the rumbling, roaring, bellowing mob that descended upon him. *Bang!* No effect. He fired again and saw a steer stumble, to be instantly trampled by those behind, some of whom also fell. Monday fired again at a downed steer struggling to get over the first animal's body. It stayed down. He picked another disabled steer and put his last two remaining rounds into it.

Without holstering his pistol, Monday dived under the nearly still hooves of two of the wounded animals and wedged himself under the bodies.

The world around him dissolved into thunder. Dust rose into his nostrils. He wanted to pull up his bandana, but his arms couldn't reach his face. He felt the thud of heavy hooves through the bodies piled on top of him. One panicked steer stepped on his right boot. He moaned through clenched teeth, but dared not open his mouth because of the dust. He'd lost track of time, but the brown wave must have rolled over him for nearly a minute.

The thuds of hooves around him gradually became fewer, but Monday's ears still rang with the rolling rumble. He lay still for another minute. No more thuds. He tried to back out of the pile of dead steers that had accumulated around his position, but it was no use trying to go that way. He laboriously moved one leg of a dead animal from his right side, then rolled a little and brought both arms to bear. He pushed and pulled and finally got his head out.

All around him was swirling dust. Monday coughed a few times. He tried to spit, but a trickle of saliva only made a muddy track down his chin. There was blood on his right sleeve, but he checked his arm. It wasn't his blood. He squirmed into a sitting position and surveyed what he could see.

The last of the cattle were straggling to a halt maybe two hundred yards away and were beginning to mill around. That was a good sign, Monday told himself. Cowboys must have stemmed the tide and brought the cattle to a halt after a run of only about a mile. Monday dragged himself out of the tangle of stiffening legs, wobbled, and fell to his knees. He tried to stand, but tripped and fell again. He looked at his hands and they were shaking. Was it fear? Why would he be afraid now, when the danger had passed?

Monday had no doubt someone had started that stampede to kill him. Three of his leading suspects—Smitty, Ben, and Sandy—were out here on the trail with him. Only Suzanne and Reese Bowman could claim alibis for this one. He'd have to see which of the three had been armed with rifle and pistol this morning. But first he'd have to walk a bit and try to hail the chuck wagon.

He heard the chuck wagon coming up behind him before he saw it. Bastiano the cook saw him first. The old man hadn't tried to keep up with the stampede, knowing they generally involved short spurts of running by animals that didn't like to run. All the cowboys must be up with the herd, Monday thought. He couldn't even see the *remuda,* the cowboys' extra horses that usually brought up the rear. That gave him an idea. He tried to jog to the approaching wagon, but his lungs and sore foot weren't up to it.

Monday wanted to exploit the uncertainty of his whereabouts and of his survival.

Bastiano brought the wagon to a creaking halt. Monday stepped past him to the water barrel and untied the lid. He resisted the temptation to put his head into it and instead drank a couple of dippers, heedless of what he spilled on his shirt. Finally, he was able to speak.

"*Bastiano, ayudame, por favor,*" he asked the old man. Bastiano had cooked for all three drives Monday had ridden on; they respected each other. "I think someone tried to kill me deliberate by starting that stampede. Will you help me for a few minutes?"

"*Si, Senor Lunes,*" the old man said. "What you need me to do?"

Monday told the cook what he intended, then moved to the rear of the chuck wagon. He could see a rider or two begin to emerge from the settling dust. They rode slowly, scanning the ground and not looking at the wagon. Monday let down and secured the gate at the rear of the wagon that protected the chuck box and served as Bastiano's food preparation table. He quickly surveyed himself. Blood-soaked right sleeve, muddy chin that might as well mean bodily fluids squashed out, and generally covered in a thick coating of dust that he hadn't disturbed. Perfect.

He laid himself out on the tailgate, letting his legs dangle. When he called out a quiet "OK" to Bastiano, the cook started the horses again and waved to the approaching riders. Monday heard them coming. At the last moment, he thought of two other things to look more like a dead body. He put his hat on his chest and pushed his pistol behind a flour sack. He turned his head toward the flour sack just as the first riders circled around the wagon.

"Shit!" somebody said, followed by more expletives and curses. Pretty soon, it sounded to Monday like a dozen riders must be milling about. Some asked Bastiano where he'd found Monday. No one dismounted. He heard the sound of one horse galloping into the group, sounding like it scattered the rest of them. The rider must have kicked out of the stirrups before the horse stopped, because a breathless voice said, practically in Monday's ear, "Oh, God, no!"

Monday recognized the voice of Ben Rollins and willed himself to be still. Ben poked at him and touched his bloody right sleeve. "Damn it all," Ben spat. "How could this happen? Monday was too experienced to let a nag like Jingo throw him. What am I gonna tell that schoolteacher?"

Monday held back a grin. A sneering voice cut into Ben's distress. Smitty.

"Well, there ain't a horse that can't be rode. But there ain't a man that can't be throwed. What did you expect? He was only a middlin' drover. Probably started the stampede through some damn fool screw-up he made. Reckon it was his last." Smitty sounded like he was gloating. But that didn't tell Monday anything; he could have predicted this reaction. He wondered where Sandy Sutter was.

"Bastiano," Smitty shouted. "Where's your shovel? If his last remaining friend is so concerned about Monday Malone's carcass, he can be the one to bury him."

"You bastard," Ben shouted. "We ain't gonna bury him out here on the trail like he was nobody." Monday heard the sound of a shovel being thrown into the dust.

"You skirt-chasin' no-good layabout," Smitty snarled. "You know we always bury dead cowboys where they fall. You can bury him and then get your bedroll outta the wagon. Think you can sass me? I don't care how many of these cows your folks own. Clear out." Monday heard the sound of a shovel being picked up. He'd played this hand maybe a little too far for Ben.

Monday sat up and cocked his pistol, pointing it at Smitty, who was about to hit Ben with the shovel.

"I reckon that'll do, Smitty." The foreman had no way to know Monday's pistol wasn't loaded.

Ben's head snapped around so quickly, his hat slid over one eye. Smitty had spun at the sound of the click before he even heard the voice.

Monday called Smitty a bastard in return, and laid in a few other choice expressions about the foreman's mother and about horse manure. "Now, you want to come over here with that shovel and try me? I don't think you can fire a county deputy sheriff."

161

"So," he snarled. "You still don't know how to stay down, boy. Big talk from an armed man." Monday kept his eye on Smitty, let his pistol off cock, and holstered it.

"I'm game," Monday said, sliding off the tailgate and testing his ankle. "Think that shovel will give you an advantage?" Smitty moved in, making a big back swing. At the far end of the swing, a shot rang out and the shovel blade rang. Smitty dropped it. Bastiano stood beside the wagon and worked the lever on his rifle.

"Thanks, Bastiano. I'll see to it he don't fire you, neither." Turning to Smitty, Monday said, "And I don't reckon you're gonna fire Ben, since some of his folks' herd is in here with Circle M stock. I want everybody working today to draw their full pay when the ranchers pay you off." All the drovers' eyes were on him now.

"I just witnessed a crime in progress right here." Monday indicated the shovel on the ground. "An assault, I think they call it. But I won't take you in, Smitty, if you play fair by all these boys. Looks like the only loser this morning has been Jingo and about four or five head of cattle. Why don't everybody get back to work? We're only an hour or two from Mitch Cullinane's Lazy C. I'll get a wagon out for that beef."

"And I'll take 'em out of our head count," Ben said, coming over to slap both Monday's shoulders. Dust rose from Monday when he did it and they both coughed. "I never expected a man to come to the barbeque for his own wake, but I reckon if anyone could do that, it'd be you." Ben beamed at seeing Monday come back to life. That was a point in his favor, Monday thought.

"Thanks for sticking up for me, Ben." Monday raised his voice as horses began to move. "But before any of you ride off, let me see who's wearing sidearms and carryin' a rifle today." Hardly any had either a pistol or a rifle. Ben had both. So did Smitty. Sandy Sutter was nowhere to be found, but Monday remembered seeing him put his rifle in its scabbard this morning.

Monday asked to see both Ben and Smitty's pistols, but it was a wasted effort. Both guns had empty cylinders; riders with pistols would be expected to fire into the air to try to turn the leaders.

"Now that hurts," Ben said, going to the water barrel. "Being compared to Smitty. I thought you just got done thanking me for being ready to haul your carcass down to Warbonnet."

"Sorry, Ben, but I had to check yours and Smitty's guns. It don't mean I suspect you. But I put my trust in the wrong person last year when I was trying to solve my first murder and it all blew up in our faces—me and Miss Kate's."

Ben went with Monday while he went to the *remuda* to check on Lightning. He looked at the horse's bruise again. It could have been made by somebody striking the leg with a pistol butt. Maybe whoever had hurt Lightning had done so in order to put Monday on a less capable mount today. The stampede had been rigged. He walked Lightning over to Jingo's body and, with Ben's help, retrieved his saddle and dressed his own horse.

"Ride with me into Warbonnet, Ben. I plan to let Lightning favor that leg and then have Joe Fitch look after him." As they crested the next hill, Monday could see the Platte River spread out below them. He told Ben how the stampede had started and what he'd done to save himself.

"I can see then why you'd want to talk to Sandy Sutter, too, since he had a pistol this morning when he left to ride right flank," Ben said. Monday didn't say anything. Ben's reaction to Monday's death had been expressed in front of a big group. Monday didn't want to think it had been staged for their benefit. He could play maybe one or two more cards at the right time that might clear Ben—or convict him.

They came down to Fitch's livery stable. Half the herd and hands, Smitty included, peeled off at Cullinane's ranch, while the other half pressed on to Dave Masterson's Arrow Ranch, north of the river. While the drovers watered the cattle in the river, Monday took Ben to his office. He stopped Ben in the street outside and pointed to the sign: "Sam Taggart Jail and

163

Marshal's Office" read the first line. "Monday Malone, Marshal" read the second, smaller line.

"I wanted you to see that sign before we came in," Monday said, after they entered his office. He dragged a two-foot-high cross out from under his bunk and set it on the desk where Ben could read it. "Monday Malone, Manzanita, Texas."

"Jesus," Ben breathed.

"So this ain't the first time I've been dead, Ben. Had to pretend to be Sam Taggart while Miss Kate and I searched for his killer last year. It was Miss Kate's idea to put my name on his grave."

"And you keep it under your bunk now? That's awful."

"It don't bother me none. It reminds me that was the second time I died. First time was four years ago in Manzanita." Ben would remember Mary Ellen's death. The way Monday had wanted to die with her out there in the street that afternoon.

Monday treated Ben to the noon meal at Martha Haskell's. They were a little late, but she didn't seem put out. Afterward, they stopped at the saloon for a couple beers. Monday bought again. He used the time to catch up on news from Chet Stratman, the saloon owner. They detoured one more time on the way to the stable, so Monday could check to see if Kate had sent him a telegram as she said she might. When they went back to Laramie, he'd bring some mail for her with him. No telegram for him.

The two men finally went to the livery. Monday left Lightning in Joe's care; in a few days, he'd probably be fit. Monday saddled up the big bay mare Sam Taggart's wife had sold him. Not a cow pony, but then he didn't plan to do any roping or cutting this afternoon. He wasn't on anybody's payroll.

It was mid-afternoon when they rode into the Arrow Ranch yard. Rosalee was preparing supper for the cowhands and would take it out to them in a wagon if they weren't finished working with the herd by mealtime. Monday and Ben rode on to Dave's northern range to watch the festivities. Well, Monday planned to watch. He knew Ben would have to work.

Delivering cattle to new owners wasn't like putting them into stock pens for the railroad. Nor like spring roundup back home. They'd already run the tally. Dave Masterson was just finishing paying Sandy Sutter and writing him a receipt. Sandy didn't stick around, but rode south immediately, probably under orders to bring the money and the receipt to Smitty at Cullinane's. Monday knew Sandy had seen him, but he wouldn't meet Monday's eye. That left Ben in charge. Ben made sure the branded cows and calves were sent off west a mile or so. The unbranded stock included a couple dozen maverick calves.

Monday found Corey Masterson in the thick of things, riding down and roping cows. When he led the mother over to the branding irons, the calf generally followed. The hardest part was getting the few unbranded full-grown steers onto the ground on their right sides and immobilized, so the branding iron could be applied to their left flanks. This job took the full-time efforts of nearly a dozen men, Corey included.

Dave Masterson handled the branding himself, no mean feat working on half a ton of scared, angry longhorn. Monday appreciated what they were going through; he'd been through half a dozen roundups and had had enough of these particular steers stepping on him today.

Monday found Becky tending to the calves. She didn't look like any darling of the dance floor today. She wore jeans, one of Dave's old shirts knotted at her waist, sleeves rolled up, and her favorite hat. Her forearms, nose and cheeks looked a little sunburned.

Still, as much as Becky dressed like a cowboy, her charms weren't lost on the drovers. A couple of them came over and tried to talk to her. They didn't stay long. Besides branding the calves, Becky was castrating the males. The efficiency with which she handled this task caused a few riders to go pale and return to the less disturbing work of wrestling grown steers.

Monday stayed to talk with her. As cowboys brought her calves, Becky alternated between castrations and branding, wiping her hands on a bloody rag. She had a half-filled bucket of testicles beside her.

She looked up at him and smiled. "You staying to have supper out here? Mama's cookin', not me."

Monday looked in the bucket. It didn't help his appetite any, although he'd had "prairie oysters" enough times. He was watching Becky take obvious pleasure in her skill. She caught his glance.

"No, we ain't gonna eat these tonight. I understand Mama's got some beef coming in from those steers our fearless marshal shot this morning. These," she indicated the bucket, "are for breakfast tomorrow morning. Been a long time since you ate breakfast at our place, Monday." She wiped perspiration from her upper lip with the back of her hand, then took a long drink from her canteen. Some of the water dribbled down her chin and into the front of her shirt. She grinned and wiggled a little. He knew it was for his benefit.

"No, I doubt I should stay for supper, Miss Becky. I been away a week and Chet tells me there are a couple official matters that need tendin' to. I'll ride back and fetch your mama and the wagon if these boys ain't done in another hour or two."

He turned his horse and rode over to see how Dave was getting along. Becky shouted something after him and laughed, but he couldn't hear her words over the bellowing stock.

# # #

Dave's work went slower than Becky's. He still had another dozen steers to go. Monday looked over at Becky's fire, but she was finished and gone somewhere. Monday got down to spell Dave, so he could rest. It took him an hour to finish the last dozen steers as they were brought in. He was nearly as tired as the cowboys looked. He looked down at his shirt. The sweat had turned his dusty faded red shirt to the color of new mud. He was glad Kate wasn't picking up his laundry tomorrow. He'd hear no end of it from Martha Haskell. Monday said his goodbyes and headed south. He

166

figured he'd see Ben and the hands from both herds at Warbonnet's Alamo Saloon tonight.

Rosalee Masterson went past him with the wagon. She asked him to stop by the ranch house on his way to town and make sure Becky had pulled the last two pies out of the oven. She was to bring them along for the cowboys' supper in a little while.

Monday pulled up at the Mastersons' corral and gratefully dismounted. He was still sore in a couple places from this morning's trampling. He tied off his horse at the trough and worked the pump to bring up some fresh water, catching some in a cup for himself. As he looked over the edge of his cup, Becky came out of the barn.

She led Darby, her black pony, into the corral. Monday ducked through the corral rails and went over to her while she finished currying the horse. He admired the seat of her jeans while she worked. The pigging string she'd used to tie the calves' legs dangled from one rear pocket jumped and wiggled as she worked. He grinned.

"Your mama sent me by to make sure you took the last pies outta the oven. But I think you did already. I can smell 'em clear over here."

"What a talented nose you have, Marshal. It's a shame it doesn't work so well on the smell of its owner. You are in sore need of a bath." She worked with her back to him.

Monday eyed his shirt again. "Reckon you're right, Miss Becky. This shirt's been trampled on, bled on, and sweated through twice. Guess I'll . . . ." He trailed off as Becky turned around. Her shirt was still tied at the waist, but all the buttons were undone. Contrary to saloon talk in Warbonnet, Monday noted, her freckles did not go all the way down to her waist.

"Why don't we go soak for a while in the stock tank?" she asked, nodding toward the big wooden tank that Dave's new Halladay windmill kept filled. "Just the two of us. Nobody else around." She looked him in the eyes. There wasn't even a trace of her usual smile.

Bathe with Becky! Memories of Mary Ellen came flooding back to him. He realized that flirting with this girl wasn't just

167

a harmless game. Monday took Becky by both arms and stopped her from untying her shirt.

"We'd best not. Reckon I ought to be getting back to town now. You got those pies to take to them cowboys." He released her and stepped back toward the corner of the corral.

"There's only one cowboy I want to please tonight," she said, stepping forward. All at once, he felt a corner post of the corral jar his shoulder blades. Becky smiled. She had him cornered.

She stepped in close to Monday, under his arms as he tried to push her away. He didn't want to cross Dave Masterson by getting involved with his daughter. And especially not the way she intended this evening.

Becky stepped up on the first horizontal rail, so her head was even with Monday's. She wrapped her arms around his waist and got a grip on the corner post, so he couldn't get away. She pressed her chest against him and kissed him. Monday found her arms but couldn't break her grip. She was stronger than Kate, he decided. And she kissed stronger than Kate, too. He figured he'd better try a trick, if he was going to get out of this snare, so he put his arms around her shoulders and surrendered to the kiss.

"Ah, ha," Becky cried, breaking her lip lock on him by three inches or so. "I knew it. I knew you liked me as much as Kate." She tried to kiss him again.

The mention of Kate gave Monday new strength. He grabbed Becky just above each elbow and pinched hard enough that her fingers went numb.

"Ow, not so hard!"

He gently walked her off the low rails and back two steps, then bent and stepped backwards, bending through the corral rails.

"Listen, Monday, I just put out fresh straw in the barn. Mama won't be looking for me for nearly an hour. Why don't you and me go in there?" Monday didn't reply, but untied his bay mare and swarmed aboard.

"Dang you, Monday Malone! You can't treat me like this. Come back here! I mean it. Come back or I'll tell Kate you stole a kiss from me. I'll tell her you stole more than a kiss!" She was shouting at him now as he rode out of the ranch yard.

"You're a coward, Monday Malone! You hear me? A coward!"

As he rode out through the Arrow Ranch gate and made for the road to town, Monday remembered Kate had been upset with him for some reason before she left Warbonnet for the Hayden expedition. She hadn't even wanted him to help her into the wagon. Women!

What else could he have done just now? He didn't want to make Dave Masterson angry. He'd made Becky mad, but that was nothing new. She'd been angry at him before. He knew one thing for certain. He'd rather face a stampede with no bullets than have Kate that mad at him.

22

Warbonnet

Monday finished his breakfast and carried plates out to Martha Haskell's kitchen. He balanced his coffee mug on top of the stack and, after putting everything down carefully, poured himself the last cup from the big pot on the stove. He sighed and set the cup aside to cool a bit. He began to stack and scrape plates, then added a little more hot water to the washing tub.

Martha came back into the kitchen through the back door. He figured she was grinning behind his back. But he was only cleaning up after himself. Didn't matter to him that he was also cleaning up after a half-dozen other people at the same time. He'd told Martha he didn't know the first thing about housework or mending and was a poor range cook. But he did know how to wash, dry and put away dishes. Martha had told him that in Kate's absence, she was grateful for any volunteer effort; Sally and Buxton had other chores.

Martha tucked a gray lock behind her left ear and stepped up next to the rinse tub. She began to set dishes and cups to dry. He hoped she was pleased that he knew enough to wash the cooking gear—the big skillet and pancake turner—last.

Monday washed in silence, intent on getting the job done, so he could get on to other chores. He wanted to confront Smitty and Sandy Sutter today at Mitch Cullinane's ranch about the stampede yesterday. He'd spent a restless night, stirred by thoughts of Becky Masterson's freckles—and her

170

mouth. That was the first time he'd kissed her. Hope she got over her spat yesterday, so it wouldn't be his last.

"We miss her, too, you know—and not just at wash-up time." Martha's voice broke into his thoughts.

"Who? Oh, Kate. Well, I didn't think I was the only one who missed her, Martha." He passed her the last soapy fork and turned his attention to the massive skillet. First Jonah Barnes, now Martha. Could everybody read his mind when he thought about women?

"I know every man in this town, married or not, misses her. The children too. And speaking for the women's sewing circle, I guess Warbonnet is unanimous on the subject.

"Are you worried some about Kate, Monday?" When he nodded and didn't look at her, she went on. "Us too. Or at least Sally. She had this terrible nightmare the other night and woke up screaming. I couldn't get anything out of her but the name 'Kate' over and over again."

Monday sighed. What with dreaming of Becky last night and planning his moves for today, he hadn't thought of Kate this morning, and that disturbed him. He usually thought of her as he got dressed. She did his laundry. But she'd been gone for so long now. Had he been taking her for granted? Her long golden hair, her cheerful disposition, her easy laugh, that faraway look he observed sometimes. He used to get that look when he thought about giving up Montana. Was she wishing she was back East when she looked like that?

"She'll be back soon enough, Martha," Monday said, placing the heavy pan carefully so it would dry. "I trust Sean Finnegan to keep her safe." He didn't tell her about the dream he'd had about Kate the night before last. Some kind of danger, but he couldn't tell what kind. And Sean Finnegan hadn't been there to protect her. He wondered what this dream meant, and if it was related to Sally's nightmare.

"I'd trust Sean Finnegan not to spill a drop of whiskey or a glass of beer," Martha said. "But I'll be sure to look for any signs of wear and tear on her when she gets back."

Monday laughed and scrubbed at the pancake turner. "I hope I get to see her first in Laramie, Martha. I won't ask her to let me conduct a top to toe inspection, though. I'll let you handle that."

"I probably shouldn't tell you this," she said. "But I've been in touch with Kate's mother, back in Buffalo. Cribbed the address from one of Kate's envelopes. Anyway, Mrs. Shaw tells me Kate's been feeling homesick and believes she doesn't measure up to what Wyoming expects of its women. She's thinking of going back East."

Monday nearly dropped the pancake turner he'd been working on. Go home to Buffalo? Why would she want to do that? She had friends here. Rode with Becky and Corey. Laughed and danced with Jonah Barnes.

"Her mother said Kate had heard from Sean Finnegan so much about the beauty of Yellowstone that she'd make up her mind if she got to go there."

Did this mean she might come back from Yellowstone and go right on through on the same train? Would he see her in Laramie after all?

"I've been keeping an eye on her for months now. Watching her moods, including her in everything women in this town do. Keeping her busy."

"Sort of like I'd do with a young horse," Monday said. "An easy hand on the rein and bit keeps a horse's mouth soft, so he's more responsive when you need him to be."

Now it was Martha's turn to laugh and almost drop a plate. She inspected the results of his washing effort and let him go.

"Comparing Kate to a horse," she snorted as he left.

Monday went to his office and collected his bedroll, rifle and shells, and canteen. He put his only clean spare clothes into his saddlebags. After he visited the bank, Joe Fitch set him up with Taggart's bay mare again. Joe said Lightning should rest that bruised leg some more. Monday decided he'd raise that issue with Smitty and Sandy, too. Never mind his own skin. It would go hard with whoever had lamed Lightning.

# # #

172

Cowboys who'd spent the night at Masterson's ranch north of town were trickling in to the Cullinane place when Monday got there. The Alamo Saloon had done a roaring business last night and many of the cowboys moved slowly or held their heads. Bastiano was still pouring coffee and had a pile of flapjacks on the tailgate. Monday took another cup and a sourdough biscuit and sat on the ground next to Ben Rollins, who was starting a second plate.

"Just like home, huh?" Monday sighed and nibbled the biscuit.

"Not exactly. Mama don't use sourdough, like Bastiano does. I saw him give you a pot of his makin's last evening. What'd you do with that? You ain't much of a cook, as I recall."

Monday grinned. "I don't claim to be. I passed it along to Martha Haskell. She said she wanted some to try. Bastiano said Barbara Cullinane asked for some starter, too. Good thing he still had enough for breakfast this morning."

Monday looked around. "I wanted to talk to Smitty and Sandy again this morning. They up yet?"

"Up and gone," Ben said, eating the last of his flapjacks and picking up his coffee mug. "Sandy lit out before first light. Smitty was pissed when he found out. He took an extra horse and went off about an hour ago. I don't know why they're in such an all-fired hurry to get back to Laramie."

"Smitty pay the boys off last night?" Monday asked, finishing his coffee.

"Nope." Ben stood up easily out of his cross-legged position. "Said he'd pay off in Laramie. Reckon that's good for your peaceful little town. They'll blow off more steam and spend more money in Laramie. A few of 'em are still a bit hung over. We'll head for Laramie with Bastiano and the wagon soon."

"Ben, how would you feel about ridin' down to Laramie, just you and me? I ain't hankerin' to wait around for Bastiano and these boys to leave. I doubt they'll be underway by noon."

Ben agreed and went to get his horse ready. He said he'd leave Curley Howell in charge of the outfit riding south.

They rode out of the ranch yard and followed the swath of trampled grass that marked the cattle trail they'd blazed from Laramie.

Monday started the conversation on the subject of the Circle M foreman. "Smitty take all that cash with him this morning?"

"Yeah, Curley said he did. I know what you're thinking. He's takin' a hell of a risk ridin' alone with all that money." Ben looked at Monday in alarm. "You don't think Sandy left first with the thought of holding him up and taking it, do you?"

"How would Sandy know Smitty intended to ride down to Laramie alone? Smitty didn't say last night he was gonna do that, did he?"

"Naw, Curley told me Smitty acted kinda surprised by Sandy's leavin' early. Smitty musta decided on the spur of the moment. He just saddled two horses and lit out. He didn't even wait for breakfast. He's as ornery as ever, just like you remember him. I recollect a couple of hands sayin' he'd got married last spring. But it don't seem to have mellowed him none."

Interesting, Monday thought. They both left early, but only Smitty was in a hurry. What woman in her right mind would marry Smitty?

"Sandy take a spare horse, too?" he asked Ben.

"Curley said he must not have thought of it. One or two of the other boys left this morning with Sandy, once they heard the payoff was gonna be in Laramie." Ben grinned. "Course, those boys only worked down here at Cullinane's place yesterday. They didn't get a look at Miss Becky Masterson. I had to practically rope and drag some of the boys at the Masterson place this morning to get 'em to come down here with me. They wanted to hang around to gawk at her even after breakfast was over. Reminds me. We expected you to come up for

174

supper with Miss Becky and those pies last night. What happened to you?"

"I got, uh, waylaid by official business back in town. I'll bet Becky was able to ride to your camp with those pies all by herself, wasn't she?" Monday hoped to change the subject.

"You should have seen the balancing act she done. Her horse just ambled up with no reins and stopped when she gave him her knees. Then she got down without using her hands and never tilted a pie. That's a right fine rancher's daughter there. If I wasn't spoken for . . . ."

"Oh, that reminds me." Ben grinned. "Miss Becky sent along some breakfast for you." He passed Monday a small paper-wrapped parcel. Monday said nothing and opened it. Inside were two fried calf nuts. Precisely two. He understood the message they carried, but ate them anyway.

A little before noon, they cut across tracks that indicated Roy Butcher's freight wagon was ahead of them. Monday knew he'd have left Warbonnet early this morning. The wagon tracks showed fresh over yesterday's cattle trail.

Monday didn't bring up the stampede yesterday. If Ben was the one who'd started it in order to kill him, Monday figured this riding alone would give him another opportunity. He did try to draw Ben out on his money, however. The young cowboy shook his head.

"I don't rightly know what to do, Monday. With the payoff from this leg of the cattle drive, I might have enough left to pay Danielle's room and board at the hotel. But not enough for a train ticket to San Francisco. Danielle swore she wouldn't let Fricker make her do anything more than sing 'til after I got back." He looked at the trail ahead and sighed. "I'm thinking of robbin' the candy store and headin' back to Texas."

Monday was instantly alert. "Wouldn't be a good idea to become a holdup man, Ben." Maybe the confession he was looking for was coming.

"Oh, I don't mean the bank or nothing. I just meant if I could pay off Danielle's hotel bill and get her a horse, maybe we'd skip out on Fricker. Leave him holding the bag. Danielle made me promise not to beat him up for some of the things he's said to her. Short of that, stiffing him would suit me fine."

Monday thought Fricker had probably done more than just talk nasty to the girl, but he said nothing. He didn't want to give Ben a motive for murder if all he wanted to do was elope. He only offered lame counsel.

"You know, Ben, it's a long way to ask a woman to ride a horse from here to Texas."

"Yeah," he sighed. "And I don't even know if she feels strong enough about me to do that. I mean, I been taking care of her and all, but I ain't tried to press my advantage. I held her hand a few times, but I ain't even tried for a kiss yet."

Monday was surprised at that, but reassured. How could a man like this have killed Francine or tried to kill him? Monday was about to return to the subject of money, when Ben pointed up the trail ahead. A lone cowboy was standing next to Roy's wagon talking to him.

"Damn," Ben said, with his hand to his hat brim. "That's Big Bob Hooper. He's a good wrangler. I wonder how he got throwed by a gentle horse. He took Babe this morning."

They came up to Bob, who slapped his leg and cursed a blue streak. He told then he'd been riding along just behind Sandy when Smitty passed them both, riding hard and leading a spare horse. Sandy was startled by being overtaken, Bob said. When Bob laughed and suggested there must be a race to Laramie, Sandy got the drop on him and took his horse, leaving him afoot. Bob had been walking back to meet the Circle M outfit when he met Roy with the freight wagon.

"Wonder why those two are in such a big hurry," Ben wondered aloud.

Monday said, "Well, I can understand Smitty maybe wanting to race down there and get that money into a Laramie bank, but it don't seem like Sandy was in a hurry 'til Smitty passed him." Why had Sandy changed his mind and taken Bob's horse when it looked like Smitty was intent on getting to Laramie first?

"Oh, Smitty probably wants to be the first one to get to town and be a big spender before the rest of us—" Ben broke off, cursed, and stood in his stirrups.

"What's the matter, Ben?"

"I'm such a fool! Smitty's gone to see Fricker. He'll be the only one of us with enough money to pay Fricker off. He wants Danielle for himself. That's what he's ridin' hard for. Damn it! *Hiyaah!*" Ben spurred his horse and dashed away up the wagon track.

"Ben, wait!" Monday spurred the big bay mare after him. His horse was stronger and he overtook Ben after half a mile. He reached out and grabbed Ben's reins, slowing him to a trot.

"Hold it, Ben, stop and think! You can't ride this horse to death and beat them there. Stop a minute and let me help." Ben slowed his horse to a walk. There was murder in his eyes.

"Ben, listen. You need to ride with a spare horse, just like Sandy and Smitty are doing. Back there is Roy Butcher with the freight wagon. I can wait for him to catch up here and I'll let you take this horse. I'll ride down with Roy." Some of the anger went out of Ben.

The young cowboy was grateful for Monday's offer and accepted some provisions he could eat while in the saddle. Monday reached into his vest pocket and passed Ben a little bag.

"What's this?" Ben asked. "More ammunition I can use to shoot Smitty?"

"Well, it is ammunition of a sort. Put it to good use and keep your gun in your holster. I mean it, Ben. I don't want to ride in there and find you dead—or in jail."

Ben made no promises beyond pledging to take good care of the bay mare and leave her at Dillon's livery stable. He rode off at a good pace.

Monday wondered who would win this three-man race. He also wondered if he'd done the right thing. But if Ben was right about Smitty's intentions toward Danielle, he couldn't just sit by idly. Who would get there first and what would happen? And where did Sandy figure in this rivalry?

Guess he'd have to learn that patience Kate was always telling him he needed. He'd certainly have to wait patiently for Roy and the wagon. He found a fair-sized rock and sat down in the shade.

23

Near Yellowstone Falls

Kate Shaw's eyes flew open. Sean Finnegan leaned over her cot, his gray beard brushing her face and his hand on her shoulder.

"Kate, wake up now. You musta been havin' a dream. I heard you groaning. I wouldn'ta come in otherwise. Are you all right? Does your shoulder hurt?" He took his hand away and stood back. Kate could read the concern deeply etched into the scout's lined and weathered face.

Kate felt her own face. It was still flushed from the dream. She'd had it again. Every night this week. She'd been afraid to go to bed the first few nights after the bear attack. She'd tried to think of other things—more pleasant things—as she drifted off, hoping the nightmare of the bear wouldn't return. And it hadn't. Every night, the events in her posing for Schonborn had advanced further and further. This latest one . . . . She caught Sean looking at her with worry.

"No, I'm fine now, Sean. Really, I'm fine. Just a nightmare." As she spoke, she glanced down at herself. She was relieved to see she had the blanket pulled up to her chin. Under the blanket, her shift was bunched up between her knees again, like it had been every morning this week. There had been so many unexpected things in this latest dream. She had to say something more to Sean. Her heart was still racing.

"Thank you for your concern, Sean. Is it time to get up now?" The birds were chirping loudly. He'd probably

179

indulged her and let her sleep longer than the men of the camp.

"Uh, yes, Miss Kate. The teamsters are wanting to take the pack mules away now and I didn't want that clatterin' to wake you up sudden. There's still a mule for our stuff, but they want to take your canvas fly and cot here." Sean had repaired her cot that the bear had damaged. He'd also appropriated a spare canvas fly for her from Jackson's supplies. It was like a small tent that went from roof beam to near the ground with no side walls. She undressed each night in the dark while Sean stood guard. It was awkward that there were so many men about when she woke up these last few mornings in full daylight.

The distant roar of Yellowstone Falls came to her. She sat bolt upright. That's right. This really was the day. The day she'd agreed to pose for Anton Schonborn.

"I fear I've slept in too late again this morning." Sean went out and turned to stand with his back to her in order to keep any men in camp from passing that way. Kate had selected today's clothes last night, but only put on her robe and gathered up the clothing. She called softly to Sean when she was ready.

"Kate, this is our last morning here at the falls. We're gonna go down to the lake, then see some more o' them geyser things in a day or two. Are you still bound and determined to stay behind here with Schonborn for a while?" He looked even graver now.

She bit her lip. "I appreciate all the advice you've given me the last few mornings, Sean, but you're not my father and I wish you wouldn't—"

"Kate, we had this talk before. I done told you that man wants more than to make a sketch of you. You said you thought that, too. Are you still going through with this?"

"I said I agreed that his, um, his attentions were a real possibility. I also said I could handle that when the time came. He's a well-known and respected artist, Sean, with many friends in New York. I can't afford to pay anyone for a portrait, so this seems the best way . . . ." She held up a hand as

180

he tried to speak. "And he has promised that he will leave enough detail out of my face that I will not be recognizable. I trust him to keep his word as a gentleman."

"Kate, in some ways, he ain't no more a gentleman than I am. You know what kind of chance you're taking. He could leave you with a lot more to remember him by than a sketch."

She knew exactly what he meant.

"But I intend to go through with this. I've thought about it all week. As you said, any Wyoming woman who can face down a band of Sioux ought to be able to handle one man."

"You had more company then, more protection all around you. I ain't sure that your stayin' here alone with that man while the rest of us move down canyon . . . ."

"As you said, Sean, we've already had this conversation. I cannot have you or any other man remain behind while Schonborn sketches me. I don't want anyone else to see me and I don't want you pointing your rifle at him again."

"If I have to point it at him again, I'll shoot. Don't look at me that way. I mean it."

"Sean." Kate took him by the shoulder. "Women get to vote now in Wyoming. That also means we get to make our own decisions. I appreciate all you're trying to do for me, but I have to make my own choices—and live with the results."

She didn't tell him she was considering Schonborn's offer to return East with him. To become his friends' model. She was becoming increasingly concerned about her own safety. Bands of Indians, that bear. And besides outlaws and snakes out here, the harsh weather would soon rob her of the bloom of youth. It would turn her as drab as Martha Haskell, unless she wanted to paint herself up like Suzanne and the other girls. She'd seen how they'd painted Danielle. If handled with restraint, some of that makeup could—

"All right, Kate. I can see it's no good arguin' with a stubborn woman. I ain't sayin' the right to vote has given you backbone. I think you had backbone when you come here last July. But I'm gonna be just down the canyon and sound carries real good up here." He pulled an extra pistol from his belt and laid it meaningfully on her clothes. Her eyes widened.

"No, I don't mean you oughta shoot him with this. If you just fire a shot, I'll be back here faster than an arrow. But you got to remember to cock it first." He held up a hand to silence her this time. "Don't argue with me on this, Kate. I just want you to have a way to enforce whatever decision you make about Schonborn. I assume gettin' the vote hasn't ended a woman's right to change her mind as often as she wants."

Kate's alarm softened into a smile. "No, Sean, it hasn't. If my having this pistol will ease your mind, then I'll keep it handy. Is there any breakfast left, any coffee?" She walked with him to the cook fire, now banked, and the deserted eating area. He gave her some toasted bread and a cup of lukewarm coffee. When the old scout saw Schonborn approaching, he turned his back on the man, tipped his hat to Kate, and went to add her cot and canvas fly to the last pack mule.

"Good morning, Kate," said Schonborn. He cleared a spot on a log and sat down near her. "Did you have a good night's sleep?" He looked at her eyes for any signs of puffiness.

"Sleep was a mixed blessing for me last night, Anton. As it has been every night this week. At least my stitches don't restrict my movement much now." She held her cup in both hands, hoping he wouldn't see them tremble. The man stirred the dying fire with a stick.

"Have you changed your mind, Kate?" He looked up at her now and their eyes met over Kate's cup.

"Not about posing, as we agreed. As to New York, I haven't made up my mind yet. I suppose it will depend on how our, uh, session goes." She kept her eyes on his. Maybe if she could meet his gaze now, her courage wouldn't fail her later.

Schonborn pulled out his watch and consulted it. "I've finished sketching the falls as background. We probably have nearly an hour of favorable back light to highlight your hair." He snapped the watch closed and looked back to her. He put his watch away.

"I have my reputation to think of, sir. So I don't want what we're about to do to become common knowledge around the camp. We only have a few days left before we leave the expedition and I don't want Professor Hayden to regret his decision to bring me along."

The last pack animals were moving away. Sean left her and Schonborn's horses. The old scout mounted his own horse and looked at her for a long moment.

"We won't come lookin' for you for an hour or more, Miss Kate. Let me know of any change in your plans." Sean didn't look at Schonborn as he turned his horse and rode to catch up with the others. The little topographer stood up and dusted himself off.

"I don't think Sean Finnegan likes me, Kate. I believe he feels he has a proprietary interest in you. Well, we have this lovely day and the view all to ourselves now." He gestured at the tip of his easel, just visible at the edge of the canyon. "I imagine you'd like a bit of privacy to prepare yourself. It will be your first time, after all."

"Yes, thank you, Anton. It will be." Kate was surprised at the huskiness of her voice. She cleared her throat and watched Schonborn move away. Her hands were shaking as she stood up and moved to her clothes. The pistol resting on top of them made her heart jump. Ought she to take it to the falls with her?

She reassured herself Schonborn was busy with his pencils and paper and didn't look her way as she picked it up.

She went to the falls overlook where Thomas Moran had painted the lovely cascade and the yellow canyon in water colors the day before. She had stood beside him and sketched while he worked, careful not to intrude on his concentration. The colors were so vivid and he wanted to record them perfectly for an oil painting later. Whether sketching or posing, Kate thought it was a privilege just to be able to drink in this scene and look over Moran's shoulder as he worked.

Schonborn looked up from his easel at Kate's approach. Her slippered feet made almost no sound as she trod gingerly to avoid pebbles. She was brushing the hair that fell over the shoulders of her robe and down between her shoulder blades.

"You look magnificent this morning, Kate. Not so much a dark-haired Diana, but more like blond Boadicea, the pagan queen of the Britons who resisted the Romans."

What a flatterer, Kate thought. But maybe his analogy would be appropriate. Boadicea had been a warrior queen, she recalled. She unbelted her robe and opened it, willing herself to keep her eyes locked on Schonborn's.

"How could you know the hair color of either one?"

He looked down as she opened her robe and she read his disappointment at seeing her shift.

"I have decided to alter the terms of our agreement a bit." She shrugged out of the robe and cast it two paces away. It landed with a clunk, from the weight of the pistol in the pocket. "With the bright sun behind me, I'm sure it shines right through this gauzy old shift." She pulled it away from her right hip as if to emphasize its obvious translucence. She saw he was looking at it. "You should be able to see both my limbs—legs—through it and it will leave little of me to your imagination." A cool breeze ruffled her hair, but didn't bring up goose bumps.

He stepped rapidly across to her. "Kate, it, uh, hides details. How can I do you justice or be sure to obscure certain details of your form if you—"

"You're supposed to obscure details of my face, Anton. Why should details of my form be difficult to fill in, for such an accomplished artist? Use your imagination. I am made like any other woman."

She saw his hands were trembling—with anticipation? How could he draw if he shook that way?

"Kate," he said heavily. "I cannot sketch you as Boadicea or Diana in this." He brought both hands to her shoulders and slid the straps off. Only the square neckline that stretched over the swell of her breasts kept the shift from sliding further. He held both her shoulders.

She opened her mouth to speak, but Schonborn brought a finger to her lips to quiet her and leaned in for a kiss. This wasn't going according to plan. Things were happening too fast.

24

Laramie

Monday rode back into Laramie at mid-afternoon, as bone-weary as the tired Circle M sorrel mare he rode and the chestnut gelding he led. He dismounted at Dillon's Livery on Front Street and turned the reins over to one of Tom Dillon's stable hands. He walked through the barn and looked out back. Taggart's big bay mare that Ben had promised to board was working a feedbag. Monday didn't know the other horses well enough to see whether Ben's own horse or Smitty's and Sandy's pairs of mounts were here.

The marshal took his rifle and saddlebag off the sorrel and limped slowly toward the sheriff's office. Monday knew he could have ridden all the way down with Roy Butcher in the relative comfort of the bouncing freight wagon. But Ben's urgency and Sandy and Smitty's suspicious haste had convinced him by the time the Circle M outfit overtook the wagon that he ought to get to Laramie as quickly as possible. If Lightning could have made the trip, he'd have ridden most of the night, dozing in the saddle like he'd planned. But having two unfamiliar horses had forced him to stop for a few hours' sleep the last two nights and keep up a good pace during the day.

Even so, Monday thought Sandy and Smitty had probably arrived in Laramie yesterday. Ben might have made it in last night or early this morning. Monday's first stop would be the jail. If Ben's confrontation with Smitty had resulted in bloodshed, Nate would be sure to have someone locked up this morning.

The office looked deserted. Monday breathed easier. He dumped his saddlebag and rifle on a chair, making enough noise that he could be heard in the back. Sure enough, the door to the cell area opened and Cal Egan, Nate's third deputy, came out. He was shorter than Dutch van Orden, taller than Reese Bowman, and older than either of them. His hair was cut so short that Monday wouldn't have known the color if he didn't know Cal already.

"'Bout time you got here," the deputy began. "Ben Rollins said you'd be hot on his tail." Monday breathed a sigh of relief. Ben was the only one of the trio he'd really wanted to find alive. Now if only he wasn't locked up in the back.

"Yeah, I borrowed a couple of Circle M horses and followed as quick as I could." Monday wanted to ask questions, but he oughtn't to forget his manners. He hadn't seen the Egans in a couple months. "How are Lucy and young Dan?" He pegged his hat behind the front door, and poured a cup of lukewarm coffee. Better late than never, he thought as he sipped; and better luke than cold.

"Lucy's fine, considering. You know she's got another one in the oven? Dan's gonna be a big brother." The deputy's pride was evident.

"Yeah, I recollect Dutch mentioned it. Nate must not be working you too hard if Lucy still waits up for you." Monday grinned and took another sip. "When's she due?"

"October, thank God," Cal said. "Couldn'ta timed that much better, I reckon. I'm working all my spare time making sure we're snug as we can be before winter sets in."

"Oh, here," Cal said, fishing a paper out of a desk drawer. "Boy brought you this telegram this morning. Nate said to hold it for you." He also put a letter on the desk.

Monday saw the wire had been sent to him in both Laramie and Warbonnet. It was from Kate. It said she would be arriving on the next train from the west, day after tomorrow.

Monday figured he'd used up all the polite conversation he'd been able to summon and put the telegram away and pocketed the letter. Also from Kate, he noted.

"Who all you got back there today?"

"Oh, your brother still. He ain't been released or nothin' yet. Seems I oughta remember to tell you something about him, though. Anyway, the two Hotchkiss boys you brought in are still here. And a couple of drunks from two nights ago. We'd-a let 'em go already, but they did some damage at the Alhambra. Now that they're sober but broke, Nate's gonna have 'em work it off up at the church. They wanted to work it off at the saloon. Can you imagine?" he chuckled.

Monday didn't smile. "Nobody else in jail? Everything quiet last night?"

Cal's grin evaporated, too. "Oh, yeah, you just rode in. Don't know about the shooting last night out at the Hog Ranch. Young cowboy was shot in the back. Nate and Dutch are lookin' into it. Another murder."

"Who was it? You mentioned Ben Rollins."

"Oh, not him. Some feller named Sutton."

"Sutter? Sandy Sutter?" Monday was ashamed of the relief he felt. After all, Ben might be involved in some way. But hadn't Cal just said he only had Tom, the Hotchkiss brothers, and a couple of drunks in the cells?

"Yeah, Sutter. That's it. Somebody killed him out back of the Hog Ranch after midnight. Dropped a pistol by the body. Nate and Dutch had a lot of witnesses to talk to."

"You keep sayin' 'somebody,' Cal. I take it nobody's been arrested yet?" Monday had a sinking feeling. Had the killer fled?

"Well, no, not yet. And if the leading suspect pans out, sheriff may not be able to make such an unpopular arrest." Cal caught Monday's questioning look. "Uh, Miss Suzanne. Over't the Hog Ranch. It was her derringer found next to the body. Somebody put a slug into Sutter's back at close range. Powder burns on his shirt."

"Then I guess she would be a suspect. Anybody see her do it?"

"No, but Sutter stopped by a card game and said he had a note from that new girl Danielle to meet him out the back door. The boys saw him put the note in his shirt pocket. Then he stepped out the back door and they heard the shot. Everybody went runnin' out the back.

"They turned him over, but there was no note on him. They said it'd only been a minute or two since he showed 'em the note and put it in his pocket. Maybe ten seconds between the shot and the first of them boys going out the back door. They didn't see the killer."

"So the note's missing. I take it nobody read it. Sandy just waved it around?"

"Yeah," Cal said. "That's right. And nobody's read it since, neither. It ain't been found."

"Do you know from talkin' to Nate and Dutch where some of the suspects in Francine's killing were when this happened? Where was Suzanne?"

"She come down the outside steps from the upper floor. Of course, she was already down before the boys noticed her. Said she come down when she heard the shot, but nobody saw her on the stairs. Suzanne coulda been alongside the building when the shot was fired and just said she come down after. She's the one that looked at the derringer and said it was hers. That gun and her timing on the stairs is why Nate's treatin' her as his best suspect."

"Hmmm. Was she searched for that note?"

"I reckon." Cal grinned. "I understand she only had a robe on and it didn't have no pockets on it or anything. And she's the kind of girl that don't mind being searched. Wish I'd been there." Then he added quickly, "Don't tell Lucy I said that."

"Where was Ben Rollins during all this?"

"I'm not sure. Dutch was gonna talk to him. There were only them three cowboys in town last night, two besides your Sandy."

"How about the third one, then? Smitty, the foreman."

189

"Oh, he ran out there with the boys to see what the shootin' was all about. He was with the first group that gathered round the body."

Monday kicked the corner of the sheriff's desk and sighed. If he couldn't figure out how or why Smitty had framed Tom for Francine's murder, he was hoping to find a way to show he murdered Sandy, but he needed to ask about one more suspect.

"Who was the first deputy on the scene? Reese again?"

"Yeah. Just like at Francine's murder. But there ain't nothing peculiar about that. Reese takes most of the night shifts so us married deputies can spend nights at home. And you know he has to include the Hog Ranch in his rounds. More trouble happens there than at the saloons along Front Street."

But Bowman was there again. As the first arriving deputy. Was there a connection between the two murders? Sandy had been Monday's leading suspect as Francine's killer. Kate had told him that someone with the initials A.S. might be involved in Francine's murder. Sandy was known to have been taken with Francine and was jealous of her other customers. And Monday had Sandy pegged for having tried to kill him with that stampede. Why else had he lit out for Laramie, rather than stay and face Monday's questions?

Monday was so lost in thought, he'd forgotten Cal. The deputy swirled the coffee pot again to get Monday's attention. He took a second cup of that lukewarm coffee.

"Oh, Monday. I almost forgot. Sheriff said any deputy that saw you first was supposed to tell you that Judge Beekman will be back from Cheyenne day after tomorrow. He wants to get your brother's case settled pronto. Nate said if you ain't got some other suspect to put in the old hoosegow here, Tom Malone is gonna hafta stand up for Francine's murder. Only reason the judge ain't heard the case yet is because there were so many cases to hear in Cheyenne. Your brother and the Hotchkiss boys are the only ones we got to try."

That was bad news. Maybe Monday could get the judge to try the Hotchkiss boys first, but it would have to appear to be Nate's idea. He'd talk to Nate. Then he had to find Ben and see if Nate or Dutch had already questioned him.

"I gotta go, Cal. Reckon I'll see what help I can be to the sheriff. If I don't find him, though, tell him I'm stoppin' at the Frontier. I'll either be there or in the closest bath house, right after—no, right *before* supper. I ain't fit company for anybody but criminals or peace officers right now." Cal laughed and saw Monday to the door.

# # #

It turned out Ben Rollins wasn't hard to find. He was coming out of the Frontier Hotel as Monday was going to check in and they almost collided in the doorway. Monday took him down to the Alhambra and bought him a beer.

"Seems like I oughta be buying you a few rounds," Ben said. "For all the beers you bought me the last few weeks, and for lending me your horse—and that little bag you gave me."

"Reckon you can buy me a round when Smitty pays you for that last drive. How did things go with Danielle?" Monday watched him over the rim of his beer glass.

"Real well. Just like you said it would. We were in the dining room this morning when we heard Sandy'd been killed last night. You lookin' into that, Monday?"

"Yeah, along with the sheriff and his deputies. Who got into town first in that three-way race you were runnin'?"

"Um, I reckon Smitty did. He chose the best horses and I figure he knew how to pace them—and himself. Somebody told me he got in about sundown yesterday. I heard he went straight to the Hog Ranch when he got here." Ben caught Monday's raised eyebrow.

"No, Danielle wasn't there. She was up here at the hotel. Desk clerk wouldn't let him up to her room. I confronted Fricker this morning. Sure enough, Fricker said Smitty wanted to pay him off so he could have Danielle before any-

191

body else. If you're lookin' into whether I mighta killed Sandy, you're barkin' up the wrong tree. But I coulda killed Smitty or Fricker without batting an eye. And if I'd wanted to kill Sandy, I had my chance out on the trail. I passed him about moon-rise."

"Then you got into town before Sandy? He started early, but got here last."

"No, he passed me again before we got to town. I'd just switched horses, onto your bay mare, but she threw a shoe a mile later. I had to get back onto my own played out horse. Sandy musta made it in here before midnight. I dragged in about two o'clock or so. Ruckus was over by then. I didn't hear about Sandy's death 'til breakfast this morning with Danielle."

"You know I can check that horseshoe story, Ben."

Ben looked disappointed. "I wish you were as careful checking out Smitty as you are checking out your friends. Ira, one of Dillon's boys, knows when I brought them horses in. I made enough noise when I came in that I woke him up. Ask him about the mare's right rear shoe."

Damn, Monday thought. He'd been trying to help Ben two days ago and now he was treating him like a suspect again. Sandy's murder didn't have to be related to Francine's. There could be two separate killers here. Why was Sandy killed? And was he lured to his death by that note? Or was he just bragging to the other customers and got killed by somebody else who was smitten with Danielle?

"Don't worry about Smitty," Monday told Ben. "I'll check him out later. And I'll talk to some of the witnesses. He was seen going out the back door with everybody else after Sandy was shot, so he seems to have a pretty sound alibi. Smitty probably consoled himself with Suzanne when he couldn't find Danielle."

Ben reddened and Monday decided this wasn't a good subject to be joshing Ben about. He excused himself and went off to find a hot bath. Maybe he'd see Smitty and spoil his evening by talking to the bastard. He'd have that bath and read

Kate's latest letter first, then have supper, so talking to Smitty wouldn't spoil his whole evening.

25

Union Pacific to Laramie

Kate closed her book and set it beside her on the seat of her train car. Finished. An eminently satisfying ending. She wished Captain Nemo hadn't gone down with the *Nautilus*, though. He was such an intriguing character that she wanted to read more about him. Kate usually pictured a play as she read, and the characters leaped off the page and into a stage in her head. She'd imagined the darkly handsome Thomas Moran saying Nemo's lines, Hayden as the professor, and Monday as the American harpooner Ned Land.

How absurd! She was sure Monday had never seen the ocean and couldn't possibly say Ned's lines. But she couldn't control the faces her imagination put on the characters. There was no woman in Verne's adventure novel, but she would have loved to have a part in the play this book suggested to her. Her hand strayed to her copy of Collins' *The Moonstone*. Now here was a mystery play she could put herself into.

But the time for dreaming was past. She'd better be thinking about the Tom Malone mystery again. They were almost to Laramie.

Kate glanced across to Anton Schonborn in the facing seat. He'd been watching her, but when she glanced at him, he looked out the window. He hadn't often met her eyes since they'd left Yellowstone. How odd. She thought she'd be the one to avert her gaze since the falls. Maybe Sean Finnegan, asleep on the bench across the aisle, was intimidating the man. The old scout had stuck to her like glue ever since she'd returned from the falls and handed him back his unfired pistol. He'd been disappointed she hadn't needed him to rescue her. But she hadn't wanted a rescuer. She'd wanted the experience of that morning to proceed without interruption and according to her terms. And it had.

She sighed and wondered again whether she'd made the right decision back at the falls. Would anyone understand if she told what she'd done? She couldn't tell anybody in Warbonnet, not even Becky or Martha. Maybe another letter to Lacey Ferris or Anna Green.

Kate wasn't returning to Laramie the same woman who'd left a few weeks ago. She'd left Warbonnet as just a girl, twenty years old, to be sure, but so many things had happened this summer. The black lace lingerie, spying on Monday in his bath, her daring first Moran, then Professor Hayden, to get a place on the expedition, talking with Schonborn in her bath. Then the bear attack and posing at the falls. She'd faced down so many of her old fears—snakes, Indians, the companionship of gruff and uneducated men, as well as professional explorers. And she'd held off Schonborn's intended conquest. Would the changes in her be apparent to Monday?

She rubbed the back of her scarred left hand and thought of Stuart. The last time she'd made grandiose plans for the future, reality had stepped in to crush her dreams. Instead of marrying the older brother of her best friend, she'd mourned his death in the Siege of Petersburg. That had so unhinged her that she'd considered suicide. At fourteen. When most girls were just starting to dream. Only her last-minute discovery of Stuart's betrayal had dissuaded her from throwing herself over Niagara Falls.

Kate opened one of her sketch books and considered the Old Faithful geyser. Her last night there, before the group split up and some went to Yellowstone Lake, she'd had a chance to be alone with Professor Hayden at the campfire before turning in. In the morning, they'd all ride to the lake. From there, the bulk of the expedition would circumnavigate the lake while she and Schonborn, the wagons, and their milit-

195

ary escort would return to Fort Ellis by way of another geyser basin.

"I want to thank you for making the difficult decision to allow me to come this far, Professor," she'd told him. "In the past five weeks, I've seen wonders experienced by few men. And I'm conscious that no other woman may have seen what I've witnessed. These scenes shall remain with me always. As will your kindness and the consideration of the other men," she added. "I could not have been better treated."

Professor Hayden filled his pipe before replying. "Thanks to you, Miss Shaw, I've gotten used to the idea that women as well as men, even families, might wish to travel great distances in order to see the wonders of this land. That idea fills me with hope. It encourages me to believe that we may be able to set aside these precious places—hot springs, waterfalls, geysers, mountains, and lakes—and keep them as unsullied for our descendants as we have seen them. Despite my initial misgivings, I've heard nothing to fault your conduct. And your drawings fill me with delight."

Nothing to fault her conduct, Kate thought. Only Sean and Schonborn knew about her posing at the falls. If Anton kept his word and didn't publicly display his sketches of that morning when he returned to the East, she might . . . .

"I've thought some more, Doctor, about what you said last night about preserving the views of Yellowstone Falls from rampant exploitation. I told you I come from Buffalo. Although Niagara Falls are every bit as splendid as the falls we've seen here, the boarding houses, hotels, chop houses, taverns, and other tawdry establishments that crowd Niagara's margins and spoil its views are cause for concern. Sean Finnegan tells me that some man named McGuirk is planning to file a claim on White Mountain Hot Springs soon. The bath huts and cabins there were bad enough. I've heard he also plans to build a hotel overlooking the falls."

"Not too near them, Miss Shaw, I promise you. I've heard that hotel tale, as well. There must be some nearby facilities for those who come a long way to see the Yellowstone country, but I take your point." Professor Hayden sighed and put a match to his pipe, puffing a few times until he had it going.

"I don't suppose we can put up a fence around all this vast wonderland," he continued. "But Washington will have to find a way to regulate it or lose it—and soon, as you say. I'll make some recommendations in my report. Jackson's photographs, Moran's watercolors, and your sketches, cannot but help me make a case to the President and the Congress."

Kate thanked him and stood to say good night and turn in.

"I know you're suspicious of the motives of the railroad interests," Hayden went on. "But I hope I can harness their vision of tracks all across America to pull the weight of public interest for a while. Perhaps Congress can beat Mr. McGuirk and stake a claim for all of us."

Kate smiled at the recollection of Professor Hayden's hopes. Setting aside Yellowstone as some sort of parkland appeared unlikely to her, but he knew the workings of Washington and seemed optimistic.

She was shaken out of her reverie by the conductor moving through the car to announce they would be arriving in Laramie in ten minutes. She began to gather up her books. Sean Finnegan sat up and put on his hat. Kate turned to him.

"We're almost in Laramie, Sean. Will you still do as we agreed? Let me talk to Monday first, if he's in town. I need to determine whether his brother is still alive and if Monday's already caught the killer before you worry him with your report."

"Shoot! I ain't gonna bother him none with my report, Miss Kate. If I told him everything I saw and heard or suspected, my life—and your precious Mr. Schonborn's—wouldn't be worth a nickel beer." Kate looked over and saw Schonborn blanch at this. "Don't fret now. You can talk to Monday first and tell him whatever tale you like. I won't contradict anything you say. In fact," he grinned and whispered, "marry me and I'll never be able to say nothin' against you."

Kate laughed and hugged him. This was his third proposal since they'd started their journey. Schonborn seemed a little put off by her show of affection for the scout.

197

"Cheer up, Anton," she said to him. "You're almost back to civilization—or what passes for it in Wyoming. We'll stop over long enough for you to eat."

And long enough for Kate to get that money from the bank that she'd wired for.

With great clanking and hissing, the train rolled to a stop at the Laramie station. Several passengers got off, but only a handful would remain here. Most travelers still rode right across Wyoming, but few settled. The territory was growing more slowly than moss.

Finnegan and Schonborn helped her with her things. The men left Kate on the platform while her crate—a far cry from the elegant trunk the bear had ruined—was unloaded. Kate arranged to have it left there on the platform for now; she didn't want to tell Schonborn yet that she'd made up her mind not to go on with him to Omaha or on to New York.

The old scout went off to get a drink and see if Monday was in town. As she was closing the drawstring on her reticule —how odd to be carrying a handbag and wearing a dress again after so long in the beautiful wilderness—Kate looked up to see Monday crossing the street, heading for the station.

He didn't see her standing amid the freight and Kate could watch him unobserved. She noted his easy grace and the way he tipped his hat to people as he approached the station. He had a familiar gait, the loose amble of a man used to wearing a holstered pistol. His elbow bent as his arm swung easily past his gun as he walked. In Warbonnet, she realized, Monday was nearly the only man she saw walking the street habitually armed. Here in Laramie, there were many more—and they all walked like Monday.

Just then, the young marshal saw her on the freight plat-form and changed direction.

Kate smiled as Monday stopped a few paces from her, con-scious that they were in public. She wanted him to open his arms and take her in, to hold her and tell her she'd done the right thing in going to Yellowstone. But there were too many other people around. As it was, he just said how nice she looked and how good it was to have her back. Had he missed her? She longed to hear him say it. She was on the verge of touching his arm and telling him how much she'd missed him when he popped the bubble of her mood.

"Can we go somewhere and talk, Kate? There's been another killing and it may have something to do with Francine's murder."

26

Laramie

Monday regretted the bluntness of his statement as soon as the words were out of his mouth. He realized by Kate's expression that he should have spent a little more time on pleasantries. She looked like she'd been about to say something, but had to swallow the words. Her eyes grew as wide as the circle of her open mouth. He could read disappointment and shock at the same time. Damn! He was sorry now that he hadn't asked about her journey. Maybe he could undo some of the damage he'd caused.

"You probably don't want to talk about murder or your trip to Yellowstone out here in the street, Miss Kate. Why don't we find a quiet corner over in the Frontier?" He gave her a moment to recover her composure, then offered her his arm. They waited for a wagon to rumble past and walked across the rutted street to the hotel.

Monday seated Kate on a couch in an alcove beneath the stairs to the second floor. He stepped away for a moment and ordered tea for her and coffee for himself, then returned to her. He started to sit on a chair across from the little couch, but she patted the cushion beside her and he took that seat.

"I think," she said, opening her reticule and taking out a pencil and small notebook, "that what we have to talk about will be more private if you sit closer. What was that about another death? Who was killed? Why do you think it might be related to Francine's murder?"

Monday filled her in on what he'd learned about Sandy Sutter's death from Cal Egan and Ben Rollins, including a note said to be from Danielle that had led Sandy to his death. He hadn't spoken to Smitty or Reese yet and wasn't about to revisit Suzanne for her story.

He wanted to ask Kate about her trip and knew she must be dying to tell him stories of Yellowstone. When the tea and coffee arrived, Kate reached into her handbag for money, but Monday paid for them.

"I ain't spoken to Smitty about this yet, but he looks to have a pretty good alibi. He was with the first group that gathered around Sandy's body, so he wasn't likely to have been out there when Sandy was shot. I gotta talk to him—and I ain't lookin' forward to it. The night stablehand backed up Ben's story about his getting to town after Sandy's murder."

He broke off for a moment and steadied himself with some more coffee.

"But I'm worried, Kate. I think Danielle might know something useful. I know they're in love and she might lie to protect him. I ain't gonna be very good at figuring out the truth of her yarn. This needs your touch. I think you'd have a better reason to talk to her and pick up quicker on what she says."

"Well, I'm flattered, I think." She sipped her tea. "This is a far cry from our conversation that evening in Warbonnet. I don't think my skills are just limited to questioning women, thank you. But I understand what you mean and I'd be glad to talk to Danielle. What about Suzanne? Have you talked with her? Recently, I mean."

Kate looked down at her cup.

Monday hesitated before answering. How much did Kate know about his first encounter with Suzanne?

"Uh, no. No, I ain't talked to her yet. I talked to Nate about what she said when he questioned her. Suzanne claimed she come down those back stairs when she heard the shot, but nobody really saw her on the stairs. She coulda been right there when Sandy was killed. They said she acted surprised when Reese Bowman picked up the derringer and held it in the light from the back door. Said it looked like hers. I'd hate to ask you to talk to a woman like her, though."

"Don't worry about the propriety of my talking to her. I've done that once already. But this time I'd like to talk to her on more neutral ground. Isn't this Thursday? I recall that the—um, Suzanne and the other ladies—come into town to shop on Thursday afternoons. Perhaps I shall talk to her before I see Danielle."

Monday couldn't think of anything to say. If Kate had already talked to Suzanne, the woman might have told her what almost happened when he visited her. Oh, Lord.

Kate just looked amused and sipped her tea, waiting for him to say something. When he didn't, she broke the awkward silence.

"I'd like to prove I have the skills to question men, too. But I'm not going to offer to talk to Smitty. As distasteful as you find it to meet with him, please believe me when I say it would be far more difficult for me."

Monday sat up straighter.

"I'd never want you to talk to that skunk. Nor to Tom neither. But I wormed out of Reese Bowman that you talked to Tom once already. That how you found out Sandy was involved in Francine's murder in some way?" He finished his coffee.

"No, I never said that. I just said someone with the initials 'A.S.' had something to do with Francine. How was Sandy involved? How did you get Sandy's name from those initials?"

"Uh, Miss Kate. Sandy's given name is—was—Alexander. I thought from your letter that he might've killed Francine. I'm pretty sure he tried to kill me by starting a stampede last week." He hated to tell her he'd been in any danger. He knew she'd worry about his safety now.

"Heavens. Has it come to that? Well, if Sandy did try to kill you, then I'm glad that threat is over. But how would we ever be able to prove he killed Francine and save Tom?" He could see she was thinking. She twisted a strand of loose hair around one forefinger. "I wonder if he was the blackmailer, too."

When Monday wrinkled his forehead at that, she continued. "Tom boasted that someone had been talking to him about identifying the killer for five hundred dollars. He wouldn't say who it was, but I gathered it was a man. I guess that rules out Suzanne."

Neither of them said anything for a while. Monday thought about Sandy trying to extort that money. If Tom was referring to Sandy, had the cowboy known who the real killer was? Or was he just looking to make money out of Tom's predicament? Did it mean that Sandy wasn't the killer himself, or could he have done it and hoped to throw suspicion onto someone else—Smitty or Ben? He'd said things to Monday about Ben the morning of the stampede, but had said nothing about Smitty.

He was about to ask Kate if Tom had told her anything else, especially about Mary Ellen, but she asked about the letters peeking out of his shirt pocket.

"Oh, yeah, sorry. I plumb forgot. I picked these up rather than have Roy take them to Warbonnet in a couple days. I guess you'd like a chance to catch up." Most of the letters to her were from Buffalo or some other cities in New York, but one was from Manzanita, Texas, Monday's old home town. That must be an answer to the letter Kate told him she'd sent. What did it say? Monday had wanted to open that letter himself, but hadn't dared to. He handed them all over to her.

"More tea?" he asked, anxious to give her a little privacy while she read. When she agreed, he took their cups to the dining room. As he was waiting for refills, he saw a man with dark hair and beard in a fancy suit sitting at a table by himself. Monday walked over to the table. Could this be the Moran or Schonborn Kate mentioned in a letter? The man looked up from his dinner.

"Yes, Sheriff?" he said, squinting at Monday's badge. "Or Marshal, rather. What can I do for you?"

"You just get back from Yellowstone with Miss Shaw?"

"Why, yes, I did. I'm Anton Schonborn, lately of Omaha. Miss Shaw was a delightful traveling companion. I take it you two are acquainted. Would you like to join me?"

"No thanks. Miss Shaw and I are just discussing what she did and saw on this trip. We're just getting around to talking about the artists, in fact." Schonborn put his cup down so quickly, some coffee spilled into the saucer.

"I—you needn't take everything Miss Shaw says literally, you know. She has a vivid imagination. We compared sketches on more than one occasion. I'd like to think that we had a professional relationship. A collaboration between two artists." He wiped his mouth with his napkin.

"Look, Mr. Schonborn. You don't have to throw those big words around to impress me. I charged Sean Finnegan with lookin' after Miss Shaw's safety and welfare. I ain't talked to him yet, but I'm sure he'll tell me Miss Shaw was treated like the lady she is." Monday hadn't meant to sound so stern, but he noticed the fork Schonborn was holding clanked against his plate.

"I assure you Miss Shaw had a perfectly uneventful trip— apart from the Indians. And the bear, I mean. And the wonders of Yellowstone. I'm sure she'll tell you all about them."

With that, Schonborn waved at a serving girl, indicating he was finished with his meal. Something must have spoiled his appetite, Monday thought. The cups of tea and coffee were ready. What was that about a bear, he wondered, as he carried the cups carefully out to the lobby.

When Monday returned to Kate in the alcove, he saw she'd opened two letters and was staring off into space, lost in her thoughts. Setting the cups down seemed to break the spell. She looked at him with concern.

"I was just . . . . I mean, I read some replies to letters I sent while I was in Yellowstone," Kate stammered. "They don't seem to make any sense. I got answers from two old friends about questions I hadn't asked them." She was rubbing her right hand nervously over the scar on the back of her left hand.

"One of them," she held up a sheet of paper, "actually sent back a page of the letter I sent her. It contains some of my theories about Francine's murder and some questions I thought I sent to you, ideas you might follow up on." Now her hand holding the page was shaking.

What is this, Monday thought. First Schonborn, now Kate. Was there something in the water in Yellowstone that gave everybody the shakes? What must Sean Finnegan look like now? He began to grin at that thought, but stopped cold when he saw Kate's lower lip begin to tremble.

"Did you get my last letter, the one I sent from the geyser basin?" So that was it. Here it comes, he thought. He'd been looking forward to this, but figured he'd better tread lightly.

"Yes, Ma'am, I did. And a pretty piece of writing it was, too. Mighty like poetry in a couple places. Talked just a little about your bath in the hot springs and about my bath, back in Warbonnet before you left." He looked into his cup and didn't meet her eyes.

"I didn't mind being likened to some statue you once saw named David. Why, any man would—"

He broke off at a strangled sound and looked up to see Kate Shaw's red face dissolve into creases. Tears came to her eyes and that awkward gurgle was rising to a wail. He stood up instantly and pulled her to her feet. He hugged her to him and put her face into the hollow of his shoulder. She resisted weakly, but her muffled sobs told him he'd done the right thing. Her shoulders shook. Between sobs, he heard words and phrases that didn't make sense.

"Oh, God. Punish me. Hot springs. Anton. I knew it, I knew it. God sent the bear. Sean. The letters. I never should have .... Monday. Bath. Never be able to .... "

At last the words dissolved and she just bawled against his shirt. Her shoulders shook like she was in some sort of agony. Fortunately, the lobby was deserted. Or almost deserted. Schonborn walked over to the desk at that moment, but turned at the noise Kate was making and saw the pair of them. He looked horror-stricken. He turned on his heel and dashed out.

Kate ran out of words about the same time she stopped shaking. Monday let her pull away from him a little, but he kept a strong grip on her upper arms, ready to pull her back to his shoulder. Kate's face was a wet mask of pain. Besides the tears, her nose had run and she hiccupped softly as she tried to find her voice again. Monday pulled a spare bandana from his hip pocket. Kate didn't take it.

"It's clean, Kate. I ain't used it yet." He pressed it into her hand and she buried her face in it. This wasn't working out like he'd hoped. He'd planned to tease her about the contents of the letter and watch her squirm, but he'd never figured on a reaction like this. You'd have thought he'd killed her dog. Or cat. Whatever she had back in Buffalo.

She tried to speak, but he couldn't understand her. He held the tea cup for her and she sipped a little. Eventually, she spoke in a cracked voice that didn't sound like her at all.

"I'm sorry. So sorry. For everything. For breaking down like this. For sending you the wrong pages in that letter. For things you don't even know about. I wish, I wish I could go back two weeks and erase every stupid, foolish thing I've done. You know I'd never have written you a letter like that. I couldn't afford to lose your respect. The bear, the bear . . . . " With that, she buried her face in his bandana again for a while. Then she recovered and went on.

"I must sound crazy to you. I must have seemed crazy in that letter, too. Those pages were never, never meant for you. I was writing to my friends about you and God punished me for having spied on you in your bath. First he sent Anton Schonborn to spy on me. Then that bear. I thought those things were retribution. But the mixed up letters were really my punishment, my humiliation." Kate wasn't making sense, but she appeared to be pulling herself together. The tears had left lines down her blotched cheeks.

"I need to go wash my face. But I don't have a room yet."

"You can use my room, Kate." Monday fished the key out of his vest pocket. "Two-oh-three." Kate backed away a step.

"No. I can't be seen going up to a man's room. Even when I have so compromised myself that no decent—"

"You didn't compromise nothing, Kate. This was all my fault for not telling you about that letter right away. I was hoping to use it to tease you a little. I knew I'd have to give those pages back to you. But I never figured you'd take it this bad. I'm the one should say he's sorry."

Kate brightened a bit at his apology and waved the bandana slightly. "I guess I can go up and wash my face if you stay down here and stand lookout for me. No scandal if no one sees me go into your room." She laughed at that for some reason. "Will you stay here?" Monday nodded. She took his key.

"And I should like to have those pages back. May I have them, please?" She didn't usually sound this meek. Either she'd cried out all her usual stubbornness or getting those pages back was really important to her.

"Uh, it's not like I carry them with me, Kate. You can get them when you're up in my room. They're under my pillow."

"Why would you keep them there?" Doubt had crept into her voice.

"I ain't never had a letter from you before. I'd have kept it under my pillow even if you just went on about the weather in Yellowstone. I read it a few times every night when I turn in. Brought it all the way down here from Warbonnet with me." He saw her expression harden into suspicion.

"But I'm willing for you to have them pages back. Reckon I got all your words in my head by now."

This threatened to provoke more tears, so he stopped even this mild teasing. He looked around the lobby to make sure no one was there, then sent her upstairs. He gathered up their cups and his damp bandana. Well, if she was going to take back that letter, maybe he'd keep this rag under his pillow, once it dried. What a load of tears she'd had. He felt sorry for having caused her breakdown.

Why couldn't they just work on getting Tom out of jail without always having feelings get in the way? Kate had been so happy to see him and then he'd just aggravated her with one thing and another. He wouldn't try teasing her any more, but she must've picked up a case of the shakes in Yellowstone.

Then another thought struck him. What if she were planning to leave Wyoming. Had he just pushed her over the edge of her decision?

27

Laramie

Kate washed her face and carefully inspected Monday's towel
before using it. Then she looked at her face in the little mirror
above the washstand. Puffy bags under her eyes. And the eyes
were still red. She sighed heavily and hung her head. God had
inflicted spectacular punishment on her for all her sins of the
past few weeks. She'd spied on Monday in his bath, lied to get
into the Hog Ranch, lied again to go on the Hayden
expedition, allowed a man to talk to her in her bath while she
was unclothed, written scandalous things about Monday to
her friends, and posed in a gauzy shift for Schonborn above
Yellowstone Falls. At least she'd stopped him after one kiss.

The bear should have been enough, but no. God, working
through Sean Finnegan, had seen fit to humiliate her with her
own words in front of a man whose trust she'd tried so hard to
earn. Kate wanted to be needed, as a teacher, as a friend, as a
female detective. Now all the respect she'd cultivated in
Monday lay in ruins. Why hadn't the bear just killed her?
Perhaps she should reconsider her decision on returning to
the East. She didn't need to go with Schonborn for that.
There'd be other trains.

Kate felt tears starting again and hastily rubbed cold water
under her eyes. She remembered her mission and stumbled
over to Monday's poorly made bed. Just like his bunk in the
jail. She raised the pillow gingerly and found the two pages of
her letter. She'd burn them in private. She'd been up here
long enough. Time to go down and face the music. Oh, God.

Monday stood up as she came down the stairs to the lobby.

"Uh, Kate, before we go off and, um, question the people we said, could I, I mean, would you show me the letter you got from Manzanita? I ain't heard from anybody there since I left Texas on my last cattle drive."

"The letter I intended for you to receive," Kate looked at the floor and didn't meet his eye. "In that letter, I said I'd written to your friend Zack about Cora Wallace, your brother's former fiancé. I didn't think it had anything to do with Tom's current predicament. Tom just told me, well, he said how shabbily he'd treated Cora and I wanted to know. . . . " She couldn't tell Monday what Tom had told her about Mary Ellen and Monday. Zack's letter had more in it about the lovers. She couldn't show it to him, didn't want to open old wounds now.

"Things are looking up for Cora," she said, blinking back tears. "Zack says she got married this spring in Fort Worth. He didn't know who the husband was, but said he'd try to find out from her family. It's nothing to do with this case, really." She could look up now, but only glanced furtively at him as she spoke. Would she ever be able to look him in the eye again?

Monday took her by the shoulders and made her look at him.

"I told you not to talk to Tom. There's no tellin' what kind of poison he might pour in your ears. He didn't say anything bad about Mary Ellen, *did he?*" He was staring hard at her now and squeezing her upper arms. It hurt.

"No, nothing about Mary Ellen." There was a time when she couldn't have imagined lying to this man. She gulped. "Tom told me someone said he knew who really killed Francine. He asked for money before he'd tell Tom. Did he tell you anything about that when you talked to him?"

Monday appeared to realize he was bruising her arms. He let go of her and stepped back a pace.

"Just that he was gonna have to pay this person five hundred dollars for that information, like he told you. He planned to wait until the ranchers in Warbonnet paid for their cattle. He sent the money he got in Abilene back home by draft. Reckon he'll take the five hundred out of what Smitty brought down with him. I'm gonna have to talk to quite a few folks today, Kate. Reese Bowman, Tom, even Smitty." Now it was Monday's turn to look at the floor as he finished speaking. Why would he have as hard a time talking to Smitty as she would?

Kate swallowed hard. "Do you want to meet back here this evening? I mean, just for supper? To compare notes."

They agreed to meet at six o'clock and Kate watched Monday walk off toward the jail. She remembered she had her own errand at the bank. She hoped there was enough time.

The money she'd directed by telegram be transferred from Warbonnet was waiting for her at the Laramie Bank and Trust. Thank God. Maybe she could salvage something from this horrible day. She hadn't heard the train whistle yet. She hurried to the station. Her crate was still on the platform, silently daring her to make her final decision. She hadn't said goodbye to Monday. With everything going on, she couldn't leave now. Fate was making her decision for her.

Passengers were still saying farewells on the platform as the last freight and baggage were being loaded. She spied Anton Schonborn putting a folded newspaper under one arm and picking up his suitcase. Kate called his name and he turned.

"I was afraid I might miss you, Anton. That the train might pull out—"

"I didn't think we had anything more to say to each other, Kate. I saw you in the hotel lobby, crying in the arms of that Malone fellow. I knew you'd probably changed your mind. If you told him everything . . . ."

"No. No, I didn't. We were discussing a murder—actually two murders." The train whistle sounded for the first time, to call passengers to the station. She only had minutes now.

"Anton, I wired for the money I needed to send with you. It's here in my bag. I want you to take it, as a down payment for the portrait." He waved his hand and cut her off.

211

"I don't want to take your money out of Wyoming, Kate. I'd like to take you away from here. Won't you reconsider? You will regret not coming to New York. If not today, then tomorrow, or next month. Certainly by next year. Wyoming is damaging more than just your fair complexion."

"I think we said all that needed to be said about New York City back at the falls." This wasn't going to be easy. She hadn't made her mind up when she wired for the money.

The conductor waved to the engineer to pull the whistle cord a second time.

"Wyoming may be hard on a woman physically, Anton, but it can be a tonic to her spirit. This territory is just an empty space on most maps. Full of Indians, but it's nearly devoid of white people. Women are scarce out here. But that renders the contributions we few women can make to this land even more valuable."

The conductor was waving to Schonborn now. At any moment, the whistle would sound a third time and the train would begin to move.

Kate thought of Monday and the respect she'd squandered. Would her words sound hollow now?

"We have a woman justice of the peace in Wyoming this year. Women are even sitting on juries." She'd heard there might be two women on Tom Malone's jury. That would not necessarily be good for him. He was going to be tried for knifing a prostitute he'd patronized. The women of Laramie would want to mete out harsh justice in any case involving the Hog Ranch.

"Kate, Wyoming is still only a territory, not a state. What did you tell me you have out here now, three thousand people? You have more than that at home in Buffalo." The man looked frantic now, tripping over his words. Were her words more than upsetting him?

"But women can't do the things in New York yet that we can out here in Wyoming. Nor anywhere else in the world." Like being able to travel with a party of men to Yellowstone.

"Wyoming needs me. And so does Warbonnet. But more than that, I need to be with the people here. They're building something grand, trying to turn this land into a state. I can be part of that. I can vote here; I can speak up. I can help make things better by teaching children, working with mothers, sometimes helping to set the innocent free. You know one woman could never make that much of a difference in New York. Certainly not as an artist's model. Or as the mistress of one painter after another. I've made my choice."

The whistle blew a third time and the train began to lurch forward. She took Schonborn's arm as he stepped onto the train.

"Goodbye, Anton If you won't take this money, send your bill to me in Warbonnet." A pale Schonborn tipped his hat and looked back until the curving track took him out of view. What would he do with the drawings of her? Would he keep his bargain or would she see herself undraped in a museum some day? A painted woman, no better than the women of the Hog Ranch.

Kate walked away from the station. Some change in the reticule on her wrist clinked, reminding her of the money. Since Schonborn hadn't taken it for artists in New York City, then perhaps Danielle would take it. Maybe she could redeem herself by saving someone else. This was Thursday afternoon. The women of the Hog Ranch would be in town shopping. Kate saw a familiar form come out the door of Ivinson's. Suzanne. Kate hurried over to her.

"Well, well," Suzanne said with smile, a hand on one hip, "If it ain't Miss Vera Jones. I forget what paper—"

Kate ignored the teasing. "You know who I really am. I'm helping Monday Malone look into Francine's murder. And the death of Sandy Sutter, too. You know, you're a leading suspect in both killings. I understand they have evidence against you for Sandy's shooting. I want to help you if I can. Do you want to go somewhere and talk?"

Kate's urgency caught the older woman off guard. She licked her lips and looked around. Was she thinking of fleeing or only seeking a quiet place where they could talk?

"What about tea at the Frontier? I'll buy," Kate said, clinking her handbag.

"Oh, no, we could never—"

"Yes, we can. I'm a paying guest and Mrs. Crout may not like it, but she won't want to lose my custom when I come to Laramie. Come on," she said in a conspiratorial tone, "this isn't a busy time for the dining room and I don't imagine the proper ladies of Laramie usually leave their homes to have tea or go shopping on Thursday afternoons, do they?"

That seemed to settle it. Ten minutes later, they were drinking tea in a secluded booth in a corner of the dining room where no one in the lobby could see them.

"This is a right nice hotel. I recall I stayed here the first night I come to Laramie. Before anybody knew what I was."

"Maybe some day you can stay in places like this again. I understand women sometimes retire from your position—your vocation, that is—get married, and lead respectable lives. You could retire, couldn't you, if you don't have to face a murder charge?"

Suzanne set her teacup down with a clatter.

"I didn't kill nobody. Not Francine and not that Sandy neither. Hell, I mean . . . . Oh, I'm sorry. I don't know too many nice words. I didn't have no reason to kill Sandy. He came to see me just before he was killed. Said he wanted to find out if Danielle had gone to work—our line of work—while he was off on that drive to Warbonnet. I told him she wasn't there."

"And did he find her that night?"

"I don't think so. He didn't find her at the Hog Ranch. He was going to see if she was at the hotel. I was just trying to change his mind, to get him to spend some of his cattle drive pay with me, when that note was shoved under the door."

The note Monday had mentioned. So there really had been a note. Someone at the Hog Ranch that night . . . .

"What did it say? Did you see it?"

"No, Sandy didn't show it to me. In fact, neither of us might have noticed it if I'd convinced him to stay with me instead of looking for Danielle, but there was a knock on the door that made us turn that way. That's when he saw the note on the floor. Nobody was there when he opened the door."

"Well, if he didn't show it to you, did he read it to you? Did he tell you what it said?"

"Just that it was from Danielle and that she'd meet him in ten minutes at the back door. He put the note into a vest pocket and picked up his hat. Said he'd just have time for a drink before meetin' her. I, well, I tried my best to keep him there, but I guess he'd been on enough rides with me. Ain't no reasonin' with a man who has his heart set on a new filly."

That made Kate think of Schonborn. How many rides had he taken with other models before he'd invited Kate to the falls?

"Did you go to see if he met her?"

"No, I couldn't. It was a busy night. I had another customer just a few minutes after Sandy left."

"Could that man have left the note to hurry Sandy along? Or did your next visitor see who left the note?"

"No, he said he came up the front stairs and didn't see anybody out in the hall. Whoever left it might have gone out and down the back stairs."

Kate remembered the outside stairs she'd seen when she played her Vera Jones charade. She pictured the back entrance, too, where Monday said Sandy had died. Two steps up from the muddy backyard and the outhouses. The outside stairs must start not far from Suzanne's room at the other end of the hall. That was the way she reportedly came down after hearing the shot. Could the murderer . . . ?

"How was it you could come down so soon after hearing the shot?" Kate asked. "Weren't you still . . . . engaged?" She touched her cheek. The woman who returned from Yellowstone didn't seem as prone to blushing as the girl who'd left Laramie a few weeks ago.

"Not with that one, dear. He always goes off half-cocked, so to speak. If my time is worth anything, he's never gotten his money's worth. He went down the front stairs again to send the next man up."

"Was that your derringer they found by the body?"

"Reckon it was. I seen it that evening, on my lamp table next to the bed. Most of my customers knew I had one. Kept it loaded after what happened to Francine. I went back to look for it after I saw Sandy dead, but it was gone."

"If you saw it earlier, then someone must have taken it that evening. How many customers, I mean, who could have . . . ? "

"I think I had six or eight by that time. All regulars. No strangers. Reese Bowman for one. And that Smitty for another. He was mad not to have found Danielle there, too. Said he'd just come from wavin' a lot of money under Fricker's nose. Fricker said she told him she had the Curse of Eve that night. Fricker was fixin' to start her off the next night with the highest bidder, so he let her go back to the hotel after a few songs."

"Were Smitty or Reese in a hurry, too, so to speak?"

"Reese is Reese. He always wants the same thing and it takes me a while. Smitty took his time, but he was rougher than usual, as if he was taking his disappointment over Danielle out on me. He muttered under his breath the whole time. I couldn't make out words or nothing. But he left with a smile on his face and gave me a two-bit tip, too. He's never done that before. He must've figured he'd be top bidder on Danielle the next night."

That would mean Smitty could count on having a lot of money. Could he have been planning to keep some of the trail drive payoff? Or had he collected from Tom Malone? Was Smitty the blackmailer? Monday said Smitty was Tom's most frequent visitor in jail. As foreman of Tom's ranch, he could have been in to see his boss every day or so.

"I hoped it might be Francine's derringer when I seen it. That would mean her killer had killed Sandy, too. But when I found mine missing—"

"You mean Francine had a derringer like yours?"

"Like mine, hell. She gave me mine. It was a pair to the one she had. Brought 'em both with her from N'Orleans. We got along pretty good for the first few days after she got here.

Then Fricker gave her my room and she took more of my regulars."

A second gun. That raised the possibility—

"Were your guns absolutely identical? Did either one of you put your initials on the handles or anything like that, so that someone could tell them apart?"

"Nope, not up to the time Francine died. And I haven't done anything to mark mine. They had such nice pearl handles."

"Had? What happened to Francine's derringer?"

"Don't know. But it weren't with her things after she was killed. This is pretty good tea. You reckon we can get another pot, Miss Shaw?"

Kate was already scribbling a note. She waved for a serving girl to find a boy to take it to Monday Malone. And to bring them more tea.

28

Laramie

Monday put the note Kate had sent him in his vest pocket and stepped up onto the walk in front of the jail to look in the front window. Reese Bowman was seated at the second desk, playing Patience. Monday grinned. He'd hadn't expected to catch the little deputy alone. Why was Reese on day shift? His usual tour was late night, in order to make the rounds of all the saloons and the Hog Ranch.

Monday opened the door. Reese guiltily scooped the cards into the open desk drawer in front of him before he saw who his visitor was.

"Damn it all," the little deputy said. "Couldn't you knock? I was winnin' this time."

"How much did you have bet with yourself?" Monday asked with a grin.

Reese grinned back. "Nothin'. You better not a-brung any beer this time. Sheriff'll be back any minute. You come to talk to your brother again? Judge got done with the Hotchkiss boys real quick today. Wanted to start Tom's trial, but Nate reminded him he'd agreed to tomorrow."

"Well, of course I aim to talk to Tom, Reese. But I'd like to talk to you a little, too. How come you're here in broad daylight and not restin' up for tonight's rounds?"

"Sheriff said he wanted to talk to you about that. Ain't my place to tip his hand before he does."

The little deputy wasn't inclined to talk today. Monday hoped this wouldn't be like pulling teeth. Maybe he'd try a little flattery, starting with what Kate had learned about a second derringer.

"Fact is, Reese, as I get more crime up in Warbonnet and I'm spending more time down here as a county deputy, I was thinking about the need for a back-up gun. Dutch and Cal don't carry any, but I figured an experienced lawman like you would have some notion—"

"Them two don't even understand the idea of a hide-out gun. They used to make their rounds with shotguns before the town council decided it wanted its lawmen to impress travelers with how safe Laramie is and had 'em put them long guns away. I can't tell you how comfortin' it is to have a second gun when you may need it."

"Well, what do you recommend? I thought maybe a second Colt .44 for balance. Maybe even a Schofield?"

"Naw, what you need is a pocket pistol or a derringer. I used to carry a pocket pistol, but it got hung up in my pocket when I practiced with it. What you oughta consider is a little beauty like this one."

Reese pulled a shiny little derringer two-shot from his left vest pocket and placed it on the table in front of Monday.

"Now, of course, it ain't very accurate beyond about ten feet, but it'll punch a big hole. Trouble-makers are just as respectful of this as they would be my Navy Colt."

Monday picked it up and hefted it, turning it as if to admire it. He carefully sniffed the muzzle and looked at the handle.

"Not fired recently. You haven't had to break up many fights with this, I take it. What about these pearl handles, Reese? A little fancy for a tough deputy, wouldn't you say?"

"Aw, nobody can see the handles when I got my paw wrapped around it. I faced down one or two rowdies with it, but I ain't had to fire it yet. Ammunition's easy to come by, though."

219

"It looks kind of familiar, Reese. Ain't I just seen one like it, not too long ago?"

The deputy reached out and took the little pistol, slipping it back into his vest pocket.

"Yeah, well, maybe you have. Gamblers and fancy women favor these."

Monday got up and walked over to Nate's desk. He pulled open one of the right side drawers and, after a moment looking in an evidence folder, pulled out another shiny derringer with pearl handles. He broke open the action to make sure it wasn't loaded. Then he sniffed the muzzle and tossed it on Reese's desk. It had been fired recently.

"Lucky for you yours don't smell like this one. They seem like twins. Two peas in a pod, wouldn't you say?"

Reese looked like his lunch had disagreed with him.

"Well, what if they do look a little alike? These little guns is as common as—"

Monday sat on the edge of Reese's desk.

"That won't cut it, Reese. I don't have to hold 'em side by side, do I? We can talk about this now, just you and me. Or we can wait for Nate to come back here. Which'll it be?" He used the sheriff's first name just to see its effect.

"I, uh, we wouldn't have to bother the sheriff none about this. I just found this here pistol and picked it up. I coulda bought one, but . . . ." It must be obvious Monday wasn't buying this.

"I saw Suzanne had one just like this when I was up in her room a couple weeks back," Monday lied. "I suppose anybody would have trouble telling these two pistols apart. We know the one I plunked on the desk just now was the weapon used to shoot Sandy. But the other one could have been switched for it. Come on, Reese, 'fess up. You've got Francine's little pistol, don't you? How did you come by it? And just as important, when?"

Reese gulped nervously and looked like he was planning to make up a story. At that moment, heavy boots sounded on the boards out front and Nate Boswell's black-coated form walked past the first window. He stopped in front of the second window, however, accosted by some unseen person.

"You better talk fast, Reese."

"Um, yeah. You're right," he said nervously. "I got that gun from Francine's room the night she was killed. Didn't do her any good and I figured nobody would miss it. But the fact I took her gun don't make me her killer. She was knifed in the heart, not shot. And I don't have a knife like them cowboys use."

"Now don't get a burr under your saddle about this." Monday glanced out the window, where Nate was talking with someone. "I ain't sayin' you had anything to do with her murder. I'm just trying to account for some items that came up missin' in her room. Things that shoulda been there, but weren't. What about her night's take, Reese? Don't make me dig this out of you. You wouldn't like it if it was still up in the air when Nate comes in."

"All right, all right. I took her money, too. There was twenty-eight dollars there. She wasn't gonna have no more use for it. Fricker probably woulda kept it. And if it went to the other girls, they'd only get a couple bucks apiece."

"Four dollars, Reese. They each woulda got four dollars. Well, did you put it to better use than they would?"

"Damn right. I put it back into the business, you might say. Re-invested it with Francine's friends. They each got their dollars and I got special treatment from every one of 'em. I don't normally have much money and they don't give anything away for free. Ever'body came out ahead, you might say." He acted almost smug. And since the money was all spent, Monday couldn't very well challenge him on this story. Reese would just deny it.

As Nate opened the front door, Monday managed to squeeze in one last jab at Reese.

"Yeah, everybody came out ahead, except Francine, I reckon."

Monday palmed the little derringer from the desk and as Nate hung up his hat and frock coat, he was able to slip the weapon back into the sheriff's desk drawer.

"Glad to see you, Monday," Nate said, rolling up his sleeves as he came over to his desk chair. "Has Bowen been filling you in on our temporary shortage of deputies?"

"Uh, no, I ain't, Sheriff. I figured you'd want to do that."

"Well, I had to send Deputy van Orden over to Ogallala on the train with the Hotchkiss boys. Much as we'd like to have kept them in the local lockup, the judge had an order that they're suspects in a gang that's been robbin' trains between there and Cheyenne. You recall that young lady's uncle who died after a robbery a few weeks ago?"

"Sure, Nate, I met her a couple times," Monday said. "But the Hotchkiss boys were mining near Warbonnet when that happened, getting ready to rob the assay office. How could they—"

"Word is," Nate said, "that they ran with that gang in Nebraska last fall. Judge wants to hold them in Ogallala for a few days and see if they'll talk. Anyway, I had Dutch take them this afternoon. First return train will be late tomorrow. I pulled Reese here onto dayshift. Would you consider walking rounds tonight? Reese is off tomorrow and Cal will be on day duty then."

Monday thought for a moment. He and Kate had planned to meet this evening and share anything they'd found out over supper. He'd regret not talking to Kate, but she'd been upset with him the last time they'd talked. Maybe he could speak with her over breakfast.

"Sure, Nate. Glad to help out. I'll just go over a few particulars with Reese before I start rounds. Shift starts at six, don't it?"

Nate agreed on the time. Monday stood up and unbuckled his gun belt.

"All right if I go in and see Tom for a while first?"

"That'll be fine. Deputy Bowman, why don't you wait and tell Monday about night rounds when he comes out? You can get the prisoners' suppers and have your own after six."

Reese let Monday into the back, then locked him in.

Tom Malone was standing, looking out his window, when Monday came around the empty cells.

"It's tomorrow, ain't it? They're gonna try me tomorrow and find me guilty and string me up the next day, aren't they?" Monday thought he'd come in quietly and was startled to find Tom had heard and identified him.

"Uh, no, nothin' that quick. They gotta call a few witnesses. Trial should take 'til Saturday and they don't hang nobody on a Sunday. That ain't civilized even in Texas. And we're a far cry from Texas here."

That brought Tom around from the window. He moved to the bunk and sat down. Monday thought his movements were a little unsteady.

"What's wrong, Tom?"

"Wrong? What could possibly be wrong? I was countin' on somebody bringin' in the name of Francine's real killer. If not you, then Sandy Sutter. Now he's been killed without namin' names and your face says you ain't got a name for me neither. I'm tired of this jailhouse food, but not so tired I'm ready to have 'em shovel dirt in my mouth."

Sandy Sutter! Then it was Sandy who offered to name the real killer if Tom paid him. But had Sandy really known something or had he just hoped for an easy payoff? If the court couldn't prove anything against the person he might have named, Sandy probably figured he could keep the money while he watched Tom hang.

"I see by your expression, Monday, that you hadn't figured out Sandy yet."

"No, I hadn't settled on him. But I was casting about for who might have started a stampede near Warbonnet that was meant to kill me. I had that down to Sandy or Smitty. I wanted it to be Smitty, so I could arrest him for it. Or have him draw on me. That'd be even better. But now that I think on it, Sandy had a good reason to want me out of the way. If I

223

came up with the name of the killer on my own, he'd be out his five hundred dollars."

"Well, if you're gonna come up with the name on your own, I hope you get some *in*-spiration tonight. It could affect my *res*-piration tomorrow."

Monday thought for a while. The five hundred dollars would also explain Sandy's hard ride back here to Laramie. He thought about the other two. First Smitty and then Ben had been intent on getting back to Fricker and laying first claim on Danielle's virginity. So who had Sandy been going to name? And would it have been the real killer? Maybe so. Had Francine's killer then shot Sandy before he could collect his money from Tom? The jail had been closed at that late hour. All the other suspects were in town that night—Reese, Suzanne, Smitty, even Ben. Monday had only Ben's word that he'd gotten in too late that night. Maybe Kate would get confirmation from Danielle. Tom interrupted his long silence.

"You're doin' a lot of thinkin' over there. You gettin' any place, little brother? If so, I hope you'll tell somebody a name before you get shot, too."

That sobered Monday. How had the killer known Sandy had promised Tom he could provide that name?

"Uh, I'm thinking on it. I got Miss Shaw workin' on it, too. And she's a damn sight smarter than I am. Which reminds me. I told her not to come in here and talk to you. What did you tell her? Did you tell her about me and Mary Ellen?" Monday got to his feet.

"What if I did? Wouldn't that have soured her on you and spoiled whatever plans you got to treat her like Mary Ellen? You talked to her lately? Is she still speakin' to you?"

Monday sat back down. Kate hadn't shown any revulsion toward him. All that crying in the hotel lobby was a different matter entirely.

"All right then," Tom went on. "The closest I got with her to our time in Manzanita was when she asked me why I hadn't married Cora Wallace. Damn, but don't that beat all? I didn't marry Cora and treated her like a whore. So she became one.

Then I got over that and asked another whore to marry me and I was gonna make her respectable."

"Marry her? Marry who? Were you gonna marry Francine, Tom? You didn't tell me that before."

Tom ran his hands through his hair and looked at the floor.

"I didn't want you to laugh at me. You knew how I treated Cora and you'd have thrown my plans for Francine right back in my face. It don't matter now, I guess."

"Maybe. Maybe not. When did you ask her? Did anybody else know?"

"I asked her the night she got killed. She didn't believe I was serious. Said she got a lot of proposals all the time. How'd she know I'd really do it? How'd she know I had as big a ranch as I said I did?"

"Well, I give up. How?"

"She was real proud of this readin' class some preacher was runnin' for them girls. Dared me to put it in writin'. So I did. 'I, Tom Malone, intend to marry Francine . . . .' I had to ask her last name and she told me her real name wasn't even Francine. Gertrude Fortnum. Can you imagine a woman like that bein' named Gertrude? Oh, I forgot, you never saw her. Anyway, I had to cross out Francine and write in her real name. She took it as evidence of my bona fides, but she said she'd ask some of the Circle M boys how big my spread was, how many head of cattle I had, and how many I'd sold so far."

"So you gave her this note? What become of it? There was no mention of such a note in with her things."

"I don't know. I left it with her. She said she'd ask some of our boys about the land and cattle. Promised she wouldn't mention my proposal 'til she'd confirmed how much I was worth. So I didn't tell anybody, either. I just had a few drinks after leaving her. Too many drinks. I was a mite peeved she didn't say yes right off." Tom looked at the small barred window.

"I remember walkin' the streets and singin' for some time. Then climbin' the stairs to my room at the Frontier with

Sandy. Is it important that we were gonna get hitched? I didn't tell anyone else."

"I don't know. Probably not. But Miss Shaw will know if it's important. I'll be talking with her tomorrow morning and —"

"Tomorrow morning! Couldn't you just go knock on her door now and get her started on this? I'm runnin' out of time."

Monday stood up. It was still hard talking to Tom, but at least his brother had finally said he needed Monday's help.

"Sheriff's got me working tonight. I'll see if I can contact her somehow. I'll be back in the morning, Tom."

"Well, I expect you'll see me in court, then. I understand this judge tries early and hangs early, too." Tom had a point. The judge and jury might not believe the left-handed knife story that had cleared Tom with Monday and the sheriff.

With that, Monday left. He checked his watch as Reese was handing him his gunbelt. Already six o'clock. He was on duty. Kate would have to wait.

Reese was heading out to get supper for Tom and another prisoner. Monday wrote a quick note and asked Reese to give it to some boy who could find Kate. He apologized for missing supper with her and proposed they compare notes at breakfast tomorrow morning.

After Reese left, Monday thought he should have told Kate about Tom's offer to marry Francine. He wanted to repay Kate for her telling him about Francine's gun. Oh, well, he'd tell her about that at breakfast. Provided he saw her then. He recalled Tom's warning with a shudder. Get the killer's name before Monday himself got shot.

29

Laramie

After seeing Suzanne out the side door of the Frontier, Kate considered her next move. Maybe this would be a good time to talk to Danielle.

The desk clerk acted like he didn't want to be seen talking to Kate after she'd walked Suzanne out. He was bound to report Suzanne's visit to Mrs. Crout. Kate managed to worm out of him what room Danielle was in. She headed up to Room 209.

The girl opened the door to her knock. Kate frowned in disapproval. A young woman alone, especially an attractive young woman, should never open her door without asking who was calling. Just as Kate couldn't mask her feelings, neither could Danielle hide her obvious disappointment.

"Oh, Miss Shaw. I thought you might be Ben Rollins. I mean—"

"Has this hotel sunk to allowing young men to visit ladies' rooms?" She couldn't sound too preachy on this subject. After all, hadn't she herself made a teary scene in the lobby today, then blithely invited Mary Magdalene to tea? And who was she to talk, after the events of the past few weeks? Maybe Mrs. Crout wouldn't want Kate's business after all.

"I quite understand, Miss Shaw. I'm sorry I seemed so eager to see Ben, but he's been so kind."

"May I come in for a while? I'd like to talk to you about Ben. I haven't seen him since I got back to Laramie. Is he all right? Monday Malone told me Ben had a hard ride back down here from Warbonnet. I've ridden down a few times myself. I know how grueling it can be."

Danielle showed Kate to the only chair in the small room. She sat on the edge of the bed.

"You have no idea. When he got down here, he barely stopped to see to his horses, then came straight to see me."

"But wasn't that quite late? How did he get in? He doesn't have a room here, does he?" Kate was conscious she was probably overwhelming the girl with her rapid-fire questions.

"No, he didn't have a room, and still doesn't. I have to sneak him up the back stairs. Isn't that scandalous? But what can you expect from a woman in my situation? The people of Laramie think the worst of me already, for singing in that place."

"How did he get in when he came back from Warbonnet? You couldn't have been expecting him so soon. I understand he rode like the wind."

"Ben knew my window. He just threw some pebbles at the pane to get my attention. I came to the back stairs door and let him in."

"What time was that?" Kate persisted.

"I really don't know. Neither one of us had much thought for a timepiece at that moment. But we told the sheriff it was two o'clock. I didn't want Ben to be suspected in that cowboy's death."

That wasn't exactly endorsing Ben's alibi, Kate thought.

"I won't probe any more about how long he stayed that night—"

"That's all right, Miss Shaw. He stayed all night." Kate frowned at such an open admission, but Danielle continued.

"It's what *I* wanted. He didn't propose it. I could see he was dog tired. When I pulled his boots off, he sprawled back on the bed. By the time I stood up, he was fast asleep. He didn't even get undressed or under the covers. I just lay down beside him. It's not like anything happened that night. He lay

228

there asleep and I lay there awake." She glanced down shyly after she said this.

"Ben was embarrassed the next morning to find himself in my bed. By the time he woke up, I was dressed and had been to breakfast. That's how I found out someone had been shot the night before, out at the Hog Ranch. Once we found out it was Sandy Sutter, we thought Ben needed some story to cover the whole night, so he wouldn't be under suspicion. I, I said he'd spent the night here, but I had the 'curse of Eve.' My reputation only suffered a little. Ben didn't want me to tell the sheriff that, but he had no other alibi."

The girl's forthrightness on sexual matters would have discomfited Kate before, but no longer. She looked around the room and saw the half-packed suitcase and filled trunk.

"Are you going somewhere, Danielle?" Ought she to call the girl Lynn, her true name?

"Didn't you hear? Ben gave Fricker his money and settled my debt with the hotel. I'm free. I don't have to sing at the Hog Ranch or go back there ever again. Ben said there's a westbound train for San Francisco the day after tomorrow. He said he'd buy me a ticket and send enough money with me to last until I found a singing job. He's got so much money now."

How had Ben come by that money so suddenly, Kate wondered. It would take a lot of money and the only large source of funds she was aware of would have been Tom Malone's five hundred dollars. Was Ben the one who promised to identify Francine's killer? And had he?

"You don't seem as pleased about leaving as I would have thought," Kate said.

"I'm glad to be leaving this horrible situation. But I'm not so pleased to be leaving Ben behind. I think he loves me. But he said he won't come to San Francisco with me. He rescued me from a life of sin and degradation, but says he has to go home to his parents and his ranch. I just don't know . . . . " She trailed off and stifled tears. For the first time, Kate noticed a wadded up handkerchief atop the bureau.

"While I admire Ben's good sense and breeding that prevents him from taking advantage of someone in your situation, I'm concerned about what he may have done to get that money. Do you know the source of his funds?"

"No, he wouldn't tell me, Miss Shaw. I gathered he wanted the donor to remain anonymous."

Hmmm. Well, that left out Monday Malone. He wouldn't even know the word "anonymous." But she ought to talk to Monday about this as soon as possible.

"You know, Danielle, Monday's brother Tom will be going on trial tomorrow for Francine's murder. I imagine you'll be called on to testify. But if you're not going to stay beyond the first day of the trial, is there anything else you can tell me about Francine or her admirers that might help us?"

"Oh, Miss Shaw. I'm so glad to be leaving this place. I've been so scared ever since I saw Francine murdered. I've been afraid that if I said anything about it, the killer might come after me. Ben said it was all right to keep quiet. He said he'd rather lose Tom Malone than me, but I'm just beside myself, not knowing the right thing to do."

Kate was speechless. A witness? Had Danielle held the key to the murder all along, while she and Monday had ignored her? She tried to collect her racing thoughts. This could be the break they'd been hoping for.

"How could you not tell anyone? No, wait. I mean, how did you see her killer?"

"Well, I really didn't *see* him. I mean, I was in the room that night, but it was one of my times to hide behind that screen and learn what the girls do to please their customers. That's where I was sitting. When I came up the stairs that night, Francine's door was closed, so I waited. And after a while, Tom Malone came out and went down the stairs. He left Francine's door open as a signal to the next man. I went in first."

Kate's heart sank.

"And was she lying there dead?"

"No, she was up and humming a tune as she redid her hair. I helped her straighten the bed, but she didn't tell me why she was so happy. We heard footsteps on the stairs, so I got behind the screen real quick. Mr. Fricker didn't want anyone to know I was sometimes in the room. He thought a customer might want to have two of us at once and he was adamant that I not give up what he called 'my pearl' except at great price. All the girls knew I was learning things behind the screen, but I don't think any of the men ever knew."

Kate sympathized. Danielle must have had a rough time of it. Kate wasn't sure she could have survived in such an environment. The old Kate couldn't have. Maybe she could now.

"So who was the next to come in, the killer?"

"Oh, no. Two or three men came and went before I dozed off. I sometimes peeked between the screen fabric and the frame to see what was going on, but, well, forgive me, Miss Shaw, but after you've seen dozens of men's bare backsides, you aren't much interested in a few more." She smiled gently but didn't laugh.

Kate swallowed hard. She and Danielle seemed beyond blushing now.

"So how much of the murder could you see, Danielle? Shouldn't I call you Lynn, now that you're going to go to San Francisco and start a career?"

"I don't think I want to be Lynn again until I'm well out of Laramie, Miss Shaw." She took a dry handkerchief off the dresser and unfolded it.

"I think I woke up when Francine squealed a little. The bedsprings were creaking very loudly and the man was grunting. He asked her why she made that noise. I couldn't recognize his voice. Francine said she had some news for him and he should hurry up and finish. She wanted to show him an important note.

"I heard the squeaking springs stop, the rustle of sheets, then the crinkling of paper. The man grunted again and took the paper over to the light of the wall lamp, next to the rack where everyone hung their clothes and their gunbelts. I could see just a little of him between the screen fabric and the frame.

"He crumpled up her paper and swore. I couldn't hear what he said, except for the words 'marry him,' so I turned my head to the fabric to hear better. That's when he must have gone to his gunbelt. I heard a little rasping sound, like my comb makes when I pull it out of its case. I was alarmed, but I looked around the edge of the screen and his pistol was still hanging in its holster."

"What happened then?"

"Well, I heard him say something to her. It must not have been anything like 'congratulations,' because she spat back to him 'you bastard.' Then I clearly heard him say: 'Let's get back to business. I reckon I'm gonna get my money's worth one last time.' Or something like that. After that, there was only one squeak of the springs. After that, no one said anything. That was odd. Francine and her men always had something to say when they finished. They would get dressed and she would clean herself."

Kate shuddered at what the silence might have meant.

"Then the man got off the bed. I could tell by the way the springs squeaked. He walked over to the clothes rack again, but he didn't get dressed right away. He pulled out one of the loose nails—I saw his hand—and walked back to the bed. In a minute or so, I heard the springs squeak again. I thought it was Francine getting up this time, but I wondered why no one spoke. Then the man came over to the clothes hooks and I heard him getting dressed. I stayed back and quiet, so he wouldn't see me. I didn't know anything was wrong then. I just didn't want anyone to know I was behind the screen. He buckled on his gunbelt, took his hat, and left."

"Could you tell if he was right-handed? Tom Malone is left-handed. When this man hung up his pistol belt, could you see his holster? Was it on the right side?"

Danielle thought for a moment.

"Yes, it was. I recall now. But I couldn't identify either the man or his gunbelt. I crept out and intended to ask Francine about who she was going to marry, but then I saw the knife in her breast and her eyes wide open and staring at the ceiling and, and I screamed. I couldn't help myself. I don't know how I didn't faint. I just knew I had to get out of that room."

So that was the scream that Suzanne and the men downstairs had heard. How was it that no one saw her?

"Did you leave by the outside stairs?"

"Yes. And I ran all the way back to town. It was dark and all and I was sure I was being chased by whoever killed Francine. I ran and fell down, and ran on again. By the time I got back to the hotel, I couldn't talk, let alone scream any more."

Kate couldn't think of another question to ask the girl. If she couldn't recognize the killer, why had she kept silent all this time? But she knew the answer to that. The killer might not believe she couldn't recognize him. Him. This appeared to rule out Suzanne. But it meant that Ben, Sandy, Smitty, or Reese Bowman still could have done it. And who was Francine going to marry?

"Is there anything else you can tell me, anything at all odd that you noticed afterwards that might help Monday and me identify the killer?"

After a moment, she said, "For a week after the murder, Reese Bowman had more money to spend. He was always hanging around and each girl would see him once a week as a kind of bribe to keep the law handy if any of their customers got rough with them. After the killing, though, Reese had enough to pay for a lot of time with each girl."

Too much information, Kate thought. What a horrible journey this girl had had to make to womanhood.

# # #

After getting a glass of water in the dining room and fanning herself a little to cool down, Kate went to the lobby. That's when she read the note Monday sent saying he wanted to meet her over breakfast and share what they'd learned. She went to the jail, but Monday was out walking his evening rounds.

Sheriff Boswell himself let Kate back into the cells. She was surprised that he would do so, given what Reese had said about Nate's prohibition before her first visit. When she asked why the about-face, the sheriff told her Monday had said it was all right for her to talk to the prisoner now. It was Monday's change of heart, the sheriff said, not his own. From his gruff manner, Kate thought the sheriff wouldn't have lifted the ban.

Kate waited while Reese brought in supper for Tom and another prisoner. She sat on the stool outside Tom's cell while he ate. He didn't seem to be enjoying it.

"If they find me guilty, I'm gonna ask for a big steak and a couple beers for my last meal." He grinned weakly at her. There wasn't a hint of humor in his eyes.

"I've just come from talking with Danielle. She knows, but I don't think anyone else does, that someone was going to marry Francine. Was it you? Did you give her a note to that effect? I know you visited her the evening she died." He looked up from his meal.

"Yes, I proposed to her. But she also wanted a note from me. To get it in writing, she said. She knew two other girls in New Orleans who'd had similar promises and then the men backed out. She said if I gave her a note, she'd say yes the next night, provided some of my hands vouched for the size of my spread and the number of cattle I still owned after the two drives this summer. So I wrote it out and left it with her. She read it out loud. Acted proud of her readin' lessons."

So that was how there came to be a note. Since it hadn't turned up, it was fair to assume the killer had taken it. That ought to make jealousy the likeliest motive. But if an admirer had been jealous of Tom, why hadn't he killed him instead? Why kill Francine? And why make it look like Tom had done it? That must have taken some quick planning and a crafty meanness. Monday would immediately suspect Smitty, but couldn't . . . ? Tom shook her out of her thoughts.

"Will I see you at the trial tomorrow, Miss Shaw?"

"Yes, certainly. I hope your brother or I can shed some light on the likely killer by then. If we don't show up at the start, it may mean we're working on something. Or one of us may come, but not the other. Can you tell me anything else that may help? Was Ben Rollins the one who offered to name the killer for five hundred dollars? Did he? And did you pay him?"

"Ben? No. It wasn't him. It was Sandy Sutter who offered me that deal. And now that he got himself killed without giving me the name, you and my kid brother are my only hope."

Then how did Ben get the money to pay off Fricker?

"Did you loan Ben some money so he could pay Fricker and rescue Danielle? That was a far, far better thing to do, Sidney Carton, considering your circumstances."

Tom paused with a fork halfway to his mouth.

"Huh? Who? Not me. He never asked me for any money. Ben did pay me a visit yesterday, though. Said he was sorry I was still in here. Read me a letter from his folks saying they had faith in me." He finished that bite, but paused before taking another.

"Nope, Smitty was gonna put all the rest of that money in the bank here today, since he paid off the hands this morning. If I leave here in a pine box, the bank has instructions to turn that cash into a draft so he can carry it back to Texas. I told him to give a couple hundred to Monday and give the rest to the hands. Cora will get the ranch."

"Cora? I thought—"

"I know what you think of the way I treated her. Fact is, I never changed the will Pa had me make out back in '66, when it looked like I was gonna marry her. He had me and Monday make out wills when he did his own. If anything happened to Monday, he was gonna split his share between me and Mary Ellen. I named Cora in my will. Never changed it. Too lazy, I guess. Funny how things work out. I wasn't too kind to her in life. Maybe in death, she'll forgive me for that."

Kate was barely listening. She fished her watch out of her handbag. The bank would close in five minutes. She wanted to get her wired money put safely away, since she hadn't had to give any of it to Schonbrun or Danielle.

"I've got to go to the bank myself before it closes. Monday and I will see you tomorrow. Have faith. What you just told me about providing for Cora shows you really are a better per-

235

son than you think you are. And Monday is better than you think he is. We'll figure something out."

I hope we will, she thought. I really do hope.

# # #

Kate practically ran to the bank and arrived just as the manager was locking the door. She shamelessly used her wiles to get him to reopen and waited patiently while he wrote her a receipt and a draft, so she could redeposit the money in War-bonnet.

She asked the manager if he'd be glad to have a quiet day after so many cowboys had been paid off and the big Circle M cattle drive funds had been put away.

He looked at her and raised an eyebrow.

"Cowboys don't put their money in banks, Miss. They generally blow what they've got as soon as they get it. There won't be a town as big as Laramie between here and Kansas on their return trip to Texas. And I don't know anything about any draft of Circle M funds. No one deposited any Circle M money here today."

As he showed her to the door, Kate wondered what that meant. Had Smitty just been slow in depositing the funds? He had instructions from Tom. He couldn't be planning to carry all that money back to Texas as cash, could he? Maybe it would be easier to pay off Ben and the other hands, as Tom had said, if he still had cash with him. He probably anticipated ranch funds would be tied up until Tom's will went into effect. He had no faith in Monday or in her.

Stop that, she told herself sternly. If she got to assuming Tom would be hanged, she'd run out of ideas that might save him.

30

Laramie

Monday paid attention to little details as he walked his rounds. This was a much bigger town to look after. Twelve saloons in Laramie, not including the Hog Ranch outside of town. It took him more than an hour to drop in at all twelve. He didn't dare have a beer at any of them, like he did sometimes back in the Alamo in Warbonnet. He wasn't sure of Nate's rules about an occasional beer on the job.

He figured between the ride out to the Hog Ranch, the time spent there, and the ride back, he'd be starting saloon rounds about every hour and a half. He wondered how Reese did it. If he spent too much time at the Hog Ranch, he wouldn't be able to "show the badge" in each of the saloons more than two or three times in a night.

The Hog Ranch was quiet the first time he checked. No gunplay at any of the saloons. On his second visit, the Hog Ranch was much livelier.

There were four card games going and Monday couldn't see the balcony at the back for the thick haze of smoke. In fact, he had trouble even seeing the bar when he began strolling among the tables. Small stakes. No big winners. Except at one table.

Smitty was playing with three other hands from the Circle M and one Monday recognized from Ben Rollins' folks' spread, the Rocking R. The foreman had just raked in a substantial-looking pot. High stakes for cowboys, Monday thought, even if they had just been paid off for their drive to Warbonnet.

The Rocking R hand finished his drink and announced this game was too rich for his blood. When he left, the three Circle M hands looked up anxiously at Monday. Maybe they didn't want to be in this game, either. Monday sat down in the empty chair.

"Deal you in, runt?" Smitty asked. "Ain't you on duty?"

"Nothin' wrong with my sittin' in for a couple hands in a nice, friendly little game while I listen for any trouble. And this is a nice, friendly game, ain't it?" They were playing five-card stud. Monday tried to remember everything the Major and Old Jesus had taught him about the fall of cards and filling straights. He anteed up and looked at his two hole cards. A seven of hearts and a king of diamonds. No one opened and Smitty dealt everyone their first up card. Three of spades for Monday. He remained expressionless. Smitty got a jack and put in two bits. Everyone called and waited for their next up cards.

Monday got a seven of diamonds this time. Smitty got one of Monday's kings. The foreman's jack and king were two powerful up cards. One cowboy folded, but Monday and the other two called Smitty's fifty cents. The last up cards dealt gave Monday the ace of clubs. Smitty got a nine and one of the other cowboys got an ace, too. Smitty didn't seem pleased at that, but he might have a straight if he had a queen and a ten down. Monday knew how hard it was to fill a double inside straight.

Monday bet a dollar. One cowboy folded, but the one with the ace called. Smitty put in a dollar and raised a dollar. The other cowboy evidently didn't have a second ace and folded. Monday called and showed his pair of sevens. Smitty threw in a queen and a six to go with his king, jack, and nine. He'd narrowly missed bluffing a straight and wasn't pleased.

Monday collected his winnings while one cowboy sitting to Smitty's left, name of Bridges, took out a plug of tobacco. When he reached for the knife on Smitty's left hip, the foreman knocked his hand away. Monday recalled Smitty had always been reluctant to loan out his equipment. He'd seen Smitty knock Sandy down over at the bar once for borrowing his knife without permission.

"Use your own," Smitty growled, and gathered his winnings.

"Ain't bought one," said Bridges. Monday drew his knife and slid it across.

"Much obliged," said the cowboy, acknowledging Monday's help.

Smitty got up in disgust.

"I'll be back. Gonna spend some of this upstairs. Air's better up there," he said, looking pointedly at Monday. He moved off and collected a bottle of whiskey at the bar. Monday lost track of him in the smoke near the balcony stairs.

"You boys look like you could use a little relief, too. Smitty make you sit in on this game?" He shuffled the deck, but no one looked interested in cards.

Bridges, the older cowboy, broke the awkward silence.

"Smitty always tells us to play when he's feelin' lucky. None of us are much good at cards. And you don't say no to Smitty."

"Were you playing with Smitty the night Sandy Sutter was shot out back?"

They looked at each other. The youngest cowboy spoke up.

"Well, yeah, I was. A couple of us left Warbonnet before Sandy and Smitty and got in before them two arrived. Sandy come by my table and said he had this note from that little Miss Danielle that she was gonna meet him out back in about ten minutes. He kissed it and put it in his vest pocket."

"What did Smitty think of that? I understand he wanted first night with Danielle for himself."

"Um," said the cowboy. "He wasn't actually sittin' with me at the time. He went to get more whiskey and I saw Sandy talkin' to him on his way over to our table."

"Did Smitty come back while Sandy was here?"

"Nah. I don't know where he went. At any rate, he moved away into the smoke and I lost track of him."

"But you saw him later, after you found Sandy's body. Wasn't Smitty with you then?"

"That's so. He come out behind us right after we poured out the door. He hadn't been out back. Didn't come up from the outhouses."

Hmmm, Monday thought. He'd have to go out back and look at things himself.

Monday excused himself and headed for the back door. He stepped out and took a breath of less smoky air. His relief was tempered somewhat by the closeness of the three out-houses. He pulled the back door toward him so some light would spill out here. There were railings on both sides of the two steps. The door bumped against one rail. Monday looked behind the door. There was room enough for someone to stand there if you wanted to ambush somebody.

From here, Monday couldn't see the outside stairs that came down from the second floor, so he let the door close and walked around the corner of the building. The outside stairs showed pale in the moonlight. No one could have seen Sandy at the back door from the landing at the top of the stairs, or even from the foot of the stairs. Was that important? Smitty didn't come that way, but Suzanne could still be a suspect. Something more to think about tonight on his rounds. He went back through the building to the front and collected his horse.

# # #

About an hour into his next round of saloon visits, Monday had two more saloons to check. As he crossed the street to the Alhambra, he saw a lantern farther down the street, near the last saloon, go out. Was it out of oil, he wondered?

Ten minutes later, Monday found out. He walked from the Alhambra toward his last stop and noted that a light from a second story across the way illuminated the end of the next alley he was set to cross. The lantern he'd seen go out hung at the mouth of that alley. He paused, reached up for the lantern, and shook it gently. Still had oil in it, but the wick had been turned too low.

What would Sam Taggart do in a situation like this, he asked himself.

Monday drew his pistol and cocked it, but kept it next to his right leg, so it wouldn't show in silhouette. He took two steps down from the boards to the alley, two steps forward, then leaped back suddenly.

A gunshot split the night and a tongue of flame lit the alley for an instant. A bullet whizzed past Monday at chest level. He fired from the hip up the alley but heard his round strike wood somewhere. He crouched at the corner and cocked his pistol again. When he looked up the dark alley, he couldn't see anything. But he could hear hoofbeats. Someone was riding behind the building, heading back in the direction Monday had come from. Back in the direction of the Hog Ranch, too. Monday cursed and ran up the street, heading for where he'd left his horse.

Customers came out of the Alhambra to see what was going on. The two shots would be sure to rouse Nate Boswell and probably Cal and Reese, too. Monday spotted a man he'd talked with in the Alhambra and asked him to tell Nate he'd traded shots with someone and was headed out to the Hog Ranch.

Monday had to take a roundabout way in order to avoid being ambushed on the dark road. When he reached the Hog Ranch, he carefully checked each horse at the rail for any that might be breathing hard. None of them were.

Inside the building, it was as smoky as ever. No one here could have heard any shots from town. Smitty was playing poker with the same three Circle M hands. Monday went directly to his table. Not a very big pile in front of Smitty this time.

"You been in that chair long, Smitty?" Monday asked.

"Long enough. Ain't I, boys?"

The other three looked terrified as they nodded their heads. He wasn't going to get anything from them.

"Then you won't mind hoisting out your cannon for me, will you?" Monday asked, drawing his own gun and moving to where he could see Smitty's right hand.

Smitty sneered and stood up. He slowly undid his hammer loop and took out the pistol, handing it to Monday.

"Go ahead and check it. Won't do you no good."

Monday sniffed it. It hadn't been fired.

"How'd you know what I wanted it for," he asked, handing it back.

"Just guessing. It's like playing poker. You get good at it if you stick with it. You want to try any other guesses tonight, Deputy?"

This was going nowhere. Smitty could have a second gun, a hideout gun like Reese. And Monday could search the dark woods out back all night without finding someone's winded horse. He holstered his pistol and resumed his rounds. His schedule was no secret and anyone could have left the Hog Ranch to set an ambush for him. He'd have to be much more careful when he headed back to town for his last rounds.

Last rounds. That sounded so final. He just wanted to survive this night shift and get some sleep, but he needed to see Kate first thing in the morning.

31

Laramie

Monday paused at the entrance to the Frontier dining room and watched Kate Shaw sitting at a table by the window. She didn't see him and was intent on writing something. Monday looked forward to moments like these, when he could watch Kate without being seen. He loved to see her do little things like she was doing now, twisting a lock of hair around a finger while she concentrated, sip from a little teacup, even frown and root through her handbag. Looked like she'd had a good night's sleep. She pulled out her little watch, looked at it and sighed, then looked out the window toward Front Street.

Her hair was haloed by the morning sun. She hadn't put it up in a bun and it shone like it was freshly washed and brushed. Although Monday had faced plenty of danger, he was glad this had been a safe investigation for her so far. Not like last summer, when she'd almost been killed. No matter how many moments he enjoyed watching Kate like this, he'd always remember what she looked like last August—wounded, disheveled, dusty, tear-streaked, and riding a stolen horse, trying to save his life.

A waitress bringing Kate fresh tea looked up and spotted Monday yawning in the doorway. Her look caught Kate's attention. She turned, saw him, and stood up.

"Thank God you're all right," Kate said as Monday walked to her table. He'd never seen her look so relieved. "I heard those shots last night. The sheriff told me a little while ago that you'd been ambushed while making your rounds."

Monday was pleased to see Kate had worried about him. He took her hand awkwardly for a moment before releasing it.

"Yeah, I'm all right. But I didn't catch whoever did it. I think he—or she—went back to the Hog Ranch, but I couldn't find any hard-breathin' horses there. I checked out Smitty's pistol, but it hadn't been fired. It's just like this damned investigation. 'Scuse me. I keep thinkin' I'm getting close to the truth, but it's always out there someplace just beyond my reach."

"I hope that doesn't mean you're thinking of giving up. Your brother's trial starts in a short while. They won't call us to give evidence, but I mean to drag Danielle over there. I'll tell you why in a minute. I know you'd like to be in court. I mean, I'd think you'd want to be there."

"Miss Kate, there's likely to be lots of disturbing things shown and said. I don't think you ought to—"

"I know all about the manner of Francine's death and a lot more about what goes on in that establishment than you give me credit for. This is Wyoming and it's 1871, for heaven's sake, not the Dark Ages. You don't have to worry about every little thing that might distress me. Be more concerned for your own safety. That's what scares me most right now. If someone tried to kill you, then someone must think you're close to figuring out who really killed Francine."

"Hmmph. I can't see that I'm all that close. Maybe you are. I have faith in your mind, Kate. You see things before I do. You got a head for details that are out of place, things that don't make sense. If we figure this out, it'll be because you didn't listen to me when I accused you of wanting to interfere. I'm glad you don't listen to me sometimes."

Their eyes locked across the table. He couldn't tell what she was thinking, but her eyes softened and the corners of her mouth trembled.

The spell was broken by the waitress returning with coffee for him and, without his asking, his usual breakfast at the hotel: ham, eggs, and biscuits.

"Anyway," Monday went on. "What I was trying to say is I've been running all I learned through my head and I can't see a trail that leads us to the killer. If we're gonna solve this before Tom hangs, it'll be you that does it again, just like last year. I'm fresh out of miracles."

While he ate, Kate rearranged between them some torn open envelopes she'd been studying. She was writing notes on the back of her mail, Monday noted. There, that was one detail that hadn't escaped him. And she had four envelopes. A lot of mail. No wonder she seemed so happy this morning.

"I've tried to write down what we know about each of the suspects on the back of an envelope. I didn't have a fifth envelope to use for Sandy Sutter, but since he's dead, maybe we can just keep track of him in our heads."

"That's good. Looks like a system," Monday said, around a bit of biscuit he had dipped in egg yolk. "Want to tackle Sandy first, then?" Without waiting for Kate's reply, he put a forkful of ham and egg into his mouth.

"All right. We can start with Sandy. We know he, um, patronized Francine quite a bit. Two people have told me they thought he was in love with her. Sandy took Tom back to his hotel room that night when Tom was too drunk to get there himself." She paused for breath and consulted her notes.

"Did your brother tell you he left a note with Francine saying he wanted to marry her? Tom might have told Sandy he was going to marry Francine. Sandy had access to Tom's knife when he put him to bed. And didn't you tell me Sandy and Smitty were the two you suspected of trying to kill you with that cattle stampede?"

Whew, that was a lot. Kate certainly was well set up, Monday thought. He motioned Kate to wait while he washed a bite of breakfast down with the last of his coffee.

"All that's right, Kate. But there's two more things to add to that list. Tom told me Sandy was the one who offered to tell him who really killed Francine. And if Sandy was in love with Francine himself, why did he react like a kid at Christmas to a note saying Danielle would meet him out back the night he was killed?"

"A note nobody else saw," Kate reminded him. "Tom Malone also left a note with Francine, Danielle told me. So far as we know, nobody saw it but Tom, Francine, and the killer. That note hasn't turned up either—and probably won't. I can't see the killer keeping those around. Oh, wait. There was a third note in this case, but that hasn't disappeared." She dug in her bag for a moment and brought out a small slip of paper, which she unfolded and handed to Monday.

The waitress poured him more coffee.

"'To Francine. A.S.'," he read aloud. "You reckon this is from Sandy? Who did he send it to? And how did you get it?" He watched Kate bring her cup to her lips. She wasn't quick enough to cover the faint flush that spread up her cheeks. She looked down at her plate, not at him.

"I think that note was meant for Francine. It was folded in some, uh, garments that were somehow placed inside that parcel you brought me from Laramie. I found out those items came from the Hog Ranch. They were Francine's. Suzanne told me she put them in my parcel."

Monday sprayed hot coffee onto the tablecloth and his plate.

"*Suzanne?* She told you that? When was this?" Oh, Lord. He hadn't wanted Kate to know anything about the Hog Ranch, but if she talked to Suzanne soon after he . . . . Lordy. He wiped up the mess with his napkin and sneaked a look at Kate. She had a knowing smile on her lips this time.

"Oh, just after I came down here to meet Thomas Moran and take the train to join the Hayden expedition. Suzanne only talked to me about Francine. We didn't speak of any other matters."

Monday let out the breath he'd been holding.

"She said those garments were given to Francine by some unknown admirer the week she was killed. Suzanne said nothing of Francine's would fit her, so she hadn't opened them after the murder. She said she sent them to embarrass me. I don't know why. I can't think how she'd know I even existed— or how she could get access to that parcel you picked up for me." Kate turned her eyes to her plate and the last of her breakfast. Monday reached for his coffee cup and his shaking hand spilled some of it over his saucer and onto the table.

"My," Kate said, sipping her tea. "You're awfully nervous this morning, Marshal. Perhaps you should drink a little less coffee, if it makes you jittery like this."

"Let's forget about my breakfast," Monday said, throwing in his napkin. "Let's get back to Sandy. So you think he gave Francine that stuff and sent the note? If those garments you mentioned were frilly underwear, that kinda stuff was available in Abilene and some of the other cow towns the Circle M outfit passed through. Sandy or any of the other boys coulda picked 'em up." He was pleased to see her grin disappear.

"I focused on Sandy originally because of the jealousy motive," Kate said.

"I'm satisfied that the items came from Sandy," she went on. "Now that we know Sandy was hoping to get that money from Tom, I'm really confused. Ben Rollins paid off Danielle's debt with Fricker. I thought Ben must have been the one, but Tom said he didn't give him that money."

"No, he didn't, Miss Kate. I gave Ben what he needed to pay off Fricker. I took some money out of the bank in War-bonnet and meant to give it to him down here. But when he wanted to go hell for leather down here chasing Sandy and Smitty, I passed it to him up on the trail. I figured if he had enough cash to get her off the hook, maybe he'd leave the other kind of ammunition in his pistol belt. I don't know if he did, though. What did you find out from Danielle about his alibi for the night Sandy was killed?"

"That's a little complicated," Kate said. "Neither Danielle nor Ben knew what time it was when he put up his horses at Dillon's livery and came to her hotel. He spent the night with her, but she says he did nothing but sleep. She was willing to risk her reputation for him because she loves him. I believe her. It was hard for her to put forward a reason why they didn't have relations that night. But it's an excuse a woman would understand. You'll forgive me if I don't elaborate."

Monday shrugged.

"I trust your judgment, Kate. If you tell me something is true, then it must be so. But before we get too far along Ben's trail, tell me what you found out from Danielle about Francine. Did she know anything else that could help us?"

Kate consulted the back of one envelope for a moment.

"Yes, she did. I should have told you about this first thing. Danielle saw the whole thing. She was in the room at the time of the murder. That's why I want her to talk to the judge. She knows that a man did it, not a woman. That takes Suzanne off the hook."

"*What?* How could she have been in that room when the killer knifed Francine? He'd have killed her too."

"No, he didn't see her. And she really didn't get a look at him, either. She was hiding behind that screen in the corner. Fricker made her observe what the girls did with their men from time to time, sort of a training experience for her. You remember how you told me the chair in Francine's room was found behind the screen?"

"Yes, and I recall Dutch telling me the chair was knocked over. I guess that would explain. . . . But how did she keep quiet? Why didn't the killer hear her? How could she not see him?"

Kate quickly related how Danielle hadn't been aware there'd been a murder, how she'd heard the killer take Francine's note to better light, and how she'd heard the scraping sound as he returned to the bed.

"I think she heard the killer take his knife out of its sheath. I didn't dare suggest that to Danielle. She's nearly frightened to death already. She wants to take tomorrow's westbound train out of here. No one knows what she heard and there are no plans to call her to court. But I think we ought to arrange that with the judge. She also knows the killer was right-handed." Kate went on to tell Monday about the right-handed gunbelt Danielle had seen. And how the killer had returned to the clothes pegs and taken a nail out of the clothes rack for some reason before returning to Francine's bed.

"So let me get this straight," Monday said. He was having trouble keeping up with Kate's mind. As usual. "Danielle didn't see the killer, but could tell from the gunbelt and grunts and groans that it was a man. That clears Suzanne and just leaves us with Sandy, Smitty, Reese, or Ben himself." He was ticking suspects off on his fingers. "But Reese didn't have a knife like we cowboys carried."

"If it were Ben, I can't believe she wouldn't have recognized his voice, even the few snatches she did hear. He told us he was saving his money to help Danielle at that point, so why would he spend two dollars on Francine? Besides, if Danielle had any idea Ben had done it, why would she have told me what she knew?"

"All right, then, Kate, let's look at Smitty. He used Francine, too. Liked her a lot, I understand, and spent more time and money on her than on any of the other girls. He was at the Hog Ranch when Francine and Sandy were killed. Plenty of men saw him before Sandy went out and was shot. I checked that back door. He must've been with the first men who responded to the shot. The next group was hot on their heels."

"Kate, doesn't that point to Suzanne? Maybe she really did kill Sandy that night, coming down the outside stairs. If she did unwrap that parcel of underwear and saw Sandy's initials and thought he'd killed Francine because she was gonna marry Tom—"

"But we don't know if Suzanne knew about Tom's proposal or his note. I'll admit Suzanne's story about her missing derringer is just a little too convenient. What if Suzanne was lying about how she got the gun? What if Sandy knifed Francine and gave that derringer to Suzanne and she later killed him with it? Oh, God. I don't want to be thinking like this. That would be so tragic, so . . . so Romeo and Juliet."

"Huh? I don't know nothing about any Ramon and Julia. But I do know where Francine's derringer went. There were two of them little guns. Reese Bowman stole Francine's after he found her body. He also took the girl's money for that night. Said he blew it on the other girls the next week. He's still got the gun. He showed it to me."

"Then it actually was Suzanne's derringer that killed Sandy," said Kate. "Sandy must have been bluffing about naming the real killer. I wonder when Suzanne found out he'd done it himself. Oh, the ironies in this case."

She must have been able to read the puzzlement on his face.

"Oh, I'm sorry to speak so like a schoolmarm. Do you know what irony is? I'll show you some more." She turned over envelopes until she found the right one.

"You don't have to use hard words to make me think you're smarter than me, Kate. Uh, is this irony something to do with blacksmithing? Horseshoes?"

She grinned at him as she found what she was looking for.

"No, it just means an amusing or bittersweet coincidence. Here, listen to this. I got Zack Hibben's second letter yesterday after I left the bank. Remember how he told us Cora got married last spring? Well, here's irony at work again. She married an A.S., too. Take a look at his name." She pointed to one line.

Monday read, with difficulty, "All-oy-see-us. Schmidt . . ." He squinted. "Mister. Or meester."

"The first name is pronounced Alo-wish-us. And I'm no expert on German names, but I think the last name would be pronounced Schmidt-myster. I'm happy for Cora, but you'd think anybody with a name like that would have had to change it just to survive. I mean, tough men and bullies would have—Monday, what's wrong?"

"*Damnation!*" Monday pounded the table with his fist. Kate's empty cup jumped off the saucer with a clatter. Everyone in the dining room looked in their direction.

"Of course! Now I see it. What a *fool* I've been!" He grabbed his hat and stood up. "Come on. Get your envelopes and let's get over to that courtroom."

32

Laramie

Kate hated being dragged down the street by the left hand like
she was a child. Monday was half running and she was having
to run to keep up. Her right hand was holding her hat on her
head and the reticule hanging from that wrist kept bouncing
against her face. The stitches in her left shoulder hurt. She
should have had a free hand to gather up her skirts. At any
moment, she would stumble and fall—

Monday stopped short.

"Bridges," he panted to an older man who was just coming
up the street. "We're running a little late. Whew. Can you tell
us . . . what's happening down there?"

"Well," the cowboy said, staring unabashedly at Kate's disarranged hair and the ruffle of petticoat that showed at her
ankles. "First, they called the deputy who found Francine's
body. Then they called the doctor. I didn't rightly follow what
he said about her being stabbed twice. Then they started calling some of us to testify about Tom and Francine. They even
wanted to call Sandy to say what he told us about taking Tom
up to his room. Course, Sandy can't talk so good any more.
Hope he plays the harp better than he did the harmonica." He
grinned.

"What about Smitty? Was he there? Did he testify, too?"

"No, they didn't seem to mind that he wasn't there. Ben
Rollins was there, though. Told me he'd seen Smitty's horse

being led out of the barn by one of the stable boys this morning."

"Stay here, Kate!" Monday growled, dropped her hand, and took off at a dead run for Dillon's.

Kate wasn't about to be left behind at this point. She nodded to Bridges, gathered her skirts in one hand, held onto her hat, and ran after him as best she could.

Up ahead, she saw that Monday didn't slow down until he neared the stable. He was breathing hard as he bent to tie down his holster with the leg thong. Then he released the thumb loop and drew his pistol. He checked the loads and caps on his pistol, turning the cylinder to rest on the empty chamber. He holstered his weapon, but didn't put the loop back over the hammer.

"I told you to stay there, Kate. This may be dangerous." He spoke in short sentences, still catching his breath.

"You always want me to stay . . . out of the way . . . when you face danger." Kate could only speak when she exhaled. "Maybe you'll need a witness. What's this all about?"

"This may be hard on you, Kate," Monday said, his breathing coming easier. "But just this once, for God's sake, let me do the talkin'. I don't want you to get ahead of where I'm going until I get there."

They rounded the corner of the barn and saw Smitty buckling saddlebags onto his horse.

Monday stopped Kate with his left hand and walked a few paces closer. Kate stood by the tailgate of a little wagon. A horse that was hitched to the far end turned to look at her.

"Going somewhere, Aloysius?" Monday's voice betrayed none of his breathlessness now.

Smitty slowly turned from the left side of his horse. Kate and Monday could see his holster and gun hand.

"Leaving mighty early, aren't you?" Monday went on. "You think the trial, the verdict's a, um . . . ."

"Foregone conclusion?" supplied Kate.

"A sure thing? Well, do you, Smitty? There's only one reason I can think of that you'd be certain Tom would be found guilty and hang. And that's if you killed Francine and you're sure you set up things to put the noose around his neck."

"Mighty big talk when you're hidin' behind a badge," the big man snorted. "And a skirt," he said, looking past Monday to Kate. "You got nothing on me. But I've got something I'd like to have on her, if she'd just go back out to the Hog Ranch." He sneered at Kate.

"Damn it! I'll kill you for that!"

"Monday, don't provoke him!"

"Kate, stay outta this!"

"Better listen to her, you scrawny bastard. I had nothin' to do with the trouble your brother's got himself into."

"Oh, yeah? And it's just one of Miss Kate's coincidences that you married Cora Wallace last spring, huh?"

"Who says I done any such thing?"

"Zack Hibben found out about the marriage. And when I heard your last name, all the pieces of the puzzle fell right into place. You remember how you gave me my first split lip and black eye? Me and some of the hands teased you about your 'Schmidt-something' name when my Pa hired you to replace Jim Squires as foreman. When Kate showed me that Aloysius name, everything made sense. We never knew your stupid first name. No wonder you kept it a secret."

"All right, so what if I did marry Cora? She's a proven per-former in her line of work now. And I like my women . . . ." He stripped Kate with his eyes. "Experienced."

She saw Monday was controlling himself with difficulty, flexing his gun hand.

"I don't know much about Texas law, Smitty. But I recall when Pa had us fill out wills before, before Mary Ellen . . . . Anyway, a long time ago. Seems that if a man wants to leave his property to his wife, he don't have to name her in his will—"

"But if he does name someone who's not his wife and she later marries someone else," Kate filled in.

"Then that woman still inherits," Monday said, with obvi-ous exasperation.

"Unless Tom got married," Kate gasped. She couldn't help herself. Now she could see the motive clearly, too. If Tom had married Francine, Smitty would have lost the ranch that Cora would inherit from Tom's will.

Monday went on. "You probably planned to kill him on the way back to Texas or on the trail to Warbonnet. Make a stampede look like an accident. When Francine showed you the note that said Tom wanted to marry her, you had to move fast, before he acted on his pledge. But you couldn't just kill her, could you?"

"Not until I finished what we were right in the middle of," Smitty leered at Kate again. "But you can't prove nothing. You ain't got the note."

"Nothing? I, uh, *we* can prove motive now. You killed Francine and planted a knife you made to look like Tom's. We have a witness who'll testify to the killer marking the murder weapon. Then when Sandy found you had Tom's real knife and was gonna expose you by telling Tom, you killed him with the derringer you took from Suzanne the night you rode back here."

"And how'd I do that? Nobody saw me take her pistol or shoot Sandy."

"You wrote that note to him about Danielle. Then you left and waited behind the back door. It opens outward. When Sandy came out, you shot him in the back. You just had time to drop Suzanne's gun and take the note from his vest pocket. Then you stepped back behind the door before the first men came rushing out and found the body. You stepped up right behind them. That's why they thought you ran out there with them."

"And why would I shoot Sandy? We rode together."

"Since he saw you had Tom's knife, Sandy was gonna tell Tom who the real killer was. He hadn't done it yet. Tom had no reason not to trust you, so he told you Sandy planned to give him the name for five hundred dollars. On the drive to Warbonnet, Sandy thought maybe I'd figure out the killer and give the name to the sheriff, so he tried to kill me by starting that stampede. When I turned up alive, he jumped the gun

254

and left early to ride back to Laramie. He wanted to get to Tom before I could, but the jail must've been closed when he got here. Ben and I thought you took off to get to Danielle first, but you knew you had to kill Sandy. Too bad I didn't see it at the time."

Smitty slowly reached down and took the hammer loop off his pistol, then stepped away from his horse. He wasn't smiling or sneering now.

"You got no proof of any of that."

"Maybe not to pin Sandy's murder on you, but I've got proof about Francine—and about the shot you took at me last night. You won't scare any of those hands we were playing poker with, once you're in jail."

"On what charge? Even I know you gotta have some call to haul me in."

"How about theft? Kate told me you didn't deposit Tom's money in the bank. You got one of those saddlebags stuffed with cash? Planning to head out before the hanging and take the news to Texas? As Cora's husband, you'll take over the ranch she gets. What you got planned for her, you snake? How long you gonna let her live?"

"Until I get tired of her. I've heard about enough of your suspicions. You got nothing on me but wild ideas. All right, Malone, let's settle this."

"Monday, don't. You can't—"

"Be quiet, Kate! I know you mean well, but don't say what you're thinking. Let me handle this. Stay back!"

She was hurt by his harsh tone, but considered. She'd been about to say he couldn't kill Smitty or they could never prove a case and Tom would still hang. To her horror, she realized if she'd completed the sentence, Smitty would figure Monday couldn't shoot him. He would draw his weapon and either he'd kill Monday or Monday would be forced to kill him. She kept quiet. But Monday's ordering her about still rankled. She was stunned by the level of his anger at this man; it was as if he couldn't focus on anything but his hate.

255

Quicker than she could blink, Monday drew and cocked his pistol. Smitty looked startled. He'd only touched the butt of his own gun. He slowly took his hand away from it. "Let's settle this a different way, Aloysius. How 'bout you unbuckle that gun belt with your left hand and toss the whole rig over here? Wouldn't you rather talk about this without all that iron, the way you used to handle me?"

Smitty sneered. He slowly unbuckled his belt and tossed the whole thing underhand to land at Monday's feet. Monday picked it up in his left hand and held it out beside him.

"Kate," was all he said.

When she came forward and took the heavy belt from him, with its holstered pistol and sheathed knife, he asked her to go put them in the little wagon.

She did as he asked, but he had another request.

"Take out his knife, Kate, and tell me what you see on the handle."

As she drew it out, Monday continued. "From what you told me about everything Danielle saw and heard, I figure Smitty here read that note, then pulled out his own knife. I reckon he went back to, uh, finish his time with Francine. Then he must have stabbed her in the heart. You said Danielle never heard a sound out of her.

"Smitty must have figured he could pin this on Tom. So he went to the clothes rack and took out that loose nail Danielle mentioned. He must've scratched Tom's initials on the handle and put the knife back in Francine. That explains the two wounds Doc noticed. Smitty never put his initials on his own knife like most of us did after we bought them. But, being right-handed, he scratched the T. M. into the wrong side. After the murder, Smitty went to Tom's unlocked room and took Tom's knife. But Sandy saw Tom's initials at the Hog Ranch when he borrowed your knife, Smitty. I saw you knock him down."

"Monday, I'm sorry," Kate said, unable to hide her disappointment. "But I can't see any initials on the handle. It's blank."

"Both sides? Did you check both sides?"

"Yes. I'm so sorry. I wanted to believe what you figured out."

"Haw, haw." Smitty just sneered and hooked his thumbs in his pockets. "Blondie, if you'll just hand me back that pistol belt, I'll be on my way."

That galled Kate. His easy familiarity with her, his lewd innuendoes, his obvious lack of remorse for the lives he'd taken.

"Wait a moment, Monday," she said. "I have an idea. Keep him covered." Kate pulled her pencil and an envelope out of her reticule. She put the paper over one side of the handle and rubbed it lightly with her pencil. Nothing. Oh, God. Then she turned the handle and the envelope over and did the same thing. The initials T. M. appeared on the envelope.

"Monday, I've got it. The initials are there. He must have rubbed bootblack or something on the handle to conceal them. Did Tom carve the periods after his initials to look like little diamonds?"

"Yeah, Kate. I'd recognize his initials on that knife and so would a lot of the other hands. I reckon we've got all the evidence we need now for the court to hang this skunk. He must have gone direct to Tom's hotel room after he killed Francine and took Tom's knife before the deputies arrived. The initials on the murder weapon and Tom's empty sheath were nails Smitty tried to put into Tom's coffin."

All the swagger had gone out of Smitty. He glanced at his horse and licked his lips.

"But we're not finished yet, Smitty, you and me. Kate, put that knife back in the wagon and come over here." He was barely controlling his anger, she noted. What was he planning?

Monday untied his leg thong, then unbuckled his own gunbelt and lofted it into the wagon bed. The horse snorted a bit at the clatter and the wheels turned a little. Monday let down the hammer on his weapon.

"Here. Take my pistol now. Remember how I fired it at target practice? It's heavy, isn't it? You may have to use two

257

hands to hold it. Now, I want you to keep it pointed at Smitty. We're gonna have a little fight here, him and me. If he tries to get to his gun in the wagon, shoot him. If he tries to get to his horse, he's going for the rifle in the scabbard. Shoot him. If he wins, if he beats me, shoot him. Got that?" Monday tossed his hat in the wagon and began to roll up his sleeves.

"Don't do this, Monday. You don't have to prove anything to anyone."

He touched her cheek with his palm. His hand was trembling.

"Except to myself," he said.

"Pretty brave of you, runt, but by giving her that gun, you're still hiding behind her skirt." Smitty rolled up his sleeves and slowly circled to his right. Closer to the wagon, Kate noted. She raised the heavy pistol with both hands and he stopped, then circled in the other direction.

Smitty said some more bad things to Monday, probably to make him angry. His language made Kate's ears burn. But Monday said nothing and moved in closer. He struck first, landing a one-two punch to Smitty's midriff. Smitty grunted, but moved forward and hit Monday on the chin. Monday turned his head and let the blow slide along his cheek, then punched twice again. When he tried to back up, though, Smitty stepped forward and grabbed Monday's left fist in his larger right hand. Then he hit the younger man twice with his own left fist. Each blow snapped Monday's head to the side. Kate winced.

"Stop that! Don't hurt him," she called out to Smitty. This was senseless. Monday didn't need to take this risk. They had Smitty dead to rights.

Smitty just laughed and made a kissing sound in Kate's direction, then hit Monday in the stomach with his third blow. It was hard enough to double the younger man over and when Smitty released Monday's fist, the latter fell to his knees. Smitty drew his leg back for a kick.

"No!" Kate screamed.

Monday fell flat before the kick connected. When Smitty's foot sailed over his head, he rolled into the bigger man's other

258

leg. Smitty went down on his back. Monday put both hands together and brought them down hard on Smitty's midriff. The first few punches to that area hadn't worked, but this one did. Kate could hear the air whoosh out of Smitty and he rolled away from the young marshal. Monday staggered to his feet. As he turned to face Smitty again, Kate could see blood on his cheek.

She'd always thought it would be romantic to have two men fight over her, but this wasn't about her and she wished she didn't have to witness it. It was brutal and ugly and senseless. Why was Monday subjecting himself to this? She knew Smitty had beaten him up when they rode together, but hadn't he learned anything in the time she knew him? He could let the law be the instrument of his revenge.

Smitty moved in more cautiously this time. Monday must know better than to trade the bigger man blow for blow. She saw him feint, hoping to draw Smitty off balance. No such luck. Smitty hit Monday and rocked him back on his heels, but he recovered and came in low, hammering more blows into Smitty's midsection. After the third one, Smitty brought a roundhouse left into the side of Monday's head and he went down hard.

Shaking his head, Monday got to his knees. Surprisingly, Smitty didn't try to follow up on his success. He was wheezing and holding his belly. He took two steps backward and fell down. But he fell in the direction of the wagon. Smitty rolled over onto his belly and began to crawl on hands and knees toward the wagon. Monday tried to get to his feet, but fell over.

Kate swung the pistol around toward the crawling man.

"Stop! Stop right there! I'll shoot." He just grimaced at her and crawled the last few feet.

"I mean it! I will! Don't make me shoot you." Smitty began to haul himself up the wagon spokes like they were a ladder. He was on his knees, reaching for the rim of the wagon.

Kate held the pistol out in front of her, pointed it at Smitty, squinted in anticipation of the noise, and pulled the trigger.

Nothing happened. She pulled it again and again. Nothing. Not a sound. What . . . ?

Smitty reached over into the wagon bed with one hand while holding onto a spoke with the other, scrabbling for his pistol. Out of the corner of her eye, Kate saw Monday rise to one knee, cock his arm, and throw a pebble.

The stone missed Smitty.

But it hit its intended target.

The pebble smacked the horse's rump and it skittered forward a few feet. Smitty was thrown to the ground as the wheels turned. The rear wheel ran over his right arm and he cried out.

Monday crawled over to him on his hands and knees. Kate could see blood covered his chin. As he passed her, he said through clenched teeth, "Cock it first. You gotta cock it."

Oh, dear, that was right. She had seen him do that. It was hard to cock his pistol, though. She had to use both thumbs, but the hammer snicked into place. All the way back. Now she was ready.

By this time, Monday had crawled over to the writhing Smitty. The latter got to his knees and they faced each other that way. Smitty swung his right arm, but there was no power in the blow. Monday blocked the punch and hit him hard. Smitty toppled over.

Monday was on him in an instant, snapping a right, then a left to Smitty's head. There was a rock embedded in the ground next to the foreman's head. Monday grabbed Smitty by both ears, lifted his head and smacked the back of it against the rock.

"Stop it, Monday! Don't do that. You'll kill him. We need him alive." Monday ignored her and continued to hit Smitty's head against the rock.

In desperation, Kate pointed the pistol at the ground to the left of the pair and squeezed the trigger.

Bang! The bullet plowed up a puff of dust. The gun kicked so hard, Kate nearly dropped it. Monday released Smitty's head and grabbed his own left ear, rolling away to one side.

"Damn it, Kate. I didn't say to shoot me."

"You would have killed him. I had to stop you."

"What?" he cried back, still holding his left ear.

A minute later, Deputy Cal Egan ran around the side of the barn, pistol drawn. He was followed by some other men. Monday tried to talk to him, but couldn't make himself understood through bloody lips. Kate told Cal what he needed to know and made sure he took Smitty's gun belt and the knife and the envelope with him. Two men carried the unconscious Smitty away. Kate promised she and Monday would come talk to the judge and the sheriff in a few minutes.

She put Monday's pistol in the wagon, then went over to help him to his feet. He stank of sweat and blood and leaned heavily on her. No, not romantic at all. A good thing she'd never had men fight over her. The victor would have been just as distasteful as the vanquished.

"Well, you proved you could beat him. Are you satisfied? I thought you'd be happy that you outsmarted him by figuring out he was the killer. Why did you have to descend to his level and brawl with him?"

Monday looked at her and just grinned. The skin over his cheekbones was puffy and he had a black eye. At least he hadn't lost any teeth and his nose didn't look broken.

"Come on," Kate said, leading him away gently. "I'm going to have the doctor look at you. Then we'll clean you up and go talk to the authorities."

They were halfway to the doctor's office when Kate remembered she ought to say something more.

"Congratulations on solving this case. You thought I'd figure things out, but it was really all your work, once you heard Smitty's real name. You should be proud. Nice job, Marshal."

33

Laramie

Monday Malone felt like hell the next day. His ribs hurt, his jaw ached, and he still had a ringing in his left ear. All his parts felt worse now than they had after the fight. He remembered his bronco-busting days and grinned. Smitty hadn't been as punishing as some of the worst rides he'd had— Saber, Yellowtop, old One Sock.

He helped Ben Rollins load Danielle's luggage onto a buck-board in front of the Frontier Hotel. It wasn't until the two of them manhandled her heavy trunk into the little wagon that Monday remembered his knuckles hurt, too. He'd split the skin across two of them yesterday and, sure enough, hauling the trunk had broken them open again. He sucked the bloody knuckles while Ben toted the last two suitcases out of the lobby and down the steps. The young cowboy began to lash everything securely in place.

"You don't need to be that fancy, Ben, for a short haul down to the station." The westbound train had blown its first whistle a few minutes earlier.

"That ain't where she's going. Didn't you listen last evening over supper?"

"I think I was drifting in and out last night," Monday said. "Too much of that wine. My head hurt. I remember Kate and Danielle being excited about something."

"That's right. She ain't goin' to sing in San Francisco. I bought this rig. We're taking it all the way to Texas. She's comin' home with me to meet my folks. We're gonna get married." He finished the last knot and stood beaming at Monday. He pushed his hat back on his head, and sunlight fell full on his pleased face.

"Then did I remember to clap you on the back last night? I don't recall. Anyway, which one of you dragged a loop and who stepped in it?"

"I reckon I been draggin' a loop for her the last few weeks," Ben said. "I'd been pinin' for her and doin' every little thing, every courtesy I could think of, to get her to fall in love with me. When Tom's trial broke up yesterday morning and you and Kate testified against Smitty, I went to the station, bought her a ticket to San Francisco, and took it to her at the hotel." He took his hat off with his left hand and rotated it with his right.

"That's when we had it out. I told her I didn't want her to go, but I wanted her to be happy, even if she went somewhere else. Looked like she was waiting for me to say something more, so I blurted out that I loved her. That I'd always loved her. I loved her enough to let her go to San Francisco, if that's what she wanted."

"And that did it? That little 'I love you' was all it took to change her mind about the big city?" Monday thought about Kate and wondered what she missed back East.

"She said she wanted to change her mind, ever since I paid off Fricker. But she really wanted me to say enough to get her to change it. Women! Here I thought all along she just liked me. Maybe liked me better than the other hands from the Circle M. Turns out she loved me from the first time I talked with her on the hotel porch and dragged this great big trunk back into the lobby and paid for her room. I don't know when she was gonna tell me that. I guess she was waiting to hear it from me first." He put his hat back on.

At that moment, Danielle and Kate came out of the hotel and stood at the top of the steps. Last night's brief shower had left soft spots around the little wagon.

Kate cleared her throat and said to Ben, "My, what a rain we had last night. It certainly looks muddy down there."

263

Monday didn't understand why she spoke louder than she needed to.

In a flash, Ben shucked his vest and spread it between the foot of the steps and the side of the buckboard. He took Danielle's hand as she reached the bottom, let her step gingerly on his vest and then took her by the waist and lifted her into the wagon. When he retrieved the garment and came around the back of the wagon to go to the driver's side, he winked at Monday.

"Miss Kate was telling me last night about Sir Walter Raleigh. Said an act of chiv'ry like that would earn me a kiss from Danielle later. Probably a long kiss." He flipped the dirty vest into the back of the wagon. It clinked.

"Damn," Ben said. "Almost forgot. Look," he said, pulling the vest back and fishing in one pocket. "Here's the money back from that train ticket she won't be using." The train sounded its second whistle as if to punctuate Ben's remark. He dropped a bag into Monday's palm. "I'll send you what I spent for the hotel, Fricker's payoff, and the cost of this buggy after we get home."

Monday pocketed the bag without looking at it.

"No hurry, Ben. That's what friends are for. Just invite me to the wedding, will you? If I can get away and get down there, I'd like to come."

"You got a deal," Ben said, shaking Monday's outstretched hand. "Long as you remember to invite me to yours." He glanced past Monday to where Kate was chatting with Danielle. Monday turned and Kate made eye contact with him. Had she heard what Ben had said? He gulped.

The jingling of tack and the sound of many horses coming from behind them reminded Monday that the whole Circle M outfit was leaving this afternoon, too. Smitty had been found guilty this morning and sentenced to hang on the day following the Sabbath. No one wanted to be here to provide any familiar faces the despised foreman would see from the gallows. There'd probably be only Fricker, one or two of the Hog Ranch girls, and Nate and his deputies.

264

Monday shook his head and returned to the subject of Kate.

"I don't know if that'll ever happen, Ben," he said quietly. "I mean, well, you met Corey Masterson. He's tall, good-looking, and his daddy owns one of the two biggest spreads around Warbonnet. And there's this preacher comes through every four weeks. He's got an education and can sing good and dance even better. When he's in town, Kate spends nearly every waking minute with him.

"It's gonna be years before I get enough land and can afford a decent herd," Monday went on. "By that time, she'll have stepped into somebody else's loop." He looked across at Kate as he said this, certain he was speaking softly enough that she couldn't hear him over the sound of the approaching horsemen. She said goodbye to Danielle and hugged her. Kate looked impossibly lovely in the afternoon sunshine and Monday's heart joined the list of aches that his body was tallying today.

"Tell her," Ben shouted into Monday's left ear as the noisy cowboys and the clattering chuck wagon pulled to a halt close to them. "Remember what I said. She wants to hear it from you." They shook hands.

"What?" Monday called as Ben went forward and climbed into the little wagon. He still couldn't hear well out of that ear and the approaching horses made such a jangling racket. Kate came around the back of the wagon. He was going to tease her about walking through mud that Rolly guy wouldn't touch, when a hand came down and touched his shoulder.

Monday turned to find Tom looking down at him from his horse.

"I need to thank you again for what you did." Tom gestured to the assembled outfit and to the buckboard. "You made all this possible. I, uh, left something behind for you at the livery. I recall how you always hankered for Mary Ellen's little roan gelding, Opie. He's yours now."

"Shoot. You didn't ought to do that, Tom. You said everything you needed to yesterday. I reckon that's what

265

brothers are for, to do things for each other with no thought of thanks."

"Yeah, brothers," Tom sighed. "Well, I ain't treated you like that for years. I'll be a long way from you, but I'll keep in better touch. Might even learn how to write a letter. I aim to rewrite my will when I get home. According to Pa's will that I hid from you, half the Circle M should be yours, you know."

Monday blinked and looked down at his boots. Must be the angle of the sun.

"Much obliged, Tom, but I reckon my future's here in Wyoming now, not back in Texas."

"Well, if that's so, Monday, it looks like you're a top hand at this new lawman job, as good as you were cowboyin' in Texas. How'd you figure out all that stuff you said at the trial —how Smitty married Cora to get the ranch, tricked up a knife to look like mine, and stood behind that door to shoot Sandy?"

"I had a good teacher," Monday said. He felt a smaller hand reach into his palm. He didn't have to look to see whose it was. *"Vaya con Dios."*

"Mr. Malone," Kate added from next to him. "Remember what I said yesterday about Cora. Look her up when you get back. I don't think she was aware of her status in your will. Smitty just took advantage of her. Like men have been doing to her the last few years. Reach out to her and her child. I don't know how she'll respond, but I know you'll feel better."

"I reckon I'll do that, Miss Shaw," Tom said, tipping his hat to her and then showing even more respect by taking it off entirely. "And I'll write you about what happens. Thank you for everything."

"And you, little brother," he pointed at Monday with his hat. "A word of advice from the head of the family. Marry a woman with brains enough for two and you'll get by just fine." He swatted Monday with his hat, put it back on and whistled to the outfit. After what he'd said, Monday didn't dare look at Kate.

The cowboys spurred their horses, but kept behind the moving buckboard. They liked Danielle too much to make her eat their dust all the way to Texas. She'd probably sing to them all along the way. Kate and Monday moved aside as the chuck wagon lurched past them at the end of the parade. Kate waved her left hand and Monday his right. She hadn't let go of his hand.

While they stood there waving, she said to him, "Did you hear what Danielle told Ben over supper last night? I didn't think it registered with you. It was the sweetest thing."

Monday shook his head, but gently. Even the hair on his head still hurt.

"We were just getting used to calling her Lynn again. We thought she'd probably want to leave the name Danielle and all its memories behind her here. She said the other night she wanted to do just that, leave Danielle behind and become Lynn again. But everyone, including Ben, had gotten used to that name. She said if Ben wanted, she'd always be Danielle for him. Isn't that a romantic thing to say?"

Monday couldn't think of anything more romantic to say than "Uh-huh."

At last, when the line of wagons and horses turned at the end of Front Street, they stopped waving. Kate brought Monday's left hand up in a tight grip to where she could look at it.

"I thought so. Blood. Your knuckles are split again. Come on," she said, leading him by the hand toward the hotel. "I'm going to bandage that hand. I told you these cuts would open up again. You're going to have scars." She took charge, sounding like the doctor's daughter again. Monday resisted.

"That's all right, Kate. I want a reminder of how I finally got the best of Smitty. Besides, a man don't mind scars on his hands."

He regretted that the instant he said it. Kate moved her scarred left hand behind her hip, out of sight, and dropped his left hand like a hot branding iron. Damn! Why did he always have to say the wrong thing? They went into the hotel in silence.

At the desk, Monday said, "I'm sorry for what I said out there. I'm not thinking too clear today. Will you still have

267

supper with me before I leave tomorrow to ride back to Warbonnet? I don't intend to be a face in the crowd that Smitty
might recognize."

"No, nor I. But yes to your question. Yes, I'll have supper
with you. And I don't want to wait until Roy Butcher comes
down here with the wagon next week. Would that roan gelding Tom gave you be gentle enough for me?"

Monday's heart soared. There was no one in the world
he'd rather spend three days on the trail with. But reality had
a way of moving in and souring the milk of dreams.

"Uh, Kate. Miss Shaw. We really can't ride all that way
alone. Think of your reputation."

"Oh, f-f-fiddlesticks!" She stamped her foot. "Everyone in
Warbonnet knows me well enough by now. My reputation
won't suffer one whit. Besides, if I ride back on the wagon
with Roy Butcher, I still wouldn't have a chaperone. I'd rather
ride with you."

Monday grinned at that.

"Well, then, I guess it'll be all right. Yeah, little Opie will
suit you just fine. He's a damn smart cowpony, but I'll teach
you how to handle him. You don't want a horse tellin' you
what to do, any more than you like men to do that."

Kate laughed and said she'd have to make arrangements to
have the freight master at the train station hold her trunk and
most of her Yellowstone baggage for Roy. She said she
planned to travel with just a small valise again. But she still
hid her left hand. He'd never pried, but when would she tell
him how she'd got that scar?

"I'd better see to packing my valise and make sure I have
enough clean laundry for the journey. Thank you, Monday.
I'll see you at supper."

With that, she gathered her skirts and climbed the stairs.

Monday watched her go up, admiring her ankles at every
step she took. No petticoat showing today. But she'd wear
that tight-waisted, hip-hugging riding skirt tomorrow. Damn.
His mouth went dry and he thought about a beer. Then the
picture of another woman came unbidden to his mind.

Becky. Becky Masterson. She'd probably tell Kate upon their return that Monday had kissed her, not the other way around. Should he take advantage of the next three days and tell Kate what'd really happened before Becky told her version? He considered that for a moment and remembered how Becky had called him a coward as he rode away.

No. He wouldn't tell Kate. That would be the coward's way out, ratting on Becky. Let her make up her story and tell it to Kate. If Kate trusted him, she'd believe what he told her. And if she didn't believe in him, then maybe she wasn't the right woman for him. Besides, he thought, Kate's being alone with him for three days and two nights on the trail would put a real burr under Becky's saddle.

He chuckled to himself and headed for the door, intent on getting a beer or two down at the Alhambra, but stopped short in the doorway. The face of another woman came to him then.

Mary Ellen. He stood looking out at the street. It was just like coming out of the hotel in Manzanita with her and Lassiter standing in the street. His dry mouth became painful. He was about to spend three days on the trail with Kate. When he'd spent three days alone with Mary Ellen, they'd conceived a child. Was he doing the right thing by allowing Kate to ride with him? Of course he was. Kate wasn't about to grant him any favors in a situation like that. She'd act like she was in charge all during the ride, just like she always did.

Still, he reflected, recalling Kate's long, hard kiss last year when she found him alive after thinking he was dead, she could raise a man's "interest" without even trying. He'd better not stare at her skirt too much or start conversations with her, just to hear the sound of her voice. He'd try hard to keep his feelings under control. He knew she could.

34

The Trail to Medicine Bow and Warbonnet

Kate and Monday prepared to ride out early. It was a warm morning, fragrant with the promise of rain. Without a word, Monday lashed a yellow slicker around the blanket and the little valise behind Kate's saddle. The slicker didn't look new. Kate was afraid to ask where he'd gotten extra rain gear. It might have been Smitty's. She shuddered. They mounted up and headed northwest.

It was a long while before they spoke to each other. Kate knew Monday thought she talked too much at times, so she bit her tongue and waited for him to speak. The effort to keep quiet was killing her. She wanted so much to tell him about the wonders of Yellowstone. Kate's moment finally came when Monday halted above the bank of a little stream. He took the canteen from his saddlehorn and unscrewed the top. Still silent, he handed it to her to drink first.

"Yes, thank you." She drank deeply, wiped her mouth, and handed the canteen back, conscious that Monday had been watching her the whole time. He made a move to wipe the rim of the canteen on his sleeve, appeared to think better of it, and just drank.

"You been pretty quiet this morning," he said, taking another sip. "Smitty on your mind? I been thinking about him, too." He recapped the canteen and hung it back where it belonged.

"No, not at all. I imagine by this time tomorrow, justice will have been served. I was thinking of Tom, of Ben and Danielle. I mean Lynn. Whatever she wants Ben to call her. And I've been thinking about you. Are you all right with the way this turned out? Are you disappointed that you didn't get to kill Smitty yourself? I've never seen you so angry."

Monday tilted his hat back on his head and rested both palms and his reins on the saddlehorn.

"Well, I thought I might regret not killing him when I had the chance. But I made my point. I mean, I showed Smitty I could outdraw him. I won a hand of poker from him. And I finally beat him in a fair fight. But I was still sore about some of those things he said about you. I thought it might feel good to go and see him in jail last night and, uh, gloat." He looked over to see how Kate might react to that.

"I walked in quietly as Cal was collecting the supper dishes. I went to where I could see him through the bars of a couple cells. There was a little light through his window. I stayed back where he couldn't see me. I never said nothing, just watched him a while. He paced a little, then sat with his head in his hands. After a bit, I reckoned I really had nothing to say. I got Cal to let me out."

Kate relaxed a little.

"After all he did to you and Tom," she said, "I suppose it was natural to look in on him before his execution. I'm glad you didn't berate him on my account. What he thinks of me or said about me is of no consequence."

"It's of some consequence to me, what folks say about you," Monday said, looking at her. Then, more calmly, he added, "But he wasn't gonna spread any more poison. He couldn't aggravate me any more. So I could just walk away. Leave him and a painful chunk of my past behind."

One painful chunk of his past. There was another painful chunk Kate knew about.

He took up the reins and looked to see if Kate was ready. They continued the walking pace he was setting for her. Opie had a gentle gait and a perfect girth that didn't tax her leg muscles.

271

"What about Yellowstone, Miss Kate? Wanna tell me about what you saw, some of what happened? You said something about a bear, but you must have seen some of the sights you hoped to, like waterfalls, and them hot springs and fountains you told me you'd read about."

Ah, Kate thought, a safe subject. But why was he so formal with her? He only called her "Miss Kate" around other people. There was no one to hear them out here.

She told him about being accepted by Professor Hayden when Sean and Moran spoke up for her. She went on at length on safe subjects—White Mountain Hot Springs, Yellowstone Falls, and the enormous geysers, Old Faithful most prominent among those she'd seen—but said nothing about Schonborn at her bath, the nervous man at his easel, or the cool breeze against her skin. It was safe to tell Monday about the bear, and his concern for her touched her. He asked so many questions about the attack that she was sure he gave no thought to Schonborn. Her secret would be safe. Thank God Monday hadn't received any of the posing pages from those mixed up letters.

Kate looked over at Monday and bit her lip. Was it right to tell him new information about his past? Would she be helping him or just hurting him by bringing up what he thought was his own deep dark secret? In any case, she didn't plan to say anything until tomorrow night, when they'd camp at the old site on Box Elder Creek.

# # #

They spent the first night in Medicine Bow, just as they had during the ride to Warbonnet a year ago. Kate got to sleep in a bed at the Farleys' house while Monday unrolled his blanket on the porch of the general store and saloon across the street. He hadn't turned in yet as Kate prepared to go to sleep. She could see his boots and legs across the way in the lamplight that spilled out of the windows behind him. She knew he wouldn't try to sleep until after the saloon closed up. She wondered how much sleep he might get and whether he'd be tired tomorrow.

Rain came that night. Kate rose to close her window a little. In snatches of cloud-scattered moonlight, she could see Monday sleeping across the way. He'd unrolled a slicker over his blanket, but the rain was light and there was no breeze. She went back to bed and wrestled with thoughts of Tom Malone, Cora, and Mary Ellen until she drifted off.

# # #

The rain was over by morning, but clouds hung low and threatened more drizzle. They rode out early again, as if Monday were eager to get her back to Warbonnet. How did he feel about their camping at Box Elder Creek tonight, Kate wondered. Besides the memories that might linger there of Sam Taggart's murder, she'd be spending the night by a camp-fire with him completely alone. She'd been sincere when she told him this journey wouldn't adversely affect her reputation. But was he comfortable with this situation? She was gambling on his being enough of a gentleman not to take advantage of her. But what did she want to happen tonight?

35

Box Elder Creek

They made camp at Box Elder Creek just before sundown. As Monday hobbled the horses and removed their tack and saddlebags, Kate went off to wash up in the fading daylight. She didn't remove any clothing, just rolled up her sleeves and washed her hands and face in the creek. Her face was hot when she applied the cool water. She was thinking about how Monday had spied on her while she was washing up in this very spot last summer. That made her think of Sam Taggart. On the way back to their campsite, she looked for the rocks on which the old marshal had bled out his life. She couldn't find a trace. A voice stopped her search.

"I, uh, turned over all the rocks with Sam Taggart's blood on 'em when I came through here a month ago. I didn't know we'd be back here together again, but I didn't want to leave any unpleasant reminders . . . ." Monday trailed off.

"Now I understand. That was very considerate of you. It was morbid of me to try to find the exact spot again. Thank you for that bit of chivalry." She didn't feel as contrite as she tried to sound. She needed to patch things up a bit before the important conversation she wanted to have with him. He appeared to accept her remarks at face value and returned to their campsite.

Monday spread her blanket and saddle over some willow boughs on the opposite side of the campfire from his own gear. He dragged an old tree trunk up to one side of the fire to use as a bench. As she watched, he built a fire, lit his kindling, and soon had a creditable blaze going. Without asking, he began to prepare their supper. Good. She doubted she'd be able to make a decent meal in these surroundings. The sky had cleared in the afternoon. There would be no threat of rain.

After they ate, she took the frying pan and utensils from him and said she would wash up. His cooking was no better than hers would have been, but she complimented him on his skill. He fetched wash water and they cleaned up together.

Afterwards, as the sun was sinking behind the mountains behind them, Monday sat down on the tree trunk facing the fire. He absently patted his vest pockets as if looking for the makings of a smoke. Kate hoped he hadn't tried to take up the habit again. His consistently futile efforts to roll a decent cigarette were the stuff of legend in Warbonnet, and of much good humored banter among members of Martha's sewing circle. After a moment, Monday appeared to recall that he had no makings and put his hands on his knees. This was the time she'd been waiting for.

Kate rose from the fireside, gathered her skirt, and stepped over the log Monday sat on. She sat down with her back to the fire next to him, positioned so she could see his face clearly in the firelight.

"I have some things to talk about with you this evening. It's part of the reason why I wanted us ride up here together without waiting for Roy and his wagon. First off, I wanted to tell you I'm sorry I didn't do what you said about not talking to your brother."

"That turned out all right in the end, Kate. If you hadn't talked to him and found out about Cora and sent your letter to Zack, well, Tom would be hanged by now and we never would have, I mean, *I* never would have figured out why Francine was killed. I admit I thought at the time that you were meddling. But I reckon you were smarter than me again."

"I am not! I mean, I'm not one whit smarter than you are. You recognized the name of the man Cora married. You determined how Sandy was killed. And you figured out how the murder weapon was made to look like Tom's knife. I was just the catalyst for your deductions."

She saw his look of puzzlement. Oh, no, she'd done it again. Sounded too superior.

"I mean, I just provided the kindling, so to speak. Without your spark, we wouldn't have had a fire. We wouldn't have figured out anything." She could tell this praise had pleased him. She watched his face. This was the moment.

"I wasn't entirely truthful in something I told you back in Warbonnet," she said softly. "When I talked to Tom the first time, he told me everything." Monday looked sideways at her suddenly. "Yes, *everything*. He told me how Mary Ellen was carrying your baby. I understand why you could never tell me that. But she wasn't actually your sister. You were raised together. I think I could have understood, if you had trusted me."

Monday turned from her and looked at the fire.

"Tell me about her, Monday. Please. What happened? How did you come to love her?"

He took so long to answer that Kate thought he might have been offended by her request. At length, Monday reached down for his canteen, took a swig, and started. He didn't look at her as he spoke, addressing his remarks to the fire.

"She was beautiful. She had long hair like yours, but it was dark brown, almost black. Her eyes were black, too, but not flat like coal. They sparkled. They had these little specks of color in them. I never noticed those specks until, until we were close together." He sighed.

"It was April of '67, just before my birthday. Spring roundup of all the cattle for branding. That meant we had to break some new horses before we rode out for the roundup. That was my job. I was good at it. Not yet nineteen and I'd broke more than fifty horses with only a broken collarbone to show for it. But that spring, a horse named Bart's Bandit threw me and I hit my head. Didn't come to for some hours. Doc from Manzanita said I might have scrambled my brains a mite and wanted me to take it easy for a week or two."

276

"Concussion," Kate said, trying to be helpful. "A possible concussion."

"Yeah, I think that's what he said. I felt pretty good, unless I tried to stand up too quick. Anyway, Pa and Tom and Jim Squires, our foreman at that time, and all the hands went on the roundup without me. Told Mary Ellen she had to stay home to nurse me. She usually went on the roundup, too, so she was as put out as I was. Said she was damned if she'd nursemaid a perfectly good wrangler. Only one left with us was Old Jesus. We always left him behind on roundups and trail drives. He looked forward to staying drunk for that week. I felt well enough to follow the outfit, but they didn't leave us a single horse."

He put the canteen down, glanced at Kate, and looked back at the fire.

"Anyway, the morning they left, Mary Ellen said I needed a bath, so I went down to the wide spot in the creek where Tom and me and the cowboys always horsed around. It was pretty cool water that April, I recall. I hadn't been in the creek long when Mary Ellen came down with a big basket of clothes and said she was gonna do the laundry since Old Jesus couldn't. I threw stones at her to get her to leave, but she just laughed. Asked if I'd brought a towel. Of course, I'd forgot and she laughed some more. She hung a towel for me on the limb of a young cottonwood.

"That was bad enough, but then she had the gall to take the clothes I'd just got out of and tossed them in the creek to wash them. They were my last halfway clean clothes. When I squawked, she said I could just wear my towel 'til my pants dried. I shouldn'ta done what I did next." He shook his head, but grinned.

"I brought up a handful of mud from the bottom and flung it at her. Hit her skirt, her blouse, and her cheek. At first she acted real mad and called me names I didn't know she knew. But then she laughed. She pulled her blouse over her head, took off her skirt, and before I could do much more than say her name, she shucked her drawers, too. Flipped 'em all into

277

the creek and added them to the wash, saying now she was in the same condition as me."

"That must have been . . . awkward."

"I couldn't take my eyes off her. I never seen a woman nekkid before. After she washed our clothes, she rinsed 'em, wrung 'em, and put 'em back in the basket. Then she got in the water with me. Walked right up to where I was standing in the deep part and asked what I was going to do about the mud on her cheek. I washed it off. It was like my heart was in my throat. Then she kissed me and let me wash her. She washed me, too.

"I never thought Mary Ellen would be interested in me. At the town dances, she always danced with Zack Hibben, Ben Rollins, and boys from other outfits. She only danced with me once or twice when I had no partner. I thought she only did that out of pity. She could always find better partners than me."

Now it was Kate's turn to pick up the canteen. She didn't notice her own hands were shaking until she made the cap chain on the canteen rattle. She tried to control her hands enough to take a drink, but the cool water sluiced down her chin and soaked her bosom. She sat the canteen down with a clunk, hoping Monday hadn't noticed.

"Mary Ellen got out of the creek and used the towel. She said I should dry off and we'd go back to the house. I came out slow, trying to cover myself with both hands, but she gave me the towel and stood there smiling. I asked how we were gonna get back to the house with only one towel. She said we wouldn't need even one towel, since Old Jesus was passed out on his bunk. She hoisted the basket and walked back to the house, nekkid as a jaybird. I followed her, the towel flapping around my knees.

"In the kitchen, she picked up a handful of clothes pins and took my towel away. I thought she'd go right out to the wash line without a stitch, but she looked at me and smiled and just dropped the pins onto the wet clothes. Said she reckoned the wash could wait a little while longer. Then she took me by the hand and led me to her bedroom."

Monday hesitated, as if considering whether to continue.

"Anyway, we were together for three more days 'til the out-fit came back. It was the best time I ever had. It was like my birthday and Christmas and the Fourth of July all rolled into one." Monday blinked rapidly, probably to keep tears at bay. Drifting smoke.

"She swore she'd always loved me. I only realized then that I'd always loved her too. But I never would have told her. Could never have . . . ." Monday tried to stand up, but Kate took his arm and pulled him back to his seat.

"Don't get up. Don't walk away. I know that must have been painful to recall. But I learned something else from Tom that I have to tell you. What do you remember about the day Mary Ellen died?" Kate kicked the canteen and heard it topple, its contents gurgling away. She'd fill it again in the morning. She didn't want to break eye contact with Monday now.

"A couple a months later, when she was pretty sure she was gonna have a baby, we both went to tell Pa. Tom wanted to kill me, but Pa wasn't upset. Said Ma would have wanted us to get married, even if it had to be like this. He took Mary Ellen into Manzanita for Doc to confirm her condition and see the preacher about an early weddin' date. I think I told you the Lassiter gang took over the town while they were there. Mary Ellen and Cora and Maria and Angie. . . . " Monday put his head in his hands. Kate waited a while.

"I learned something about that day I have to tell you," Kate said. "Your brother Tom told me what Cora said to him after the shootings. He never told you what Cora confided to him, so what I have to say may be upsetting. I've been think-ing all day about how to tell you."

When Monday raised his head to look at her, Kate took his right hand in hers and held it against her thigh. She held it tightly, so he couldn't pull away.

"Cora said Mary Ellen told her about the baby. She said the doctor warned her not to engage in further relations with you. He told her your mother had had more than one miscar-riage before Tom was born and he feared Mary Ellen might

279

also have a delicate constitution. You know what happened to those women in the saloon that night, don't you?"

Monday nodded and tried to pull his hand away. Kate hung onto it with both hands.

"Cora said those men took turns with them. All night, with no sleep. One of them strangled Angie when she wouldn't stop screaming. At one point—" She paused for breath.

"Oh, God. At one point, Cora and Mary Ellen were together, held—held down—on top of adjoining tables. Mary Ellen began to bleed. A lot, Cora said. Those men left her alone after that, and, and used Cora and Maria. About daybreak, they let the three women alone and went off to get breakfast. Cora held Mary Ellen while she cried. Mary Ellen told her she was sure it was the baby. That those men had made her lose it. Did she tell you that? Before the end?"

Monday wiped his cheek with the back of his hand.

"I recall now she must've been tryin' to tell me. But someone or something, gunshots mostly, kept interrupting us. I never thought to ask her and then it was too late."

"Do you remember what happened out there in the street? When Lassiter called you out?"

"I could never forget. It's branded on my brain. I couldn't get a clear shot at him, the way he was holding Mary Ellen with that big knife in his left hand. I knew he was gonna shoot me, so I turned my left shoulder toward him. I couldn't see Mary Ellen for a moment. Then his bullet hit me and I went flying. Everything sort of runs together after that." He turned away to look at the fire.

"Tom said Cora told him what happened when you couldn't see Mary Ellen. Cora could see everything from the walk in the front of the saloon. Mary Ellen must have known Lassiter would kill you. He and his men had already killed her baby. She probably couldn't bear to think of life without you and without your child."

Kate caught her breath, gasping for a moment. She knew exactly how Mary Ellen must have felt. All that fall of 1864, Kate had longed for a baby from Stuart, then found out he'd died at Petersburg just before Christmas. How she'd wanted

280

to die herself all that winter. Mary Ellen had lived Kate's months of Hell in just one night. No one could stop her the next day, once she'd resolved on a course of action in a matter of seconds.

"Cora said Mary Ellen called out your name, then took Lassiter's hand in both of hers and pulled the knife into her. She screamed just as he fired the shot that hit you. The combination of the scream and her sudden weight on his left arm may have thrown his aim off. Cora said that was his last shot." Kate blinked rapidly, but her lashes were already wet.

"Mary Ellen did what she intended, Monday. She gave you a chance at life by giving up her own. Tom told me he'd never said anything about this to you and Cora moved away, and, and . . . . I'm sorry to be the one to tell you all this. I know it's painful, but you need to know."

She held his hand fiercely as he tried to stand, tried to pull away.

"Don't you understand, Monday? You didn't kill her. You don't have to blame yourself any more. Lassiter didn't kill her either. She killed herself trying to save you. She wanted you to live, to have a life after she was gone."

Kate couldn't say any more. Her tears flowed so quickly, they threatened to choke her. She released Monday's hand and, before he could stand, pulled him to her and buried his head in the hollow of her shoulder. His body shook as she held him. Her own tears raced down her cheeks. She tasted the salty drops and knew her nose must be running, too. Monday never made a sound, but Kate could hear her own wailing. She hadn't cried like this in years. Not since she'd gotten the news of Stuart's death.

Kate lost track of how long they held each other. After a time, the fire popped loudly and she felt a sudden burning on her back. She started and felt Monday raise his head and beat at a spark that had settled on the back of her blouse. They pulled apart a little, still sitting hip to hip on the log. Monday was red-eyed, but his cheeks were dry. Kate knew her face from eyes to chin must be streaked with tears. She raised a hand to wipe her face, but Monday caught her hand. He pulled her to her feet and held her tightly by both upper arms, his face only inches from hers.

"I know why I'm feeling this way, Kate. But why are you crying? You didn't know Mary Ellen." Despite his rough manner and husky voice, he was studying her face intently.

"She and I could have been sisters. I know all I need to know about her. All I'll ever need to know. She loved you so much, she gave up her life for you. I understand that."

Monday looked hard into her eyes, and Kate couldn't help but blink, then close her eyes. Her tears and the woodsmoke burned her so. She could feel Monday's breath on her face. She knew she must look awful, but all she could think was, *Yes, yes. Kiss me. I know you want to. Just kiss me.*

As if he could read her mind, Monday kissed her lips lightly. She opened her mouth and tasted her salty tears. Oh, God, why did he have to pick this moment when she must look horrible? But he didn't seem to mind. He held her tighter and his kiss became more insistent. Kate had trouble breathing, but she'd be damned if she'd break this kiss first. She'd wanted this for so long.

All at once, Monday released her and stepped back from the log, stumbling away awkwardly. Kate was so limp she almost fell.

He said, "I gotta see to the horses before we turn in." He was gone.

Kate found her handkerchief and vainly tried to clean herself up. She had to wring it out and dab at herself again. Finally, she blew her nose three times. Oh, why did she have to bawl like that? Kate staggered blindly to one side of the fire, intending to go to the creek to wash up. She kicked the nearly empty canteen and thought it might have enough water for her needs. She wet her handkerchief with the little water that remained and applied it to her face.

She was so warm now and the night was so close. She looked to be certain Monday wasn't returning yet and stripped off her boots, stockings, blouse, and skirt. She slipped under her blanket just as he came back. He went to the fire and added some of the fuel he'd brought.

"Will that be necessary?" she asked. "It's so warm tonight."

Monday cleared his throat.

"We're pretty high up here, Kate. It'll get cooler before dawn. Be a lot easier for me to stir up coals than to get a fire going again about three or four in the morning." He stood up.

"Thank you for telling me all that. I'll sleep easier because of it. Better dreams. Maybe not tonight, but for the rest of my life. I'm sorry we had so many disagreements the last few days." He was about to leave for his own bedroll when he stopped and noticed the blouse and skirt on top of Kate's boots. He mumbled a hasty good night and retreated.

"Good night," Kate called softly after him. She wished now she hadn't taken everything off. She hadn't meant to further complicate Monday's feelings toward her. But still, she told herself, it was warm tonight. She closed her eyes and surrendered to sleep.

But sleep refused to accept her surrender. When it finally did, Kate's dreams were not peaceful. She replayed and elaborated on her confrontation with Anton Schonborn that morning at Yellowstone Falls. All the things she said or wished she'd said. In her dream, she left him no room to reply to her points.

# # #

She remembered her fear, standing there at the lip of the falls, with a man preparing to strip away her last scrap of clothing. Her robe and the pistol in its pocket seemed like a continent away. She could have decided the issue just by stepping backwards into the gulf above the torrent. How easy that would have been. Like what she'd planned to do at Niagara after Stuart's death.

Instead, when Schonborn had tried to pull the shift down over her breasts, Kate pulled the straps back up.

"No, you mustn't. We can't do this. Part of me says it would be glamorous and exciting to have you sketch me nude, but we both know that after a few minutes you'd put your

283

hands on me again. And after I'd allowed your eyes to travel over all my secret places, I couldn't resist your next attempt to kiss me.

"If I let you have your way with me today, I might run away to New York. I couldn't return to Warbonnet and be a simple schoolteacher again. The lure of the big city, art, culture, being part of an educated circle, would seduce me as surely as your attentions.

"But it wouldn't stop there, would it? Your artist friends would also want to paint me. And one by one, they'd have their way with me, too. Until one day, I'd find myself with a child on the way and no real idea who the father was. At that point, I'd either have the baby or do away with myself. I would long since have cut all ties to a family that had given me up for dead. No matter whether I did it then or years later, we both know I'd bleed out my life in some gutter."

When he'd tried to deny all her imaginings, to comfort and console her, she'd become even more adamant.

"No, Anton. You can't see all of me that you wish today. You're an artist. I know this threadbare shift lets the morning sun behind me show you the outlines of my entire form. Use your imagination to fill in the rest. It will have to do. We will not have relations today. Not ever. I don't know why I was so weak or so foolish as to entertain the idea. I'll get you some money for a down payment. I'll pay for a portrait for my parents somehow. Whatever your friends' fees might be."

"I know you'll be disappointed today, but you have a great future, having been the topographer of this famous expedition. All you have to do is sketch me and return to Omaha. I may not have a glorious future in art, but I'll have a life I can be proud of."

As one type of painted woman, but not as the other kind.

# # #

She recalled how cold Schonborn's hands had been on her shoulders. Kate felt chilled now and came suddenly awake. She was sleeping on her left side. The blanket had slipped from her shoulder and was now under her right arm. Monday

284

had been right; it had turned cold, whatever time it was. She decided to pull the blanket up, but froze at the sound of a breaking twig somewhere nearby.

Monday knelt by the fire in his long johns and set down some extra fuel. He carefully added some more wood and brushed off his hands. As he began to look Kate's way, she closed her eyes to slits and feigned sleep.

Kate watched Monday rise and walk over to her. She glanced down in alarm. Was she in an immodest state? Her breasts had nearly spilled out of her camisole. They rose and fell dramatically with each breath. Breathing more shallowly did little good.

Monday stopped in front of her and knelt. Oh, God, was he going to—

He bent forward and she could feel his warm breath on her head. What was he doing? Then it came to her. He must be smelling her hair, something he would never dare to do when she was awake. What else would he attempt with her in this situation? She was sure she'd encouraged him by opening her mouth to his kiss.

He reached out for the blanket under Kate's arm. She took a deep breath and held it. Oh, God. This was it. She felt him take the edge of the blanket and pull it down. She closed her eyes and stifled a gasp.

Then Kate felt the rough scrape of wool against her arm as Monday pulled the blanket up over her shoulder and laid it against her cheek. His knees popped as he stood up and gravel crunched as he made his way back to his own bedroll. She watched him lie down on the other side of the fire.

Kate let out the breath she'd been holding. Why hadn't Monday taken advantage of her when he had the opportunity? Schonborn had been ready to do that. Kate was sure Monday had seen the pile of her clothing. The sight of her bosom and the smell of her hair should certainly—

There was no escaping the conclusion. The rude Texas cowboy-turned-lawman must be more of a gentleman than the artist.

She rolled onto her back and lay looking up at the stars. The same stars she'd seen through her torn tent in Yellowstone just a couple short weeks ago. How close she'd come to throwing away her future on a whim. Considering becoming an artist's model, then a mistress. What a fool she'd been.

Kate blinked, but she was out of tears tonight. She'd cried them all for Monday and Mary Ellen and had no more left. Just as well. A Wyoming woman ought not to cry for herself.

ABOUT THE AUTHOR

Robert Kresge is a former senior intelligence analyst and founding member of the Central Intelligence Agency's Counterterrorist Center. He lives in Albuquerque, New Mexico.

Rob holds a Bachelor of Journalism from the University of Missouri and a Masters in International Affairs from George Washington University. He helped found and is a former president of the "Croak and Dagger," the Albuquerque chapter of Sisters in Crime. He also founded a writers group at CIA in 2000 that had, upon his retirement, 180 members and is still active today. Rob is also a member of the Rocky Mountain Chapter of Mystery Writers of America, the Historical Mystery Society, and Western Writers of America.

Further information on Rob and the Warbonnet mystery series can be found at www.robertkresge.com. Books in this series can be ordered from Barnes and Noble, Books-a-Million, IndieBound bookstores, and from www.amazon.com. The novels are also available at www.abqpress.com and on various e-book platforms.

CPSIA information can be obtained at www.ICGtesting.com
Printed in the USA
LVOW060743091011

249685LV00004B/3/P